The Riddle of the Sphinx

ALEXANDRE MONTAGU

The Riddle of the Sphinx

PERSEPOLIS PRESS   NEW YORK

Published by Persepolis Press, New York

For information, including permission to reproduce this book or any portions contained therein, please visit www.alexandre.montagu.com

This book is a work of fiction. Any references to historical events, real people, or real places are used fictitiously. Other names, characters, places and events are products of the author's imagination. Any resemblance to actual events, places or people—living or dead—is pure coincidence.

ISBN 978-1-7326021-0-6
EBOOK: ISBN 978-1-7326021-1-3

Cover and book designed by John Lotte

For Mark and Michael

THE SPHINX: *What creature is it that goes on four feet in the morning, two feet at noon, and three feet in the evening?*

OEDIPUS: *Man*

Prologue

IN THE CONFERENCE ROOM ON the forty-ninth floor no one was paying the slightest attention to the spectacular views of Central Park and the iconic spires of the Empire State and Chrysler buildings. Instead, the occupants of the room were riveted by a wholly different image—that of a man, the hero of the hour. Up until now, he had been celebrated as an artful and perspicacious lawyer, zealous and intrepid in his advocacy, industrious and resolute in approach, discerning and sagacious in judgment, the type of person junior lawyers aspired to be, a paradigm of the partner the firm strove to display and clients liked to see. However, this occasion was different; he now had played an instrumental role in the largest M&A transaction in the history of the firm. The team of lawyers and paralegals who had negotiated the merger agreement had gathered at the request of the firm's chairman, who in an unprecedented gesture, had left his imperial perch to address employees whose names he did not know, unaccustomed as he was to interacting with anyone in the firm, other than his fellow equity partners.

"I wanted to thank you all," he intoned, as the room fell silent, "for all the hard work you've put into what is without question, the most important deal that our firm has completed this year, perhaps ever. Our client's CEO called me this morning to thank us and mentioned that without Eric's guiding hand, the deal wouldn't have closed. Well done, all of you, and in particular Eric."

With that, he left the room with regal aplomb. A king among men. All the eyes in the room now spun to Eric, like sand in an hourglass. He was relatively short, no more than five foot eight, with dark brown hair and hazel eyes deeply set against skin the color of ivory. He cut a handsome figure, and though he was forty-four, he looked as if he were in his mid-thirties and, in fact, was often mistaken for a senior associate by the junior lawyers and nonlegal staff who didn't know him. He was a full equity partner who had joined the law firm directly from law school. Initially, he had been repelled by the firm's culture and atmosphere; the partners, aloof and callous, oversaw and tacitly encouraged savage competition amongst the associates. The firm's ambiance, together with the lengthy working hours, had inflicted tremendous psychological and emotional distress on him. He had considered leaving but had sense enough to know that a job at another law firm would be no different, only less prestigious and less lucrative. Moreover, the firm had agreed after eighteen months to sponsor his application for a green card, which had also compelled him to stay as he had no desire to return to Paris, where his parents lived and where he had grown up. His U.S. law degree would be virtually ineffective in France, and besides, he didn't want to live near them. His Iranian stepfather was an unpleasantly sententious and narcissistic man. His mother, whom he did love, was so enthralled by her husband and his very large family that she had become part of them.

But those days were long since past; now he was a partner, indeed he was "the" partner, who had just closed the largest deal in the history of the firm. He was about to address the team that had worked under him for more than a year on the transaction. While the culture of the firm had remained the same, his position had changed, permitting him, if not fewer hours in the office, at least some control over his schedule. The attitude of junior lawyers toward him had changed on its own.

He rose to address his team:

"I couldn't have done it without—" Just at that moment, his cell phone rang. He looked down at the phone and recognized the number.

"Excuse me," he said, "I have to take this." He stepped away and answered the call. "Yes, I'll be there," he said, trying to whisper into the phone. "Of course I didn't forget."

There was an uncomfortable silence while his caller was speaking. They heard Eric say:

"I'm in a meeting and can't really speak right now." Silence. "No, I promise not to be late—" Silence, and then, "No, I'm not always late." Silence. "I'll be there on time."

Eventually, he hung up with a sigh.

"I'm sorry," he said with a smile and a roll of the eyes in an attempt to disguise his unease. "That was my wife. Our daughter is in a play, and I've promised to be there."

The others were uncertain how to reply. Eventually, the most senior lawyer ventured a hesitant laugh and the others followed suit. It was not a hearty laugh, as a group of friends would share over a joke, but one of those deliberate laughs that remind you of a courtier's consummate snicker. Discussing personal matters on firm time was frowned upon; alluding to a personal engagement as a reason to leave the office, no matter what time of the day or night, was considered heresy. That is why Eric's colleagues, all of whom were his subordinates, had been unsure how to react to his statement. As for Eric, he had been visibly perturbed by the call and sensed that he had to diffuse an awkward situation. He also felt sufficiently senior to break the rules in the right circumstances, but was relieved by the laughter and, to everyone's relief, decided to join in. The forced laughter turned into mirth.

When the room went quiet, he continued to thank everyone for their contribution to this monumental deal and gave a stock speech about how valuable each and every one of them was to the firm. He then took his leave. "I must go now. As you have no doubt ascertained, I've been summoned," he said with a grin.

On the way down in the lift, he encountered a distinguished looking, silver-haired gentleman in a charcoal grey suit and sporting a red Hermes tie. He had a solid stature, a handsome face of transparent paleness, high cheekbones, and piercing blue eyes. But a lifetime as a law firm warrior had left its marks: his shoulders sagged, his cheeks were hollow, and his teeth yellowed. However, it was his eyes that revealed the awful attribution. They were, as Shakespeare said of Henry V, "cold as stone."

"Hullo there," said Eric. "Didn't expect to see you here."

"Why not? I still have an office and come from time to time. I'm not dead yet, Eric, you know."

"I wasn't suggesting anything of the sort. Just that we don't see you here as often as we'd all like."

His name was Michael Landauer. He had been the chairman of the firm for more than twenty years and had retired two years earlier. Like many retired partners, the firm offered him a small office and the honorary position as "of counsel." He was also Eric's father-in-law.

"Harrumph," replied Michael and then, "Anyway, I hear congratulations are in order. You closed the Chrysalis deal," he said as if he were congratulating Eric on the purchase of a new pet.

"Oh, thank you, Sir," replied Eric. "It took a bit of time, but we got there in the end."

At this point, the lift had reached the ground floor, and they began to walk out together.

"Are you going home? My driver's outside. Shall I drop you?" asked Michael.

"No, thanks. I'm going to Susanna's school play. I think I'll walk. It's nice out and I wouldn't mind getting some fresh air."

They shook hands and parted ways.

It was one of those cool, sunny days typical of early spring when you want to cast off overcoat, hat, and gloves, but the wind reminds you that winter won't be dismissed so readily. Now that he had closed the deal, he should receive a larger draw and could use it to pay off the mortgage on their house in the Hamptons. Why hadn't the chair already assured him of the bonus? Why didn't he have a bigger say on the bonus pool?

Unlike publicly owned corporations, which have a clearly defined organizational structure and whose top executives' compensations are a matter of public record, law firms are private partnerships with opaque structures. The hierarchy within a law firm's partnership is largely determined by control of client relationships. The higher the revenues generated by the firm by a partner's clients, the higher that partner's take and the more prestigious his position.

When Michael retired, Eric had inherited his client relationships, propelling him to the very summit of the law firm because his clients now generated more revenues than the clients of any other partner. Yet Eric was troubled by the sentiment that he was deprived of the rank and compensation that should accompany the highest grossing partner in the firm. He felt that his partners would never trust him; that they would always consider him a foreigner, not one of their own. He suspected that beneath the flattering comments and sycophantic smiles they thought him undeserving of his position, that he owed it all to Michael, who had bequeathed Eric his roster of clients. He thought they believed that he had been handed everything on a silver platter: the clients, the position, the glamorous life, the palatial apartment on Park Avenue, and a house in Southampton.

Yet Eric now felt that it had come at enormous cost. The financial burden alone was crushing. It wasn't just the debt on the properties; his wife, Celia, did as she pleased. She spent as she desired, on household furniture, expensive antiques, works of art, and haute-couture outfits, not only for herself but also now for their eldest daughter who had just turned fifteen and mimicked her mother. In the rare event that he protested, she would peremptorily close the conversation by reminding him that he owed it all to her; that if it weren't for her, he'd be toiling as a service partner in some second-rate law firm. She exploited his insecurities as if she were ripping open a freshly healed wound. Ironically he hadn't even wanted to be a lawyer. Eric had majored in comparative literature at Princeton and had wanted to write, to be an artist. He had been a great admirer of French literature, of Proust's *Remembrance of Things Past,* of Flaubert's *Madame Bovary,* the poetry of Baudelaire. What had happened to him? Where had he gone wrong?

He was pulled out of his ruminations by someone shouting behind him. As a New Yorker, his initial reaction was to ignore such noise. The city is too large, too cacophonous for any one sound, however distinct, to stand out. But the shouting was persistent and appeared to be coming closer. Soon he realized that it was a voice repeatedly calling out a name. As it rose above the humming din of the city, he realized this person was calling out a name he hadn't heard in more than thirty years— his childhood name, which no one in New York even knew, one that he had almost forgotten.

When he turned around, Eric saw a middle-aged man with dark wavy hair, an olive complexion, in a long brown overcoat, out of breath from walking quickly, and waving in his direction. When he caught up with Eric, he said, "Aren't you Keyvan?"

"Yes, I mean no, I mean, I was ... I guess, a long time ago. How do you know that name?" stammered Eric.

"I recognized you. I'm Ramyar. Don't you remember me? We were in primary school together, Iranzamin."

Eric stared at him. He didn't recognize him, but in an instant his mind traveled through the alembic of time to another land, a different era that had long ceased to exist, except in his memory. Images of Iranzamin, which was the International School in Tehran in the 1970s, passed in quick succession through his mind, like a slide show, but not in any particular order.

"Yes, I remember now," he replied, recalling the name but not the face. "How are you?" he continued, almost mechanically, as his mind groped about in the past.

"I've been well since I last saw you," replied Ramyar with a laugh. "Would you like to sit down to a drink?" He had the presence of mind to move them out of the noisy, crowded street.

"I'm on my way to a school play. For one of my daughters." He smiled sheepishly and added, "I have two daughters." But he wasn't going to pass up on this chance encounter and said, "I have time for a quick drink. The Princeton Club is across the street. Let's go there."

As they were suitably dressed for the Club, they walked in and sat down in the mahogany grill room and ordered two glasses of Bordeaux.

"So how long have you been in New York?" Eric asked.

"Only recently, and I'm not sure for how long." He hesitated, then added, "I am producing a movie, and this is one of our locations."

"Congratulations. That sounds great."

"And you. What do you do?" Ramyar asked.

"Oh, I'm a corporate lawyer, have been for years," Eric said, and then smiled at how people define themselves by their occupations and social class, and wondered, "is that really who I am?"

And so they spoke and caught up on their recent pasts until their conversation turned to the one subject they eagerly wished to discuss.

"So when did you leave Iran?" Eric asked.

"About a year after all of you left."

"What do you mean by 'all'?"

"Well, when the Revolution began in earnest, you know, around the time the Shah went into exile, the families of a lot of the kids in class left. Yours included."

"Yes," Eric said, wistfully and almost to himself. "I left Iran in December 1978 never to return. But tell me, who else left? Or should I ask who stayed behind? I'm not in touch with anyone."

"I don't remember exactly, but I do recall when our teacher took roll calls that winter term, fewer and fewer kids would respond when their names were called."

"What was it like, I mean the school, after the Revolution?"

"Well at first it wasn't too bad, but then all the foreign teachers left and were replaced by Iranians. Khomeini's government used the teachers to get kids to spy on their parents. You know, if the parents talked badly about Islam or the regime, they would ask the kids to tell them. And then the Revolutionary Guard would arrest the parents."

"That's terrible. What about the curriculum? Did they continue with English and French?"

"Are you kidding? Only Farsi. And some Arabic in religion classes, where the Quran was drummed into our heads. It really was a shock for the holdover students. I mean, there were a lot of new students, and they didn't seem to mind. But I hated it. My life changed overnight, just like Iran did. Under the Shah we had all this freedom and progress; it was like living in London or New York. We could listen to music, go to movies, do what we wanted, and then we got this nightmare; they banned music and movies completely. Oh, and they segregated the boys from the girls. We weren't allowed to hang out with the girls anymore. It was a lot worse for the girls actually. They had to wear the hijab, which was painful for most of them. Remember how the girls used to love wearing the latest designer clothes, the Calvin Klein jeans, the mini-skirts, the sandals? Well, no more. They had to be covered from head to toe, even in summer, when it was hot. At least for us boys, it wasn't as bad, though we weren't allowed to wear shorts anymore."

"And to think that to this day, the Western press portrays the Shah as this dictatorial ogre," Eric added, shaking his head. "I mean, we were the most progressive country in the Middle East. Our women were the most emancipated of any near Eastern country, and that included Turkey. The Shah had female ministers in his cabinet and in the Parliament."

"I know, poor Farrokhroo Parsa, the education minister. You heard that Khomeini had her executed?" replied Ramyar.

Eric shook his head. "Yes, I heard, the savages. They executed members of my family too—my cousin Hoveyda, the former Prime Minister."

Ramyar nodded his head sympathetically. "Do you remember Haleh?" asked Ramyar.

"You mean the really tall girl with auburn hair?"

"Yes, her!"

Eric remembered her well. She had been in his class for a whole year. The teacher had a habit of lining them up according to height. She and two other girls were the tallest in the class, rather like Mnemosyne and her sister muses. He also remembered that she played the piano well. She must have been good because the music teacher, a very stiff Englishman who berated the students for even minor mistakes, always encouraged her to play for the class.

"I remember her. She was only eleven, but she played beautifully. But what about her?"

And then Ramyar told him the chilling story.

He was standing on the second-floor balcony one day with one of their friends, Eddie, when they saw Haleh and her friend Susan crying. The two boys had looked at them from across the way and had pretended to cry, dabbing their fingers to their eyes in a mocking gesture of preteen infantile naivety, as if they could attract the aloof damsels by such a misguided display. Suddenly the girls ran toward them with expressions of fury, and when the boys retreated, they gave chase. Ramyar had been perplexed by their uncharacteristic belligerence; after all, they used to treat the boys as if they didn't exist, not even vouchsafing them a disdainful glance.

As he was running away, he felt something moist and warm hit the back of his neck. He reached around and felt for the missile that had been hurled at him. It was a handkerchief, and it was so drenched that it was almost heavy. It took him a moment to realize that it was thoroughly soaked through with tears. Later that day, someone told him that Haleh's father had been executed the previous evening before a firing squad.

There was a long silence, after which Eric, visibly shaken, asked, "What happened to her?"

"I don't know. She was still there when I left. You know my family escaped, or I would have been drafted into the war with Iraq."

"How did you do that?" Eric asked.

"We made a mad dash over the Turkish border. Luckily we made it out. Most didn't."

Eric knit his brows and looked away; it was obvious that he was thinking of something else. Ramyar took this as a cue that Eric would have to leave soon. But Eric was thinking of himself, of what would have happened if he had been stuck in Iran, like Haleh or Ramyar, of another life and another fate. Then suddenly, he asked, "Do you remember Farhad?"

"Yes, I do. You know he was drafted into the war and died clearing the minefields?"

Eric held his breath. The words "died clearing the minefields" reverberated in his mind, like an echo in a canyon. Something strange happened; he released his breath, or rather he noticed his out-breath. He thought it strange that he was alive and breathing and Farhad, who would have been his age, could have been a man just like him, perhaps with a family, friends, and coworkers, and who would be loved by some, envied by others, perhaps reviled by a few, was no longer. Farhad, who had been his age; had gone to school with him; had played, laughed, and cried just like him, wasn't breathing any longer, hadn't taken a breath in quite some time.

"I'm sorry," said Ramyar, who read the distress on Eric's face, "I thought you knew ... I knew you were close but didn't realize that you—"

Before he could finish the sentence, the head waiter approached them.

"I'm very sorry, Sir, but we're setting up the room for a conference. Would you mind moving next door? They should have told you before you were seated."

"What conference?" asked Eric reflexively, as if in a trance, for his mind was still elsewhere, at a different time and a distant location.

"A poker conference."

"You mean, poker, as in the card game?" asked Eric, not sure that he had heard him correctly.

"Yes, Sir, mostly professionals."

"What? They're going to be playing poker? Here at the Princeton Club?"

"No, Sir, it's an instructional conference called, "How to Play and Win Every Time."

"Play and Win Every Time" echoed in his mind and intermingled with "died clearing the minefields," creating a resonance between now and then. Time became telescoped as if he were in a dream. Farhad had lost, decisively, conclusively. "And I suppose I have won," he murmured to himself looking around the Club's plush surroundings, suddenly mystified, as if he were living an illusion, but if this was how victory felt, then life must be a sham, just like a game of poker.

First Noble Truth of Buddhism:
All existence is suffering.

PART

I

Tehran Late 1970s

1

O N   T H E   W A Y   T O   the Mehrabad International Airport in Tehran, on that cold morning in the winter of 1979, Keyvan had no inkling that his life was about to be turned upside down and that he would soon find himself in a nightmarish ordeal that resembled Joseph K's in Kafka's distorted world.

Life had been very stable for him, filled with harmonious routines alternating between a rigorous trilingual education at Iranzamin and a comfortable home attended to by servants, with a driver who ferried him to and from school, the tennis club, and birthday parties. All of this was punctuated by holidays at the Caspian Sea and at the Riviera resorts, ski trips in France and Switzerland, and fun-filled weekends at his grandparents' country house in Karaj, a sleepy village in the outskirts of Tehran, where he and his cousins would play from dawn to dusk.

He lived with his mother, Lili, in a house they rented in the center of town, an area that once was considered the best neighborhood, but was fading fast. In the 1960s and 1970s, Iran was in the midst of an oil boom, and nowhere was this more apparent than in the Tehran real estate market. It was as if a new mansion appeared daily, one more sumptuous than the other, the changes reminiscent of Newport in the gilded age of the 1920s. In this respect, Tehran, rather like Evelyn Waugh's New York, expanded northward as the rich and fashionable abandoned the south and central parts of the city for areas that once were suburban countryside.

The migration north caused not only a geographic divide between north and south Tehran, but also separated the two parts of the city into different social classes. In the North lived the aristocracy and newly wealthy merchant classes in grand houses with gardens and pools, behind the brick walls so customary in the Middle East. The southern parts of the city were becoming increasingly the domain of the poor, who lived in apartment buildings, as well as shantytowns and slums which, while undeniably impoverished, were not nearly as squalid as their counterparts in Delhi or Karachi, or as dangerous as those of Harlem or South Central Los Angeles. This comparison held for the houses in the northern part of the city which, while undoubtedly opulent, did not have the grandeur of the mansions in Bel-Air. Even Niavaran Palace, where the Imperial Family lived, didn't compare to Buckingham Palace in its pomp and opulence.

Keyvan's house was large and very comfortable with a garden and even a small swimming pool. Like all houses in Tehran, it was ring-fenced by a tall, brick wall, an architectural feature that is rarely seen outside the Middle East. This was perhaps a vestige of the days when men maintained harems and wanted to shutter their multiple wives away from the unwanted gaze of strangers.

Even as a child, Keyvan had read about Darius the Great, the famous Achaemenid king who maintained a large harem in Ecbatana, where his shrewd and scheming first wife, Atossa, plotted to keep the King's other children from the Peacock Throne. Supposedly, she never left the palace grounds in her entire life, other than perhaps to travel in a golden carriage to another palace where she lived behind the same gilded walls. While the harem dated back twenty-five hundred years to the beginning days of the Persian Empire, its demise was recent. The current Shah's father, Reza Shah, a progressive king who had endeavored to free Iranian society from the shackles of Islamic superstition, had instituted reforms that eventually led to a burgeoning women's rights movement and the concomitant collapse of laws that maintained male hegemony. The pace of change was vertiginously fast.

By the time Keyvan was born, male polygamy was virtually abrogated and the harem obliterated. His mother's companion, Farzad, had grown up in a harem thirty years earlier. Farzad's father, Nezam, had been a Royal Prince who had become infamous for having sired thirty-four children. Together with his seven wives and multitude of servants, valets, grooms, and drivers, they lived in an enclosed compound in south Tehran. Nezam's first wife had been a Royal Princess; the other six were of different classes, a downward sloping gradient on a social map whose byzantine topography was crystal clear to the seven wives and their offspring. Farzad's mother, who was widely known to have been the maid of the Royal Princess, was at the bottom of this uncompromising conjugal food chain. The class demarcations within the family were exacerbated in a society where every gesture, accent, tone, and item of clothing functioned as a signal, a veritable and societal semiosis, reminiscent of Proust's *Le Côté de Guermantes*.

The ramifications of this intra-familiar class distinction were profound. When Farzad's eldest brother was a student in Paris, he took apartments at the Ritz hotel and had a chauffeur-driven Rolls Royce at his disposal. "If he would see us playing football in the compound," recalled Farzad of his older brother, "he wouldn't distinguish us from the groom's children." When Farzad's father had his thirtieth child, the eldest son complained to the king that his father was dissipating his inheritance with so many offspring and asked that his father be threatened with imprisonment lest he sire more children!

Growing up in such a distorted environment had an indelible and psychological impact on Farzad; even in old age he would remain a victim of a warped and rigid childhood, unable to escape the talismanic trances of those early years— a Freudian family romance within a Prince's household.

Just how completely that old world had been transformed in a short space of time was evinced by the contrast between Keyvan's childhood and that of Farzad's. Keyvan's parents had divorced after a brief and fractious marriage. His mother was a single working parent; their life resembled the movie *Kramer vs. Kramer* in its portrayal of the changing fabric of the modern American family as a result of women entering the workforce. His mother complained that his father didn't provide sufficient alimony, and she had to rely on her own father to subsidize their lifestyle. Even more surprising was his mother's relationship with Farzad, whom he referred to as his stepfather but who was, in fact, not married to his mother. While they lived separately, they functioned in every other aspect as a couple; they socialized and were invited to parties and events as a couple; they each attended the other's family gatherings as a couple, and traveled together. Farzad had a daughter and a son from a prior marriage. His daughter was married, and his son attended a University in California.

Keyvan's grandmother Parto and her siblings had come of age just as Reza Shah was modernizing Iran. Like much of Iran's elite, Parto had heartily embraced the King's progressive ideas, even though her marriage to Keyvan's grandfather Massoud had been arranged by her parents. They had had three children—Lili and her two brothers, Cyrus and Darius, all of whom had been educated in the United States. As a child, of course, Keyvan was unaware of the historical and political forces that shaped his family's behavior. All he knew was that they celebrated Nowruz—the Persian New Year—on the first day of spring, and he looked forward to those festivities and the gifts of gold coins customarily handed out. As his paternal grandparents had died by the time he was born, family gatherings, including Nowruz celebrations, were held at his maternal grandparents' large, beautiful house, which had a garden and crystal blue swimming pool in the southern part of the city. Like all Iranians, Keyvan's family celebrated Nowruz with enthusiasm, decorating their house with the traditional table settings made of the seven Ss, together with delectably fragrant hyacinths, a goldfish bowl, and golden coins.

Keyvan and Lili had lived in this house for a number of years after Lili had divorced Keyvan's father, Kamran. Keyvan loved the house, especially because his cousins, who were all around his own age, would come over and play games all day and spend the night sleeping on the floor in the same room. In fact, Keyvan considered his grandparents' house as his home and had been devastated when they had sold it to move to an apartment in one of the new and fancy high-rise buildings in the northern part of Tehran.

They never attended any Islamic religious celebrations. Keyvan had not even seen a mosque, let alone gone into one. By the time he was born in the 1960s, his parents had fully forsaken any religious inclinations they might once have had. His grandfather had progressive ideas about Islam, and his father's religious education was not as rigorous as might have been imagined. In fact, his father had attended a secular school in Tehran, followed by University in France. Whatever that early education imbued in him, by the time Keyvan was born, there was no observance of Islam in his nuclear or extended family.

When the religious unrest of the late 1970s infiltrated their home, with some female servants wearing the hijab to cover their heads and necks, Keyvan had gone to his grandmother Parto for an explanation. She had clarified the inconsistencies at the heart of Iranian culture, which would soon baffle those in the West. This story dated back more than one thousand years to when Persia was conquered by the Arabs in the eighth century A.D. The Sasanian Empire was economically and culturally advanced and had withstood the assaults of Imperial Rome, but fell to the Arabs. While they imposed their religion, Islam, on the Zoroastrian Persians, they largely left alone their cultural institutions. In fact, the Arabs appropriated and exported many of Persia's artists and artifacts. The Alhambra in Spain features many Persian architectural designs, such as the seamless melding of interior and exterior spaces, intricate mosaic work, and beautiful fountains.

Parto explained that the Arabs had permitted their conquered subjects to continue to celebrate their Pre-Islamic traditions. Nowruz, a Zoroastrian festival that long predated Islam, was still faithfully celebrated by all Iranians; in fact, it is the most popular and beloved tradition. Chaharshanbe Suri, a celebration of life held on the Wednesday preceding Nowruz, during which many pyres are lit for people to jump over, dates back to Zoroastrian times when fire was revered as a symbol of the life-giving sun. Keyvan loved this festival, when they would arrange small, multiple bonfires on the large pavement of his grandparents' garden and he and his cousins would jump over them, yelling and screaming in ecstasy.

However, while the conquering Arabs may have provided liberties in the domain of art and culture, they did not do so when it came to their faith. Islam became the religion of the Iranian people, on which it had imposed a stranglehold. Despite the progressive reforms of the Pahlavi era, to this day, Iranians remain profoundly religious, and many adhere to the teachings of Islam with the fervor and zeal of true believers. This dichotomy, between Pre-Islamic traditions and a resolutely sacred belief in the tenets of Islam, defines the fabric of Iranian society today, she told Keyvan.

"The Shahnameh, whose fabulous tales I've often recounted at bedtime for you, is one of the seminal works of Persian literature," she continued. "It's a mytho-epic poem written by Ferdowsi in the eleventh century A.D. While the Shahnameh is undoubtedly a cultural and literary masterpiece, it also has functioned as a significant political symbol. The poem does not include a single Arabic word among its sixty thousand lines of verse, a deliberate endeavor by the poet to save the Farsi language from annihilation by the Arab invaders. By writing the Shahnameh, Ferdowsi resurrected Farsi from the ashes of the Sasanian Empire. The distinction between Farsi and Arabic is key to understanding Persian cultural identity," Parto insisted, "because it is part of a peaceful, yet powerful historical resistance of Persians to Arab rule. Like many Iranians today, Ferdowsi believed in the cultural superiority of Iran over its Arab neighbors and conquerors. The Shahnameh was a cultural bulwark against a militarily superior, occupying power. The poet succeeded in his struggle; today Farsi, not Arabic, is the language of Iran. Iranians of all classes are familiar with the figures and characters of the Shahnameh—the hero, Rostam, reared by the mythical bird Simorg and the evil king of Turan, Afrasiab. Children learn the epic's stories from an early age." Keyvan remembered going to nursery school one day with a paper crown that he referred to as Afrasiab's emblem!

"On the other hand, *Namaz* or *Salat,* the daily prayer, is traditionally recited in Arabic, a language most Iranians cannot read or understand. This is not to underestimate the power of Islam on Iranian society, best dramatized by its recent resurgence," his grandmother added.

"In the twentieth century, Iran struggled between the profound pull of Islam and an increasing secularization and westernization that adopted and incorporated its Pre-Islamic traditions. The Pahlavi kings, Reza Shah, and his son, Mohammed Reza Shah, glorified Iran's Pre-Islamic empire. The chador—the Islamic veil that had covered Iranian women for more than a thousand years—was rendered illegal to wear. The emancipation of women signified a waning of the Islamic pull in favor of pre-Islamic traditions. In 1970, when the Shah celebrated the two thousand five hundredth anniversary of the Persian Empire, there were no signs of Iran's Islamic heritage, as the king paid homage to Cyrus the Great at his tomb in Persepolis.

"Yet," Parto continued, "less than a decade later, Islam is leading a resurgence led by fanatical foreign troublemakers."

"What will happen, Grandmother? Will they do away with Nowruz and Chaharshanbe Suri?" he asked.

"Over my dead body," Parto replied.

But the religious forces aligned against the Shah and the aristocracy would leave a bloody trail behind them.

2

KEYVAN'S FATHER WAS THE youngest of twelve children and had Keyvan late in life. His once prominent family was now on the decline. Keyvan's paternal grandfather was revered and respected to a point that shops in Tehran all had closed on his death in the 1930s. One of his uncles, Jamal, was a member of parliament and had famously opposed Prime Minister Mosaddegh in his struggle for power against the Shah in the 1950s. When the Shah returned triumphant from exile, he rewarded Jamal with a level of trust and familiarity that propelled his family to the very top of Iranian society. He was awarded ambassadorships in India and Great Britain. His daughter Farideh married Prime Minister Ali Mansur, who was assassinated on the street by Islamic militants; and his other daughter Leila married Prime Minister Hoveyda who later was executed by Khomeini shortly after the Islamic Revolution in 1979. Keyvan's father was one of the king's twelve chamberlains and a regular at the Imperial Court, especially at Princess Ashraf's, the Shah's powerful twin sister, who hosted a lunch every Friday. Keyvan would hear his mother complain that at these lunches no one listened to anyone else, and everyone was on the lookout for the arrival of the King and Queen so that he or she could be the first person to catch the sovereign's eye and bow.

Nevertheless, by the 1970s his family's star had diminished considerably. Jamal had died, as had Farideh, after leaving Iran for Switzerland. Keyvan's father had a falling out with his niece Leila, who herself had a turbulent on-again, off-again relationship with the Prime Minister, marrying, divorcing, and remarrying him within the course of a decade. While his father remained as Chamberlain and had a good position as the chief officer of the agricultural bank, he lost his intimacy with Princess Ashraf, and his invitations to the Imperial Court declined to a point where he only was asked to attend official occasions. By this time, Lili and Kamran had divorced and Keyvan was living at his grandparents' house.

The social, political, and economic forces that were sweeping through Iranian society and buffeting his family's position were mostly immaterial to Keyvan. The idyllic rhythm of his early years in Iran was punctuated by personal, rather than political dramas. One such event took place on a ski vacation when he was five years old. Every year in winter they would take at least one trip to Dizin, a ski resort about one and one-half hour north of Tehran in the Alborz Mountains. The road trip itself was always filled with excitement and anticipation. On that particular trip, as on virtually all others, the designated driver was Parto's stalwart chauffer, Khaleel. At five foot nine, Khaleel was considered tall. His grey hair was decidedly thinning, revealing an increasingly visible bald spot. He had been with Keyvan's grandparents for so long that he had become part of the family; Keyvan had never known life without him. He was a quiet, solemn man, but with a sense of humor that Keyvan had begun to notice as he was getting older. His passengers that day consisted of Keyvan and Lili, his cousin Lars and his mother, Caroline. Lars was the brother that Keyvan never had. As Keyvan was an only child, Lars and Keyvan typically played together at family gatherings and often would go on holiday together, as they did that Wednesday afternoon while Khaleel drove out of Tehran toward Dizin. Their school observed the Iranian calendar and closed for the weekend on Wednesday evenings and reopened on Saturday mornings.

The drive out to Dizin was a scenic one, though Keyvan and Lars were too busy playing games in the car to notice the scenery. A narrow two-lane road wound its way in concentric circles up the snow-covered mountain, like a tall, corpulent lady in white, and then down again in the same circular journey. At one point they were driving by the banks of a narrow river dotted with maple trees, their brown, barren branches stenciled against the vast canopy of silver snow that blanketed the entire landscape.

The road was rarely plowed, and just when they thought they couldn't go any farther, Khaleel would get out and place chains around the Land Rover's tires to push through. Lars and Keyvan were brimming with excitement as they helped with the chains, though they were more hindrance than help as they frolicked in the snow, and Keyvan's mother would reprimand them. Khaleel remained unperturbed, a deep grin blossoming on his face, as he focused on the task at hand as if it were as effortless as the flapping of a bird's wings. The road continued through the alpine wilderness with not a trace of humanity other than the occasional car that would first appear in the distance as a circle of light on the horizon, then gradually morph into two approaching headlights as it struggled through the snow. For Lars and Keyvan the experience was exhilarating, though for Keyvan's mother it was at best tiresome, and sometimes a harrowing ordeal. In any event, they all shared in their excitement when the silhouettes of Dizin's two hotels appeared in the distance.

One hotel had been built in the 1960s, the other was a more recent addition and had a very contemporary 70s feel to it with shag carpets, mirrored walls, and even a disco ball in the nightclub. The resort itself had been the brainchild of his majesty, Mohammed Reza Shah, who was an expert and avid skier, having attended Le Rosey secondary school in Switzerland. His queen was also a proficient skier, and if the idea of the ski resort was his, her influence, if not her hand (she had been an architectural student in Paris) was visible. It could be seen not only in the late modernism style of the structures and decorations but in the choice of retail establishments such as its exquisite French restaurant and the Studio 54-esque nightclub. Down the road from the hotels were a half-dozen brown-brick ski chalets that dotted the gleaming snow, reminiscent of the postcards one receives from friends on ski vacations in Switzerland. They had always taken rooms at the hotel, first in the older one and when construction was completed, at the newer hotel. On this occasion, however, they had booked one of the chalets because of the size of their group.

Massoud was already there when they arrived. He was a burly squat man with a fluff of white hair that resembled cotton

candy, olive skin, deeply set hazel eyes, a small aquiline nose—
unlike the large Roman noses that typified most Iranians—and
a mouth that was always on the verge of smiling. If it weren't
for the olive tone of his skin, he would have made the consummate Santa Claus, which is perhaps why he repeatedly played
that role at Aunty Caroline's Swedish-flavored Christmas parties. His preternatural affability complemented his Santa Claus
appearance, though it was sometimes punctuated by a temper
as fulgurant and thankfully as ephemeral as a lightning flash.

Keyvan was always happy to be in his jovial company
because he so rarely saw him. He traveled frequently in
Europe, often to Caux in Switzerland, a center for meditation
and yoga, activities that he pursued as avidly, though perhaps
more openly and freely, as he did the company of younger
women. He spoke five languages; German, his strongest,
and spoken almost like a native. He had studied in Weimar,
Germany, in the 1920s and had received a PhD in chemistry.
Exactly how and why he had arrived in Germany were details
that were shrouded in mystery, as were his return to Iran in the
early 1930s and two intriguing month-long visits to Berlin, with
his wife, in 1933 and 1936. In his teenage years, he had been a
student in Beirut, which at the time was known as the Paris of
the Middle East. Rumor had it that when the money from Iran
was delayed, he and his brother survived on coconuts.

Keyvan's grandfather had brought Mohammed along, a
handsome young man who worked as a groom and gardener at
the house in Tehran, to help with domestic chores at the chalet
and to play with Keyvan and Lars. The previous summer,
Mohammed and Keyvan were by the pool at his grandfather's
house in Tehran. Keyvan had lain on Mohammed's stomach
and had developed a crush on him. Since then Keyvan would
always ask if Mohammed would let him rest on his stomach.

Whenever he agreed, Keyvan would lie there for a long time and never understood why Mohammed would be nervous about this game and didn't want him to tell anyone. Keyvan didn't know that this was the sort of thing that adults would vehemently object to. All he knew was that he liked it and wanted it to continue.

Keyvan's father arrived in the early evening, trudging through the snow in his Wellington boots from which one could surmise that he was not a skier but a fisherman. This was the first occasion on which Keyvan had seen his parents together after their divorce, which had occurred when Keyvan was three. His father took the large bedroom at the back of the chalet. While Keyvan was excited by his arrival, he was anxious about being in the presence of both parents because he behaved differently with each of them in an effort to please them individually. Now he was perplexed as to how he should conduct himself and therefore felt ill at ease. To his surprise, his father's arrival did not focus any attention on him or his disquietude; rather the conversation centered around the comforts of the chalet, unpacking, closet space, and his mother's questions concerning domestic matters.

Then they received an unexpected visit. Keyvan's aunt Shahla, married to his mother's brother, was staying at the hotel and came down for a drink before dinner. She was in her early thirties, had hair as black as red grapes that fell below her shoulders, deep black eyes set against an olive-toned skin, and a voluptuousness reminiscent of an odalisque. His mother didn't like her, and there had been quite a bit of history between them.

She sat down in the living room as tea was brought in by Mohammed. Keyvan's mother and father joined her, but his grandfather remained absent. When Keyvan's mother left the room, his father engaged in banter with Shahla that bordered on flirting, leaving Keyvan bored and daydreaming about the games he wanted to play. Suddenly his father said, "Look at Aunty Shahla's boobs. Look at how round and rosy they are." Keyvan was startled out of his daydream by this unexpected invitation to focus on his auntie's tits. Before he could inspect them, he heard his mother's scathingly irritated voice scolding his father from the doorway, "If you want to flirt, leave the child out of it."

"What's it to you?" he growled defiantly in a low baritone like a lion distracted from his kill by hyenas.

She continued to shriek at him, and he suddenly leapt from his seat and hurried toward his bedroom muttering, loudly enough to be heard, "I'll get my gun and I'll shoot you and your little puppy." In Farsi, calling someone's child a puppy suggests that the father of the child was a dog and is considered a tremendous insult to the mother, as well as, of course, to the child.

Keyvan went into the kitchen, which was across the hall from the bedroom.

He saw his naked grandfather bolt out of the bathroom where he was showering and follow his dad into the bedroom. His mom and Shahla followed, and all he could see was the back of Shahla's head. He asked Mohammed if he could take his shirt off and let him lie on his stomach.

"Now is not the time," said Mohammed gently, though Keyvan couldn't understand why. It seemed the ideal time since he needed a refuge from the chaos and disarray that was unfolding across the hall, a situation too complicated for him to grasp intellectually, but which nevertheless inflicted tremendous emotional anxiety. He sought comfort and reassurance in Mohammed's arms to placate the unpredictable and chaotic violence that, like the eruption of a volcano, had unexpectedly just arisen for no apparent reason.

His father emerged from the bedroom, not with a gun as threatened, but with a suitcase, and without even a goodbye, left the chalet and the resort and drove back to Tehran. Later he would hear that his father did indeed reach for a gun, a silver-plated antique that was more of a decoration than a weapon, and that his grandfather had wrested the gun from him.

Mohammed took Keyvan and Lars to play in the snow. They made a snowman and decorated it with a hat and a scarf; there was so much snow that they would slide down a gentle slope, falling as if into a bed of feathers and squealing with laughter.

3

I N 1978, one hundred thousand Americans were living in Tehran, virtually all of them in the northern part of the city. While their embassy, a large enclave with beautiful gardens full of old cedar trees, was in the south of Tehran, most Americans sent their children to ACS (short for American Community School) or Iranzamin. The latter, whose campus had only recently moved from the south to the northern part of the city, was truly international. Each year the school celebrated United Nations day and invited pupils to stand when the name of their country was called out on a loudspeaker. The process took approximately an hour. The majority of students were Iranian, but by the numbers that stood up on that sunny day in 1978 as the United States of America was called out, it appeared as if there were half as many Americans at the school. That year UN day was celebrated at the end of the school year. Report cards were handed out and the school closed for the summer holidays, not to reopen again until September.

When the celebrations were over, the students went to the allocated classrooms to collect their reports. Iranzamin followed a curriculum similar to the American school system and handed out an international baccalaureate to its graduates. Like American schools, the classes corresponded to the year or grade of the pupil. The sixth-grade class that year had approximately eighty students and was divided into four homeroom classes: 6B, 6G, 6K and 6W—the letter corresponding to the last name of the teacher instructing the class. The pupils of 6B hurried to their classroom to collect their reports. As they arrived, Keyvan noticed that their teacher, Miss Branch, was absent and an administrator, a Filipino named Tito, was handing out the reports.

"Where's Miss Branch?" asked Keyvan as he approached Tito to collect his report.

"Not here today," she replied with a marked Filipino accent.

"Where is she? I wanted to say goodbye to her."

"I don't know." Tito mechanically looked up Keyvan's name and handed him his report.

Just then, Michael and Hossein came in for theirs. Michael was a tall, lanky kid with dark brown hair, brown eyes, a fair complexion, and a wild but kind manner about him. He was half American and half Iranian, and his parents had been very friendly with Keyvan's mother. Hossein wasn't much taller than Keyvan, and was a good-looking boy with brown hair and eyes, fair skin, and large metal-rimmed glasses. The three of them had become great friends that year. While Keyvan and Michael had attended Iranzamin since the age of three, Hossein had recently enrolled, having previously studied at a school in London where his father had been sent on assignment. Their friendship had blossomed one day when they were paired up in soccer, and to their great surprise beat the opposing team five goals to one.

Keyvan and Hossein were the top two academic students of 6B, and unbeknownst to either one until United Nations Day, they were two of the five students in grade six who would receive highest honors that year. Neither of them expected to win at soccer on that sunny day in September 1977. Whether the victory was the result of the confidence the two found in each other—academics and excelling at soccer—or some other factor, neither of them spent much time thinking about it. Instead, they relished their newfound success on the soccer field, and from then on became virtually inseparable. What natural academic rivalry sprung up between them was overcome on the playground and in soccer games with their peers. Keyvan was even more surprised at this victory than Hossein. In first grade, when his classmates had played "boys chase girls" and "girls chase boys," Keyvan had always wanted to, and often did, side with the girls. This hadn't surprised or fazed the others who had, in good nature, accepted the fact that Keyvan played on the girl's team. He, in fact, had assiduously explained this phenomenon with the flawless logic of a child to a bewildered substitute teacher who had tried to get Keyvan to play on the boys' team. "The girls are more fun to play with."

From the chase game in first grade to soccer in sixth, Keyvan seldom had excelled or distinguished himself at sports. He sometimes wondered if his newfound confidence in soccer was a natural extension of his innate competitive nature, or was the result of his friendship with Hossein.

Though initially shy at his school in London, Hossein excelled academically and played a variety of sports, which in the UK, unlike at Iranzamin, had been organized by the school and were mandatory. While he didn't know much about Keyvan or the rest of the students, he already had seen that the boy did well in class. Whether it was Keyvan's genuine, good-natured camaraderie, or that he sensed a bond with another intellectual and potential outcast, Hossein picked him as his teammate from that day forward, and together they won the vast majority of the games.

Later that school year, after one of their soccer games at recess, Keyvan overheard one of the other boys say there had been acid attacks on the street. He didn't understand the meaning of this statement and looked around to the others. When the teacher began speaking, the class fell silent. When he arrived home, he questioned his mother, "What exactly is an acid attack?" She didn't provide a satisfactory response, too distracted by her relationship with Farzad, party dresses, jewelry, and gossip to explain such an attack to an eleven year old. He understood that it meant someone would throw a liquid into someone else's face; he had learnt about sulfuric and hydrochloric acid in chemistry class. Yet he was curious as to how you would carry the liquid. He pictured a beaker containing acid. But, wouldn't they spill it? And what would it do? He asked his chemistry teacher, Mr. Prewett, what would happen if he were to accidentally spill acid onto his hands. The response was that, while it would depend on the type of acid, it may cause burning and scarring. He could imagine the dire effects of the scarring on one's face.

If Keyvan was curious about the meaning and mechanics of such an acid attack, its underlying significance eluded his mother and apparently everyone else. The storm clouds that announced a Revolution that would abolish a monarchy that was over two thousand five hundred years old went unheeded. The ruling class—the old aristocracy and the bourgeois technocrats recently promoted by the Shah—were too preoccupied with jockeying within the system to discern the dangers that would topple the monarchy and devastate their lives. Farzad's brother Missid typified that mentality. He was one of the thirty-four children of the Prince, who despite the concerns of his eldest royal children, had left all of his offspring a tidy inheritance. In addition to that, Missid had parlayed his connections to create a thriving business that enabled him to amass a fortune estimated to be in excess of one hundred million U.S. dollars in the 1970s. His children went to the best schools, including Ivy League colleges in America. He had multiple properties around the world and a very prominent position in society. Nevertheless, Keyvan had heard him complain that he was made to wait two hours by a minister whose authorization for a building project he had sought. "These worthless cronies of the Shah," he would grumble, his pride wounded by the perceived slight. His delusion of grandeur had reached a point that he couldn't see that the minister, perhaps, had other urgent matters to which to attend; Missid didn't realize that he was one of the primary beneficiaries of a system that he now condemned. Blinded by his narcissism, he even joined some of the anti-government Revolutionary protests which, in the end, led to the confiscation of all of his Iranian properties as well as a death warrant that he narrowly evaded by fleeing into exile.

He wasn't the only one who was addled by delusions; the

King himself would succumb to the same form of psychological infirmity when, to quell the rapidly escalating demonstrations and protests, he would imprison some of his most loyal ministers and advisors, including Keyvan's cousin, Prime Minister Hoveyda, to placate the people. It had the opposite effect. And when the Shah fled into exile, he would leave behind bars the very people who had served him, now themselves served up on a silver platter to Khomeini's Revolutionary firing squad.

In early September 1978, Keyvan celebrated his twelfth birthday with a pool party at his grandmother's house. He invited friends from school—Hossein and Michael included, as well as cousins and others. The most notable guest was Prince Ali, who arrived with an escort of a dozen soldiers. A few weeks earlier, the Rex Cinema in Abadan—a huge theater that seated more than five hundred people—had been set on fire. The doors had been mysteriously locked from the outside, and virtually everyone inside had perished. The BBC, which broadcast reports in native Farsi on the radio from the Persian Gulf, repeated rumors that cast suspicions on the SAVAK, the Shah's secret police. Years later, it would turn out that Khomeini's followers had burnt down the cinema and locked the doors to incite the people against the government, a tactic that proved successful. The cinema fire became a galvanizing force for the Revolution; demonstrations erupted all over the country as a stunned public demanded an accounting for the arson. Blame was placed squarely on the government's shoulders. The Shah, ill with cancer that would eventually kill him, equivocated. Eventually, he named a quasi-religious man by the name of Sharif-Emami as prime minister in the hope that his premiership might quell the protests. However, he was an incompetent who did little to placate the situation.

For Keyvan and his friends, the soldiers' presence outside added to the excitement of the party, which unfolded flawlessly under a brilliant sun with swimming contests, soccer, and a game of Monopoly. His mother was less sanguine and inquired of the colonel, who led the soldiers and had been invited in to join the birthday party, whether there might be cause for concern.

"His Majesty's government is as stable as the Rock of Gibraltar," was his response. Four months later, the Shah would leave Iran, never to return.

Those four months marked a turning point in the two-thousand-five-hundred-year history of Iran. From the founding of the Persian Empire by Cyrus the Great to the twentieth century, Iran had endured its share of geopolitical, religious, and cultural turmoil; yet the monarchy had survived. What Alexander the Great, who destroyed the Persian Empire and burnt down Persepolis; the Romans who waged a multi-century war against the Sasanians; the Islamic Caliphate in Arabia that conquered the entire Middle East; the Mongol hordes of Genghis Khan in the twelfth century; the Ottomans at the peak of their power, nor the British who had colonized the world in the nineteenth century and coveted Iran's newly discovered oil, had been unable to achieve, an obscure seventy-nine-year-old religious cleric from Najaf succeeded in bringing about in a relatively short time frame, the fall of the Peacock Throne.

———

THE FIRST DAY OF SCHOOL was the day after Keyvan's birthday. There were five sections in his year, and when he arrived at his assigned classroom, he was pleasantly surprised to see Hossein.

"We're together again!" exclaimed Hossein.

ayed soccer on the same team at recess and won.
their new teacher, Mr. Brown, a relatively young
, who told them all about the English football

Michael was in a different class, but they would meet and play at lunch time or other off periods. One day Michael said to Keyvan, "I heard that yesterday you got here before everyone else and locked the classroom door from inside?"

"Only for a few minutes and then I opened it."

"What were you doing there? Why did you lock the door?'

"Nothing. I was just resting."

"Oh come on, tell me what you were doing. Were you going through your teacher's papers?"

"Well it's a secret, but I'll tell you if you tell me a secret."

"Okay, a deal."

"Well, I did go through his stuff."

"Wow. Actually, I've done the same thing in my class. After Ms. Gorsky leaves, I go through all her papers."

"Really? What have you found?"

"Oh, nothing really, just the papers that she's marking and some other teacher stuff."

"Hmm," Keyvan thought to himself. That's odd. He'd found all sorts of things in Brown's desk, including copies of future tests and answers that he'd cribbed.

"Now, your turn. What's the secret?'

Michael reflected and then said, "Oh, here's one."

"Let's hear it!"

"There's this religious guy called Khomeini who says the Shah is bad and needs to go."

"That's a terrible thing to say," responded Keyvan, taken aback "but that's not a secret. Tell me something that relates to us."

"I don't have anything right now."

"Oh Michael, think of a better secret next time you ask me to tell you one. Come on now, let's go and play."

As the autumn drew on, the demonstrations against the government escalated and wildcat work strikes broke out all over the country. Periodic electricity outages caused blackouts.

"Can I light the candles? Please let me light the candles," Keyvan exclaimed excitedly one night.

He was fascinated by a gas lamp that his mother had pulled out of an old closet. It was fueled by paraffin, and he had learnt how to light it.

One evening, when the lights had gone out and Keyvan had proudly lit the gas lamp and was doing his homework, a large demonstration passed by their house.

"Death to the Shah. Khomeini is our leader," the crowd outside chanted.

Keyvan, Lili, and Mohammed ran into the garden. Like most other houses, theirs was surrounded by a brick wall. Lili made sure that the door was locked and bolted. Mohammed wanted to go outside, but Lili forbade him and so he climbed a tree to watch the demonstrators. Lili walked around nervously, ushering Keyvan inside.

"What's going on? Why is Mohammad climbing the tree?"

"Don't worry, darling. It's nothing. Just finish your homework. It's almost time for bed."

She went over to the phone and started calling her friends.

Eventually, the demonstration passed by their street. Silence fell over the house, punctuated by distant and uncertain noises.

Keyvan stayed up late, working on his homework. When he eventually went to bed, he slept soundly. The next day he went to school as usual.

"How long did your homework take last night?" Hossein asked him.

"Forever. The math was particularly tough. And then the Farsi essay."

That year they had a brilliant Farsi teacher, Mrs. Rezvan. She was one of the traditional school teachers, steeped in literature and poetry, who cared deeply for her students and genuinely wanted each and every one of them to share in her delight of Persian poetry and literature. She was particularly fond of the thirteenth-century poet Saadi, whose entrancing rhymes she made her students memorize and recite. Even more remarkable was her ability to explain to her young wards the profound philosophical and spiritual teachings that underlie Saadi's poetry. Humans, she had explained, are not separate beings disconnected from each other as in self-contained vessels, but part of a larger whole. Saadi had likened humanity to the limbs of a body: the pain in one limb infects the others, just as the suffering of one person affects the whole. Saadi, she told them, was a deeply spiritual poet. His references to the "beloved" did not designate a remote and fearsome sky god, but rather the underlying spiritual force that unites all of nature, to which humanity is inextricably linked. "This force permeates the whole universe; it *is* the universe of which we are a part. But we are in a sense blind to it because we do not see clearly. Like two rays of the sun, so far removed from their common origin, we ask each other 'where are you from?' It is this ultimate delusion that is the source of our suffering." In this, the teacher further explained, Saadi's poetry overlaps with Buddhist teachings.

When he had heard the reference to Buddhism, Keyvan had raised his hand and asked, "I've heard my grandfather speak of Buddhism and meditation. What does that have to do with Saadi?"

"That's an excellent question, Keyvan. And, while you might yet be too young to fully understand it, I'll try to give you an answer. Your grandfather spoke of Buddhist meditation because the Buddha thought that mankind's suffering arises from the wandering mind that clings to external things in a futile quest for happiness. Instead, happiness can come from turning inward, looking inside yourself. Why? Because that's where you will recognize that self-same essence about which Saadi sings in his poetry." She paused, and from the blank stares of Keyvan and her students, realized she had lost them, but couldn't resist one last thought. "Don't worry. Hopefully you'll revisit all of this when you're older. But for now, let's turn to our weekly essay."

Every Tuesday she would hand out an essay topic, and on Wednesdays she would ask the class to write the essay in class. Most of the students, if not all, would ask their parents for help and some, like Keyvan, would ask an adult to write the essay, which he or she would then memorize and write down in class. In fact, one of Keyvan's essays had been deemed so good by his teacher that she had asked him to read it aloud. It was a true story, based on two parrots that had been gifted to him. The female had choked on a nut, and the male had become inconsolable. He wouldn't eat or drink. Keyvan had even opened the bird cage in the hope that liberty might give him some hope, but to no avail. One day, when Keyvan came home from school, he found that his parrot had died. He had cried, as touched by the suffering of the male parrot as by its death. The essay, written by Keyvan's grandmother, had recreated the parrot's anguish, Keyvan's efforts first to assuage and then to save him, and his eventual descent into grief when he realized that his parrot had perished.

The essay, when read aloud by Keyvan, brought some girls in class to tears. But one girl raised her hand and said, "Khanom, Mam, when you hand out the topics, the kids get their parents to write the essays for them, and then they come and regurgitate them here in class."

One of the sobbing girls interjected, "That's rubbish. He wrote that essay himself. Why do you always say such a thing?"

"Quiet please," responded Mrs. Rezvan, and then turning to the girl who had complained, she said, "Do you not know the very value of that memorization?"

Of course, she had known all along that her students would receive help. But to her, memorization was not only a skill that trained the mind in a certain way; she used it to teach her students to write. She felt the more you memorized great prose or poetry especially in youth, the better writer you became.

It was to this essay that Hossein had made reference and, of course, it had taken Keyvan some time the previous evening to memorize the essay that his grandmother had dictated to him.

The gathering storm of Revolution had not yet interfered with Keyvan's routine. The only thing that he began to notice was a change in his friendship with Hossein. At first, he saw Hossein going off to play soccer after school.

"Who are you playing with? Can I come?" he asked.

"Just with some friends," was the response but with no invitation for Keyvan to join.

Then at recess, Hossein didn't want to play, or, if he did, he played on another team, with some older kids. When previously they had compared answers after tests, showed each other their marks, and shared everything, now Hossein pulled

back, became reticent, and used the pretext of other commit-
ments when asked why. One day, when Keyvan volunteered
his answers and asked to see Hossein's, he snapped, "You
really shouldn't do this. It's against the rules. Our answers are
private."

"What? We've been doing this for more than a year. What's
going on with you?"

"Nothing. It's just that we're not kids anymore, and we
should behave responsibly." He then walked away.

Keyvan was disappointed and hurt. He could see his friendship with Hossein slipping away and he didn't know why.

He asked Michael, "Have you noticed anything strange
about Hossein?"

"No, like what?"

"Oh, I don't know. He seems different. So distant. Less
friendly."

"I haven't felt that. Why do you say that?"

"I dunno. Maybe it's me. Maybe I've done something to
upset him, but I can't think what it might be. I mean he doesn't
want to play soccer with me after class or share things like we
used to."

"I've heard that his family is political and critical of the
Shah," Michael said.

"Really? I didn't know that. Anyway, why would that make
him less friendly?"

"Well, it's just a guess, but you invited the Shah's son to
your birthday. Maybe that has something to do with it."

"Oh, come on. That's grownup stuff. It doesn't affect us."

"If not, then I don't know. Maybe he'll come around."

Michael had been right. Hossein's family, highly political to
the point of radicalism, had exhorted Hossein against his friendship with Keyvan.

As the term drew to a close, the demonstrations began to increase in number and size. Curfews were instituted and martial law was declared. Rumors drifted like dark clouds presaging a storm: Troops had fired into the crowd; no they had fired into the sky, it's a different sound;

The imperial guard—the elite band that protected the Shah—had become involved; no they hadn't; they protected the person of the Shah;

The United States will never let the Shah fall; they know Iran will fall prey to communism; no, Jimmy Carter doesn't like the Shah because of his human rights platform.

The Shah, himself, ill and uncertain, sought guidance from the American Ambassador, William Sullivan, who assured him of his country's support. Yet, in the United States, the Carter administration was deeply divided. The U.S. Secretary of State, Cyrus Vance, was against the use of force and eventually became convinced that the Shah had to be removed. The National Security Advisor, Zbigniew Brzezinski, recommended crushing the riots by force and negotiating from a position of strength. The internal disagreement within the U.S. cabinet resulted in conflicting and confusing messages to the Shah—"be firm but don't use force"; "we're behind you but won't send you any anti-riot gear." Two of the Shah's generals begged him to let them gather up and execute approximately one hundred religious ringleaders and promised that this would put an end to the uprising. The Shah refused; he didn't want to spill his own people's blood.

In the final days, U.S. President Jimmy Carter dispatched General Huyser, who circumvented the Shah and went to the top Iranian generals. The Shah was outraged, not just at the disrespect but also because he felt that Huyser would be inciting the generals to a military coup d'état. Whether or not that was

Huyser's intent, it never happened. Perhaps Huyser didn't realize the extent of the top military brass's loyalty to the person of the King. Weakened by cancer and depression, betrayed by a childhood friend who would lace his drinks with soporifics and tranquilizers, unaware that the major powers had sealed his fate at a summit in Guadeloupe, the Shah left Iran in late January 1979 never to return.

The front page of the daily *Kayhan* announced this extraordinary event with two words:

"SHAH RAFT"—the Shah is gone.

4

EVEN BEFORE THE SHAH'S departure, Keyvan's friends and their families were hastily leaving. Each day, when the teacher took roll call, it seemed as if another student's name went unanswered. Other friends, even family members, were leaving early for Christmas vacation and not returning. Farzad, who had taken his two children skiing in Zermatt, had delayed his return. In fact, Lili was quite upset that he hadn't invited her and Keyvan; he claimed that he wanted to have some time alone with his children. Lili and Keyvan had gone skiing at Dizin, while Aunt Shahla and her two children had not returned from France where they, too, had gone skiing during the holidays.

The Shah left the government in the hands of Shahpour Bakhtiar, an urbane aristocrat and intellectual who had openly criticized the Shah's rule as too autocratic. His appointment was a last, desperate effort to placate the rising tide of the Islamic Revolution, but it failed to quell the demonstrations or the wildcat strikes. Panicked by the Shah's departure and the ensuing disorder in the city, Lili decided it was time to leave the country. She discussed it with her parents and her brother Darius who agreed that they should all leave until the chaos settled down. Of course, they believed they would be gone for only a month or two, at most until summer. It didn't occur to any of them that they might never return and should perhaps take their belongings and pack up their houses.

Keyvan had very mixed feelings about leaving. On the one hand, he would miss his friends, his grandparent's house, his dog, and his classmates. Yet something had changed since the first term that year: was it just Hossein's distant behavior, Cynthia calling him a sissy, or was it the academic program? It seemed more difficult to maintain his number-one position this year; he had to work so much harder, and he wasn't even first in all the subjects. Perhaps leaving now wouldn't be so bad after all. Attending school in France might be better, he thought. His mother had talked about a boarding school in England; he wasn't thrilled with that idea but didn't give it much thought as it had been only a passing reference. And then there was the panic and upheaval inflicted on his family by the Shah's sudden departure. While he was yet too young to grasp its true significance, the aftermath caused a sense of great disquietude in him that he imagined, perhaps not even consciously, would be resolved by their departure.

Leaving now, however, was no longer a guarantee. The airport was as often closed as it was open, and more importantly, they might not let you fly out. Apparently a list had been drawn up of people who wouldn't be allowed to leave, and of course, if your name was on the list, then you were stuck. No one knew who was on the list. Then there was the matter of booking seats. The next available flight wasn't for another ten days, and even then they had to call in favors to secure tickets; anyone of prominence who could travel was leaving.

The plan was for Lili, Keyvan, and Parto to depart together and for Massoud and Darius to follow soon thereafter.

On the appointed day, Khaleel drove them to Mehrabad Airport. They had never seen the airport in such disarray: luggage strewn all over, a huge crowd of passengers standing around, or walking and bumping into each other, many anxiously hurrying to join the long check-in queues that snaked out of the airport and into the parking lot. After a two-hour wait, they finally approached the Air France check-in counter, where an Iranian man in Air France's blue uniform asked for their passports and tickets. Lili let out a huge sigh of relief when he handed them their boarding passes and checked in their luggage. They said goodbye to Khaleel, who had accompanied them into the terminal, and proceeded to the gate.

At Mehrabad Airport in the 1970s, there were no security checks, so they thought that they could just proceed to the gate and board the flight. However, it appeared that they had to pass through a passport control desk, which they previously had never encountered. When they handed over their passports, the attendant looked down at some papers and then asked them to wait; he left his position with the three passports. They waited. Behind them, people started to grumble. Some even moved into the other queue. The man eventually returned and asked them to follow him to a separate area, where they were made to wait. There were no chairs. Others were waiting there nervously.

Eventually, after about half an hour, they were ushered into a small windowless room with two foldout metal seats and a desk behind which sat a corpulent bureaucrat, rifling through some papers. He didn't look up as they entered. The room was stiflingly hot, and Lili felt faint even before the creature informed them, matter-of-factly, that Lili wasn't allowed to leave the country.

"Why?" she protested."

"I don't know," he replied. "You'll have to inquire at the Foreign Ministry."

She pleaded with him, tears streaming down her face as the thought of missing the flight and being stuck in Tehran assailed her; Parto joined her in beseeching the man to let them all board the flight.

"It must be a mistake or misunderstanding," Parto kept repeating. "Our papers are all in order. We haven't done anything wrong. Why are we forbidden from leaving to go on holiday?"

"Khanom, Mam, you and the boy are free to go. It's this lady here," gesturing toward Lili, "who is on the government's list. But, if as you say, it's a mistake, then I'm sure you can clear it up at the Ministry," he said, impatiently. "But now you must leave; as you can see, there are other people waiting for me."

Back in the terminal, Keyvan watched as his mother and grandmother argued. "Maman, mother, you and Keyvan leave, and I'll follow with Massoud in a few days when we clear this up."

Parto shook her head and insisted that they wait and all leave together. Suddenly, it seemed to Keyvan that time had stopped or split and that his fate hung on the balance of this decision.

He wanted to say, "I want to go now," but he was overwhelmed by the gravity of the situation and reluctant to contradict his grandmother, still living in a past that had been suddenly swept away and clinging to her false sense of entitlement.

Nobody asked him, and the decision was made to stay and wait it out.

They left in a taxi, leaving behind their checked baggage.

"Let's get out of this hell-hole. I'll send Khaleel after the bags," said Parto.

"What's going to become of us, Maman?" sobbed Lili.

"Don't worry my darling. We're going to fix it. We'll get in touch with the minister and sort it out. It has to be some sort of bureaucratic mistake. Why would you be on the list? It makes no sense."

"What minister? The Shah is gone. What's left of any ministry? Hoveyda is in the gaol. For all we know the foreign minister himself is either gone or imprisoned. It's my bad luck; it's my fate. We should have left over Christmas while we could," she lamented.

Keyvan listened to them as they drove away from the airport. "Fate, her fate," he thought. What about his?

Lili didn't understand why she was on the no-fly list. She had never held a government post, let alone a major position that would put her amongst the handful of ministers and important government officials who had been jailed or precluded from leaving the country in a misguided endeavor to placate the Revolutionaries. Just because those in her family were in that category, why condemn an innocent woman?

Their efforts to reach various ministers were in vain. The

ones they knew had either left the country or languished in prison. The streets were chaotic; cars no longer obeyed traffic lights—the police were nowhere to be seen; stores were looted; covetous servants laid claim to their masters' property. Rumors were rife with reports of Khomeini's imminent arrival and that there was a secret plan to shoot down his plane.

A few days later, he disembarked, robes flapping in the air, the signature turban wrapped tightly around his head, with an entourage of reporters and followers. The national airline of France, a country whose government that had been a vocal ally of the Shah, now conveyed Khomeini from Paris, safely and soundly, into the bosom of a delusional crowd who thought that he would be their savior. Like a house of cards, Bakhtiar's government collapsed and the monarchy gave way to an Islamic Republic, a theocracy that would obliterate the progress of the last half-century and plunge Iran into a medieval dystopia from which it has not emerged to this day.

A somber mood descended on Parto's house where Lili and Keyvan had taken refuge. They were astounded and appalled by the popular support and celebrations garnered by this old religious man. They couldn't conceive how their country had arrived at this point: The Shah gone; the country in the hands of a maniacal mullah. Like *Alice in Wonderland*, they didn't want to go out amongst "mad people," and yet as the Cheshire cat said in the story, "You can't help that, we're all mad here."

"There's no reason to panic. None of us has done anything wrong. We've never held high office." Massoud continued to reassure them, unconvincingly. After some discussion, they decided that Parto, Lili, and Keyvan should go to Karaj, a rustic village an hour outside Tehran where they had a house. The schools in Tehran were closed, and it was dangerous to move around in the city. It would be safer to sit out the turmoil of the next few weeks in Karaj. Khaleel drove them at night when the roads were quieter.

But no sooner had they arrived in Karaj than they had to turn back. Keyvan's father, Kamran, had passed away. He had been sick with lung cancer but hadn't told anyone. He had died quietly in the middle of the night. When they returned to Tehran, they went directly to Parto's flat. As soon as they arrived, Parto's maid, Soltan, came in, panicked.

"They've arrested Mr. Darius," she blurted out.

"What? When? Why?" Parto asked.

"I don't know, Khanom, Mam. It was early this morning. I heard a lot of noise in the hallway and looked through the peephole and saw Revolutionary guards from the Committee. I was worried they were coming here, but then I saw them go toward Sir Darius's flat across the hall. Sir Darius was at home when they knocked, and when he answered the door, I saw them drag him out and take him away."

"Oh my God, the brutes. Where have they taken my son?" lamented Parto. Overcome with grief, Lili suddenly thought of the ring, the flawless D-rated diamond ring that Darius had purchased from the jeweler Fred in the South of France. She knew it was in his safe.

"Maman, quick. Do you have the combination to Darius's safe?" she asked. She knew that the guards would be back to lock and seal the door to his apartment if they hadn't already done it.

"Yes, I have it written down."

"Quickly fetch it," she said, as she stepped into the hallway to check on the door. Luckily they hadn't sealed it. She stepped back into her apartment, but then heard the lift rising and footsteps in the hall.

It was the guards.

"Oh, no, they've come to seal the door."

She looked through the peephole. There were two of them, and they were having a hard time opening Darius's door. Their key didn't appear to be working. After about five minutes, they went back down in the lift.

"It's now or never," thought Lili as she rushed into the hallway and opened the door to Darius's flat with her mother's spare key. She went to the safe in the bedroom and tried the combination. It didn't work. Her hands were trembling; she knew that the combination lock was extremely sensitive. She tried it again. It still didn't work.

"Maybe Maman gave me the wrong combination. What if they come back? They would arrest me on the spot," she thought.

She gave it a third try, and, click, the door opened. She looked inside and saw some papers as well as cash in British pounds and American dollars but couldn't find the ring. Exasperated, she rummaged in the safe and was about to give up when her hand touched something smooth. It was a small black, velvet case. She opened it and there was the ring, gleaming in the dark. In the landing outside, she saw the light above the lift door turned on indicating that it was coming up. She hurried across the hall and inserted the key into Parto's apartment. It wouldn't work. Wrong key, must have been Darius's. She checked her pockets but couldn't locate the right key. She rang the doorbell and banged on the door. Parto opened the door, and Lili flung herself inside just as she heard the "ding-dong" sound of the lift stopping on their floor and the footsteps of the guards.

———

A NEW INTERIM GOVERNMENT was now established, headed by Prime Minister Bazargan, though chaos continued as different political factions vied for power. Tensions rose between the Islamic Marxists or "Tudeh" party and the conservative religious clerics who had joined forces to bring down the Shah's government. Each group vied to seize the upper hand in an ever escalating cat-and-mouse game that eventually broke out into open armed conflict. The religious faction retained the thugs who would later become known as the "Quds" Force; they would beat up, arrest, shoot, and kill the Tudeh party members, who tended to be younger and more idealistic. Every night groups of people were rounded up by the dozen and bused to Evin prison where they would be summarily executed.

Revolutionary Tribunals were set up to arraign and try members of the prior regime, some of whom languished in gaol. On the day that Khomeini arrived, all the prison doors had been opened and the prisoners set free. Keyvan's cousin, former Prime Minister Hoveyda, had not left his cell. The former mayor of Tehran, Nikpey, who did escape, was later arrested and executed. Hoveyda was tried by Ayatollah Khalkhali, the infamous hanging judge, who sentenced him to death. He was executed by a firing squad. The former head of SAVAK—General Nassiri—was taken to a schoolhouse where Khomeini had set up his headquarters upon arrival in Iran; his vocal chords were torn out before he was shot.

The new government, calling itself the Islamic Republic of Iran, had issued new passports. The airport had reopened, but exit visas were required to leave the country. The visas were issued by the Ministry of Foreign Affairs, which, although housed in the same building, was now run by different people. In fact, no one knew who was really in charge. The source of power and authority appeared elusive and ever-shifting, reminiscent of Kafka's *The Trial*.

Lili and Parto decided to go to the ministry and chance their luck. They needed new passports as well as exit visas. By the length of the queue that snaked out and around the building, it was apparent that thousands of others had had the same idea. They decided to wait and joined the back of the queue. Some two hours later, when they finally arrived at the allotted desk, they were given forms to fill out for the new passports and visas.

"At least someone is still doing something," said Parto, when they were back in the car.

"Or pretending to. He said to expect our new passports in about a month. I wouldn't hold my breath."

"So what do you want to do?"

"I don't know, Maman, why do you even ask me that?" replied Lili, annoyed and exasperated.

"My darling, we've seen such hard times before, but none like this," Parto said in a low voice, almost to herself.

"I know. Let's just get home. I'm exhausted."

After a few days, Keyvan's school reopened as did the corner shops and businesses. For a moment, it strangely appeared as if things were normal again. Keyvan went back to school where his classes resumed. The Imperial Club was open as usual for lunch and tennis.

At school, many of Keyvan's friends, including Michael, had left. Hossein was still there, though he had grown even more distant toward Keyvan, barely acknowledging him with a faint smile and a brief hello hurrying away as if on an important mission. One day, he ran into Haleh, the tall girl in his class who played the piano so well. She was inconsolable and in tears. When he asked her why she was crying, Haleh said that they had executed her father the prior week. Stunned, Keyvan hadn't even known how to respond to her loss.

New teachers had arrived to replace the ones who had departed. His history and geography teacher, an English lady who had been married to an Iranian, was replaced by an Iranian woman who spoke no English. She wore a veil around her head and told her class they had a duty to report their parents if they were un-Islamic.

When Keyvan reported this to Lili, she decided it was time to leave, by any means. Despite jammed phone lines and tapped calls, she had been in regular contact with Farzad, who was now in Paris. He told her, in highly coded language, that his brother, Missid, was in hiding in Tehran but had plans for an escape. He was staying with a friend, Dara, whom she knew well. When she called Dara, he invited her over that evening. She thought it risky to visit, given he was harboring Missid, who was a fugitive, but decided she didn't have a choice.

It was after 9:00 P.M. and very dark as Lili drove herself to Dara's house. She parked outside on the street and walked quickly to the front entrance and rang the doorbell. Dara himself came to the door to let her in. Like two people stranded separately on a desert island who come across each other, they gazed back in amazement.

"Come in. I told Missid you were coming, and he's waiting to see you."

In the living room, Missid, gaunt and forlorn, opened his arms to hug Lili; fear had apparently robbed him of his usual pomposity. He recounted how he had been at his office when his loyal manservant called him and told him that the Revolutionary Guards had come to the house to arrest him, and not finding him there they were on their way to his office. He had immediately run out the door, under the pretext of a doctor's appointment and had come to Dara's, who, at great risk to himself, had given him refuge.

"Farzad told me that you might be escaping via the border?"

"He told you that?"

"Yes, and I was wondering if you might be able to guide me to do the same."

"Why do you want to escape? You can just leave normally, can't you?"

"No, I can't." Lili summarized her recent travails at the airport.

"I see. I'm so sorry. But you know it's not easy and can be very dangerous."

"I know. I mean I don't know but I can imagine, but I can't stay in this wretched country any longer."

"I can understand that. Very well. I can put you in touch with the people who are helping me." He handed Lili a piece of paper with a name, "Mr. Javad," and a phone number.

Out of discretion, Lili didn't inquire any further concerning the details of Missid's own departure. She took her leave, hugging Missid and Dara, not knowing if she would ever see them again.

5

KHALEEL DROVE THEM TO THE Grand Bazaar, a vast maze of alleyways dating back to the Saffavid period in the sixteenth century, which housed shops, cafes, restaurants, banks, hotels, and hammams, or saunas—a veritable city within a city. Located in the southern part of Tehran, neither Keyvan nor Lili had ever been there, though Parto, who accompanied them, appeared to have some familiarity with the place. The two women felt obliged to wear scarfs over their heads. While the chador had not yet become obligatory, they had been advised to "dress appropriately," which meant that women should cover their heads with at least a headscarf. The Bazaar had provided strong support for the Revolution. The bazaari, or merchants, were traditional Islamic and suspicious of the West and any ties to the former regime. Wearing makeup, skirts, high heels, or being unveiled not only would be frowned upon, but it would also raise suspicion. Traffic was heavy and it took them more than an hour to arrive there. Khaleel let them out, and Parto asked him to return to collect them in an hour.

Keyvan had never seen anything like this Bazaar. There were so many people walking around, with shop after shop selling everything from spices to carpets, clothes, toys, and gold; it also had its money exchanges and banks, restaurants, and guest houses. The women virtually all wore the traditional black chador; men were mostly unshaven, wearing cheap collared shirts and trousers in drab colors and the traditional Persian slippers known as "giveh." Some of them fingered prayer beads. None wore a suit or other clothes that Keyvan was accustomed to seeing; people appeared saturnine, almost hostile, dragging their feet and bumping each other without excusing themselves, as they rushed past. However, none of this was unusual. The Grand Bazaar had been this way for hundreds of years, and until very recently it was a big tourist attraction. But for Keyvan, it was an entirely different universe, whose otherness was the very incarnation of the dystopia that had suddenly sprouted around him. The irony that they would come to the very heart of this darkness to seek an escape from it was lost on them, given the desperation of their visit.

They made their way to a tiny shop that displayed ceramic tiles and vases. The shopkeeper greeted them with a smile and offered to show them his wares. Keyvan's grandmother asked for a Mr. Javad. At his name, the man slid off his stool and asked them to wait while he opened a door in the back of the shop and called for someone. In a moment another man emerged from the back room and nodded his head in a polite gesture, identified himself as Mr. Javad, and asked them to follow him through the door. After exchanging a worried glance with Parto, Lili took Keyvan's hand and followed Mr. Javad into a cavernous space full of ceramics. On one side of the room were sofas and a coffee table, where Mr. Javad asked them to have a seat. A woman in a black chador appeared with a tray on which there were four small Persian tea glasses and some sugar. She set the tray down on the coffee table and left without speaking a word.

"Welcome. Please have some tea," he said, deliberately avoiding eye contact with the women, a practice common among observant Muslim men. He was tall, perhaps in his late thirties, with a mustache, but no beard. He was wearing a suit without a tie and black leather shoes.

After a few preliminary niceties, they came to the subject at hand.

"Mr. Malek tells us you can help arrange for our holiday abroad," ventured Parto.

"Yes, indeed. Mr. Malek is a great gentleman and a great friend of our house and family."

"Excellent. Perhaps you could tell us what would be involved."

"Well, we thought that it would be more scenic if we went to Urmia and then traversed the Ararat Mountains into Turkey. The terrain is spectacular."

"But Agha, Sir, how can women and children cross a mountain chain?"

"Don't worry Khanom. Mam, we do it all the time. Our brothers in Urmia are well equipped and can handle everything to make your vacation as comfortable as possible."

"How long does it take, and can you tell us how it would work?"

"I can't give you specifics for your own safety, but I can tell you that we would drive out of Tehran to Urmia, and then we'll go on horseback across the mountains into Turkey. It shouldn't take more than four days at most."

"But we don't know how to ride horses," protested Parto.

"Khanom, Mam, as I mentioned, our brothers will handle everything for you. But, if you're worried about the details, perhaps you don't want to go on holiday, and we can leave it at that," he replied, with a tinge of exasperation.

"No, no, we want to go; we'll go," Lili interjected. "It'll just be me and my boy here. He's eleven."

"Have no worries Khanom, Mam. You will be in great hands with my brothers who have already helped many of Mr. Malek's friends on their vacations to Turkey."

"I don't mean to sound indelicate, but what would such a journey usually cost?" asked Parto.

"Khanom, Ekhtiar dareen, Mam, it's our pleasure; there is no cost for such esteemed friends of Mr. Malek."

"No, I insist Agha Javad, Mr. Javad. We can't accept that."

After the customary back and forth or "taroff," Mr. Javad finally divulged the astronomical figure of fifty thousand U.S. dollars, half to be paid up front, the rest on completion of the journey. Parto gasped, but Lili accepted.

"How soon are you ready to leave?" asked Mr. Javad, more matter-of-factly, now that terms had been agreed and the transaction concluded.

"We can be ready next week."

"I'll call you with a list of things to bring. It's very important to travel light. Please bring only those items that I mention and absolute essentials." By this he meant money and jewelry.

"We understand. Thank you."

Khaleel was waiting for them at the appointed place. To avoid any possible suspicion, they had decided to discuss with friends their upcoming travel as a trip to the Caspian Sea. Lili was now very excited, talking eagerly about their packing and discussing whom they have to visit before departing. Parto planned to leave the country by flying to Paris after Lili and Keyvan were safely in Turkey. She would have her packing to do and her own goodbyes, though of less urgency.

The week went by fast. As promised, Mr. Javad called with his list, which included a change of clothes, a warm coat, and comfortable shoes or boots. Meanwhile, they visited Keyvan's old aunt, Ameh Badi and her daughter, whom Keyvan affectionately called Zooz. They hugged Keyvan and broke into tears on parting, not knowing when they would see Keyvan again. Lili knew they could be trusted with their secret and had informed them of their true plans. On the night of their departure, they had dinner at Parto and Massoud's house. Cyrus, Keyvan's other uncle, joined them. They talked about how they would soon all be meeting in Paris and escaping the daily nightmare that was their life in Tehran these days. Cyrus and Massoud would stay behind for a while to see if they could sell their lands and other assets and transfer the funds out of the country. Though filled with anxiety and tension, Lili tried to remain positive, even cheerful, ostensibly to avoid alarming Keyvan, who was too young to grasp the perilous nature of this undertaking, but in reality, it was to reassure herself.

At 5:30 A.M., on the morning of their departure, they got into the car with Parto. The plan was for Khaleel to drive them to an allocated spot where a car would be waiting to take them out of the city. This would avoid raising any suspicion with the servants or nosy neighbors. As instructed by Mr. Javad, they carried a small bag in which they had packed the few items of clothing, as well as Lili's less important jewelry, and ten-thousand U.S. dollars and fifty-thousand tomans. She left Darius's diamond ring, as well as a ring made of Burmese rubies, and the sapphire pendant with Parto, hoping she would eventually be able to carry them out of the country.

A blue Paykan (a typical Iranian car) was parked at the corner of the designated street. A man wearing a brownish-grey collared shirt was at the wheel. In the back seat, a woman in a black chador was holding a little girl in her lap whose pigtails were visible from beneath a small scarf.

Keyvan and Lili embraced Parto and Khaleel, breaking into tears as they took their leave. Parto hugged her daughter and grandson and didn't want to let go.

"I love you, I love you," she sobbed.

"Maman, we'll see you in a few days," whispered Lili, trying to sound confident.

"Khanom, Mam, we have to get going," said the driver, who had left the car and approached them, though keeping a respectful distance.

Tears started to stream down Keyvan's cheeks. He was confused, and though they had concealed the dangers of their impending journey from him, he sensed the restive anxiety in his mother and grandmother and sobbed uncontrollably, clutching at his grandmother as she held him tight while she fought back her own tears. Lili began to feel agitated and raised her voice:

"Come on, we have to go. There's no time to waste."

Suddenly Keyvan felt a great unease as if looking at a dark storm cloud heading their way. "I don't want to go," Keyvan insisted. "Please, we must stay."

"No, no, we must go. It'll be okay, pesaram, my son,

I promise. Your grandmother will join us in a few days," she said, as she pulled him away and toward the car. He gave in to his mother, but turned around in the backseat of the car to wave goodbye to his grandmother. She sent kisses back to him by blowing into her palm.

It wasn't until they were completely out of sight that he noticed the little girl sitting on the woman's lap, the driver, and in the passenger seat, a nondescript man of whom he saw only the back of his head. Keyvan was sitting between his mother and the women. They were silent until the driver spoke up.

"There's a checkpoint coming up on our way out of the city. Please be silent, no matter what happens."

Lili adjusted the scarf on her head and pulled Keyvan toward her. He looked at her with alarm. She gave him a reassuring smile, though she was more frightened than he. The other woman remained impassive, staring forward, and the child on her lap didn't utter a word. There was no doubt that this wasn't her first such journey and that she had been trained to be silent.

At the checkpoint, the cars slowed down to a crawl and two guards in military uniforms, holding machine guns, scrutinized each car as it passed by, occasionally stopping a car for a closer inspection. Keyvan could feel the intense gaze of the guards as if it was palpable, but they went through the roadblock without hindrance.

"They know what they're doing," thought Lili of her companions. "They made us look like two working-class families going on a holiday. Perfect!" She smiled, relieved rather than cheerful.

Once outside of Tehran they drove west toward Qazvin, but then turned north and drove all the way up to the coast of the Caspian Sea. As they descended the mountainous road, Keyvan felt the scent and humidity of the sea envelope him.

The familiar fragrance and sensations catapulted him back to happier days when they had taken a road trip with his family to the shores of the Caspian Sea. The earlier trips had marked the beginning of the holiday season to which he had looked forward with great anticipation. Once there, he enjoyed the carefree and innocent play as only children can, in the sand, by the sea, under the sun, with laughter abounding, while surrounded by a family who loved him. He thought of that while he now sat in a car full of strangers facing an uncertain future. Perhaps one day he might recall this trip and realize how the birthright of all children, one free from worry and regret, had been stolen from him and the children of Iran by the dark cloud of this Islamic Revolution.

They made the nine-hour drive to Ardabil stopping only when necessary for bathroom breaks, twice for food, and once in the historic town of Qazvin and then in Rasht, the birthplace of the Shah. Neither city appeared as bleak nor as menacing as Tehran; they didn't see any patrols on the streets, and people appeared to go about their business as usual, without the anxiety and apprehension that pervaded the streets of the capital. In Qazvin, they had a glimpse of some of the historic sites such as the Jame' Atiq Mosque, which had been turned into a museum. Lili asked if they could take a short break to visit the magnificent edifice, but the men wouldn't let them leave the car. Instead, the man in the passenger seat went to a store and brought back kebabs with warm "lavash" bread. Lili asked again in Bandan Pahlavi where Keyvan wanted to go to the beach, but was rebuffed.

Now that they were on the road again, the woman started to speak, as if she had been resurrected. She complained about the new government, lamenting that they had promised to help the poor and underprivileged, who had received nothing. That the Revolution had provided them with a lucrative career in human smuggling, an occupation that had brought in sums that previously she could only have imagined in her dreams, did not appear to alter her perspective. Lili thought her lamentations typified an attitude, or rather a mannerism, common among working-class women who instinctively, or as a result of cultural atavism, bewailed a dark destiny, no matter how fortunate their circumstances. The men didn't speak with them at all; they only conversed with each other, and did so rarely.

They had the radio on for much of the way which, since the outbreak of the Revolution, didn't broadcast any music; the only programming was news and tiresome religious chanting. When one of the men lit a cigarette, Lili asked if he wouldn't mind refraining from smoking in the car. He didn't respond and continued to smoke. Thinking that perhaps he hadn't heard her, she repeated her request, this time louder and impossible not to have been heard, even with the radio on. Still no response. She gave up. None of them had introduced themselves, other than the little girl, who told Keyvan her name was Mina, though her mother tried to hush her up.

They arrived in Ardabil in the early evening, the two of them exhausted as much by the car ride as by the radio and the smoke. They checked into a simple, nondescript motel where Lili and Keyvan had their own room with two beds and, surprisingly, clean sheets. They spent an uneventful night and were awakened at five in the morning to continue their trip. After six hours they reached Lake Urmia, where they turned off the main highway and after a short while travelled up an unpaved road, where the dust billowed behind the car. They pulled up to an isolated two-story mud house in the middle of what appeared to be a farm. Hens, roosters, ducks, geese, sheep, cows, and two donkeys roamed the land. The men asked them to leave the car. The driver opened the door to the house and carried their luggage inside for them.

Then, without a word, he turned around, shut the door, and left. They heard the engine start and soon the car was gone, leaving them behind in this desolate house. They walked around cautiously. Downstairs there was a single room with a tattered sofa in front of a large wood-burning fireplace, a dining area with a square table covered by a traditional paisley tablecloth across from an archway that led into a kitchen with a brick oven and a stove on which two large pots sat. There was a tiny bathroom, with a deep, square-shaped bathtub, a sink, and a squat toilet with a plastic water pitcher. "How horrible," Lili gasped when she saw the hole in the ground in the bathroom. A stone staircase, with unevenly paved steps, led up to the first floor, where a small landing opened onto two tiny bedrooms with windows overlooking the farm.

Unsure of what to do, and since it was still daytime, they ventured outside. Keyvan enjoyed chasing after the geese, and the hens and roosters, while Lili walked around anxiously ruminating about dangers that lay ahead. After about half an hour, she went back inside and sat on the sofa trying to read a small book that she had brought with her. It was Jane Austen's *Emma*. But she was unable to concentrate, reading and rereading the same page over again, as her mind raced from the turbulent events of the recent past to the uncertainties of the future. Keyvan came in and was hungry and thirsty. Lili poured two glasses from the tap but then hesitated, unsure if the water was clean. They drank it anyway, but decided against touching any of the food. Another hour went by without incident. Lili looked around for a telephone but there was none. She was then startled by the braying of a donkey.

"I'm bored," Keyvan complained.

"Now's not the time to complain; you see the predicament we're in; please try to be helpful," she snapped at him.

"But I'm hungry," he protested.

"I'm sure someone will be here soon, and we'll have some dinner. Why don't you try to lie down and rest a little? We've had a long day."

"I don't want to rest. I've been sitting down all day."

Suddenly, the front door swung open, and an old woman carrying a basket stepped inside. All three let out a cry.

"Who are you? What are you doing here?" she said in a Turkish dialect spoken in North-Western Iran. Lili, who had previously heard this language spoken, understood the gist of her question and ventured in Farsi:

"We are friends of Agha Javad from Tehran. We were driven here today and asked to come in and wait."

"Oh! We didn't expect you until next week. Agha Kamran, Mr. Kamran, told me you were coming next week," she replied in Farsi, but in a regional dialect that was barely discernible. She had a heavily lined forehead, which made it seem as if she were perpetually frowning, with thin lips and a squint that made her appear at once angry and worried.

"What do you want us to do?" Lili asked.

"We wait until Agha Abbas, Mr. Abbas, comes home."

"Who's that?"

"Who is Agha Abbas? Who do you think he is? He's the man of the house, my husband."

"Oh, I see. I'm sorry, and meant no disrespect."

"I'm going to get dinner ready. You can join us."

"That is so kind of you, but can you tell us what the plans are?"

"What plans?" she asked.

"Our plans. You know, who is coming to take us over the mountains."

"I don't know anything about that; maybe Agha Abbas—" she said, and then stopped without finishing the sentence and hurried into the kitchen to prepare dinner.

There was no electricity in the house. The stove was wood-burning, and when night fell, she lit several gas lamps that used kerosene as fuel. Meanwhile, her husband, Agha Abbas, arrived. He was a brawny man in his mid-fifties, though his sunburnt hands and wrinkled face made him look older. He was tall, with dark hair and hazel-green eyes. Dirty boots, which he had removed before entering the house, mud-stained clothes, and pungent body odor indicated that he had just come off the farm. Unlike his wife, he was a jovial man, with a broad smile that appeared fixed on his handsome, bearded face.

As soon as he walked in, the wife started, "You told me they were coming next week. Well, they're here now!" she complained in the same Turkish dialect.

"Ha, ha, ha," he bawled, with a hearty, peasant laugh that revealed several missing teeth. "Crazy, forgetful woman," he said jovially, as he put an arm around his wife. "I told you to expect them today." He turned to them. "Salam Khanom, hello Mam, and welcome to our humble abode," he continued in the same Farsi dialect that his wife had used.

"See what he does to me," protested his wife, looking up and raising her hands, palms open, to the sky, addressing God. This was delivered in Farsi rather than Turkish for their benefit.

"Woman, stop complaining about the life that God, in his mercy, has given us and put some food on the table. I'm starving!" he exclaimed, as he walked up the stairs. "Please come upstairs," he said to Lili and Keyvan, who followed after him.

He showed them one of the bedrooms, which had two small fold-out beds that had been opened and fitted with sheets and threadbare blankets.

"Come, honorable guests. You'll stay here with us tonight."

"Thank you," Lili ventured. "What happens tomorrow?"

"Tomorrow, my cousin will come and fetch you early in the morning, but now come and have some supper," he said and walked downstairs.

Dinner consisted of a Koofteh Tabrizi, a large meatball stuffed with rice, prunes, leeks, onions, split peas as well as turmeric, parsley and cilantro, which makes this an incredibly flavorful and aromatic dish. It was so delicious that even Lili, who was on a perpetual diet that excluded carbs, finished hers. There were extras, and Agha Abbas helped himself to two additional servings, and Keyvan had half of another one.

"What time is your cousin coming in the morning?" Lili asked.

"At around 5:00 A.M.," he said, between mouthfuls.

"Is he coming alone? Where will he take us?"

"I don't know, Khanom, Mam, but you will be in great hands and trust in the merciful God."

After dinner, they went upstairs to their room and got ready for bed. Keyvan went back downstairs to use the bathroom and heard the husband and wife whispering in the kitchen. She was doing most of the talking, in a plaintive voice; his responses were brief, often just one word, and his tone was one of exasperation but resignation. Keyvan reported this back to Lili who decided to go downstairs with the pretext of using the bathroom, but they must have heard her coming down and broke off the conversation.

Lili became very nervous afterward. Instinctively, she didn't trust the woman and worried that perhaps she was scheming to extract money from them, or even worse, inciting her husband to attack them in the middle of the night for their possessions. There was no lock on the door, so there was nothing that she could do to keep him out.

Keyvan noticed his mother's agitation and asked her what was wrong. She said she was just concerned about tomorrow, though he could sense that it was more than that. They went to bed and Keyvan fell asleep, but Lili stayed awake, tossing and turning, despite the fact that she knew there was a long and arduous journey ahead. She heard the husband and wife enter their room and presently all noise in the house died down. It was completely dark out, and the only noise was the blowing of the wind outside.

"Even the animals have gone to sleep," she thought to herself. "There's no one here to help us, nothing I can do if they decide to attack. What sort of arrangement is this? That bastard Agha Javad. Telling us it's safe and there's nothing to worry about. And even if we do survive the night, what's going to happen tomorrow? Who are these people coming for us?"

She rolled over on her side toward Keyvan's bed, although she could not see him in the dark. "I have to stop thinking about this. There's nothing I can do. Why did I do this? I can never do anything right. We should have left a long time ago when we could. It's all Farzad's fault. If he hadn't said we should stay, we would have left on vacation to Switzerland before all these crazies took over. These bastards, making me wear a headscarf. I'd rather die than wear a chador. Why did this happen to us? What am I going to do when we get to Paris? Will I have enough money? Will Farzad look after us? He's probably shacked up with another woman. Men, they're all selfish." She then thought of her ex-husband. "Didn't even lift a finger for his son. How can you call that being a father?"

Lili heard something and thought someone was outside her door. She rose up on her elbows and listened intently but there was no sound. She was sure she had heard someone at her door. She listened more closely. Only the wind and the sound of leaves rustling outside the window. She didn't realize that the volume of her silent thoughts was so loud they had drowned out most external sounds. "It must have been a door shutting or something like that," she decided and was soon lost again in the same circular and repetitive thoughts and worries that robbed her of her faculties and blinded her to the reality that surrounded her.

They were fast asleep when a gentle knock on the door woke them. Lili, who thought she hadn't slept all night, jumped out of bed.

"Who is it?" she asked.

"I'm sorry to wake you, Khanom, Mam, but it's time to get ready."

"What time is it?"

"4:30."

Downstairs the husband and wife rose from the table as they approached, and offered them some breakfast tea as well as bread and local white goat cheese. They could hear some noises outside, people talking, men's voices.

"My cousins are here. Do you have all of your belongings?"

"Yes, thank you," Lili said, and she went to give the man some money.

He refused to take it. She now felt bad about doubting their sincerity.

"God be with you and your son, Khanom, Mam."

The wife was standing by silently and held a Quran over their heads as they left the house, a custom that was meant to put travelers under the protection of God.

6

OUTSIDE there was an ambulance and three bearded men who motioned for them to get in the back. They were dressed in traditional peasant clothes, their trousers held at the waist by elastic bands, but their boots appeared to be sturdy. They reeked of opium. One of the men stepped in behind them. There were two stretchers and he motioned for them to lie down on each. They did and the ambulance drove off, though they didn't hear a siren. Keyvan felt uncomfortable lying down in a backward position and started to get car sick. He looked over at his mother who shook her head.

Lili was more concerned about where these men were taking them. They couldn't see outside the ambulance, but the jarring motion of the ride indicated they were travelling along an unpaved road. They hadn't travelled an hour when the ambulance came to a stop, and the man in the back opened the door to let them out.

They had pulled up in front of a structure made of mud, where a boy who couldn't have been more than fifteen years old was waiting with two horses. Two of the men approached the boy and took the reins of the horses and then mounted them; the third man and the young boy helped Lili and Keyvan climb on behind the riders. The horses now scampered up the mountain trail. It was dawn and the sun was just rising. An orange hue enveloped the mountains as its rays gently caressed them, but their fear and anxiety prevented either of them from feeling the sun's warmth or enjoying the splendor of this magnificent landscape. Keyvan held tightly onto his horseman, feeling at every turn that he might be flung off the animal.

The horses appeared very familiar with the terrain, turning at every juncture on the trail without direction from the riders. "How long will this ride last?" Lili asked the horseman but he didn't answer her. She screamed when two wolves approached them, but the men beat them back with sticks and a whip. A few hours into the trip, they arrived at another mud hut and got off the horses and went inside. The men knew the woman who greeted them, and for the first time, Lili and Keyvan heard their escorts speak, returning her greeting in Farsi with the same Turkish dialect as Agha Abbas, their cousin. The younger of the two was tall, about six foot, with dark hair and hazel-green eyes; his handsome features were obscured by a thick black beard and a sunburnt face. The older man, who must have been in his late thirties, was short and squat, though his brawny physique was visible beneath the loosely fitting clothes.

The woman set out their lunch of rice and chicken, and they sat down and ate. The men talked about the unemployment in the region, which had reached close to fifty percent among the youth, many of whom turned to smuggling as the mainstay of their livelihood. They didn't openly discuss their trade, but the stories they told in a light-hearted banter revealed that before the Revolution, they had mainly trafficked in weapons and bootlegged alcoholic beverages and drugs. Now, they smuggled mostly upper-class Iranians who had supported the Shah, such as Lili and Keyvan, or so they assumed.

By the time they left the hut, Lili felt more relaxed, whether as a result of the genuine complaisance of her escorts, or a realization that their goal was near, or perhaps both. She was struck by the savage beauty of the mountains. It was as if she were seeing this landscape for the first time. They must have climbed halfway up the mountain for below them she could see the green pastures of the steppe, a verdant sea from which rose the brown mass of limestone, with patches of grey and rust, or perhaps vermillion. At the very top, there were sprinklings of white, remnants of snow that had no doubt blanketed the whole mountain in winter, but had melted away in the spring, only to return now. A juniper tree seemed to be beckoning to her and below that were the Persian oaks, her favorite trees; how could she have missed them on the way up the trail?

Lili stood still, and as she took in the majestic silence, she was strangely at peace, transfixed. She breathed out, almost a sigh, but of relief, not anguish; she felt, for the first time that day, the warmth of the sun and slipped off the jacket that she earlier had clutched in fear; she felt the whisper of a gentle breeze. In the distance, she saw the rocks gleaming, like multi-colored giants, looking back at her as if to welcome her to their pristine abode. At that moment, and it was only a brief moment, time itself stopped, for time is a construct of the human mind like the thoughts and fears that it churns.

They climbed back on the horses and continued on their way up. They would have to climb virtually to the very top of the mountain, an elevation of approximately nine thousand feet, before descending toward the Turkish border. As they climbed higher, the trail narrowed and Keyvan closed his eyes, while Lili started to pray silently as they approached a treacherous pass. "We're going to die here," she thought. "Why did I do this? Why did I bring us to this dangerous place?" But the horses navigated the pass dexterously, confirming that they had made this journey countless times.

By the time they rode down to the valley below, it was dark with a chill in the air. They had already slipped on their jackets, and while they were both exhausted—a fatigue that caught up with them—they extended their necks and scanned intently for signs of a border crossing in anticipation of their deliverance. "Are we almost there?" asked Lili.

"Yes, Khanom, Mam," her escort replied, "don't worry, we will get you there safely."

In the darkness, Keyvan saw a form approaching. It was another horseman. "Don't be afraid; he is with us. He will help guide us to a safe house across the border." The man greeted the two escorts in Turkish, and all three horses continued along the trail.

"We're almost at the border," said Hasan. "A few more minutes and we'll be on Turkish soil."

"Thank God," sighed Lili.

At that moment they saw a light pop up ahead of them. Their guides pulled up the horses and started to talk among themselves.

"What is it?" asked Lili anxiously.

"He says it could be border guards, but that would be unusual. This is a very remote place. There's usually no one here. It's probably a shepherd or something."

"Can't we go a different way?" Lili asked.

"Yes, that's what we're going to do."

They turned the horses around and started in a different direction. It was hard to see which way they were going, but it looked like the light was still moving in their direction. As they continued, the light appeared to be moving faster, bridging the distance between them. The guides didn't gallop away, probably to avoid making noise that would attract attention, Lili thought. She was hoping that whoever it was would eventually disappear. Yet they kept coming closer and closer, and then suddenly they heard a voice shout in Farsi:

"Who goes there?"

The guides now dug their heels into the sides of the horses who took off at a gallop. The others gave chase and they heard:

"Stop, halt, or we'll shoot," they shouted.

They kept coming after them. Gun shots rang out behind them.

"Oh my God, oh my God. God, please help us; we're so close to the border, please have mercy on us," the voice in Lili's head rang out.

Keyvan clasped the waist of his guide. He felt the up-and-down motion of the horse as it galloped off. The gunshots had terrified him, but he was now strangely at peace with himself. He felt the cool, crisp air around him, sensed the stillness of the mountains. Intermittently this was pierced by gunshots and

the voices of their pursuers, but while coming closer, the
distant to this moment. He felt his weight on the horse and his
legs dangling on the side, the fragrant scent of lavender and rose
caressing his nostrils. Whether it was the unfamiliarity of the
situation or sheer exhaustion—physical, mental, and emotional
fatigue—or the monumental, yet inscrutable danger they faced,
his mind had transcended these concerns at that moment. The
usual voice of fear in his head had vanished, leaving only physical
sense perceptions. That moment was perhaps the calmest, the
most delicious moment of his life. Later, when looking back, he
might understand it as a collapse of the ego mind that allowed
his true self to emerge, one beyond fear and all emotion, at one
with nature—an expression of universal harmony.

More gunshots rang in the air, and then suddenly the cry of
a man—that raw, piercing sound of anguish and distress that
most people have never heard except perhaps in a war film.
The horse that Keyvan rode suddenly stopped and reared its
front legs neighing loudly; it shook off the guide and Keyvan,
who fell hard to the ground, feeling a sharp pain in his left arm.
They came to a standstill and their attackers slowly approached.
There were seven of them wearing the green fatigue uniforms
of the Iranian border patrol.

"Get down," they ordered, and the guides and Lili climbed
off their horses. When they shined a bright torch on the area,
Lili saw Keyvan on the ground and ran toward him; but one
of the guards hit her with the butt of his rifle and she fell to the
ground screaming in pain.

"Shut up, woman," he barked.

One of the guides—the one who had just joined them—had
been shot and killed, and the horse carrying Keyvan was shot as
well. It now lay there, not quite dead but bleeding out. The two
remaining guides were on their knees, almost prostrate, heads

bowed and silently seeking clemency, knowing that they were in danger of being shot on the spot. Smuggling was highly illegal, and they knew that border patrol had orders to shoot to kill.

One of the guards shot the wounded horse and used a scarf to sling Keyvan's injured arm. They now had the two guides mount their horses, with Keyvan and Lili behind them, and were escorted to a military jeep where they were loaded in the back and transported to the local kalantary or police station. Lili pleaded with the guards to release them, offered money and jewelry, promised untold riches when she returned to Tehran, but they were unmoved by the bribes and remained silent. At the station, the two of them were handed over to a female guard. Keyvan had excruciating pain in his left elbow and whimpered. Sobbing quietly, Lili begged the woman to see if there was a doctor who could attend to him. The guard turned out to be a kind and compassionate woman. She comforted Keyvan and asked him to show her where it hurt.

"Unfortunately, we won't be able to see a doctor until morning, but I can give you something to help with the pain," she said gently to Keyvan.

"What happened? Did you fall off the horse, my son?" she asked him.

"Yes, the horse was shot and he fell off," Lili said, in tears. "Please Khanom, Mam, you seem so kind, I can see it in your eyes. Please help us."

"I'll try to make you both comfortable, and then the boy can see the doctor in the morning."

"What will happen to us?" Lili asked anxiously.

"That I don't know. We have to wait for the chief to come in tomorrow. It's up to him." She now asked, averting her eyes, "What were you doing out in the middle of nowhere? Were you trying to flee the country?" she asked, matter-of-factly, in a conversational rather than interrogational tone.

"No, we were just tourists who got lost," Lili said, looking away embarrassed by the obvious lie.

The woman stared at her but didn't question Lili further.

"I have some polo khoresh if you like," she offered, referring to a stew with white rice.

They were hungry and had some stew and drank spigot water from dirty glasses. She then showed them to a spartan room with two little beds and a light bulb dangling from the ceiling.

"You can sleep here, and I'll come and get you in the morning."

Keyvan, exhausted and drowsy from the soporific painkiller, fell asleep quickly. Weary and utterly drained, Lili watched Keyvan sleeping and then collapsed onto her bed.

They were awakened early the next morning by the female guard, who had brought the doctor with her. He was an old country doctor and told them that Keyvan had broken his arm, at the wrist and perhaps also at the elbow. An X-ray would be required, as well as surgery to properly set the bone. Meanwhile, he replaced the makeshift sling with one that supported his entire arm and cautioned Keyvan against moving it. In the meantime, the chief had arrived. He sported a full, light brown beard and handlebar mustache that he twirled, giving him an uncanny resemblance to Czar Nicholas II.

"What's this we have here?" he asked gruffly as he entered the room. "Oh, hello Dr. Babak, what are you doing here so early?"

The female guard began to explain that the child had a broken arm, and the doctor had suggested having it X-rayed.

"It's a serious fracture. He may need surgery," the doctor confirmed.

"Well, they're going back to Tehran, where they came from. They can go to the hospital there. They're fugitives and need to be brought to justice."

"But that's a long trip. Can we not go to the hospital here?" ventured Lili, cautiously, almost sobbing.

Nothing disarms Iranian men more than the crying of a woman.

"Don't worry, Khanom, Mam," he said, in a much gentler tone. "We have a car going to Tehran within the hour. They have much better hospitals there and can give your son the best care."

He left the room hurriedly, obviously perturbed by this sobbing upper-class woman.

"Don't worry, my son. You'll be well looked after when you get to Tehran," said the female guard.

"But who's going to take us? What car was he referring to?" asked Lili

"We have a car that goes to Tehran once a week. It's supposed to leave today. One of the guards drives it. I think you're going with him."

"What will happen to us when we get to Tehran? Where will they take us?"

"I don't know, my dear. But you're in God's hands, and he will look after you and your son."

The drive back to Tehran went much faster; the guard who drove them—Ali Agha, Mr. Ali—was a jovial, gregarious man, and instead of the radio, he entertained them, or rather subjected them on their ten-hour drive, to fantastic stories about capturing and killing smugglers. Keyvan was in excruciating pain, and Lili held him in the backseat, trying to comfort him. Luckily the female guard had given him more painkillers that helped him sleep through most of the journey.

On the outskirts of the city, Lili asked, "Where are you taking us?"

"To the central police station. That's where we take all fugitives and smugglers."

"What do you mean fugitives and smugglers? We're neither. We are just tourists who got lost."

"Khanom, Mam, you can explain all that in Tehran. My orders are to deliver you to the police station. Besides, the smugglers who were trying to get you across the border confessed to everything."

"What do you mean they confessed?"

"They told us how you and your family had hired them to help smuggle you and the boy across the border."

"How could they say such a thing? It's a lie."

The man shook his head. "No Khanom, Mam, it's the truth; they would have been shot on the spot if they hadn't confessed. Now they have a small chance of not being executed."

Lili gasped.

"Many people like you try to escape. Most don't succeed. Sometimes, the smugglers don't even know where they are taking them; they abandon them in the mountains, and we find them days later, hungry, thirsty, and desperate. You were actually very close to the border. We don't usually patrol that close. It was pure chance that my colleagues spotted you at night."

Lili didn't protest any further, but thought about their fate, and especially that of her son, who had wanted to leave the country with his grandmother. What had she done? What harrowing future had she secured for him?

In Tehran, he took them to a police station from where they were taken directly to Evin prison, a notorious gaol in the north of Tehran that had been built by the Shah but, in an ironic twist of fate, now housed many of his loyal supporters. Fenced off from the world by tall, thick brick walls, the prison had become infamous for the tortures, summary executions, and other barbarities that had come to define the nascent Islamic Revolution.

Lili shrieked and wailed as they separated her from Keyvan, who cried, calling for his mother, "Mummy, mummy, don't let them take me."

She kicked, scratched, bit, and yelled, but was brutally restrained and fainted as Keyvan was taken away.

They took him to a clinic within the prison where he was told to sit and wait on a wooden chair. An oppressive scent of disinfectant and dried blood filled the air. Severe-looking veiled nurses hurried about the ward. Men and women with dreadful-looking wounds lay in bloodstained sheets on narrow makeshift cots. He felt alone, bereft, and frightened. Pain shot up and down his arm. An hour passed. The pain had become intolerable, and his voice joined the chorus of groans and wails. He called out to one of the passing nurses, but she ignored him. He began to feel lightheaded and nauseous, and was on the verge of fainting and vomiting when, finally, a doctor came over to him.

"What's the matter?" he asked.

"My arm, I think it's broken," was all that he could manage to stammer. Keyvan held out his left arm.

The doctor lightly touched his elbow and he cried out in pain, almost falling out of the chair.

"Oh, it is broken all right. Let me see," he said and examined the arm more closely.

"Okay, you're going to need surgery. Wait here."

After a few minutes, a woman in a black chador approached him and said, "Come with me."

"Where are you taking me?"

"To the hospital."

They left the clinic, and the nurse took him through the

front gate of the prison to an unmarked blue Paykan, with a man at the steering wheel.

"Let's go," she said to the driver.

"Where to?"

"The hospital."

It was approaching midnight; the streets were very quiet and dark. They drove a short distance to a hospital where the woman stepped out of the car and took Keyvan inside. They went up two floors to a desk staffed by two veiled women at a nurse's station. The woman in the chador appeared to know them and they exchanged pleasantries. She explained that the prison doctor had examined the boy who had an arm fracture and needed surgery. Then she left.

One of the women came around from the desk and took him to a private exam room.

"What's your name?" she asked in a gentle tone.

"Keyvan."

"It's your left arm, is it?"

"Yes, it hurts a lot."

"You poor thing. We'll sort it out for you. The doctor will be right in to see you."

"Can I call my grandma, please?"

"Let me see about that. Meanwhile, here's a painkiller. Take two tablets. It'll help you."

She left the room. He took the pills and laid down on the exam bed. His whole body ached, but it was the shooting pains in his arm that had become intolerable. He started to drift off into unconsciousness. A rapid succession of images passed through his mind: mountains, a smoke-filled car, guides and horses, the Caspian Sea, his mum in tears, the horse rearing up.

"Maybe I'm dying," he thought. "Death would be better than this pain; anything would be better."

The doctor in a white lab coat walked in, followed by a veiled nurse. He was a young man, no more than thirty years old, strikingly handsome, with jet black hair set against alabaster white skin and deeply set brown eyes. He examined Keyvan's arm and said he would schedule the surgery for first thing in the morning.

"I have a lot of pain," Keyvan whimpered.

"I know. You've fractured your arm. Did you take the painkillers?"

"Yes."

"They should help with the pain. They'll put you to sleep soon. We'll operate and fix your arm."

"Can I call my grandma?"

"Yes, go ahead."

"But, doctor," the nurse interjected, "they brought him here from Evin."

"I know. He's a frightened boy. Let him call his grandmother."

Keyvan followed the nurse out into the hallway and to the reception desk, and she showed him to a rotary phone.

"Go ahead," she said, but waited there.

He dialed his grandmother's number which he knew by heart. The phone rang ten times, but there was no answer. He held on and let it ring. On the fifteenth ring, someone picked up. A decidedly sleepy woman's voice said, "Allo?"

"Soltan? It's me. Keyvan. Please get Grandma. It's very important."

"Khanom, Mam, is sleeping. Where are you?"

"I'm in the hospital. I'm very sick. Now go and wake her up."

"Okay, okay. Hold on," she said grumpily."

A few minutes later, while he was still waiting for his

grandmother, the nurse told him to hurry up, that she had patients to attend to.

"Allo, Keyvan jounam, my darling Keyvan, where are you?" Parto asked over the line.

"I'm at the hospital."

"Which hospital? Where? Where's your mother?" she asked anxiously.

"I don't know the name. Hold on."

"Khanom, Mam, what's the name of this hospital?"

"Imam Khomeini Hospital," she spat out impatiently.

Keyvan repeated the information.

"You're in Tehran? What are you doing here? Where's your mother?"

"I don't know. I mean, it's complicated. I have a broken arm. They're going to operate on me tomorrow."

"Oh my darling, I love you. I'm coming over right now. Which room are you in?"

He asked the nurse, who told him his room number.

"I'm in room 109. I have to go now."

"I'll be right over."

The nurse showed him to room 109, a double room but the other bed was empty.

"You can sleep here. We'll come and get you in the morning for your surgery."

"But my grandma is coming. Will you show her to my room?"

"If they give us permission," she said and walked out the door.

Keyvan went over to the bed and laid down. "What if they don't let Grandma up? What if she forgets the room number and can't find it?" he asked himself feeling increasingly drowsy.

The nurse had given him codeine together with a soporific sedative, and he soon fell asleep.

When he woke, he found his grandmother sitting in the chair next to his bed. When she saw him open his eyes, she gently stroked his hand.

"Keyvan jounam," she said softly.

"Grandma," he responded. "I'm so happy to see you."

He groaned as pain shot up and down his left arm. "My arm really hurts."

"I know, my love. They're going to fix it today."

At that moment, the door opened and the doctor came in with the nurse. Keyvan noticed that it was the same tall, handsome doctor from the prior evening. The doctor greeted Parto and said, "It's time to go."

The doctor's entrance excited Keyvan. He felt curiously at ease in his presence; the way he moved, the timbre of his voice, his gestures, all exuded a gentle confidence. He giddily chatted with the man, as they wheeled him out into a maze of hallways, down a lift and through other corridors, and eventually into the operating room. He had even forgotten to say goodbye to his grandmother. The doctor told him that he would feel no pain because they would be putting him under general anesthesia, but Keyvan just gazed at him. Explaining the procedure, the doctor patted Keyvan's hand as he continued to reassure him. When Keyvan grasped his hand the doctor held on to it reassuringly as they prepared him for the operation. The physical pain in his arm and the suffering wrought by the appalling events of the previous days melted in the physician's touch. He imagined the doctor embracing him, protecting and nurturing him as unconsciousness slowly engulfed him, and the doctor let go of his hand which fell limply to his side.

7

THERE WERE FORTY OF THEM, perhaps even more, in a single cell. At night Lili had to shift on her side because there wasn't enough room to lie flat. Her fitful sleep was often interrupted by gunshots and screams. She knew it was the firing squad, killing more people in the prison yard. They were bused in and shot on the spot, the young Marxist leftists, for whom the Revolution had been so full of promise and hope but had delivered only suffering and death. In her cell Lili would join in with the morning and evening prayers, muttering under her lips because she didn't know the Arabic words to be recited. The food,

, was surprisingly good—as far as prison food went—
rice with a variety of meat stews, but she rarely touched hers.
At least I'm losing weight, she thought, the only silver lining
in her troubled confinement. Though her body ached from
sleeping on the hard cement floor, her emotional suffering had
somewhat numbed her to the physical pain.

How had she come to be in this awful place? What had
become of Keyvan, all alone in the hands of these fanatical brutes? It was all her fault. What made her think that they
could escape like that, over those treacherous mountains, without being detected by the vigilant border patrols? It was all a
ploy to extract what little money they had left. And why hadn't
they let them out of the country in the first place? She blamed
everyone: her parents, her brothers, and Farzad for her predicament. If only they had been more helpful, more consider-
ate. She was aghast at the Revolution and the devastation it
had inflicted on her and her family. How had this happened?
she wondered. The Shah was gone, the throne collapsed after
twenty-five hundred years. Who would have thought this even
possible? A Revolution in this day and age. Why? How? She
was caught in the middle of some historic upheaval that was
beyond her comprehension, even beyond her imagination. And
now she was here, in this hellhole. These thoughts circulated in
her mind over and over again, with no respite, causing further
anxiety and more sleepless nights.

As she didn't say much or eat anything and took up so
little space, the other women in the cell left her alone, as did
the prison guards. No one paid much attention to her at all.
One of the older women, who was obviously from the same
social class, had tried to speak with her, to encourage her to eat
some food, but Lili was too listless, too burdened by sorrow,
to engage in conversation, or even eat. Twice a day, they were

allowed to walk outside in a walled prison yard. She went out at every opportunity; it was the only thing that kept her sane.

She wasn't permitted any calls or visitors, but about a month into her imprisonment she received a package. It contained some fruits, a piece of chocolate and most importantly, a note from her mother and one from Keyvan. He wrote that his arm was healing and that he was back in school. He missed his mum and wished that she would come home soon. Parto wrote that they were all doing well, but that she missed her daughter. She didn't provide much detail about their life; they both knew that the correspondence would be scrutinized. But Lili could read between the lines that her mother was trying her very best to obtain her release.

Two months after the first care package had arrived, she was discharged, unceremoniously. It had been totally unexpected. A prison guard came into the cell, called out her name, and told her to pack her things. When she had inquired why, the guard simply responded, "You're being released."

When she walked out of the prison gate, her parents, Keyvan and Khaleel, were waiting for her. Keyvan ran up to his mother and hugged and kissed her, as did Parto and Massoud. Tears streamed down her face; Khaleel drove them home to Parto's house.

"You've lost so much weight, my darling," Parto said while hugging her daughter as they sat in the living room.

"I couldn't eat or sleep. I was so miserable. But the important thing is that Keyvan and all of you are okay. I can't believe they released me. What did you do? How did this happen?"

Parto explained that she had gone from one ministry to the next, knocking on every possible door. They had no connections now; there was a new government in place if it could be called that—mostly marauding religious brutes with machine guns. At first, she had gone to Evin Prison every day hoping to visit her, but they wouldn't permit it. By chance, one of her friends, someone she played cards with, knew a relative of a powerful Ayatollah. This person, Agha Hossein, Mr. Hossein, had taken an enormous bribe and arranged for Lili's release. When Lili heard how much Parto had paid, she went pale and exclaimed, "Maman, you shouldn't have. We have nothing left. How will we live?'

"My darling, the important thing was to save you from that place. God is great and we will manage."

"God is great? How can you say that after all this?" she asked defiantly.

"Don't talk like that. We are alive. We have a roof over our head. Come and have some tea and buttered toast. You haven't eaten in so long."

Lili acquiesced. She ate the toast, and then some leftover stew.

"Oh, and by the way, I found out why they wouldn't let you fly out at the airport."

"What?" replied Lili, "What was it?"

"It was the policeman you had slapped last year. They started a file on you and put that in it. But now it's been removed. You see, this regime doesn't like the Shah's police-men, so they think you did well to slap him."

"Are you telling me I got put on the no-fly list under the Shah's regime?"

Parto nodded her head. Lili took a deep breath. She recalled slapping the policeman. He had been impertinent and she believed he deserved it. But to be on the no-fly list because of that? Before the Revolution? She closed her eyes and shook her head in denial. She was about to spiral into confusion and despair, but then another thought brought her back. Parto had said, "It's been removed."

"So, do you think they'll let me leave now? Even after I tried to escape?" she asked, with a glimmer of hope.

"Yes. You need to, we all need to get new exit visas, which Agha Hossein has told me can be arranged, eventually, once you get a new passport."

The old passports, issued under the Shah's imperial seal, were considered invalid. The new passports bore the emblem of the Islamic Republic of Iran.

Lili took another deep breath and sat back in her chair. The realization that she didn't need to escape the country, that she had inflicted this suffering on herself and Keyvan tempered the joy she felt that they may soon be free. She had been too hasty in her decision to escape. If only she had waited, she could have obtained her clearance and left. But who knew at the time? Lili now looked back and realized that Keyvan had been reluctant. His words at their parting now haunted her, "I don't want to go," her son had insisted. "Please, we must stay."

If only she had listened to him.

Eventually, her mind having been cleared to some degree, she said, "So let's get new passports and exit visas."

"Lili jan, my darling Lili, you've just been released from prison. Why don't you try to rest a little; eat some food, recover your strength. And then we can go and get the exit visas and leave."

"But what about Keyvan? His school? He needs to get a proper education."

"He's still learning. Aren't you?" Parto queried Keyvan.

"Yes, school is fine, mummy. It's more or less the same. Some of the English teachers are gone, but they've been replaced. Some of my friends have left too, but I'm okay."

Keyvan had returned to his school at the beginning of September. They had begun to separate the boys from the girls in different classes, but this didn't concern him in the least. Many of his friends had left, including Hossein, whose departure had surprised but not disappointed Keyvan. They had ceased being friends, though Keyvan never found out why; he had assumed it was because Hossein supported the Revolution. His departure was perplexing to Keyvan. But he didn't spend much time thinking about it as he had become close friends with a boy named Farhad, whom he had previously known and played with.

They were in many of the same classes and had been spending much time together outside of class, eating lunch, doing homework, and playing games. One day, in science class, when Keyvan was bent over looking into a microscope, Farhad had come from behind and rubbed himself against Keyvan. He had done it very discreetly as if he were impatient to look into the microscope, which was meant to be shared by two students. Keyvan enjoyed the sensation without understanding the full context of Farhad's conduct nor his own feelings. All he knew was that he liked it. From that moment on, he would find excuses to turn his back to Farhad and bend over, such as when washing his hands in the sink, or fetching his sandwich out of his lunch box, or books out of his case, and sure enough, Farhad would rub himself up against Keyvan. Eventually, he dropped all such pretexts and would simply turn his back to Farhad and wait for him to come up behind him. Their conduct, in plain view of everyone, had not caught anyone's attention because it was done very quickly and discreetly.

One day, however, they happened to be in a classroom alone at the end of the day doing their homework. Keyvan had as usual bent over, and Farhad had come over and rubbed himself against him, but this time he didn't pull away as quickly as he had in the past. He stayed in position, his crotch against Keyvan's arse, and he reached his hands around and pulled Keyvan's back into his own chest, holding him tightly from behind. For an instant, Keyvan thought the boy was horsing around and was about to push his hands away, but he didn't. This was different. It wasn't the usual playing around, and Keyvan stayed in place and let himself fall back into his arms. They stayed in that position for a while, their bodies pressed against each other. Keyvan felt Farhad's crotch push against him; something about this felt incredibly good, like nothing he'd ever experienced. He didn't want it to stop; he wanted to do more but wasn't sure what to do. Uncertain what to do next, Farhad peeled away. Keyvan turned around and they looked at each other. They knew that something had happened, something that went beyond friendship, which felt all right, and yet should be disavowed. Neither spoke, unsure of what to say, what to do, or even what had just occurred. They then decided to return to reading their books as it was getting late.

———————

THE NEXT SEVERAL WEEKS were spent trying to obtain new passports for Lili and Keyvan. News had also arrived from abroad, from Farzad and Shahla. Farzad was in his apartment in Cannes on the French Riviera. A friend of Lili had told her that it was widely known that Farzad was dating another woman, Vida, who had moved to Nice with her two sons. Lili was enraged when she heard this gossip and confronted Farzad on the phone, but while he denied his betrayal on the call, his actions confirmed it. He called Lili infrequently and rarely answered her calls. When they did speak, he sounded distracted and was inattentive to her concerns. Despite all this distancing, she clung to him, refusing to accept that he would abandon her in her hour of need, though that is exactly what he had done.

Shahla meanwhile was as unconcerned about her husband's incarceration as she was incensed at the loss of their possessions. She blamed her husband's family. And while she didn't explicitly accuse her mother-in-law and sister-in-law of theft, her tone and conduct was that of a person betrayed. She had all but refused to speak with Lili and had even intimated that Lili had deserved her imprisonment.

Lili was a determined woman; the abandonment by her lover, while devastating, did not shake her resolve to leave the country with Keyvan and make a new life for them in Western Europe or America. She persevered in her efforts to obtain the necessary documents to secure her departure. First, they needed a passport, and then she had to obtain an exit visa and finally, but no less challenging, she had to obtain a visa for France, England, or the United States to visit there.

Her endeavors were set back by the calamitous takeover of the American embassy in Tehran in October 1979. This event, which shocked the world, caught U.S. President Jimmy Carter's administration and the American public by surprise, but only because they had no conception of whom they were dealing with. Anyone who was familiar with Khomeini's book—the *Velayat-e-Faqih on Islamic Government*, freely available in pamphlet form on the streets of Tehran—would have realized that, despite the many assurances of his supporters, themselves perhaps duped or self-deluded, Khomeini had no intention of establishing a democracy. It was a grim theocracy that he envisioned for Iran with no room for American-style liberalism, human rights, women's freedom, and other cornerstones of the Western democratic ideals. The siege of the American embassy was a concrete manifestation of the ideology that would come to grip Iran. Mehdi Bazargan, the prime minister and an early supporter of Khomeini, resigned his post in protest over the hostage-taking at the American embassy. He like the others—Abolhasan Banisadr, Sadegh Ghotbzadeh, and Ibrahim Yazdi, to name just a few, all backers of the Ayatollah, and each instrumental in bringing about the Revolution—fell victim to the Islamic dictatorship that engulfed the country. The street clashes among the left-wing Marxist groups, the Mojahedin-e Khalq and Fadayeen-e Khalq, and Khomeini's supporters continued, but Khomeini had the upper hand and would eventually destroy his opposition.

The chaos that ensued during the occupation of the American embassy delayed Lili's plans to obtain her documentation. The government offices would close their doors with no warning; there was no certainty or predictability in official matters. Most Western embassies, including the British and French, were shuttered. The ones that remained open kept a skeleton crew but evacuated their nationals from the country.

Remarkably, in the midst of this crisis, Keyvan was leading a relatively normal life, to which his growing relationship with Farhad added much joy. At school, Keyvan didn't mind the drastic change in curriculum and the segregation of the boys from the girls. He spent all his free time with Farhad. They had moved past the initial befuddlement of their first intimacy and had cautiously embraced. It had felt so natural that they soon sought each other out at every possible opportunity and would hug and kiss. Empty classrooms and their respective bedrooms at home provided the necessary privacy for these encounters. Consumed by the events at hand, Farhad's parents, like

Keyvan's mother and grandparents, paid little or no attention to the friendship of their sons.

More often than not, Farhad and Keyvan would go home together after school to one or the other's house, under the pretext that they needed to do their homework together, and would spend the night sleeping in the same bed. They had started to explore each other's bodies and the mysteries of the male sex organ, and the white liquid that emerged when they rubbed it. It was the first adolescent crush for each of them, and while they were too young to distinguish between love and friendship, they knew instinctively how deeply they felt for one another. The chaos of their external world had had the effect of reinforcing and cementing their relationship. For now, they drew closer to each other and felt safe in each other's company, and when they embraced, the madding world outside would fade as if it were a distant land.

8

Months went by and Lili eventually secured their passports and exit visas. All they needed now was a visa from the French or British consulate, which had reopened in Tehran. Their applications had been duly submitted, and Lili was cautiously optimistic that they would be able to leave the country before the year was out. Meanwhile, Keyvan and Farhad spent a month in midsummer at Keyvan's grandparent's house in Shomal. Keyvan had never been so happy. They would go swimming and splash each other and horse around in the sea. They also spent hours playing football with

the local boys, or trekking around the empty beaches and sur-
rounding land. The beach was so sparsely populated in those
days that they often found themselves alone in the midst of the
coastal trees and bushes, and often their playing would turn
into caresses and heavy petting that would end in the emission
of the white liquid. They discussed how they would be friends
forever and would do everything together, even work together
as adults. They would be firemen, or perhaps lawyers or bank-
ers, or maybe even enter the foreign service. That these dreams
might prove to be problematic in light of the events unfolding
in Tehran was not the least of their concerns. Every once in a
while, Keyvan would think about their plans to leave the country, and sometimes he would express his concern to Farhad.
The boy had confided in him that his family, too, had plans
to leave, that they had obtained their passports and exit visas
and were only waiting for their visas from the British consulate. They would be immigrating to the United Kingdom where
they already had some relatives. The boys began to discuss how
they would both move to London and see each other every day
there. From then on, Keyvan became intensely interested in
the status of their visas and lobbied his mother in favor of the
British option.

———————

WHEN SCHOOL RESUMED IN SEPTEMBER, they went back
to class and continued to see each other as they had the previous year. In October, Farhad's family's British visas were
issued, and he informed Keyvan that his parents were making
arrangements to depart in the next few months. At first, the
news caused great consternation for both of them; but rather
fortuitously, two weeks later the British visas for Keyvan's
family arrived as well. Lili was ecstatic and immediately began

to inquire into flights to London. The two boys were thrilled; they dreamed of a life in London, where they would go to primary school and eventually to university together. As the days passed, each family made their separate arrangements to move. Farhad and Keyvan were even cautiously optimistic that they might be on the same London-bound flight.

One day soon after, when Keyvan went to school, he didn't see Farhad. He looked for him everywhere and asked his classmates, who told him he hadn't come in. That was strange because the two of them had spoken on the phone the night before, and Farhad had said nothing about missing school. In fact, he had indicated that they would see each other at school and would spend the following evening at Farhad's. Keyvan had packed his pajamas and change of clothes in his book bag for this purpose. He wanted to call Farhad but didn't have access to a phone. He did manage to send a message home for Khaleel to come and collect him from school. As soon as he arrived home, he dialed Farhad's number and reached his father, who answered the phone clearly shaken. When he heard Keyvan's voice, he told him that he had awful news. The Revolutionary committee had come early in the morning and forcibly taken Farhad away to fight in the war against Iraq.

Keyvan was dumbfounded. "But Farhad was still in school," he protested, "he's not old enough to fight in a war."

"I know, Azizam," replied Farhad's father. "But we couldn't do anything. His mother fainted and has taken to her bed. There was nothing we could have done."

"But why Farhad?" Keyvan asked himself plaintively. "Why my friend?"

"I wish I had some answers Keyvan jan, my dear Keyvan. He's our only son and we are bereft. I'm going to do everything to get him back, everything."

"I want to help you. What can I do? He's my best friend."

"Thank you Keyvan jan. I'll let you know. I won't rest until we get our son back."

After he had hung up, Keyvan sat motionless in the chair. Tears began to stream down his cheeks. He had heard that war had been declared against Iraq but thought nothing of it. How could it intrude into their lives? They were just children. He was going to find Farhad and rescue him. They were still going to move to London together.

When he informed his mother of Farhad's fate, she didn't react the way he had hoped. He had wanted to enlist her help in finding Farhad and bringing him back. Instead, she had panicked, forbidding him from contacting the boy's parents, as she began thinking of ways to hide him until their departure. She thought it best if he didn't go to school but, to avoid suspicion, she told the school administrator that they were going on holiday and Keyvan would be gone for a few weeks. He would attend class for two more days, after which they would go to Shomal while they waited for their departure from the country. Parto thought they should leave immediately, but Lili felt that would be suspicious given that Farhad was just taken. Keyvan was furious; he cried and screamed and slammed the door to his bedroom. He wasn't going to leave without his friend. How could his mother be so callous and uncaring? Lili tried to explain that being taken by Revolutionaries was a death sentence, but this distressed him only more.

"But he's my friend. We can't just leave him behind."

"He's got his own family. I'm sure his parents will rescue him, and you'll see him in London. Besides, there's nothing that we can do for him. We can only save ourselves, save you."

Keyvan realized that it was hopeless trying to convince his mother to delay their departure. He thought of running away, but where would he go? And how would that help Farhad? Who could save him? Did he know anyone? Like a house built on sand, his whole world, his dreams, hopes, and aspirations came crashing down on him.

The next day at school he was listless and inattentive. He drifted from class to class, as if he weren't there. In math class, the teacher happened to notice and asked him to stay after class. He then said to him:

"What is it Keyvan? You seem so distracted today. Not your usual cheerful self."

"I'm sorry. I'm just not feeling well today. That's all."

"Does this have anything to do with your friend Farhad by any chance? He hasn't been in the last two days, and I've noticed that you sit next to each other and appear to be great friends."

At the mention of Farhad, Keyvan perked up. At last, here was someone who was showing some interest and expressing a modicum of concern about his friend.

"Yes, in fact, his absence has been trying. He's my best friend, and I don't know what's happened."

Despite his emotional state, Keyvan had sufficient presence of mind not to disclose to the teacher that he knew Farhad had been taken by the Revolutionary committee.

"I thought so. Would you like to know where he is and what he's doing?"

"I most definitely would," replied Keyvan, excitedly. "Do you know where he is?"

"I do," responded the teacher softly. "He's very happy right now."

"He's happy?" stammered Keyvan incredulously. "But I thought—" He checked himself, "I, I, I mean, how do you know that?"

"What did you think?" continued the teacher, in the same gentle, paternal tone, trying to elicit more of what Keyvan knew of his friend's sudden departure.

"No, I mean nothing. I thought he was happy here at school. I don't know why he would leave."

"Would you like to see him? Talk to him? He'll tell you himself how happy he is."

"I would very much like that. But can that be possible? I don't even know where he is."

"I'll take you to him."

"You know where he is?"

"Yes, I can take you to him at lunchtime today."

———

PROMPTLY AT 1:00 P.M., KEYVAN went to his math teacher's classroom, and they walked to the school's car park. He drove Keyvan to a compound that resembled an army barracks. There was a barrier manned by some soldiers, but when the math teacher identified himself, they waved him inside. He took Keyvan into an ante room and asked him to wait while he went to fetch his friend. Keyvan waited. He was so excited to see Farhad and talk to him. He hadn't believed the math teacher when he had told him that his friend was happy. But what did that matter? He was going to see Farhad and together they would find a way of getting him out of here.

But when the door opened, it wasn't Farhad or even the math teacher who stepped inside. Instead, it was a short, squat mustachioed man, dressed in some sort of military uniform. He had a gruff manner about him and appeared to be holding a bright object in his hand, which he twirled repeatedly.

"So I understand that you want to join your friend Farhad," he stated.

"Yes, Agha, Sir, I would like to see him."

"Like many of his countrymen, Farhad has chosen a most sacred and gratifying path."

Keyvan didn't understand this pronouncement and simply nodded his head.

"Do you see this?" The man showed Keyvan the shiny object he was playing with. It was a large, ornate key, the handle in the shape of an ace of clubs.

"Yes," replied Keyvan, perplexed by the turn of this conversation.

"Your friend Farhad has one of these, and I am going to give this one to you," he said, as he handed Keyvan the key. He was surprised by the lightness of the key; it was made of plastic, not metal. "Why is he giving me a plastic key," he thought to himself but remained silent.

"And now that you have accepted the key to paradise, you will join the Imam's army and God willing, shall be martyred and go to paradise, where this key will open the gates for you and you will have the comfort of the houris, those beautiful young virgins who accompany the Muslim faithful in paradise." And then he started to mutter a prayer.

The golden keys to paradise had been Khomeini's Machiavellian endeavor to defeat Iraq's Sadaam Hossein. The formidable Iranian army that the Shah had spent years assembling and fortifying was now in shambles, its commanders either executed or in exile. In a move reminiscent of the levee en masse, or forced military conscription, after the French Revolution, Khomeini instructed that large groups of children should be gathered and sent to walk on the minefields to clear the way for their soldiers. To justify his diabolical strategy, which in the end resulted in the death and maiming of more than one million children, Khomeini had to overcome a major theological obstacle, which was Islam's strict prohibition against suicide. The Quran's categorical admonition against suicide was beyond debate. The dictum was that God had created man and was the only entity permitted to take his life.

To overcome this sacred prohibition, Khomeini resorted to a very cunning argument that drew on the concept of martyrdom in Shiite Islam. When the prophet Mohammed had died in the seventh century A.D., there ensued a power struggle between his father-in-law and close friend Abu Bakr and Ali, Mohammed's cousin and son-in-law, to determine the succession. This struggle led to a schism that ultimately split Muslims between Sunnis who followed Abu Bakr, and Shiites who followed Ali. The two factions waged battles in the seventh century; Ali was murdered in 661 and his son and successor, Hussein, was killed two decades later. The deaths of Ali and Hussein established a cult of martyrdom amongst the Shiite, who, to this day, mourn them in very public ceremonies and processions, often involving self-flagellation and reenactments of their martyrdom scenes.

The overwhelming majority of Iranians are Shiites. Khomeini seized on the history of this martyrdom to decree that self-immolations are insufficient penance; what is required to vindicate the memories of Ali and Hussein are actual martyrdoms in the defense of Islam. In this way, Khomeini diabolically twisted the tragic fates of Shiite Islam's sacred figures to overcome the scriptural prohibition against suicide and successfully mobilized a vast army of mostly children to clear the fields that had been mined by the Iraqis. The golden keys were to ensure that the "martyrs" entered paradise, as Ali and Hussein had obviously done. Khomeini's radical interpretation of the concept of martyrdom under Shiism supplied the ideological and theological justification to overcome Islam's strict dictates against suicide. This later paved the way for the suicide attackers, which prior to Khomeini's interpretation would have been unimaginable by Muslims.

Keyvan, who knew nothing of Islam or its history, was bewildered and started to become alarmed by this pronouncement. He said, "I don't understand. I came here to see my friend. What do you mean I will join the army? I didn't agree to that."

"Shut up. You should be grateful. Get on your knees, pray, and thank the Imam for giving you the key to paradise."

"Where is Farhad? Where is my math teacher? He promised I would see him. I don't want to stay here. You can have your key to paradise back. I don't want it. It's just a plastic key anyway." He went to return the key, but in the next instance he felt his left cheek burn as the military man slapped him hard. Keyvan reeled back in pain and shock. The man called out, and two other men came in. They were much younger than the first but dressed in the same type of uniform. He appeared to be their superior.

"Take him and get him ready for the journey," he barked and left the room.

"Come on," said one of the younger men as he pulled the boy's hand and led him out of the room.

Keyvan was loaded into the back of a military truck. There were two long rows of seats facing each other, full of boys his own age or older. He scanned the faces, but there was no sign of Farhad. There were no windows, and when the truck began to move, they were silent, but soon started to talk.

Keyvan turned to the boy on his left and asked him, "Do you know where they're taking us?"

"I don't know, but I have the golden key to paradise. Here see." And he showed Keyvan his key.

"But that's just a plastic key. They gave me one too. Surely you don't believe this nonsense."

"Don't say things like that. You will go to hell. I want to go to heaven where there are the houris, lots of them, and they all will want me."

Keyvan was stunned into silence by this remarkable statement. He wondered if all these boys actually believed this nonsense. As the truck rumbled on, he thought of his mother. What will they tell her? Will she be able to find him? And what about Farhad, maybe he'll see him, but the chances of that now appeared very remote. He sank into his seat and stifled a cry, determined not to appear weak in front of these other boys.

They drove for what appeared to be an eternity. Some bread and cheese made its way around the truck and Keyvan had two mouthfuls; his somber mood hadn't stamped out his hunger, at least not yet. Every once in a while, they would stop and would get out to relieve themselves, right there on the side of the road. They appeared to be in a desert and no one was moving about. For a minute, Keyvan thought of asking for some toilet paper but then thought better of it.

At last the truck stopped and when they got out, it appeared that they had arrived at their destination. They were still in the desert, but there were makeshift tents pitched all around a military encampment. It was dark outside, but he could make out the outline of the mountains nearby. The sky shone with many stars; it was the same clear sky he had seen as they were trying to escape to Turkey. He wondered where they were and what they were doing there. This was supposedly the military, but they hadn't been issued any weapons, not that he would even know how to use one.

They were given more bread and cheese and some water. They were issued green fatigues and told to change into them and then go to their tents and sleep. There were so many boys in his tent that he could barely sleep. They shared some blankets, but it was freezing at night. He woke up several times shivering and tried to grab the blanket back from the boy next to him who was hogging it.

When the sun came up, they arose and had a breakfast of bread and cheese and some tea in plastic cups that burned his hand, but he enjoyed the warmth of the drink. In the light he could see the encampment; there were hundreds of tents and a sea of men and boys in green fatigues. All around them was desert. The mountains, whose contours he had glimpsed the prior evening, now loomed high above them. He wondered if these were the same mountains that he had crossed. Perhaps he could run away at night and cross the mountain into Turkey. But that was a foolish thought; he would no doubt starve or freeze to death. He wondered if Farhad was in this encampment. To his surprise, there were no restrictions on walking around the camp. Everyone appeared busy. He walked around the whole compound, examining every nook and cranny, carefully scanning every face but didn't find Farhad. When he returned to his tent, he casually asked a question of an older boy, who appeared to know things. He said his name was Behruz.

"Do you know how many camps like this one there are?"

"I don't, but I know there are many. Hundreds of them, all over."

"What's the purpose of this? What are we doing here?"

"You don't know? We're in the service of Allah and the Imam. Hopefully, each and every one of us will go to paradise."

"I know that. But I mean as we wait to go to paradise,

what will we do. Will we receive training, will we be issued weapons?"

Whether it was Keyvan's tone or the expression on his face that gave him away, the older boy took him aside and in a low voice said to him:

"I can see you're not buying this crap about paradise either. They're just using us."

This came as a huge relief to Keyvan. Finally, someone who sounded sane.

"Is there any way out of here?" Keyvan asked in the same low whisper.

"I don't know. It'll be hard. We're in the middle of the desert. There's nowhere to go."

"What about the mountains? We can escape into the mountains."

"Yeah and then what? Where would we go? How would we eat or drink?"

"I'd rather risk that than this," Keyvan spat out, gesturing toward the campgrounds.

"I know what you mean. Why don't we do some reconnaissance and see where we are."

This seemed promising to Keyvan. The older boy appeared to be knowledgeable or educated. He used the word "reconnaissance," which impressed him. And at least he had found a friend in the midst of this desolation, someone who didn't buy into this crazy delusion about a paradise. Perhaps together they could find a way out; together, and become friends, like with Farhad.

Suddenly, he heard a loud blaring sound, as if from a trumpet, but in monotone, followed by a loudspeaker's voice announcing that everyone should gather for the day's exercises. Keyvan wondered what sort of exercises these might be.

He saw the boys lining up behind each other, and he drew toward his new friend.

"What's happening? He asked.

"Oh, nothing, just the usual walking exercise," responded his friend.

"They get us to walk together on a long field in the desert."

"What for?"

"I'm not really sure. I've been doing it for the last three days. They say that it's the road to paradise." And then, in a low whisper, he added, "I think the Iraqi's have buried mines in the ground, and they want us to walk over and step on them. This way they will detonate, and the soldiers can walk through these fields afterward."

Keyvan reeled around as if he had been hit in the head with a bat.

"You mean, you mean … they make us walk over mines? But we'll die—" he stammered out.

"That's the idea genius," responded the older boy with a sangfroid that shocked Keyvan.

"Why don't we run away right now?"

"Because they'll shoot us dead. Calm down. The chances you'll step on one are slim. The three days I've been here, nothing has happened and we've walked the same fields. I've talked to some of the others who say that there aren't too many mines. Besides, if you want to run away, the only time to do it is at night."

"Can we do it tonight?" asked Keyvan expectantly.

"Maybe. I was hoping to be able to store away some food or water. I already have a torch."

"Please, let's do it tonight. I don't think I can survive another day here."

l see. Now be quiet and get in line. Don't let

...ine behind Behruz and they started to walk. After about half an hour, they stopped. They were divided into groups of approximately 20 to 30 boys and, in each group, they were tied together with a long, loose rope. Each group had a leader. The leader in Keyvan's group gave some brief instructions and asked them to stand in prayer, holding their golden keys. Keyvan noticed that the boys in the other groups were all praying too. When the prayers were completed, each group began to walk in a specified direction. They walked side by side in a straight line, making sure that they followed the tempo of the leader. They walked on and on, aimlessly. Hour after hour passed and still they walked. The sun had reached its zenith and it was blisteringly hot. At first terrified, Keyvan was now exhausted, thirsty, and hungry. He wasn't sure his legs could carry him any farther. He wanted this to end. It would be better to step on a mine and die rather than endure this torture. He wanted his mother, or anybody, to save him.

He didn't realize that it was the longest he had gone without thinking of Farhad. His feet were sore. The sun blazed in his eyes, but when he closed them he stumbled and nearly fell down. No one was talking. Far off in the distance, he could see another group of people, presumably other boys. He asked the boy to his right and then to his left when they would be going back, but they didn't know. What he would give now to be back with his mother. Even to revisit the attempted escape with her, he thought; and be shot at all over again, fall off a horse and break his arm, spend time at Evin prison. All that would be preferable to this frightful torture. He thought of the doctor who had treated him in prison who had been so kind to him, and of his grandmother who had come to collect him that evening. He loved his grandmother. How had this all come to pass? Why was he here, in this forsaken place? He had only wanted to see his friend. To help another human being. How much longer will this last, or could he last, he asked himself?

At that moment, as if in answer to the unuttered question, he heard a loud bang and instantaneously a sharp pain shot through his legs and into his chest. The world went dark. That's strange, he thought, how the sun could just go out like that, and then he drifted away.

Second Noble Truth of Buddhism:
The cause of suffering is craving.

PART

II

Princeton 1980s

9

Princeton University has its own unique version of a male fraternity called "The Eating Club." Housed in ivy-covered imitation-Gothic buildings, they dot Prospect Street from one end to the other. In the 1980s three of the Clubs remained closed to women: Ivy, the bastion of the preppy gentleman; Tiger Inn, for athletes and inebriated jocks; and Cottage for guys who didn't quite fit into Ivy or Tiger. The rest of the Clubs were coed. Campus Club had a reputation for being the Club of choice for the "Euro crowd" and "Comp Lit crowd," and was viewed as a cigarette-smoking, black-wearing,

French-speaking caricature that bore little resemblance to the actual students of the Club.

At Campus Club, members took their meals in a large dining room on the first floor that was flanked by a sunroom. On the second floor was a rather old-fashioned library with shelves stacked with dusty, old leather-bound books that went unopened and unread. Rays of sun danced into the room through leaded window panes, lighting corners here and there and casting shadows of polygons on the wall. Eric was alone in the library, deeply absorbed in Proust's *A La Recherche du Temps Perdu*. A black V-neck sweater revealed only the collars of a shirt, whiter than the ivory of Eric's skin; designer jeans hugged a slim waistline and light gray socks disappeared into black moccasins. They were one on top of the other, as Eric crossed his legs at the ankles and leaned over a dark mahogany desk as he read the Pleiade edition of Proust's masterpiece.

He was particularly intrigued by the concept of anti-Semitism that runs through the novel; there appeared to be distinct parallels, if of another slant, with his own life. Though he was Iranian and had grown up in France after his family had emigrated prior to the Revolution, he didn't appear to be Iranian, or even a Middle Easterner—his origins further obscured by his Oxbridge accent perfected after many years at Harrow. For anti-Islamism or anti-Middle Eastern attitudes had become as much a matter of principle in the United States as anti-Semitism was in Europe at the turn of the century when Proust had penned his novel. The Iranian Revolution, and the ensuing hostage-taking at the American Embassy in Tehran had, no doubt, played a major role in shaping these attitudes, making Middle Easterners outcasts here. Proust was half-Jewish, yet his narrator persona, Marcel, does not carry a trace of Semitic blood and reaches the upper echelons of the closed-minded society of the Faubourg

Saint-Germain district of Paris, something to which Proust himself intensely aspired, but never quite achieved.

By his junior year, Eric was keenly sensitive to the social environment, both at Princeton and back home in Paris, as Proust no doubt had been to that of the Faubourg Saint-Germain. Princeton, or at least the part of it that interested Eric, was as unforgiving to his Middle Eastern heritage as the Faubourg had been to Semites. The social equality changes that had rocked American culture in the 1960s and the 1970s appeared to have been parked at the gates of Nassau Hall. Princeton remained the country club that Fitzgerald so aptly had named it in *This Side of Paradise*. Eric was as careful in presenting a most urbane, westernized I as did the most assimilated Jews in *La Recherche*, such as Proust's character Charles Swann. Yet, beneath the impeccable clothes, the Harovian accent, and silver-rimmed glasses, lurked the fear that a tenuous social situation might collapse this I. Eric was intelligent enough to recognize the parallels between his own fragile social construct and those that led Proust to deflect his own Semitism in a letter to Count of Montesquieu at the height of the Dreyfus Affair:

> *Je n'ai pas répondu hier à ce que vous m'avez demandé*
> *. des juifs. C'est pour une raison très simple: si je suis*
> *catholique comme mon père et mon frère, par contre,*
> *ma mère est juive. Vous comprenez que c'est une raison*
> *assez forte pour que je m'abstienne de ce genre de*
> *discussion.*

> Yesterday, I didn't respond to the question you put to me about Jews. It's for this very simple reason: if like my father and brother I am Catholic, my mother, by contrast, is Jewish. You understand that it's rather a compelling reason for me to abstain from this type of discussion.

Eric could not have chosen better words to respond to countless discussions of Middle Eastern politics and anti-Arab slurs such as the rag-head jokes, and other pejorative attitudes toward anything Middle Eastern. This generally conflated Arab and Muslim much like anti-Semitism did at the time of Proust. Eric remained silent about his Middle Eastern origins, and in extreme circumstances, he denied them.

A voice calling his name from downstairs interrupted his thoughts.

"Eric, someone's here looking for you. Are you up there?"

"Yes, but who is it?"

"A guy called Mark," was the response.

Mark, thought Eric. I don't know anyone called Mark. Who could it be, but then he said:

"I'll be right down."

————

SIX WEEKS INTO HIS JUNIOR YEAR, Mark was totally pre-occupied as he walked through Prospect Park to his Club. He had just been handed an F grade in his midterm exam in French. While that alone wouldn't ordinarily create much consternation, his tennis team had lost a series of matches that autumn, and his girlfriend had been behaving strangely the last few weeks. What's the matter with Melissa, he was thinking, trying to understand what had caused their argument the previous night. Why can't she understand that I need time alone, time with my buddies? And yet, while he faintly glimpsed the answer to his question, it eluded him each time he thought about it. For Mark didn't think long or deeply about any subject, because, like his father, a lazy torpor weighed down his mind whenever he encountered a difficult topic. Perhaps he also sensed some deep-seated fear, but like an ostrich burying its head in the sand, his thoughts moved from Melissa to the F in French. The grade threatened the minimum GPA he would need to graduate. Not graduating was unthinkable. His parents were already asking him which law schools he would be applying to in the spring.

Mark then recalled hearing that the University provided private tutors in some circumstances. Nassau Hall wasn't very far, and so he made his way to the dean's office. As he walked toward the building, his thoughts raced from his troubled relationship to his future. He pictured his father in his customary pin-striped suit, giving him that all-too-familiar censorious glance that exclaimed, "You are disappointing the family yet again, Mark." That look was more terrifying than all of his mother's histrionics and inebriated shouting. The anxiety caused his stomach to tighten, but then he was suddenly facing the large, wood-paneled door at the entrance of Nassau Hall, as if retrieved from the scary future he had conjured up. For an instant, he forgot the purpose of his visit. Why had he come here? Ah! Yes, the French tutor, he recalled and opened the door.

The reception area was a magnificent room with double-height ceilings, Queen Anne furniture, and portraits of eminent figures peering down from their majestic perches. There was no one else in the room; Mark approached the receptionist sitting behind a large French Mahogany desk with cabriole legs and elaborate carvings. A less preoccupied visitor might have been struck by the contrast between the grandeur of the dean's formal reception room and the disheveled look of the students with torn jeans and stained sneakers who paid for its maintenance and who expected to be received, if not with open arms, at least cordially.

"What can I do for you?" asked the receptionist matter-of-factly.

"Someone told me that I could, maybe, um ... get a tutor to help me in French. I'm not doing too well in that class," he said, breaking into a charming smile that he had, perhaps unconsciously, perfected to such a deep degree that it had become second nature to him.

"Yes, we do provide tutors; they are generally other undergraduates, either juniors or seniors, majoring in the subject you need help with."

"That'd be awesome," he said, as he wondered what these tutors would look like. He pictured a pale-skinned, tall girl dressed in black, smoking a cigarette as she spoke French.

"Here's a list of the French tutors. You can call them for their availability. The University will pay for up to four hours a week for one semester; you will need to apply, if needed, for a second semester."

"That's great, thanks; I appreciate it," he said, as he glanced down at the list of names on the paper handed to him. He didn't recognize any of them. There were five names; to his surprise one was masculine. Eric, he thought, "I wonder who that is." He planned to look them up in the university's picture book back at his dormitory.

He shared a quad with three others: Josh, who was captain of the hockey team; Drew, who had entered Princeton on a basketball scholarship but didn't play last season because of a torn Achilles tendon; and Kyle, who played tennis on Mark's team. The living room was spartan, with a tattered leather sofa that was obviously a hand-me-down from someone's relative, an armchair, a large TV, and the stereotypical posters of various half-clad athletic women in seductive poses. One poster showed a blonde in a white tennis outfit holding a tennis racquet in one hand as she lifted her skirt with the other, conveniently exposing a round and rosy ass cheek as she walked away from the viewer.

None of the roommates were in. Mark went into his bedroom, closed the door, and sat down with a list on the desk next to the phone:

Jennifer Miller 6902
Heather Stone 6943
Michelle Dubois 6998
Eric Richardson 6901
Deirdre Papp 6972

Michelle Dubois sounded French to him. The image of a dark-haired girl with a long face and visibly distinct gums flashed before his eyes. Eric Richardson, he repeated the name to himself, trying to attach a face to it. He went to the University picture book and looked under the Rs. Eric's picture was a simple black-and-white headshot, but the image of the whole person began to form in Mark's mind: shiny, thick black hair falling under its own weight to the left, chestnut eyes deeply set against skin the color of ivory, and an aquiline nose, like the Apollo Belvedere's; scarlet lips. He wouldn't be too tall, but not short either, of medium build with round-rimmed, silver-framed glasses—and a beguiling smile, which lingered languorously in Mark's mind. Then suddenly, he bounced the thought out of his mind as if he had hit a tennis ball across the court. "I shouldn't think like that," he thought, but the image beckoned him instinctively, an allure that he found hard to resist. He pictured Melissa in an enticing negligee, but nothing could withstand that boy's smile. He tried to envision penetrating her, possessing her, but that smile came back, again and again, as if to remind him of a part of himself that had long been neglected, long suppressed, and long denied. It was like a burgeoning wellspring that refuses to hide, like a childhood friend who reminds you of a past that is ever present, like a captivating tune that catches you off guard, only to reveal itself as a half-forgotten song.

Eric was puzzled; who would be looking for me, he thought, because anyone who might wish to see him would know to come up to the library. He went down the stairs and noticed that Matt, the prematurely balding president of Campus Club, was standing next to someone whom Eric didn't recognize.

"Hey, I'm Mark. I'm here for the French lesson."

"Oh yeah, that's right!" Eric said. He had forgotten entirely that he had arranged a tutorial over the phone. Eric had registered as a French instructor after a friend had told him that he made several hundred dollars as a tutor. While his parents provided him with a small allowance, he had thought that he might supplement his funds through private lessons. He had registered the previous semester, but by the time he received Mark's message on his answering machine, he had lost interest in the idea and had almost declined to tutor him. Besides, he had since undertaken a vast project: writing his junior paper on Proust's *La Recherche*. Initially, he had thought only to focus on the first volume of the massive work, but his advisor's reaction was to compare such an endeavor to writing a junior paper on *Madame Bovary* before she marries Charles. Eric had no option but to write on the entirety of Proust's novel, which meant he had to read all five thousand pages in French. He hadn't even made it through *A L'Ombre des Jeunes Filles en Fleures*, the second of seven parts of the book, by the time Mark's call came. He had several thousand pages of reading left, not to mention the secondary material, and then he had to actually write the paper! In addition, he had to complete the assignments for his other courses. He had returned Mark's call to decline, but when he heard Mark's baritone on the phone, he changed his mind. There was something about the timbre of the voice and its deep, warm, attentive tone that had enticed Eric to accept this person and he had suggested a time and place for their initial meeting.

Now, almost five days later, Mark was in the lobby of the Campus Club, as had been duly agreed and arranged.

"Why don't we just go upstairs to the library; there's no one there now," Eric said, recovering from the initial shock of a forgotten appointment and pretending that he had remembered all along, but also suddenly intrigued by the handsome jock who now stood before him.

It was shortly after 5:00 P.M., and already the room glowed in a pale orange haze as the sun retreated and the sky turned purple in that magical, almost mystifying moment between daylight and darkness, which is filled with anticipation and promise and yet can lead to disaster as in the opera by Wagner.

"Do you have your textbook with you?"

Mark reached into his backpack and pulled out a thick white book, illustrated on the cover by a glass of red wine sitting atop a book of verse with an image of the Eiffel Tower to the right.

"How far into the book are you in class?"

"Um ... well, I haven't been to French class this semester, that's why I need help. It's because of tennis practice."

"I see, okay. So I suppose we'll start at the beginning then," Eric said, as he opened the book to the first chapter.

"Conjugation of the verbs 'to be' and 'to have,' etre and avoir."

As he looked down to write, he became aware of Mark's eyes on him, as if he were being watched by a tiger camouflaged by the savannah's tall grass. Mark was gazing at him

directly and smiling broadly—an inviting, almost beckoning smile that he had never encountered. Eric had not known
strong desire; temptation had never laid its hands on him. It
shook him to his core and he shuddered, entranced by those
eyes, greener than any emerald. In his mind, Eric left the world
of French grammar for the more exciting pastures of a tennis
game, of boys and men stripped out of their athletic clothes,
all that young flesh, red after a brisk match on a cold autumn
day, their veins descending on muscular limbs as in a bronze
cast from antiquity, flicking towels, slapping each other's backs
and buttocks with jocular remarks about not dropping the
soap in the shower. All that testosterone-filled horsing around
from which Eric had exiled himself, consciously, deliberately,
because of the forbidden fruit that he dared not contemplate, let
alone touch, now hanging low before him—smiling, not scowl-
ing, inviting rather than dismissive. It took enormous effort to
control this desire, as in pulling reins on a runaway horse.

After a herculean effort, he was able to return to the lesson
only to realize that he had been repeating the third person sin-
gular of the verb "to be" over and over again. To his great surprise, Mark appeared completely unperturbed, perhaps even
unaware of the senseless repetition, which to any uninterested
observer might legitimately have appeared as the early onset of
madness. Mark was beaming at Eric, as inattentive to the verb
conjugation as he would be to the right side of a mathematical
equation.

The lesson continued with half attempts by Eric to explain
the basics of verb conjugations, despite Mark's own inattention,
until finally, Eric realized more than one hour had elapsed. "It's
already past six."

"I guess it's time for me to leave," Mark said rather
tentatively.

The consternation caused in Eric by the utterance of the word "leave" was comparable to standing on the shore and watching a tidal wave roll toward you. He summoned all his mental focus to prevent the impending departure, but all he could come up with was:

"Would you like to stay for dinner?"

The instant Eric said it, he regretted the invitation. How likely would it be that Mark would want to stay for dinner at the Campus Club? Besides, he might be disenchanted, if not outright repelled by some of his friends—immature literati who used the current jargon of literary theory in conversation, mistaking their pomposity for wit.

As he heard Mark reply, "sure thing," Eric was overtaken by bewilderment at the simplicity of the acceptance and his own joy, as the prospect of Mark's continued presence began to take shape in his mind.

They went downstairs and carried their dinner on trays from the buffet in the pantry to the main dining room, where they sat down at a square table for four covered by a vinyl tablecloth illustrated with a smiling sun, twinkling stars, a happy moon, and a child playing with a golden lab—reminiscent of a children's picture book. Eric had sat at the same table countless times, yet tonight the sun appeared brighter, the stars more sparkling, and the child happier. The other two seats were unoccupied, and Eric was silently hopeful that they would so remain. However, before they could take their first full mouthfuls of food, the two chairs were pulled back and Consuelo and Larry sat down.

Consuelo was a short, thin girl whose brown skin and European facial features betrayed her Puerto Rican origins. She was born and raised on the Upper West Side of Manhattan, the daughter of two intellectuals who had worked hard to send her to Brearley, where she had received, along with a superb education, a considerable dosage of hazing by the mean, white, WASPy girls who not only dominated the classrooms, but afterschool social activities. While Brearley had doubtless been the key that opened the door to Princeton, the wounds inflicted on her in her teenage years ran deep.

Larry was a wiry boy with dark hair and blue eyes, whose pockmarked skin prevented him from the acceptance he sought from the University's fashionable crowd. He, too, hailed from the Upper West Side of Manhattan, and though he came from relative affluence, he wore dirty jeans, a wrinkled T-shirt, and white sneakers turned a rusty color—a carefully cultivated image of a weed-smoking bad boy while being quite the opposite.

"Hi, Eric," they said in unison and peered at Mark inquisitively.

"Oh, hi. This is Mark. He's captain of the tennis team. This is Consuelo and Larry," he said, and preempting their questions, added, "I am tutoring him in French."

"Ah," said Larry, "which Club are you in?"

"T.I.," replied Mark in his low baritone.

"Ugh," said Consuelo. "Why would anyone belong to that bastion of male chauvinism?"

Eric's heart sank as he came to Mark's defense.

"You have to forgive Consuelo," he said turning toward Mark. "She's never afraid to tell us what's on her mind, but we still love her." He gently touched her arm, his eyes silently pleading with her to drop the subject.

"Since when do you apologize for me to your friends, especially any from T.I., which, by the way, I never realized you had."

Larry came to the rescue.

"Consuelo's just snappy today because Sonnenberg ripped her a new one in his lecture."

Theodore Sonnenberg, a professor of French and comparative literature, was a well-known author and critic. He delivered orotund lectures wearing a cape modeled after Liberace. Acutely intelligent and highly articulate, he uttered Wildean witticisms in a low monotone that made them all the more vituperative.

"Really?" said Eric incredulously, with an expression that pleaded for details. Sonnenberg was his advisor; he admired and sought his patronage and friendship. "What happened?"

"Well, we were sitting there when Sonnenberg suddenly stopped his lecture and turned to Consuelo and said, "Take off your headphones."

"Of course, Consuelo couldn't hear him because she was playing music. Everyone, I mean like a hundred people, turned to stare at her. I nudged her and told her to take them off. She did, but Sonnenberg went on to say something about who would come to a lecture and listen to music, implying that she was a half-wit, and everyone laughed."

"No they didn't," interrupted Consuelo. "No one listened to him; no one cared."

At least Larry had moved her off the topic of T.I. Eric wanted to kiss his hand.

"What class was this?" ventured Mark, who until then had maintained a silence, which was becoming more ominous by the minute to Eric.

"Proust, Mann, Joyce," spat out Consuelo, as if she were throwing a gauntlet in a challenge.

"I guess that's some kind of literature class," replied Mark, visibly perturbed by Consuelo's aggressive tone.

"Hey, guys, I have to get going. I have a paper to write by

tomorrow," exclaimed Eric, with great urgency in his voice and gestures, as he pushed back his chair and gathered his books. He had seen the expression on Consuelo's face and had wanted to preempt her pejorative response.

"I should be going too," Mark said, as he rose to leave.

"I am sorry about Consuelo," Eric said, once outside the Club.

"No big deal, man."

They stood for a minute as if glued to the ground by the unspoken desire that, like a magnet, drew them closer together. Eric hesitated as if he were facing a chasm and deciding whether to jump over it and risk his doom or salvation.

"I, um, I live off campus," he ventured looking at Mark expectantly, like a puppy waiting to play with a ball. "That's cool" responded Mark.

"Yeah, different. Want to see my place?" he held his breath as he asked the question.

"Sure."

10

E RIC RESTED HIS HEAD AGAINST Mark's chest, his right ear barely an inch from his heart whose thumping sounded like the distant drumming of a marching band. He had captured Mark's left leg between his own limbs and felt the toes of the right leg grazing playfully against the bottom of his feet, as Mark caressed him in an embrace that felt at once passionate and protective as if lover and father were merged. The past faded as in a rapidly receding tide and future worries dissolved like ice in balmy waters.

A soporiferous slumber enveloped him as he floated between sleep and wakefulness as in that moment when someone gently nudges you and whispers "you were snoring," and you protest that you could not have been because you were awake. You were not just awake but aware, keenly aware, highly sensitized and mindful of the smallest sensations, shorn of the anesthetic that numbs your senses and dulls your experience, full of vigor and alacrity. Hypnos won him over as he fell into a deep and untroubled sleep, like a child without worries. Yet the Greeks, those masters of human psychology and human tragedy, knew that such moments of bliss are mere relays along the journey of life. It was not a coincidence that Hypnos and Thanatos, the personification of death, were brothers living in the same black cave from which arose the peacefulness of sleep and the dark, empty embrace of death.

He awoke shortly after dawn to find Mark dressing hurriedly and searching hastily for his socks. He appeared agitated and mumbled, "Where the fuck are they?" as he searched under the sheets, beneath the bed, and then under the pile of clothes strewn haphazardly on the floor and chair.

"Are you in a rush? Do you want to have some coffee?" asked Eric hesitantly.

"Nah, man. I've gotta get back. Here they are," he said, sitting down on the edge of the bed and pulling on his socks.

He quickly stood up and abruptly left without even a handshake, let alone a hug or a kiss. Eric lay in bed stupefied when Mark pulled the door behind him, fleeing into the misty dawn as Daphne had before Apollo's golden arrows.

Shortly after Mark's departure, Eric rose from his bed and made coffee in a cafetiere he recently had acquired. Every morning since its purchase, Eric would look forward with excitement to his morning coffee, with the bubbling sounds of the machine, the aroma of the coffee, and the froth of the milk, producing a cappuccino instead of a dull, black coffee. On this occasion, he prepared his cup of coffee absently—not even the froth of the milk captured his attention. While Mark's abrupt departure initially concerned him, he had overlooked it as the Pompeians had once done with the first groaning of Mount Vesuvius. He imagined himself with Mark in a remote place, perhaps an abandoned island, far from the censorious eyes of the world and the inconveniences of reality.

He casually reached for a copy of the Michelin guide to the great hotels of Europe that lay on the kitchen counter. As he flipped through the pages, he chanced on Hotel du Cap in Cap d'Antibe. He had never stayed at the hotel, but had been to the beach and played tennis on the grounds. He imagined passionate embraces in their room overlooking the azure waters of the Mediterranean, tasting all of Mark as Zephyr gently blew the curtains up toward a ceiling so elaborately carved and molded that it resembled an upside down wedding cake; luxuriating in a foam bath with a glass of Cristal Champagne; spending lazy mornings in a cozy bed before traipsing down to the beach for café crème and pain au chocolat; floating together in the ozone-filtered aquamarine infinity pool; sunbathing on the large raft anchored in the middle of the sea as they watched cigarette boats slit the waters sending cascades of undulating waves shaking the raft and causing their lithe bodies to touch.

A ringing telephone broke his wistful trance. He picked up the receiver listlessly after ten rings.

"Darling, I've been ringing and ringing, but you never answer the phone. Where are you? How are you? I miss you so," his mother gushed.

"Good morning, mother," he groaned, wondering about the coincidence of this call coming after his night with Mark. "Why do you always call so early?"

"It's half past seven there. Not that early, and besides we

are six hours ahead and it seems the only time I can reach you. How are you?" she asked.

"I am well, actually. I've been very busy with my studies; I'm writing a paper on Proust, which is long and complicated."

"I know darling; studies are important. But at your age, one should also enjoy life a little. I'm sure Monsieur Proust himself would agree with that."

Eric's mother had long been accustomed to his excellent scholastic performance, but where others admonished their children to study, she always cautioned against an excessive academic focus. When she finally rang off, he glanced at his watch and realized that it was almost 8:00 A.M. and near the time for his seminar on the nineteenth-century French novel. He was momentarily perplexed by how quickly time had elapsed this morning. Mark had left more than two hours ago, and he had done nothing except make a cup of coffee, but even that hadn't taken long. His consciousness deemed two hours of ruminations about Mark as "doing nothing," oblivious to the critical and precarious terrain he was crossing by initiating this liaison.

––––––––––

As HE LEFT ERIC'S APARTMENT, Mark was gripped by a dark mood. He crossed Nassau Street and walked precipitously toward his dorm room. He felt that he had committed a grave mistake, a dangerous folly that could inflict devastation on his life. How would he explain his night's absence to his roommates? He could say he spent the night with Melissa, but that fiction could be easily exposed, backfiring to reveal the awful truth of this illicit encounter. He imagined Melissa breaking up with him indignantly, vengefully spreading news of his ignominious behavior, word eventually reaching his family. His father's silent glare that could freeze beer, and his mother's ensuing melodrama. His instant ostracism from friends and family would be ensured, as well as the loss of his position on the tennis team, and even potential expulsion from it. A shiver ran through him as he opened the door to his room. Thoughts of his impending doom were as powerful and loud as the sound of waves crashing against a cliff.

He was immediately bewildered by the silence of the peaceful room where everyone was asleep. He quickly stripped out of his clothes and climbed into bed, but lay awake wondering what his roommates would say about his absence and whether or not Melissa had called the previous night. It wasn't until after 10:00 A.M. that the first of his roommates stirred. When he heard Kyle get up, Mark jumped out of bed and started a casual conversation. Kyle offered Mark some coffee, but there was no mention of his whereabouts the previous evening. When his other roommates eventually arose, there were no questions about his late night. Mark was perplexed that no one asked any questions, though it didn't occur to him that he, himself, didn't have a single thought about his roommates' comings and goings in the last twenty-four hours.

ERIC DRESSED QUICKLY and hurried over to East Pyne, a building in the middle of campus that housed the romance language departments. He was so preoccupied with thoughts of Mark that he had wholly forgotten the agenda for the morning seminar. The subject eluded him. He had reflexively picked up his books and now glared down at the novel he was carrying. "Of course, *Madame Bovary*," he mumbled to himself. The utterance was sufficiently brief and hushed so that no one would have taken him for mad. If Eric had been more self-aware, he would perhaps have realized that our civilization does require us to not only censor the voices that circulate in our minds but to keep a tight lid on them. Minor exceptions are made in the case of very brief utterances such as his, but one was not to make a habit of "speaking their mind."

The seminar was taught by Fabien Trompet, a legendary professor whose seminal works on Victor Hugo and Flaubert had received wide acclaim even beyond the walls of academia. In France he had been interviewed on television by Frederick Mitterrand, a semi-celebrity who would go on to become the Minister of Culture.

A girl of extraordinary beauty took a seat next to him and greeted him with a kiss on both cheeks. Her name was Madeline Howe. She had red hair that cascaded to just below her square shoulders that needed no padding. Her pale skin was as clear and transparent as the waters off the coast of Calabria, where you can see the white sand at the bottom of the Mediterranean. Almond-colored, deeply set eyes, set apart by a nose that turned up at the perfect angle, produced a symmetrical effect that gave her face an exquisite feminine beauty as if she had been painted by Botticelli. Her only flaw, if it could be called that, was her petite stature which made her appear fragile, like a porcelain doll, though she was, in fact, robust and vigorous, through years of arduous and determined training as a ballet dancer. Her extraordinary talents and remarkable features had been recognized at an early age by an astute, gay, dance choreographer, who had teamed up with her unscrupulous father to enlist a sixteen-year-old Madeline in a series of ballets that had scenes deemed inappropriately licentious. The ballets had been televised and had propelled her to the status of an entertainment celebrity. However, before that notoriety could be exploited further, and in spite of her father's many remonstrances, Mattie, as her friends called her, chose to take a break from ballet and a possible film career and enrolled at Princeton.

Why she had chosen to major in French literature, where her knowledge of French was as lacking as her understanding of its literature, was a question on everyone's mind but hers. She, however, had developed a strategy for overcoming her lack of literary acumen. Her tactics, while perhaps course and unbecoming, were remarkably effective. She would spot the student in class whom she judged was the best, and would immediately strike up a friendship. She would attend to her newfound friend with such assiduous interest and charm that her target could not help but do her bidding. Her celebrity status doubtlessly went a long way in bringing about her desired goals, perhaps not only in her efforts to woo the top students but in the tacit acquiescence of the professors and the university, which turned a blind eye to her machinations.

Mattie's victim du jour was Eric, whom she had delighted with morning visits to his apartment bearing warm muffins and a night out at the *Palladium*. This was the nightclub of choice in New York City, where she had introduced him to other celebrities including the gay choreographer, whose shameless flirtation Eric had tolerated with good humor.

In return, Eric helped with her papers, which unfailingly received an A grade. So, that particular morning, she turned to Eric. "What do you think of *Madame Bovary?*" she asked, as if in conversation at dinner. At an early age, she had mastered the art of using charm like a maestro hitting precisely the right keys on a piano: the expression of her face and the timbre of her voice would strike precisely the right chord in her interlocutor, enlisting without fail the response she desired. Such remarkable emotional shrewdness provided her with tools that would serve her well after her beauty and celebrity status had long faded.

"I was thinking that it's rather interesting that she doesn't have a mother, and I wonder if there's a link there with her ill-fated romantic aspirations," said Eric.

"That's really interesting, and you know, I was wondering about that too; but of course, I couldn't express it as well as you," she said and broke into a broad smile.

Consuelo took the seat to her right and greeted Mattie with a smile and a "hello," but the girl ignored her and continued on with Eric.

"I mean, she has all these relationships with men which, as you say, are ill-fated, and that's got to have something to do with her not having a mother. I just haven't figured out what."

"Even as a young girl, she has these grandiose imaginings where she is a heroine of her own fables. She romanticizes a world where men serve as props in her continuously unfolding delusion. These stories take the place of reality for her, as she goes from one adulterous disappointment to another, where reality continuously falls short of what she imagined life would be. Perhaps in all this philandering, she is seeking the maternal security that she never had. Who knows, perhaps a maternal figure, a role model, might have curbed the excesses of her imagination and brought her back to reality as it were."

At that moment the professor walked in and silence fell over the small room with its large round table around which all twelve students and the professor sat in a tight circle. Trompet was a jovial man, one of those cultured and intelligent people whose wit and intellect sparkle through their eyes as if they were perpetually laughing.

"Bonjour, I look forward to learning all about *Madame Bovary* from you," he said with a gesture, as he placed his papers before him. "Let's discuss Emma's early life and her marriage. Anyone care to speak to that?" Silence in the room.

Discussing Flaubert in French in Trompet's cla
ing task even for the more intrepid graduate stuc
the hapless undergrads. The poor souls fell into the
Emma Bovary; they pictured brilliant discussions v 	 a celeb-
rity professor, but when confronted with the reality of actual
participation, they were dumbstruck.

Mattie cautiously raised half an arm. "Madeline!" Trompet
said in his orotund baritone, relieved that someone had volunteered and he didn't have to resort to calling on Eric as usual.
Many past seminars had devolved into a one-on-one conversation between Trompet and Eric.

"C'est interressant. It's interesting," she ventured unable
to pronounce the French r sound. "Juste avant la classe, je
parlais avec Eric que …, just before class, I was talking with
Eric about …" she paused, searching for words, "um … que
Madame Bovary n'a pas de mère, that Madame Bovary doesn't
have a mother."

"Oui, Yes," Trompet's face lit up in encouragement.
"Continuez, Continue."

She continued haltingly. "Um …" more pauses, "how do
you say link?" she muttered under her breath.

"Lien," replied Eric in a whisper overheard by everyone.

"Je me demande s'il y a un lien entre ça, et les liaisons de
Mme. Bovary? I wonder if there's a link between that and
Mme. Bovary's liaisons?"

"Un sujet très intéressant Madeline; développez votre idée,
s'il vous plaît. A very interesting subject, Madeline; please
develop your idea."

She couldn't recall the rest of Eric's ideas and turned to Eric
beseechingly, who interjected:

"En faite, en discutant justement avec Mattie, je me suis posé
la question de savoir, si Emma avait eu une mère, ses illusions

auraient-elles eu moins de force? Avec son style indirect libre, Flaubert nous étale les pensées d'Emma d'une manière si profonde— In fact, in discussing this with Mattie, I wondered if Emma had a mother, would her delusions have been less gripping? With his indirect free style of writing, Flaubert shows us Emma's thoughts in such a deep way—"

At that moment the door to the classroom opened, revealing a male student with an olive complexion and a conspicuous black mustache. He came in apologizing for being late, but with the air of someone used to deference, who apologizes not because he is sorry, but because it is the polite thing to do. At the sight of him, Eric leapt from his chair as if to offer his seat to the late newcomer, but he checked himself and merely moved to make room around the tightly packed table. His name was Ali Pahlavi, the second son of the deposed Shah of Iran. About the same height as Eric, he cut a robust figure, though he didn't exercise, and were it not for the disquieting mustache, he would have been deemed handsome. The first eleven years of his life had been primarily spent at the Niavaran Palace in Tehran, and, while in the shadow of his elder brother, the Crown Prince, he was nevertheless brought up as a Royal Prince accustomed to deference from others.

Eric and Ali had been Boy Scouts together in Tehran. The last time they had seen each other before Princeton was at Eric's twelfth birthday party in September 1978. Shortly after that Ali had left Iran with his two sisters. They had gone to their aunt, Princess Ashraf's, house in New York, before joining their parents on their ill-fated one-year odyssey around the world—to Egypt, Morocco, United States, Bahamas, Mexico, back to the United States, Panama, and finally returning to Egypt where the Shah had died. They had fled Panama at the last minute, after Ali's mother, Queen Farah, had overheard

rumors that President Omar Torrijos had made a deal with
Khomeini to return the Shah and, in return, he would set the
American hostages free. The whole world had turned their
backs on them; pusillanimous sycophants and so-called friends
had become turncoats overnight. Only one man, Anwar Sadat
of Egypt, had the courage to welcome him. Ali and his siblings
had accompanied their parents to Egypt, where the Shah had
succumbed to cancer. After that, Ali had been sent to a boarding school in Massachusetts and then on to Princeton.

Flaubert had succeeded in diverting Eric from Mark but not
for long. As soon as the discussion was finished and the seminar concluded, thoughts of Mark invaded his mind. He went
home to check his messages in case Mark had called, but there
was no blinking light on the answering machine. He inquired
at the Campus Club, but nothing awaited him there either. He
looked Mark up in the university picture book, and the black-
and-white headshot sent tremors through him. He went to
Mathey College and walked around in the hope of a chance
encounter that didn't materialize. He debated whether or
not to walk to Mark's room, even knock and ask for a different person, only to be "surprised" when Mark would answer
the door. That would be too predictably obvious. And what
if he weren't in? He wondered what his roommates would
be like. He didn't know anyone who knew Mark. "That's it,"
Eric thought to himself. He had to find someone who knows
him. But how? He didn't know anyone on the tennis team or
at Tiger Inn. He tried to think of all the people he knew but
nothing came to mind. He mustered the courage to walk to
Mark's room. The corridor was empty, and he walked past
the room hurriedly having suddenly decided that it wasn't a
good idea to be seen there, given that this would be deemed an
inappropriate act.

He asked everyone and anyone if they knew Mark, at first cautiously and then openly, perhaps even tactlessly, but none of his friends or acquaintances had any inkling of Mark, the captain of the tennis team, Mark in T.I., or Mark in Mathey College. Then the trail went cold.

He didn't hear from Mark for a while. First, a day went by and then another and then a whole week. He had thought Mark would at least contact him about their tutorial work. Why hadn't he called? They had spent an amazing night together. Had he done something to put him off? He recollected Mark's abrupt departure that morning, his frantic search for his socks. He no doubt didn't want to be found out; he had mentioned a girlfriend, but Eric couldn't recall her name. But why would he be worried about being found out? They had been completely discreet. No one had seen them. It couldn't be that. Maybe he didn't like Eric. Who was this girlfriend? Could Mark really want her more than he desired Eric, after a night like that? And why hadn't he called about the French lesson?

The questions haunted him, waking him up in the middle of the night, distracting him from his lectures, causing him to look off into space. Even Flaubert wasn't able to bring him back, prompting Trompet to ask one day, "Eric, is everything okay?" To which he had mechanically replied in the affirmative. It was as if he had been hijacked by an incubus.

One morning, as he was getting ready to leave his flat, the doorbell rang. His heart soared at the possibility that it could be Mark, but when he opened the door he saw Mattie smiling widely and bearing freshly baked muffins and coffee. "I brought you breakfast, darling."

"What a lovely surprise; please come in."

They talked of Flaubert and set a date to sit down to work on their papers together, which was of course code for Eric

writing both papers. She invited him to a lun
would include a surprise. If there had been
would have been excited by the invitation an
the surprise, today he merely nodded his head   ....ate that
he would attend.

"Well, I better go now," she said. "I have a million things
to do."

"Thank you for the coffee and muffins. It's a great way to
start my day. Oh, by the way, do you happen to know a guy
called Mark Cooper, captain of the tennis team? He's in T.I.,"
Eric asked, fully expecting a negative answer.

"Yes, I know him, or at least I know his girlfriend, Melissa.
She's in Cap. I don't particularly care for her though. Why do
you ask?"

It was as if she had thrown a lifeline to a sinking man. He
grasped it with all his might and tried to deflect the question
with a question. "How come you don't like her?"

"She's a bit of a fake and a sycophant. She wants to be seen
at all the right parties and has tried to latch onto me in a bad
way. I don't know him though. He looks like a dumb jock.
Why do you ask?"

"No reason. I've been tutoring him in French. I just wondered if you might know him."

"I'm not surprised he needs tutoring. He probably only got
into Princeton because of tennis," she said, revealing a remarkable ignorance of the reasons behind her own admission to the
university. "Why would you want to waste your time with that
guy?"

Eric looked at her and realized the deep chasm that existed
between them, or between any two individuals—a chasm born
of an intrinsic solipsism that prevents any meaningful commu-
nication. It felt like they were locked away from each other

in neighboring cells, which appeared transparent, yet their attempts to reach through the walls were unavailing.

Bewildered by the question, Eric managed to contain himself and stammered out, "I don't know; I thought it might be fun to do some tutoring; you know, earn some extra money and help someone."

"It's not like you need the money darling, and in regards to helping people, I don't think even you can help that dumb jock. Anyway, I must run, bye."

"What's her last name, I mean, Melissa?"

"Kellogg," he heard her say on her way out the door.

He rushed to the university picture book. Melissa Kellogg, Mathey College, Cap and Gown. At least he now had unmasked the enemy. More importantly, he now had found a connection with Mark, and however tenuous it may have appeared to be, it gave him hope.

11

THE F AT THE BOTTOM OF THE
page of his French test was not
accompanied by any commentary.
Mark stared at it incredulously as the
single letter silently trumpeted the
devastation that was about to befall
him if he failed this class. He walked
back to his dorm room besieged by
thoughts of failure—failure to graduate, failure to please his father, failure as a man. "I still have time to
pass it," he told himself, but he knew
he needed assistance—urgent and
substantial help. "I need a tutor."

He hadn't returned to Eric for
help, and each time he thought of
asking the university for a new tutor,
he couldn't think of a legitimate

reason for making this request. Until now, it had been more expedient to ignore the problem. However, to deny it any further was too perilous. "Maybe I should go back to Eric," he thought.

He feared Eric because his tourniquet of conscious control had come unwound in this man's embrace, and the inner wound it protected now was bleeding. A deep voice in him murmured, "You can't deny it was the best night of your life. You felt alive; you were yourself, Mark, and not some mask you wore to please your dad and his social propriety."

His mind strayed to his days in high school when he had felt the first stirrings of his homosexual attraction. He had developed a crush on a friend, Fred, who played on the football team, but had not acted on it. His desires were mere velleities, but he nevertheless had been overcome with a sense of profound shame. He took refuge from his own feelings of craving mixed with self-loathing by spending hours practicing tennis serves and perfecting his groundstrokes. In his onanistic reveries, he would muster all his strength to conjure up images of seductive and voluptuous women, but despite his best efforts, they quickly would morph into Fred. At the end of these solitary sexual fantasies, right before the climax, he experienced a moment of joy, perhaps even of ecstasy; this was when his self-judgment abated and all thought was suspended. Yet, it was a fleeting moment, soon to be replaced by such powerful feelings of disgust and shame that he would become physically nauseous.

There was a knock on the door.

"Uhhh," he sighed and opened the door to his room.

"Mark," Melissa said, waiting for him in the hallway. "I've been looking everywhere for you."

Mark looked at Melissa as if she were the lifeline needed to pull him out of his slide to oblivion. "What's up?" he replied, welcoming the distraction.

"What's up?" Melissa said in exasperation. "Urban Blight is playing this weekend at the Campus Club, and I'd really like to go."

"Okay, well that's great. Let's go," he replied.

"Well, that's just it. We can't. Not without a guest pass, and I don't know anyone on campus."

"I don't either," replied Mark, avoiding the obvious.

"But I thought you did. You told me you had dinner there a few weeks ago."

He had told Melissa that he had been to campus for a French tutorial and had stayed for dinner. At the time she had paid no mind to it, and he hadn't elaborated.

"I, I did; um . . . like I told you, I had a tutorial there."

"Great. So you know someone there who can get us guest passes."

"Melissa, I don't know the guy that well. He tutored me once, that's all. I can't go asking him for a guest pass."

"Why not? And why just once? I thought you were failing French and needed all the help you could get."

Inadvertently she had touched the wound and he growled, "I have my reasons, and besides, why are you always asking me for this kind of shit? I don't like imposing on people so you can go to a goddamn party."

"Why do you have to be such a dick about it? All I did was ask and you bite my head off."

Mark contained his rising temper. He smiled fleetingly. "You're right. Sorry. You caught me at a tough time. I just flunked my French test."

"Oh, I'm sorry, babe," she responded, calming down in response to his intemperate tone. She then inquired of his predicament. "Why didn't you say something? Didn't the tutor help you?"

"He did, but once wasn't enough, and I didn't really study for the test."

"Okay. Well, it's not too late; you can still pass if you do well on the final."

"Yeah, but I probably won't. I'm really behind."

Melissa stepped over and put her arm around him and kissed him on the cheek. "Call the tutor and get some help."

"All right, I'll do it," he said in resignation, not sure how else to respond.

"And ask him for a guest pass while you are at it," she said with a smirk. He gave her a look. "Just kidding, babe."

"No, that's a good idea. A way to mend fences. Me asking him is like apologizing for not following up."

"Use what you've got, Mark. Great charm." He nodded his head, unsure if this was a slight, but, if it were true, why begrudge it?

———

As an officer of the Campus Club, Eric was tasked with door duty on weekend party nights. Word had spread that the band Urban Blight would be playing at the Club on Saturday night, and they were bracing themselves for an all-out assault at the door from everyone on campus. A limited number of guest passes had been printed and supplied to Club members to invite their friends. Matt, the Club president, had informed all those with door duty that only members, and those with guest passes, were to be admitted. Otherwise, the Club might be in violation of fire safety rules, the consequences of which, though not clearly specified, were implied to be dire.

Eric was assigned to the door from midnight to 1:00 A.M.,

which was the peak hour when the band would be onstage. Ordinarily, he would have been dismayed by this assignment and would have preferred to mingle with his friends inside, even though he didn't particularly care for Urban Blight's music. However, he was excited about his turn at the door that night; by chance, it might provide an opportunity to interact with Mark if he should come during those hours. He was almost certain that Mark would come; the popularity of Urban Blight was such that everybody wanted to come, so why wouldn't Mark?

"He'll probably come with Melissa and some of the jocks from T.I.," he thought. "He'll be in a group and won't be able to talk to me, but at least I can let them in, and maybe catch up with him later that night." The mere thought of Mark vouchsafing him a smile at the door increased his anticipation, like a drug addict trembling at the thought of his upcoming fix. "What if he comes earlier? A lot of people will come early to beat the crowds," he thought. "Maybe I should switch to the 11:00 P.M. to midnight door? But most people will come between midnight and 1:00 A.M.; I could get to the door at around 11:45 P.M. and relieve the person early—I wonder who's doing the 11:00 P.M. to midnight shift?" He went to the list posted on the Club's notice board.

"Consuelo, great." He called her dorm room. Luckily, she was in.

"Hi, Consuelo, it's Eric."

"Hey Eric, what's up?"

"You've got the eleven-to-twelve door shift tonight, right?"

"Uh-huh."

"Can I ask a favor?" he asked as calmly as he could so as not to raise any suspicions.

"Sure. What?"

"Do you remember my friend Mark?" he asked and hesitated. He didn't want to sound too excited or anxious.

"Mark? No, I don't."

"The guy from T.I. we had dinner with one night, you know."

"Oh, the guy you were tutoring," she said. "What about him?" she asked tentatively.

"Well, I was wondering if you could let him in if he came during your shift."

"He doesn't have a guest pass?" she asked.

"I don't think so. I was just going to let him in if he showed up."

"Why don't you give him your pass; this way he can come in anytime?"

"I guess," Eric said. Of course this made sense, but the torrent of feelings about Mark showing up created so much confusion in his mind that he couldn't think straight. So, how would he get his guess pass to Mark, and what would Mark think if he showed up at his dorm room? He might be displeased that Eric would be reaching out to him. What would his roommates think? What about Melissa? She might become suspicious.

"It's just that . . . I've already given away my guest pass."

"You sound a bit strange, Eric. Is everything okay?"

"Yeah, I've just . . . got a lot of other things on my mind."

She snickered. "Why do you suddenly care so much about this guy Mark anyway? He's just a dumb jock in T.I. Why would he even want to come to an Urban Bright concert? Too cool for his kind."

A dumb jock in T.I. Did she really say that? How can anyone think that? He is the most incredible person I've met here, but someone like Consuelo wouldn't see that.

"He's actually a nice guy, and I told him he could come in tonight to hear the band."

"All right, if I see him, I'll let him in. That is, if I recognize him. I've gotta run to class, see you at dinner?"

"Sure, and thanks." Eric surmised that she had just said that to end the conversation. He was momentarily alarmed that he might have stirred up her suspicions. Consuelo was astute and alert, and now she was wondering why he was anxious to invite a "dumb jock" to the party. He recoiled as he recalled her slur again in disbelief and shock, but his thoughts quickly turned to Mark.

As Eric walked from the Club to his apartment, he wondered whether all this was just some fantasy. As Consuelo had remarked, why would Mark want to attend this concert? When he arrived home, Eric plopped onto the sofa, exhausted not by the walk, but by the marathon of thoughts and desires running through his mind. Mechanically he pressed the button for the messages on his answering machine and heard his mother rambling on about some sort of event that she had attended in Paris. He deleted the message before it was finished, his tolerance for anything that was unrelated to Mark diminishing by the day. The machine beeped and moved to the next message, and Eric bolted upright on the couch as he heard Mark's baritone.

"Hey, man. I'm sorry I haven't been in touch; I've been super busy. I need to come back for another lesson if you still have time. Also, do you have a couple of guest passes for your Club's party tonight? Melissa's been on me for it. I guess she likes the band that you guys booked tonight. Anyway, let me know and if you can't, no big deal. See ya!"

A more disinterested observer might have raised an eyebrow

at Mark's request for "a couple of guest passes" to a party that everyone on campus was clamoring to attend. However, for Eric, just the sound of Mark's voice was sufficient to create rapture. He accepted the impersonal and heartless tone of the message with perfect equanimity. But there was more: the message offered the tantalizing possibility, almost the certainty of more tutoring sessions and what that might suggest. Eric played the message over and over to ensure that he hadn't missed any of its nuances, like a child mesmerized by a new toy. He took great care to save it, unlike Mark's first message about the tutorial, which he had deleted without barely a second thought.

He considered how to supply Mark with the guest passes; should he call and arrange a time and place to deliver them, or should he simply go to Mark's room? What if Mark wasn't there? He would have to leave the passes with the roommates, which would deny him a much sought after interaction. As he picked up the phone to dial Mark's number, he realized that he only had one guest pass and needed two. He hung up the receiver and started toward the Club in the hope of obtaining one more pass. On the way, he thought of people who might not have given away their passes. He definitely didn't want to ask Consuelo and risk another interaction with her on the subject of Mark. She's probably long given hers away, he thought. Ian, Patrick, Susan, Matt would've already parted with theirs. "Perhaps Bill; that's it," he thought, "I'm sure he hasn't even collected his."

Bill and Eric had been friends since their freshman year when they met trying out for JV tennis. While neither had made the team, a close friendship had been born and Bill had visited Eric in Cannes the previous summer. He was a blond-haired, blue-eyed boy from Abilene, Texas, with handsome chiseled features, and Eric had initially developed a late adolescent crush on him. Bill had sensed that and succeeded in deflecting it with gentle candor, without losing their friendship. In his junior year, Bill was majoring in electrical engineering but had chosen to take all the prerequisite courses for medical school to keep his options open. This left him with little time for anything but his studies. He had even missed the all-important room draw, and his irate roommates had looked for him all over the campus in vain before forging his signature to keep their place on the roster of rooms. It turned out he had fallen asleep in the engineering quad after spending the whole night there. He rarely came to the parties, and Eric was now convinced that he hadn't even collected his guest pass.

Bill's room was in Blair Arch, on the way to the Campus Club, and Eric stopped in to see him. His roommate, Garry, a gregarious and slightly effete but preppy WASP, had answered the door and informed him that Bill wasn't in. Garry then launched into a lengthy monologue about something irrelevant that Eric despaired might have detained him far too long.

"I'm really sorry," he interrupted. "But I urgently need to find Bill. Do you know where he is?"

"No, I haven't seen him all day. What's the matter, has something happened?" he asked. "No, nothing. I'll explain later; see you tonight?"

As he fled down the stairs of the Grand Arch, Garry yelled out, "Do you have a spare guest pass to the party tonight?"

"That's it," thought Eric, as Garry's words registered with him. "Garry would have gotten Bill's guest pass, so Bill hasn't picked his up." But where could Bill be? In the library or the E-quad? It would take hours to search for him at Firestone Library, which was a vast structure with multiple levels and a multitude of reading rooms and other nooks and crannies. The

E-quad was at the very end of Prospect Street, a half-hour walk at least. Eric sighed at the apparent enormity of the task and decided to proceed to Campus Club in the hope that a solution might materialize there.

It was 4:00 in the afternoon and the Club was relatively empty; a few people were moving around furniture in preparation for the party. Eric casually inquired of others if anyone had any spare guest passes and was not surprised to receive a negative response.

Exhausted and confused he went to sit down but suddenly had the thought of just going to Mark's room and giving him the single guest pass. "If the roommates are there, I'll just say I was in the area and I'm dropping off a guest pass." The idea suddenly began to appeal to him, as his desires ran up against his fears, his mind working feverishly to minimize his apprehension in an attempt to realize the desire. "But what if he's not in? They'll just say to leave the guest pass, and I don't want to do that." He thought of calling to see if Mark was in. "I'd rather just go there." He considered, then rejected the thought of calling anonymously fearing that suspicion, however remote, may fall on him. "I'll just go there," he decided and went to Mark's room.

He knocked on the door, a shallow, hesitant knock that nevertheless was heard inside. He heard some footsteps and the door opened. Mark stood before him dressed in an orange-and-black T-shirt with circles of sweat under his armpits, wearing a pair of white shorts, white socks with the pungent odor of an athlete after strenuous exercise. Eric remained in a state of disconcerted silence; his typical self-confident loquaciousness overcome by disquietude at the sight of Mark, like a dog prowling the wood and chancing on a lion.

"Hey," Mark said. A genuine smile spread across his face,

evidencing pleasure at the sight of Eric, but th

"What brings you here?" The timbre of his voi.

tinged with the consternation typical in people wh   .e

themselves through the eyes of others, anxious that h. may be

seen talking to Eric.

"I brought you the guest passes you called about; or rather, a guest pass, as I only have one."

"Oh yeah," Mark responded, seemingly relieved against any insidious suspicion and potential ignominy by others. "Thanks, man." He reached out and took the pass from Eric.

"I'm sorry, but if you come between midnight and one, I'll be at the door and can let your friends in."

"That's awesome," Mark replied hesitantly, hoping that was Eric's only intent, yet not wishing for him to depart so quickly.

They remained standing in the doorway, each waiting for the other to make the first move. Though he was alone, Mark appeared hesitant to invite Eric inside, no doubt torn by conflicting emotions. Eric misjudged Mark's misgivings as concern about the imminent return of his roommates. Yet, at the same time, he sensed that Mark was happy to see him, maybe even wanted him to embrace him. This kept Eric rooted in place, giving him hope that the encounter would be prolonged, and he could further lose himself in those emerald eyes, that he could merge into him, and that all of this could freeze time. Images of Keats' Grecian Urn flashed through his mind:

> *Thou still unravish'd bride of quietness,*
> *Thou foster-child of silence and slow time,*

What was the rest? He couldn't recall. Eric pictured children dipping a vase made of glass in a stream of water in Proust's *Combray*, as if to arrest the flow of water, to capture time.

"Can I see your quad?" Eric finally ventured, emboldened by love's courage.

"Oh man, I'm kind of running late, can I show it to you some other time?" Mark replied, his debilitating fear overcoming not only desire but gratitude, compassion, even common courtesy.

Eric let him off the hook. "Sure, I understand. See you tonight." And with that, he turned and walked down the hallway and out into the day's bright sunlight, reassuring himself of Mark's desire for him, if not his willingness to pursue it.

12

B Y 11:00 P.M., THE CROWD OF people outside the Campus Club stretched along the lengthy path that led from the façade of the Club and finally spilled out onto Prospect Street. An ocean of white faces gleamed in the dark night as students hurried along to Club parties.

"It's like the siege of the Bastille," barked Consuelo to Eric, as he came to relieve her shift at the front door. A few electrified gas lamps strained to light the street, but all Eric could discern was a surging multitude: face after face smiling, laughing, serious, morose, excited; some were holding hands or jostling in undulating movement. The din muffled all voices such that Eric couldn't hear the protestations of the two herculean bouncers hired to help guard the door. The Club was already full, and in accordance with Matt's instructions, Eric was permitting entry only if someone left the Club, which no one did given the imminent commencement of Urban Blight's performance. The agitation and thrusting of the crowd increased as more people joined the line at the back in the vain hope of gaining admittance to the Club. Eric feverishly sought Mark amongst the surging, obscure faces. Though he had expected a large crowd, he was astonished at the gathering horde swarming outside and frustrated by the tenebrous night that prevented him from identifying anyone. A tall, overweight guy at the front of the line pushed his way up to the door and vehemently demanded to be let in. "I have a guest pass," he spat out at Eric.

"The Club is full. Members only at this point," he riposted, as the bouncer pushed back the ornery stranger.

"I'm gonna get you, you fucking faggot," he shrieked, as he retreated from the bouncer's outstretched arms.

"I'll never do this again," Eric lamented to himself, more dejected by the idea that the throng might dissuade Mark from coming in, than by the inconveniences of door duty or the belligerence of this corpulent boor. He began to scrutinize the morass of faces again, and suddenly he thought he recognized someone, but wasn't entirely certain. Toward the back of the line, he thought he glimpsed Prince Ali. His consternation grew as he peered into the throng, trying to put a face to the bodies silhouetted against the dark night.

"We need to let that guy in," he exclaimed to the bouncers, as he wildly gestured toward Ali.

"Which guy?" asked one of the bouncers.

"That one," said Eric, pointing and gesticulating anxiously.

The bouncer shrugged, and Eric realized the futility of trying to identify Ali. He leapt into the crowd and didn't meet much resistance as he forced his way to the back. "Your royal highness, how nice to see you both."

"What a mob scene," said Ali. "Khaled and I were just about to leave."

Eric greeted Khaled, who was the nephew of King Hasan of Morocco. Eric had met him before.

"Would you like to come in?" asked Eric looking at both the Princes.

"Well, if it isn't too much trouble," Khaled said and opened the palms of his hands toward the crowd that lined the path ahead of them.

"Come with me," Eric insisted, as he made his way back to the door, parting the grumbling crowd with his elbows as he advanced with the Princes in tow. When they reached the threshold, he asked them to enter and reassured them he would follow as soon as his shift ended. Khaled nodded his head, and they hastily entered the Club.

Forty-five minutes passed with no sign of Mark. Perhaps he had arrived earlier, Eric thought, but that was unlikely, because he only had a single guest pass and wouldn't have left Melissa behind—she was the whole reason he was coming in the first place. When the band began to play, the clamor that arose in the Club at the first twang of notes from the electric guitar was matched by an equal outcry that convulsed the deprived crowd outside, a scene reminiscent of a phantasmal painting by Munch.

The music pulsated so loudly there was almost no need to be in the Club to hear it. The outsiders began to shake and sway as if they were at a rock concert, while the blaring music attracted more and more people. As the throng outside expanded like a

hurricane gathering force, Eric was in despair over the diminishing likelihood of Mark's appearance. Because nobody was
leaving the Club, no one was granted admission, though some
implored Eric for the favor. This scene reminded Eric of Kafka's
Trial, only he didn't identify with the powerful doorman who
guarded the impregnable gateway to the inner sanctum. No, he
was, like them, a forlorn, increasingly frail supplicant, but one
bereft of the love he so desperately sought, the love that with
every tick of the clock toward 1:00 A.M. appeared as elusive as
the light to Kafka's journeyman.

Larry approached the door to relieve Eric, who told him
with a rueful sigh, "They're all yours, have at it." Eric turned
to enter the Club when he thought he heard his name being
called. He looked over his shoulder and saw Mark advancing
up the line and shouting Eric's name at the top of his voice. The
joy he felt at that moment was as intense as it was unexpected;
it engulfed his entire consciousness as it would a prisoner about
to be hanged who suddenly is saved by his allies—a joy that had
almost a tangible quality to it as when a balm soothes an aching
wound.

"Look at that crazy dude," laughed Larry. "The Club is full,
and he thinks he's getting in."

"But he's my friend. Larry; please we have to let him in,"
stammered Eric importunately, with an impassioned, almost
torrid look on his face, which to Larry appeared at once disarm-
ing yet disquieting.

"Chill out, man," Larry admonished. "It's still your time at
the door; you can let him in if you like." Eric calmed himself.
"But we're at capacity, and if Matt catches you, he's going to be
furious."

"I know, Larry, but I promised to let him in when I gave
him my guest pass," Eric pleaded, knowing full well Mark was

accompanied by at least one person, if not more. Yet, it was a facile lie, one that would be readily and promptly exposed. Eric raised his right hand and waved Mark forward. He approached the door with Melissa desperately clasping onto his arm like a baby cub.

"Hey, Mark," Eric said and broke into a broad smile. "How many are you?"

"Just me and Melissa," he said and looked around to deflect Eric's stare. "Boy, what a crowd."

"Yeah, we didn't expect this. The Club is full, but I'm off-duty now and you can come in with me." Eric turned to the doorman as they stepped up. "They're with me."

"Thanks, Larry. It's all yours. I'm done." Larry just gave him a quizzical smile, whose import was not lost on Eric, as he proceeded into the Club with Mark and Melissa.

Once inside, Eric turned to Melissa. "Hi, I'm Eric by the way."

"Melissa," she replied. "Thank you so much for getting us in. When we showed up, it looked hopeless." She turned to look over at the band. "I love, just love, Urban Blight."

"Would you like me to show you around the Club?" Eric asked.

"Well, I'd like to dance, but Mark doesn't, and I've never seen the Campus Club. So sure, that would be nice of you," she said, and then as if in afterthought, "you'd like that right, Mark?"

"Sure, sure," he grunted.

"How about a drink first?" Eric asked as he led them down the stairs. As soon as they reached the landing, Melissa exclaimed:

"Oh my God, it's Mattie," Melissa gushed.

Mattie was speaking to Ali and Khaled. "Come, I'll introduce you to my friend Ali," Eric volunteered—for him the evening was unfolding like a magic carpet.

As they stepped over, Eric made the introductions, but the music was too loud to hear anything, and everybody just nodded their heads as if they actually heard him. Mattie appeared disinterested in his friends, and with a polite smile bowed out under the pretext of going upstairs to the ladies' room. Melissa ran after her up the stairs.

"I'm glad you made it," exclaimed Eric, straining to be heard over the thunderous bass of the electric guitar.

"Me too," Mark replied. "Melissa's over the moon and I'm ..." his voice trailed off. Eric was unsure if he had deliberately hesitated, or just gave up because of the effort required to be heard.

"And you are? What?" he ventured, stepping closer.

"I'm happy to see you," Mark said placidly, though he looked surprised at his own utterance, as if the words had escaped him by mistake.

"Let's go over to the bar and get a drink," Eric stated and without waiting for a reply, he asked Ali and Khaled what they would like. Mark followed him. As they forced their way through the mob to the bar area, a great jostling pushed them together and Eric fell backward, and in an attempt to steady him, Mark held him for a brief instant against his chest. This fleeting moment, too ephemeral to be noticed by anyone else, tantalized Eric. At the bar, he summoned up his courage and moved his right leg against Mark's body as he waited to order the drinks. Mark didn't back away. As the two bartenders were overwhelmed, they remained in that position for a long while, their bodies swaying against each other in the undulations of the crowd, like two vessels tossed together in the midst of a turbulent sea.

When they returned, drinks in hand, they found Melissa, in a rather somber mood, complaining about the queue to the ladies' room, but Eric suspected that the true source of her grievance was more likely explainable by the snub of the haughty Mattie. She asked Mark to go upstairs and dance. He reluctantly agreed and followed her.

Eric stayed and continued to converse with Ali and Khaled, though Mark's departure pained him. He was unable to extricate himself from the Princes, not only because he felt it impolite to leave, but because of his innate tendency from childhood, which he himself was unaware of, to attend to royalty. He remained there for another forty-five minutes until Ali expressed fatigue and decided to take his leave. "I'll walk you to the door. Do you have a car outside?"

"Yes, thank you, my driver should be waiting outside." He led Ali to the door and bid goodbye to him. Khaled had chosen to remain.

On his return, he immediately sought out Mark. The band had taken a break, replaced by Madonna piped in via a CD player. He found Mark on the edge of the dance floor. Melissa was holding on to him and speaking into his ear. Eric hesitated. He wished to approach them but was intimidated by their intimacy. He went downstairs listlessly, and thought of having a drink but was dissuaded by the throng at the bar. He spoke to some people he recognized, but presently could endure it no longer and returned upstairs with vague and confused hopes of engaging Mark privately. To his consternation, they were not where he had last seen them. He searched everywhere, even returning to the bar area, though he knew they were not likely to be there. At last, he conceded that they must have left. Exhausted and overcome by a torpor, he decided to walk home.

A paper moon hung in the night sky as in picture books, bathing the grounds in its pale, silver light; the paths now were empty, and, as he strolled past the grand facades of the gargoyled buildings, Eric felt forlorn and rueful, a melancholy that was perhaps ephemeral, yet infinitely regretful.

Eric was a light sleeper, and if awoken in the middle of the night, he had difficulty falling asleep again. He had made his way to bed and had managed to fall asleep when he was awoken by a loud noise from outside. Very dismayed, he got up to determine the source of the din. There was someone knocking on his door. As he peered through the eyeglass, he saw Mark and quickly opened the door. Mark's breath reeked of alcohol, as he stumbled in and greeted Eric, and kissed him on the mouth.

"I failed my French test," he slurred. "I need your help." Even though he was inebriated, Mark appeared strangely confident, in control. He quickly took off his shirt and slipped out of his jeans, and led Eric, who had been asleep in boxer shorts, to the bed. He pushed Eric down on the bed and began to caress and kiss him, alternating between kissing him on the mouth and nibbling and licking his neck and earlobes. As he held Eric in his strong arms and stroked his hair, Eric held onto Mark and clasped his legs around him, feeling every inch of Mark's toned body; for him, each kiss, and each touch, registered like earthquake tremors.

They spent the whole night in each other's arms; it wasn't until eight or so that Eric started to stir. He woke up to find himself in Mark's embrace. The joy he felt was incalculable; nothing in his life compared to it. He didn't dare move for fear of waking Mark and losing his embrace; he wanted this moment to last forever. Then, concern that Mark might wake up with regret, and leave as briskly as he had done the last time, began to trouble him.

Frantic thoughts of Mark's imminent departure, and how and when he would next see him, momentarily paralyzed him. Should he offer him coffee? Or, perhaps, a French lesson. Mark made a movement and pulled Eric closer to him, and while still half asleep, he started to kiss and caress Eric and started to make love to him, slowly lowering his kisses down Eric's body. When they were finished, Eric ventured cautiously, "How about I make us some coffee?"

"Sure, that sounds good," Mark actually purred, much to Eric's surprise and contentment.

After this tryst, the French lessons went better than either could have expected. As arranged, they met once and sometimes twice a week at Eric's place. Mark was often distracted by his excitement and would start to kiss, caress, and undress him, while Eric insisted they spend an hour on lessons before making love. The weekly sessions with Mark calmed Eric's anxiety about losing him again. The distraction that had virtually crippled him earlier began to subside. While initially he fretted that Mark might cancel, or simply not appear at the appointed hour, his continued visits and their passionate love-making soon quelled these lingering doubts. He was able, once again, to return to his classwork and to resume his thesis on Proust.

Eric dared to dream of a future with Mark. With his initial desires satisfied, he began to crave more contact. He overlooked what he had read about desire in his literature studies—that it is an illusion, often evaporating to give way to yet another longing, and causing more craving, like a thirsty traveler lost in the desert and chasing after mirages. He fantasized that Mark would visit him the following summer in the South of France, where his parents had a small apartment in the town of Golfe-Juan, between Cannes and Antibes. He plotted how he would arrange it so he and Mark could spend the nights in the same bed without raising suspicion. After graduation, he might try to live in New York City, where he thought Mark would relocate to work in some sort of corporate job before applying to law or business school. He might even apply to the same school. They would rent an apartment and live together. He didn't discuss any of this with Mark of course, who remained reserved about any time together other than their weekly lessons and sexual engagements, but Eric hoped to widen that contact in the future.

13

Two months passed and the fall term's final language exams approached. Mark's French had improved but he was nervous about the exam. An F in French would spell potential disaster, personal and academic. He accepted Eric's offer to work together more frequently that week to prepare for the exam. In between verb conjugations, they would take breaks to make love.

On the day of the exam, after he had finished the test, Mark brought the questions back, and they went over Mark's answers, which had been handed in on a separate sheet. Eric estimated that Mark answered at least 80 percent of the questions correctly, which would translate into a B. Mark jumped up from his chair and hugged and kissed Eric.

As they laid there in each other's arms, Eric ventured, "Do you think we could spend a night together before the end of term?"

"Hmm," Mark said haltingly, his brows furrowed. "That might be complicated; not sure how I'd explain another ... lesson."

"It doesn't have to be here; I mean we could go to New York City. Have dinner and get a hotel room. I mean I can pay for it. We can celebrate your B in French!"

"Well, I don't have it yet," Mark equivocated, but his eyes betrayed him. He had started to fall in love with Eric, though his fear of the consequences held him back. "It'd be fun, though," he mused. "We could get a hotel room, order room service, and spend the whole night together."

"Wouldn't it?" exclaimed Eric, overjoyed by Mark's compliance. "When do you think we can go?"

"Let me check on a few things, like when I'm expected home for Christmas, and I'll let you know."

"Okay, let me know. I'm leaving for Paris next Wednesday, so hopefully the night before!"

Eric rang the Waldorf Astoria Hotel, where his mother stayed on her visits, and a helpful reservation agent informed him that they had a special rate that included breakfast. He booked the room, planning to spend the money he had earned tutoring Mark.

In his excitement, he hadn't thought about, much less discussed with Mark, how best to communicate now that the French lessons were over. Instinctively, he remained highly sensitized and mindful of Mark's need for the utmost discretion.

Eric wasn't as concerned about revealing his own sexual orientation. The precautions he took, therefore, resulted not from self-concern but were intended to allay Mark's unease. Moreover, while these concerns appeared to play on his mind at the conscious level, they actually stemmed from a deeper part of his consciousness. Eric didn't have the maturity to fathom the impulses that led to his caution, let alone the wisdom to recognize in them the perils that he himself faced.

Eric thought that he might call Mark, and, if one of his roommates answered the phone, he would say he was calling about the results of the French exam. Immediately he discarded the idea; Mark surely wouldn't want him talking to his roommates. Maybe Mark will answer the phone himself, but he may not be alone and that would defeat the purpose of the call and may unsettle or upset Mark. He didn't want to do anything to risk Mark cancelling their date in New York. While a few days before he couldn't have imagined an overnight dinner date with Mark, now he couldn't envision the possibility of not having it.

He considered walking over to Blair in the hope of running into Mark, but recalled the social hijinks of his earlier prowling and instead decided to walk to Campus Club, trusting that the familiar surroundings might prompt a solution.

At the Club, he ran into the usual cast of characters and sat down to have dinner with Consuelo and Larry.

"When are you leaving for Paris?" Consuelo asked.

"My flight's on Wednesday, but I'm staying in New York on Tuesday night." He immediately regretted volunteering this information. Yet, it was as if his deceit compelled him to tell everyone about his clandestine tryst.

"Oh? What's going on in New York on Tuesday night?" Consuelo inquired with raised antennae.

"Nothing, really. I have an early flight on Wednesday morning, and it's easier to get to JFK from there," he lied; his flight wasn't until Wednesday evening at 9:00.

"I didn't know they had day flights to Paris. Which airline are you flying on?"

"Air France."

"Are you going business?" she prodded.

"Actually yes," he replied. "My mother made the arrangements."

"Nice for some of us! Air France business class and Christmas in Paris!" she purred.

If Eric hadn't been consumed with thoughts of Mark, he may have recognized the bitter jealousy that lurked beneath her response.

"I'd rather be in New York," he countered.

"How come?" interjected Larry, who had been silent until that moment.

"I dunno. Less complicated, I guess. And besides, I've never spent Christmas in New York and would like to see the famous Christmas tree at Rockefeller Center," he added in a tone that was almost convincing since it was partially true. However, his preference was not based on seeing Christmas decorations!

"Well I've never been to Paris at all," said Consuelo, her tone a strange mix of longing and resentment.

"Trust me, it's not what it's made out to be," replied Eric.

"It's all very well for you to say; you've lived there. I'd like to see the places I'm reading about in class."

"I'm sure you'll go one day. We're all very young." Eric paused and had a thought. "In fact, perhaps you'll come and visit me at some point," he suggested, though the last thing he wanted was for Consuelo to meet his parents.

"Invite me and I'll come," she riposted, her tone suddenly

softened, perhaps realizing that friendliness was more likely to elicit a genuine invitation than hostility.

"I will," he said, as he pushed back his chair, "but now I must be off. I've got a million things to do before I leave."

"Will we see you before you go?" asked Larry.

"I'm sure you will. I'll be around the next two days."

Larry nodded his head. Eric didn't notice that Consuelo had dropped her affable smile.

In the end, it was much simpler than he had imagined. Mark called him, and when Eric described the reservations at the Waldorf, he told Eric how much he was looking forward to their evening together.

———————

THE WALDORF ASTORIA HOTEL on Park Avenue at Fiftieth Street was once the most famous hotel in the world. However, by the 1980s it was becoming faded, rather like the Hollywood celebrities it used to host and like them, in need of renovation, which perhaps explained the relatively low price of the rooms. Eric's room was on the fifth floor; it was a relatively large room with double-paned English windows that opened vertically, giving it a bright and airy feel. A bathroom, in white marble, appeared in good condition. A king-sized bed, a mahogany desk, and a Queen Anne-style armchair, which was in urgent need of reupholstering, decorated the room.

At approximately 5:00 P.M., he heard a knock on the door, and when he opened it, Mark bounded into the room, kissed him, and threw him onto the bed. They stripped off each other's clothes and made passionate love in many varied and erotic positions. Afterward, as they lay in each other's arms, Eric asked if Mark was hungry. Of course, he was; they were both starving. They looked through the room-service menu, and

Eric called down their order of filet mignon steaks, red wine, and chocolate mousse.

While waiting for dinner, they lay in each other's arms silently for a while, and then Eric asked, "What do you suppose you'll do after graduation?"

"Not sure. My parents want me to go to law school."

"What do you want?" Eric asked.

"I don't know. How about you?"

"I don't know either. I was thinking of law school myself."

"What for?" Mark asked curiously.

"I dunno. I mean, I'm no good at math and science. I think law's the only option really. I thought of perhaps teaching French, you know, like a fellowship at a University, but the idea of tenure and the whole publish-or-perish thing just scares me. Plus you don't make much money."

"That's true. This guy I know from T.I., who graduated last year, got a job with a bank doing investment banking. He makes a lot of money. Maybe I'll do that."

"What do you do as an investment banker? And I thought you needed a business school degree, an MBA maybe, for that kind of job, no?"

"I think you do eventually, but my buddy says they'll take you on after graduation; you work there for a couple of years, and if you do well, they send you to business school and sometimes even pay for it."

"I see. But what would you do there? I mean what would the work be like?"

"Not sure. He talked about analyzing investment opportunities, like buying and selling companies, or investing in new technologies."

Eric wasn't too interested in banking, but he hadn't thought about life after Princeton. The furthest into the future he had pondered was what he would write his thesis on, but that was before meeting Mark. Now all he thought of was planning a life with Mark.

"These banking jobs, they're mostly in New York, right?"

"Yep."

"So if you got one of those jobs, you'd have to rent a place there."

"I guess so, yeah."

"How about we get a place together? We could split the rent, get something really nice?"

"I guess we could. Have to think about it though," he said with a twinge. "I mean, it's way too soon to think about that."

"I know; I was just saying, if we got jobs in New York, then we could maybe get a place together." Eric had no idea what kind of job he would be eligible for with a fine arts degree, and dismissed practicalities such as his lack of a U.S. work permit. However, work didn't matter as much as a future with Mark. Everything else faded into the background, like a rapidly receding tide.

Mark also wondered about the future. He always had planned to rent a place with his college buddies, maybe a three bedroom apartment. Would he and Melissa stay together and eventually marry? It hadn't even occurred to him to live with Eric, but now that he was lying there naked, their limbs intertwined, and a part of him really, truly, wanted to be with Eric, to be able to kiss him and make love to him every day. It felt so good, so effortless, so natural. And yet, something deep down forbade him from even considering such a scenario. Eric appeared in an imaginary future, as in a movie or a dream. The real future, the practical place to be inhabited by Mark, the red-blooded American heterosexual athlete, was as closed to Eric as the Forbidden City in Beijing.

There was a knock on the door and a voice called out, "Room service."

Mark hid in the bathroom as Eric pulled on his shirt and trousers and opened the door to sign for their dinner, which appeared in cloche-covered plates on a roundtable that was wheeled into the room by a young bellhop in a red uniform.

They were ravenous and quickly consumed their dinner: Eric in his unbuttoned shirt and trousers, Mark in his underwear that he had pulled on in the bathroom. They polished off the bottle of claret and hopped back in bed, naked, and ready for another passionate session of lovemaking.

Hours later Mark fell asleep, but Eric couldn't release himself. While he was physically exhausted, as much by the packing and the journey to New York, as by the amorous acrobatics in bed, his emotional turmoil, and the sexual exhilaration he felt, were too strong and kept slumber at bay. As he looked over at Mark, who was breathing peacefully, his chest rising and falling with each breath, he was overcome by a sense of relief, as if a weight had been lifted off his shoulders. With his eyes closed and his consciousness lost in sleep, Mark no longer could escape him like sand through his fingers; it was as if Eric were able to freeze him in time, to grasp him, thereby to possess him and let this moment stretch on forever. When Mark was awake, Eric toiled, unconsciously to be sure, but rigorously and unremittingly, to find ways to delay each parting and to live in anticipation of their next reunion. Yet now, with Mark asleep next to him, immobile, their bodies lightly touching, the obsession abated and he felt calm. He reached over and held Mark's hand, and whether he momentarily awoke, or by a reflexive reaction, Mark clasped his hand and Eric eventually fell asleep while holding onto Mark's hand through the night.

They were woken by the pale winter's sun, as light darted into the room through cracks in the half-drawn curtains. They rose and had breakfast brought up.

"My flight's not 'til later this evening. Do you want to walk around the city a bit?"

Mark thought about it. The chances of being seen by friends in New York were remote.

"Yeah, sure, let's do it, but like classmates who've just run into each other."

This gave Eric pause, but knowing the importance of discretion for Mark, he nodded his head.

It was one of those early-winter days in New York before the bitter cold sets in, when the warm rays of the sun envelope you as in a gentle caress; a season that only exists in the Northeastern part of the United States, where it's known as an Indian summer. They walked across to Fifth Avenue, then up past the luxury storefronts—Cartier, Tiffany, Asprey—lost in the midst of an anonymous crowd that ebbed and flowed as in the song "La Foule" by Edith Piaf, whose refrain now echoed in Eric's mind. The crowd, that faceless, uncaring, vaguely hostile mass of people, whose untrammeled savagery Eric had always feared and artfully dodged, was now a gentle, caressing farandole that Piaf sang about, a confluence of people whirling around them, its shallow murmur a tacit approval of their unspoken love. It was as if the world had become a kaleidoscope, the wondrous "Shahre Farang" that had so captivated him as a child in Iran.

They walked up to Central Park, wandering into Sheep Meadow, where the unseasonably warm weather had drawn many people. They sat down and removed their shoes and socks, and Mark took off his coat and laid down on the grass.

They picked up a three-way Frisbee game with a young boy, and then laid down next to each other, careful not to touch, just two friends enjoying the park together. Mark fell asleep, and Eric looked over at him, beads of sweat gleaming on his brow. Eric was present in the moment with all his being. His mind didn't wander anywhere but focused on the sleeping Endymion next to him. A mysterious urge came over him to kiss him. His heart began to beat faster and his mind raced as the compulsion drew his face closer to Mark's. Despite the perils, perhaps even because of them, he knew at that moment that he had to kiss Mark, to proclaim their bond for all to behold, to affirm his own existence through love, its implicit and explicit sanction in the of eyes the universe. "I love, therefore I am," he thought as he grazed Mark's lips and made tangible the inscrutable visions of love that would at once seal their bond and his fate forever.

Their parting was more awkward than sad—halfway between a clumsy handshake and a tentative hug on the edge of Central Park, the two careful not be mistaken for two homosexuals. The tears didn't come until later for Eric. The rush of packing up, checking out of the hotel, taking a taxi to JFK, lifting his suitcase onto Air France's conveyor belt, the slight relief at not having to pay for excess baggage, and then going through security and dodging crowds to find his way to the gate had kept his mind occupied. It wasn't until he found a quiet corner at an empty neighboring gate, where the flight had already left, that the tears came—first as a sob, then despite all his efforts, an uncontrollable flood, and an almost violent stream that gushed out of his eyes and down his cheeks. Eric bowed his head and cupped his hands to his eyes to dry them and to prevent anyone from noticing him. He felt forlorn, wistful, dejected, and profoundly lonesome, yet he was surrounded by people in the airport. He made a concerted effort to stop crying; he couldn't understand why he felt this way. Hadn't he just had the most magical evening with Mark? And he was going to see Mark after the holidays. Wasn't he looking forward to spending time with his parents? Of course, he was. Yet the more he fought back the tears, the faster they came, and the more he tried to will himself back into a happier disposition, the deeper he sank into melancholy. He burned to be with Mark, to follow him to Westchester, to visit the high school he had attended, to be suffused in the ground from whence he came.

Eric reached into his carry-on bag in which he fortuitously found a pair of sunglasses; he put them on and went past the gate agent and onto the plane where he sat at a window seat next to an elderly woman with white hair who immediately tried to strike up a conversation with him. She appeared surprised by Eric's curt reply: "Sorry, no English" but left him alone for the remainder of the trip, alone with his thoughts that raged and screamed in despair.

14

WHEN ERIC CAME OFF THE plane at Charles de Gaulle Airport in Paris, his mother was waiting for him. She looked immaculate in a black sheath skirt that hugged the knees, a strapless top, also in black, from the clothes designer Jean-Louis Scherrer, who was very much in vogue at the time, and in high-heeled, red, Valentino shoes. Her face lit up when she saw her son, and she greeted him with a hug and a kiss on both cheeks.

"How was your flight? Did you manage to get some sleep?" she asked chirpily.

"No, I didn't. You know I can't sleep on flights," he responded, his tone more bland than testy.

"Why do you have sunglasses on?"

"I was told it would help with jet lag," he replied.

"What do you mean?"

"Someone told me that on an overnight flight if you keep your eyes shaded until 10:00 in morning, you won't have any jet lag, so I'm trying it out."

"I see. Well, you'll have to let me know how that works."

As they stepped into the car and began to drive to the city's center, Eric's sorrow, like a morning haze, began to lift. Even if he had only mechanically hugged his mother, something deep inside had stirred within him. Perhaps it was the sight of the familiar, or maybe the touch of someone you love, or perhaps even the hormonal changes of late adolescence. Whatever the reason, the Eric who had slipped on his sunglasses at JFK was somehow different from the person who now removed them as he entered his parents' flat for a late breakfast. If he had been more self-aware, perhaps Eric might have recalled a lesson from a class on Buddhism, explaining that our perception of ourselves as individuals is based on a common illusion— the illusion of a solid, unalterable "self," an immutable being, an "I or me," that is separate and divisible from the rest of the world. Yet, as the Buddha realized millennia ago, we consist of thoughts and emotions that ebb and flow in time, as capricious as the weather or the Duke's "la donna e mobile" in Verdi's *Rigoletto*.

Eric's stepfather, Farzad was, as usual during the day, in his study behind a huge and ornate mahogany desk. While he had been forcibly retired from his business interests by the Iranian Revolution in 1979, he claimed always to be "working," although the specifics of the work in question remained elusive.

Unlike the French and the Russian aristocracies of earlier eras, whose wealth was wholly tied up in their land holdings, the moneyed Iranian exiles had had access to more liquid assets, which they had been able to transfer out of Iran in the waning days of the monarchy. Many had large sums of money in numbered Swiss bank accounts collecting interest. They were the fortunate ones who had escaped the claws of Khomeini's regime with their money and now lived lavish lifestyles in Western cities.

In the turbulent days leading up to the Revolution, an infamous list of individuals, who had purportedly stolen large sums of money, had been published on behalf of the Central Bank. Eventually proven to be fictitious, at the time, the list had caused much consternation among the Iranian exiles because it was common knowledge that a great deal of money had, in fact, been dishonestly obtained and funneled out of the country illegitimately. In fact, the source of these people's money was the subject of intense, though furtive, speculation. Farzad's name had figured prominently on the list. It was perhaps for this reason that he was always "working," as if the mahogany desk, the phone, and the shuffle of papers stood in silent but irrefutable rebuttal to the tacit accusations leveled at him. In response to a simple "how are you," he would engage in a lengthy and boisterous diatribe on how busy he was, always behind his desk "working."

He was, in general, a disagreeable man, sententiously offering unsolicited advice, not only to adolescents who, as a result, would consistently avoid him, but even to his peers, such as his comment to one lady who had recently relocated to Paris and who was widely known to be suffering financially. He told her, "Everybody wants to live in Paris, but Paris isn't for everyone. It's an expensive city, and you need to work very hard to live here. You should move to some little town in the United States where you'd get a good job." She never forgot or forgave the comment, even after she married an old, wealthy Frenchman who died leaving her his entire fortune. However, like all the others he had so casually offended, she continued to socialize with him because his wife, Lili, threw the most spectacular parties in Paris, turning their household into the epicenter of social life for Iranian exiles. She did so on such a low budget that it would have shocked and awed these ladies had they known, all the while delighting her husband. She had found their flat after visiting more than one hundred apartments in the eighth and sixteenth arrondissements. It was a large, bright four-bedroom on the Avenue Georges Mandell, with very high ceilings and moldings typical of late nineteenth-century Hausmanian buildings and with large French windows, giving onto the boulevard. She had decorated the flat with the help of a talented gay friend who had studied theatre design. The furniture and artwork, which they had selected and arranged, complemented and accentuated the flat's understated grandeur, while at the same time giving it a cozy, intimate feeling as if one were in a familial house.

Eric went into the study and kissed his stepdad on both cheeks.

"Come, we have some coffee and toast for you," he said, smiling and rising from his leather armchair to lead Eric into the dining room, where a round Regency rosewood dining table, with beautiful inlays, had two place settings, each consisting of a white plate and matching cup and saucer made of Sevres porcelain and placed onto a black lozenge-shaped placemat. The aroma of fresh coffee emanated from a silver pot from which Farzad now poured two cups. At times, especially when he didn't feel any threat to his finances, his austere and condescending inflexibility would yield to a kinder, gentler persona. At these moments, which were rare and short-lived, he would appear solicitous, almost avuncular.

"Would you like some cream and sugar?" he asked attentively.

"No, thanks; I take it black."

"So, how was your semester?" he asked.

"It was great, thanks. I've been enjoying my class with Trompet. He's amazing, and we were reading—

Farzad nodded his head as he interrupted. "Good, good, but you know, there are no jobs with a degree in literature. You young people need to understand the importance of work. You can't just sit back and read a book and expect to make money that way."

"Well, I think you can get a job with a degree in literature," ventured Eric, as he silently plotted a graceful escape from the man's sententious snares.

"What can you do? Maybe teach. But you'll never make money."

"There are other things that matter in life besides making money. I mean literature opens your mind. It's like time travel to distant places and times."

"You young people don't understand the value of hard-earned money." He paused seeing his stepson's disinterest. "Well anyway, experience will show you." And with that, Farzad closed out the conversation to go back to his office and attend to the "mountains of work awaiting him."

While his preference was to receive immediate gratitude for the advice given, he was willing to accept a concession. However, at the slightest sign that his interlocutor may have a differing opinion, Farzad would add a preemptory assertion in the form of a sweeping generalization, which would either change the subject or allow him to excuse himself.

Eric's mother had walked in at the tail end of their conversation, and seeing Eric's exasperated look, she waited for her husband to leave before adding, "Oh, come on darling, you know him. He means well; he's just always like that. You should see how he brags about you going to Princeton and doing so well."

"I'm not sure I believe that and besides he's tiresome. I don't know how you put up with him."

"Never mind that. Now tell me all about your term. I've missed you so, and it seems we never can talk for long on the phone."

"Well, I've been really enjoying this class with Trompet. You know Ali's in it too. There's also this girl celebrity who I've made friends with and help with her essays. She's taken me to some fun events, even in New York."

"Lovely, where did you go?"

Eric explained his nights out at the Palladium and then added, "I've also met this great guy that I've become friends with. Mark is the captain of the tennis team, and we've played some tennis and spent a bit of time together. He's so nice. I think you'd really like him. I was even thinking of inviting him to Cannes next summer."

"That's nice, darling. You should invite him. I'm so glad you've met all these great people and are enjoying yourself. I sometimes worry that you spend so much time with your books that you might miss out on life, especially while you're young."

"Oh, but I haven't. Mark's gotten me out of my room and we've done lots of fun things together. I don't think I've ever had a friend quite like him."

While a more astute observer might have suspected a hint of homoeroticism in Eric's exuberant devotion to his newfound friend, his mother was genuinely oblivious to her son's homosexuality. This was, in part, cultural—homosexuality was alien to the male culture of her homeland—and besides, like the vast majority of her peers, she equated it with effeminacy, and she didn't consider her son effeminate. But a mother's intuition runs deep, and Eric's mother, in stark contrast to her emotionally obtuse husband, was particularly discerning in interpersonal matters, a trait that had served her well as the doyenne of the Persian ex-pat society in Paris. This oversight in respect of her son was perhaps explainable by her ardent desire to live a picture-perfect life in accordance with the images of that ideal in her mind. A homosexual son would decidedly mar that picture. Even if she had harbored such suspicions, she simply wouldn't allow the thoughts to take root, bouncing them out of her mind, like a ball that ricochets off a wall.

"I can't tell you how happy I am that you've found such a good friend. Tell me about him. Is he in your year?"

That was all that Eric needed. Like steam erupting from a boiling teapot once the lid is lifted, he began to talk of Mark, from their initial meeting over the French tutorial, to the parties, the struggle over the French studies which they overcame together, their celebratory evening in New York, though carefully omitting any prurient details. He finished with, "I wish you were able to meet him."

"Do invite him over next summer," she said.

"Really? I mean you mean it? You think we could?"

"Well, it's not like you haven't invited your friends to visit, darling. What would be so different here?"

"No, nothing. You're right. I'll invite him next summer."

Would Mark accept? Would he actually come? What would

it be like if Mark stayed with them? They had a two-bedroom apartment in Cannes. Mark would have to sleep in the same room as him. Two single beds, but they could be pushed together. They could play tennis, go to the beach. Maybe even to Eden Roc!

His reverie got the better of him, prompting his mother to ask, "You seem distracted, are you okay, dear?"

"Yes, yes, sorry, I was just thinking—"

"Thinking of what?" she continued.

"That I should call Ali to see if he wants to go out one evening."

"What a great idea. You really should. I hope you really use the holidays to relax, have fun, and recharge your batteries."

"Yes, you're right, mother. I do need that."

"I have to go food shopping now. Would you like to come along?"

"Actually, if you don't mind, I'll unpack and maybe take a nap to recover from the flight."

"Okay. When I'm back in an hour or so, maybe we can go for a walk in the park?"

"That's a good idea. Might even be better for my jet lag than the sunglasses!"

ERIC DECIDED TO WEAR BLUE JEANS, a blazer over a white-collared shirt, and black moccasins for his night on the town. He was going to meet Ali, who was spending the Christmas holidays with his mother in her elegant duplex overlooking the Seine on the Quai d'Orsay. When he called, Ali had asked him to meet at a club called Olivia Valere. He expected there would be others with him, but he didn't know whom. When he arrived, the Prince was sitting at a table with a young couple, both in their mid-twenties. Eric recognized Kamran, his step-brother from his stepfather's previous marriage. The woman with him was his wife, Sanam; they had been married the previous summer, and Kamran had moved in with Sanam in her palatial flat. He was tall and thin, with relatively handsome features, now socially charming, but a bully at their school in Tehran as a kid.

Kamran had gone to a third-rate if expensive university in the United States and had returned to Paris where he had lived with Farzad and Lili for several years before his marriage. He had tried to launch some sort of carpet-cleaning business that had failed before even opening its doors. Between the college fees, the failed business, and his exorbitant entertainment, he had blown through two hundred thousand dollars of his father's money. Farzad, who almost never practiced what he preached, continued to support Kamran, though not without grumbling and tiresome lectures which Kamran disregarded. He felt entitled to Farzad's money and considered his father an annoying obstacle to his happiness.

Kamran also had developed a very expensive drug addiction that required funds substantially in excess of what Farzad was willing to supply. This had caused conflict and consternation between father and son, which was resolved when Kamran met Sanam, or rather rediscovered her, as they had known each other for many years as adolescents in Iran.

Sanam wasn't particularly beautiful or charming; she had an oddly masculine look and would go around in torn jeans and leather jackets, but her dad was one of the richest Iranians in Paris. Prior to the Revolution, he had worked for the oil ministry in Iran, and his name figured virtually at the top of the infamous list. He indulged his daughter without reservation, purchasing a luxurious flat for her and allowing her copious sums of money that fueled her addictions to designer clothes, drugs, and constant entertainment. She had been sent to a finishing school in Switzerland, from which she had tried to escape by flying to Spain where she had been detained by the International Police. Because few sixteen year olds are able to run away by taking an international flight, it was believed that she had been abducted. Her parents decided against sending her back to school in Switzerland and brought her to Paris where they could keep a tight watch on her. Though Sanam had a preference for cocaine, she didn't discriminate much when it came to drugs, partaking of all the varieties available. Her drug habit was known to all except her parents, who instead chided her on her grungy clothing, her coterie of indolent friends, and the ill-kept state of her flat, which despite a full-time maid, fell far short of her mother's high standards.

"Darling, you'll never find a suitable husband as long as you keep going around shabbily dressed and with 'those' people," her mother would intone, ironically dressed in a skirt and blouse made by the same designers of Sanam's torn jeans and leather jacket.

When Sanam brought home Kamran, they were surprised yet delighted and did everything they could to encourage their relationship. They, of course, knew Farzad, whom they considered the paragon of gentility and sobriety. His son, always impeccably dressed, polite, charming, and educated, surely would make an ideal husband. They overlooked his lack of a job, or any prospects thereof and failed, or perhaps chose not, to recognize his motives. They felt that marriage to Kamran would change their daughter overnight; like Cinderella, she would become the Barbie-Doll Princess that they had always desired.

For his part, Farzad had wholeheartedly given his consent to their nuptials. While he had heard rumors of Sanam's dissolute lifestyle, her father's wealth and lavish support of her quelled his reservations.

Though polite, Sanam and Kamran barely hid their weariness at Eric's arrival, as if he were a killjoy about to ruin their evening. They considered him too young, naïve, and a decidedly "uncool" nerd, who preferred to study rather than party and hang out with the right people.

"The Gypsy Kings were meant to play here tonight, but I don't think they're coming. Why don't we go to Bain Douches instead?" Sanam suggested.

"Yeah, let's go," Ali agreed, even before Eric had taken a seat, much less ordered a drink. The others now rose to proceed to the newly proposed venue.

Eric and Kamran squeezed in the back of Sanam's latest-model Mercedes coupe; she blasted tunes from the Eurythmics on the car's radio as she sped toward the club located in the Marais district. Kamran didn't talk to him, pretending instead to be wholly absorbed by the music. They parked in a private garage where the attendant appeared to know Sanam. At the club, they expertly maneuvered past the throng of people behind the velvet black rope, which was lifted for them by the bouncer who greeted Sanam with a smile and a kiss on both cheeks.

Bain Douches was an enormous nightclub built in a space that originally had housed a traditional bathhouse, with its various hot water pools, hence its name, "Les Bains," which everyone now called Bains Douches. Decorated in black and white tiles by Philippe Starck, its iconic pool was as glittering as the international beauties and celebrities that swayed to the latest and trendiest mixes spun by its renowned disc jockeys. Bain Douches had replaced Studio 54 as the most famous club in the world at that time.

They handed in their coats at a private, unmarked coat-check where, unlike the designated "vestiaries" or cloakroom, there was no wait. Eric had to visit the men's room, and Kamran told him to meet them at the bar, but when he returned there was no sign of them. He walked around in a vain effort to find them among the thousands of people in the club. He thought for a moment that they had deliberately ditched him, but given the size of the crowd, it was easy for them to get lost. Eric thought of Mark and how he wished he could have shown off this amazing club to him; he would have been impressed and they could have enjoyed it together.

He pushed his way to the overflowing bar and ordered a whiskey sour, which was delivered by a tall bartender with model looks and an attitude to match, dressed in a tight black T-shirt and black trousers. Eric stood there, nursing his drink, not knowing what to do next, when the person standing next to him said in English, "It's rather packed tonight." He looked over his shoulder and realized that the comment was directed at him by a young man with curly dark-blonde hair, hazel green eyes, wearing a collared shirt with the top two buttons undone and designer jeans. He was strikingly handsome.

"I know. I lost my friends in the crowd."

"Are you a regular here?"

"No, I'm at University in the States. I come on the holidays. You?"

"It's my first time here. I'm visiting from London, though I'm Scottish."

"First time in Paris or at the club?" Eric asked.

"At the club, been to Paris plenty of times. Much better than the London scene."

"Where are you staying?" continued Eric.

"I'm staying at a friend's house. How about you?"

"At home, I mean at my parents' home. It's in the Sixteenth. Where's your friend's?"

"It's in St. Germain, not that far from here. I'm Campbell, by the way."

"Eric," he responded as he extended a hand that Campbell shook. He held Eric's hand for a moment longer than was customary and gazed directly into his eyes. Eric was sufficiently inexperienced that he couldn't distinguish the tell-tale signs of a gay overture, but he felt himself getting excited.

"What are you drinking?"

"A whiskey sour."

Campbell ordered him a drink and a vodka orange for himself. He wouldn't let Eric pay.

"Cheers. Great to meet you," he said.

"Likewise," responded Eric, overcome by emotions that he neither understood nor had previously experienced. His attraction to Campbell surprised, excited, and confused him. How could he find Campbell attractive when he was, in his mind, committed to Mark? The two whiskey sours didn't help bring any clarity to his self-assessment.

"Where do you go to University?" Campbell asked.

"Princeton, in New Jersey."

"I've heard of it!" Campbell laughed. "Not a bad place to hang your hat."

"How about yourself?" asked Eric. "Are you in Uni? Or, what do you do?"

"I'm working for a bank in London."

"Investment banking?" asked Eric curiously, recalling Mark's story about his friend.

"Exactly, for an American bank actually."

"Where did you go to Uni, if I may ask?"

"I was at Cambridge. I did PPE," he added, which, as Eric knew, stood for philosophy, politics, and economics. "How about yourself? What are you reading?"

"I'm doing English and French literature."

"Ah, the literary crowd."

There was a moment of silence, as neither was sure what to say and then Campbell ventured, "Let's go and dance."

Eric hesitated. What if Kamran, Sanam, or Ali saw him? But as he looked over at the dance floor, it was so packed, the lights so dim, that you wouldn't be able to recognize someone even if you stood near them. Campbell had taken a hold of Eric's hand and was drawing him toward the dance floor. Eric didn't resist. They forced their way into the middle of the swaying crowd of dancers. It was a veritable free-for-all. Young men and women, in all varieties of dress or undress, and in varying degrees of sobriety were dancing, touching, bumping, and grinding against each other—men on women, women on men, men on men, women on women, everything and anything "goes here." The Eurythmics' song *Sweet Dreams* was playing in a new remix, accentuating the bass, which appeared to touch the sweet spot of the crowd. Campbell was facing Eric, swaying to the beat while he had his eyes locked on Eric's.

"Sweet dreams are made of these..." crooned the Eurythmics.

Eric felt Campbell brush against him, then come closer until their lower bodies were touching. He felt himself getting hard and felt Campbell's hard-on push against his own. Campbell now pulled Eric into him and Eric reached behind and held onto Campbell's back.

"Some of them want to use you..."

Eric rested his head on Campbell's shoulder. "What am

I doing?" he asked himself. "I shouldn't be doing this. How come I'm enjoying this? What about Mark? I love Mark." Campbell's hand was now gently squeezing his hard-on.

"Keep your head up, movin' on—"

And then he felt Campbell's tongue in his mouth. He let himself go and allowed Campbell to kiss him passionately.

"Who am I to disagree," cooed the Eurythmics.

"Let's go back to my place," said Campbell.

"I thought you're staying with friends."

"Yes, but my friend is away. She's away for the holidays."

It had started to rain when they walked out, which normally meant it would be impossible to find a taxi, but a line of cabs always waited outside this club. They jumped into one, and Campbell hung onto Eric and didn't let go until they were in bed.

It wasn't until after 11:00 A.M. the next morning that Eric woke up. He began to dress quickly when Campbell, still half asleep, asked, "What's the rush?"

"I have to get home. My parents are going to be worried. They'll wonder where I've been."

"A bit late for that," replied Campbell lazily. "Stay for breakfast or brunch. There's a nice place around the corner."

"I can't," replied Eric. As he stepped over to say goodbye, he noticed what appeared to be some sort of a mini shrine on the dresser, draped with exotic fabrics and decorated with three figurines of the Buddha and two candles.

"What's this?" he asked, puzzled. "I didn't notice it until now."

"It's where I meditate. I'm a Buddhist."

"Meditate?" asked Eric with a quizzical look on his face.

"Yes. I meditate every day. It brings me some peace amidst the storms of life."

"Oh, Campbell, don't tell me you're part of some sort of cult?"

"Of course not. This is intensely personal, a spiritual practice for inner peace."

"What inner peace?" inquired Eric.

"The peace of knowing that no matter what happens, I'll be okay."

"If you were hit by a car, or lost all your money, you wouldn't be okay, would you?" asked Eric rhetorically. "So I don't see the point."

"I would. Or at least I'm practicing to get to that point. You see, terrible things can happen, but what's even worse is if your mind keeps fighting the situation with denial, anger, and depression. All of these are mental commentaries. Meditation allows you to drop the mental reaction and accept your situation as it is."

Eric just looked at him with tolerant bemusement.

"Now come on," Campbell insisted, "I'll take you to brunch and tell you all about it."

"No, really I have to go," Eric replied, as he hurried out the door.

15

Upon his return to Princeton, Eric was greeted by a brief, laconic message from Mark on his answering machine, inviting him to call and arrange a meeting. For a fleeting second he savored the moment, like a drop of chocolate ice cream melting at the tip of the tongue, but in the next moment, his joy gave way to guilt and self-reproach. He had felt remorseful after his indiscretion with Campbell. They had kissed and spent the night naked in each other's arms, but that was all there was to it. He hadn't given Campbell his phone number, and despite the boy's insistent pleas that they see each other before Eric returned to the states, he hadn't contacted him. Yet the more he tried to convince himself that he hadn't betrayed his love for Mark, the more he condemned himself. His mind had already tried and found him guilty, yet he kept repeating to himself: "It meant nothing. I wouldn't have done it if I hadn't been so drunk. We didn't even have sex; we just slept together and I left as soon as I woke up. It was a one-off encounter that would never recur." These feeble attempts to circumvent the inner judge's condemnation were in vain, yet like most, Eric was his own most severe critic, his thoughts like the arrows of an invading army, dipped in the poison of guilt, inflicting deep, and at times, fatal wounds.

He picked up the receiver to call Mark but groaned and put it back down. He was sullied, polluted, and was thus unworthy of Mark's affection. A tear rolled down his cheek and he collapsed on the sofa next to the phone. After a while, he made a concerted effort to stand up and unpack his bags and then decided to walk over to the Campus Club.

He joined Larry and Consuelo, who were having dinner in the dining room.

"That's all you're having, a soup?" Consuelo asked in a light, bantering tone.

"I'm not that hungry and a bit jet lagged," Eric replied.

"When did you get back?"

"Just now actually; I mean literally a few hours ago."

"You know, you're so lucky, you get to spend Christmas in Paris. What did you do?" chimed in Larry.

"Not much. Visited family. Went out once or twice."

"Oh yeah. Where did you go? What are the hot spots in Paris?" Larry persisted.

"I didn't go out like that. I mean, just to some low-key bars for a drink. What did you guys do?" he asked, trying to steer

the conversation away from the nightlife in Paris and its consequences for him.

"We hung out in the city mostly," Consuelo said and then
added, "Was Ali in Paris?"

"Um ... yeah, why?"

"No reason. Did you see him there?" she asked.

"I did actually. We went out for a drink one night."

"Where did you guys go?"

"We went to a bar called Olivia Valere," he replied, calcu-
lating that Consuelo and Larry would never find out about his
evening at Bain Douches. After all, they weren't friends with
Ali, and the only time they'd met him was when he had come
to dinner on campus with Eric.

"What was it like?" she persisted, like a dog with a rawhide
bone.

"It was nice. Quiet, not too many people. A great band playing. They're called the Gypsy Kings. They play Spanish guitar.
I really like their music."

"I've heard of Gypsy Kings," piped in Larry, who prided
himself on having tastes outside the mainstream in every sense.
"Their music is really eclectic, very cool."

"Where does he live?" Consuelo persisted.

"Where does who live?"

"Ali?"

"What do you mean, where does he live?" Eric snapped.

"Huh," snickered Consuelo. "I mean where's his house in
Paris?" She paused and looked quizzically at him. "Is that such a
hard question?"

"No, but ... I mean, why do you would want to know?"
Consuelo just stared back at him. "Anyway, he lives on the
Quai D'Orsay."

"Where's that?"

"See. That's why I was surprised by your question. Since you don't know Paris—"

She ignored his rebuttal. "I bet it's a ritzy place."

"It's nice. Overlooks the Seine. Not sure that it's ritzy." He paused. "Anyway, I'm drop-dead tired and have to get some sleep. Must be the jet lag," he equivocated, unnerved by Consuelo's cross-examination.

"Chill out, man; didn't mean to upset you. I was just curious," she said in a tone that suggested much more.

"No big deal. Like I said, I'm just really tired. Catch you guys tomorrow."

––––––––––

THE NEXT MORNING Eric had an 8:30 lecture in a physics class, commonly known as *Physics for Poets*. This was a "gut" course taken by anyone who was nonscientifically inclined, which was to say mostly, though by no means entirely, literature majors and jocks, to fulfill the science requirement for graduation. It was held in a large lecture hall, and that morning there must have been more than one hundred students in the class. He had just settled into his seat in a middle row halfway up when he turned and glimpsed Mark sitting a few rows behind him to the right. Their eyes met and Mark smiled, but just then the lecture began. Mark looked more handsome than ever. Would he be upset that Eric hadn't returned his call? But then he wouldn't have smiled, would he? Eric wondered if he should go up to him after the lecture, or would Mark prefer that he be more discreet and not speak in public? Maybe he could catch him walking out, as if by coincidence. But he was locked in the middle row, and Mark would probably be out in the aisle before him. Why had he chosen this wretched seat? He always chose poorly. Why was he so unlucky? But, if he had viewed this situation more objectively, Eric might have concluded that he was actually quite lucky that they were in the same class, or that Mark had held his gaze and smiled.

For a moment, toward the end of the class, his attention turned to the lecturer who brought up the subject of "the multiverse and parallel universes and Everett's many-worlds theory," which, of course, made no sense to Eric, his attention split as he wandered through a parallel universe of his own.

When the lecture ended, he waited until his row had emptied, not that he had a choice, but also because he was hesitant and vacillating. He gathered his notepad on which he had not written down a single word and slowly made his way up the steps to the exit. Mark was at the top of the stairs and visibly waiting for him.

"Hey buddy," he said warmly, his signature smile unfolding across his face.

"Hi," was all that Eric managed to reply.

"You wanna get a cup of coffee?"

"Uh, sure, but I don't have much time before my next class," Eric added.

"No problem. We'll make it quick then!"

"Sounds good! Let's head to the student center."

Mark's attraction for Eric hadn't wavered. It was his fear of being outed that had started to lift, the debilitating, overwhelming anxiety that had shrouded their relationship, like rays of sunlight peeking out from behind dense clouds on an overcast day. His parents had been proud of his B in French, boasting to relatives that their son was not just a top athlete, but a great student as well. Mark, who had never previously scored above a C, basked in the limelight. He hadn't told his parents about being tutored by Eric; instead, he said that a friend had helped explain a few concepts to him when he had missed classes due to practice. They had inquired about this friend, and Mark had explained that he was from France and was a top student.

"You need more friends like that, Mark," his father had intoned. "Serious men who know what they're doing; not like some of the aimless drifters you've hung around with."

And then there was Melissa and her determination to enter Mattie's sanctum sanctorum.

"We should hang out with Eric more. He's so European, so chic, and has the coolest friends," she said rather casually. "Besides, aren't you going to ask him to tutor you in French 102?"

Mark had decided to take French 102 to fulfill the second and last part of his language requirement.

"Um, not sure, but probably, yeah," Mark said haltingly.

His parents' approbation and Melissa's social climbing drive provided cover against the fear that arose in his mind at the thought of Eric.

———

MARK BOUGHT TWO COFFEES, and they sat at a small, round table for two.

"I left you a phone message," Mark said.

"I got it, thanks. I was going to call you back, but got in late last night."

"No worries, man; how was your holiday?"

"It was nice. I spent time with family and . . . old friends." He hesitated and then added, "How was yours?"

"Ah, it was awesome. My parents were really happy with my grades. Thanks for your help! I'm doing French 102 this semester. You up for tutoring me again?" he asked and winked at Eric.

"Sure, I'd like that!"

"Maybe we can do it twice a week this semester?" Mark suggested leeringly.

"That works," Eric said a bit bewildered.

"How about we start later today, like tonight?"

"Today?"

"Yeah, unless you're tied up?" he asked.

"Uh ... no, no. I have a few lectures, but should be free tonight."

"All right then, how about I swing by around 8:30 or 9:00?"

"Okay. Bring your French II book."

"Of course. Lots of conjugations. See you then."

Eric was perplexed. It was so unlike Mark to want to meet in public or to schedule two "tutoring" sessions a week. Yet the initial surprise gave way to excitement, as an almost euphoric energy suffused him and he began to approach the most mundane tasks of the day with enthusiasm, and the most tiresome people with unbounded patience. It was like someone who, after a long period of illness, rises from his bed to rediscover the joys of walking outside, breathing fresh air, feeling the warmth of the sun on his skin. He relished a one-on-one conversation with Trompet in the first class of a new seminar on Victor Hugo, prompting Trompet jovially to ask if he were a historian because he knew the significance of the dates 1815, 1830, 1848, and 1871. At dinner at The Campus Club, he regaled and charmed the table with tales of his Christmas holiday in Paris and the clubs he went to, forgetting that he had denied frequenting them the previous evening to Consuelo and Larry who were mystified not only by the wholly different version of his holiday but by the tone and manner of the storyteller. It was as if they had been speaking with a completely different person. Back at his apartment, he tidied up the two rooms over and over in anticipation of Mark's arrival, moving objects from one location to another, even though he knew that Mark could care less about the decoration of the flat. He put on a fresh collared shirt and left the two top buttons undone, then changed his mind and left only one button undone, and then decided to reverse course again and undo the second button. Eric then sat down and decided to do some reading and opened *Notre Dame de Paris*. While under any other circumstances this gothic tale of Quasimodo and Esmeralda would have enthralled him, now he read and reread the same page several times without an inkling of comprehension. He stood up and paced the room, then suddenly realized that he had no wine or beer to offer Mark. At that moment, he heard a soft knock on the door and opened it. Mark bounded inside with a big smile, and without saying a word, put his arms around Eric and pulled him toward him kissing him deeply. Without relinquishing his embrace, he gently maneuvered Eric down onto the sofa where he unbuttoned his shirt and ran his hands all over Eric's chest, pausing only to unbuckle his belt. They spent the next two hours on the sofa, not exchanging a single word. Eric drank in Mark's lovemaking, like a man in a desert who, on the brink of death, chances on the cool, fresh waters of an oasis.

"I missed you so much. I couldn't stop thinking about you," Mark confided, perhaps the first time in his life articulating such an emotion.

"Oh God, me too, you can't even imagine," Eric gushed, again feeling guilty about Campbell.

As they were getting dressed and ready for the lesson, Mark added, "Oh, Melissa wants to get together with you and Mattie. You think you could set that up?"

"I can sure try!" said Eric, not quite believing the turn of events but feeling a tinge of unease at the request. "But, you know Mattie's a bit nervous about meeting new people."

"Oh, don't worry. They know each other," Mark said, reaching over and kissing him.

16

They settled into a routine, with Mark coming over in the evenings two, sometimes three, nights a week, spending the night and leaving early. His roommates never seemed to notice his absences or, if they did, they didn't think much of them. Neither did Melissa, whose dreams and aspirations appeared to be coming true, as Eric strove for a rapprochement between her and Mattie.

After a reasonably good performance in her nineteenth-century French literature class, due in large measure to Eric's help, Mattie now had enrolled in a senior seminar on the French novel in the twentieth century where she would be reading works by Proust, Celine, Malraux, Sartre, and Camus. She had chosen this seminar because Eric was taking the class. At the end of their first session, Eric had asked her: "Mattie, would you come for dinner at the Campus with me one evening next week?"

"Sure, I'd love to," she said, as they walked up the aisle.

"Excellent. Would you mind if I invited Mark and Melissa?"

She pulled a face as if she had just smelled something rotten.

"Oh come on, Mattie; they're not that bad."

"They're asinine, both of them," she said. "Asinine" was one of her favorite intellectual words; she used it complacently like a young child demonstrating a new skill to a proud parent.

"Asinine? That's a bit harsh," Eric responded, as his face turned pale. "Just one night. For me, please?"

"Oh okay, if you're really keen on it." Mattie had tried to read the first few pages of Proust's *Swann's Way* in English and hadn't understood any of it; she would need substantial help to write an essay in French on it, and Eric was her ticket.

Eric was overjoyed but had the presence of mind to restrain himself so as not to appear too eager.

"You are simply wonderful," he said. "Do you want to have a coffee at the student center and discuss Proust?"

Mattie beamed. "I'd love to," she said, and they walked arm in arm over to the student center.

Eric arrived at Campus Club an hour before dinner to select and guard the table in preparation for the much anticipated engagement. He had chosen a four-person square table and hung his coat on the back of one of the chairs. He then waited in the Club's living room, which was almost empty at that time.

Soon the Club started to fill as members arrived for dinner. A few of them greeted Eric as they entered and made their way to the dining room. Larry and Consuelo walked in together, as usual. They spoke briefly with Eric then proceeded inside. Because Eric had dinner with them virtually every evening, they didn't ask if he would join them, assuming that he would make his way in when he was ready.

Mark and Melissa arrived first. Melissa kissed Eric on the cheek but pulled away as he went to kiss her on the other cheek, presumably because she was unaccustomed to the more European double-cheek kiss. Mark shook his hand, smiling, though Eric could tell he was nervous. Eric wondered if they should wait for Mattie or enter the dining room. He hesitated for a second but thought that it would be more natural for them to wait for her at the table. Eric directed them to the dining room where there was a self-service dinner buffet. At Eric's suggestion they went to the soft drink counter and returned to the table with two glasses of Coca-Cola and Eric's bottle of water.

"How about we wait for Mattie before we go up for our dinner," Eric ventured.

"Yes, of course," responded Melissa. "Did she say she was definitely coming?" she asked in a casual tone as if she were more concerned about the timing of dinner than the arrival of their illustrious guest.

"Yes, you can count on it."

Eric asked Melissa about her Club, what the food was like, then asked what she was majoring in. Mark smiled, but in his typical fashion said little and nodded his head mostly. After a while Eric felt that he had exhausted all avenues of conversation and invited them to serve themselves to some dinner, suggesting that Mattie was just late as usual. The thought that she might not arrive at all had crossed his mind, but his preoccupation with keeping the conversation going kept him from being too distressed.

When they were at the dinner buffet, putting food onto

their plates, his guest arrived. Eric left his plate on the buffet line and went over to greet Mattie.

"I'm so sorry I'm late. I had some calls to make that took longer than I expected."

"No worries at all. We were just about to have our dinner, so your timing is absolutely perfect," he said and ushered her to the buffet where Mark and Melissa stood, plates in hand, uncertain as to whether to proceed to the table or greet her.

"Mattie, you know Mark and Melissa, right?" Eric ventured.

"Yes, hi," Mattie said tentatively but with a smile.

"Hi, it's nice to see you outside the Club; this is my boyfriend, Mark," Melissa replied.

Since they were holding their plates and cutlery, they couldn't shake hands, which led to an awkward moment.

"How about you guys go over to the table and I'll be right over with Mattie."

After serving themselves, they walked over to the table. Mattie rolled her eyes at Eric, who opened his hands and smiled, an expression that quietly begged for her indulgence, like the figures in early Florentine paintings glancing up demurely to solicit divine grace.

No sooner had Eric and Mattie returned to their table, plates in hand, than Consuelo strolled over.

"Hi, Mattie. I didn't know you'd be here for dinner tonight."

"Oh, hi, yeah. Eric was kind enough to invite me," she responded, sitting down.

"Can we join you?" asked Consuelo presumptuously, smiling at Mattie.

While the Club was informal, and it was customary for friends to pull up a chair and sit down to dinner with others, if a Club member had three guests at a table for four, it was commonly understood that this was an exclusive arrangement.

For Consuelo, such tacit rules were niceties at best; she was too proud and egotistical to even consider, let alone respect, her fellow Club members' desires for privacy.

"It's up to Eric," Mattie replied deferentially.

"I guess so, but I thought you guys were finished, I mean finished your dinner," Eric said, giving Consuelo a look.

"Well we can have dessert with you," she persisted.

"Actually, I don't think we can fit any more people around this table," interjected Melissa rather boldly, afraid that these interlopers might scuttle the rapprochement that she had long sought with Mattie.

Consuelo stared at Melissa contemptuously.

Eric felt that his meticulously and industriously arranged evening was on the verge of collapse. "How about we join you for dessert after we've had our dinner?" he offered with a smile, hoping that this compromise might assuage her.

"Okay, that'd be nice," she snapped curtly and walked off, feeling excluded and hurt.

Eric breathed a sigh of relief.

"Who was that? *What* was that?" Melissa asked. Her emphasis on the word "what" suggested that she considered Consuelo's request outlandish.

For some reason, Mattie found her comment hilarious and broke out laughing.

"She's in our French—" she chortled, unable to finish the sentence, convulsed by laughter. It was one of those spasms that the French aptly term fourire, a "crazy laugh" that possesses the entire person, mind, and body.

Mattie kept repeating, "What was that?" and shrieking with laughter.

Even though he had not found Melissa's utterance funny, Eric began to laugh—genuinely—not the forced laughter of a sycophant, but rather a contagious one brought on by the girl's sheer mirth. This spread to Mark and then even to Melissa, who was confused and could only hope that this wasn't disparaging of her. The whole table now rocked with laughter.

Consuelo overheard it and though she had not heard Melissa's remark, she suspected that it was at her expense. These privileged white people, who had excluded her from their dinner table, now mocked her; this touched a deep-seated wound, raising her bile. "They're sickening," she uttered under her breath.

"What was that?" asked Larry.

"Oh nothing," she replied, "or, nothing that matters anyway."

Meanwhile at Eric's table, the laughter had subsided, leaving Mattie, whose carefully manicured façade had dissolved in the face of her convolutions, breathless, yet in a calm and serene mood, as after a long run.

"I haven't laughed like that in so long!"

"I know," replied Melissa, almost in a complicit tone; she sensed an opening that she wasn't about to let pass. "Sometimes you need a good laugh!"

"Don't you? I mean people should just relax and laugh more. Life would be so much better!" exclaimed Mattie, as if this were the Secret of the Ages.

"You know, you're so right. I was reading an article that said that a good laugh isn't distressing; it's actually good for your health."

"I believe it. It's like being positive and thinking good thoughts and even laughing at yourself; instead of all this negativity and idle complaints." She paused and looked around the table. "You know what I mean; like the people who always complain about this or that; nothing's ever good or good enough for them."

"Wow, that's exactly what this psychologist was saying in an article I read. You sound like you know a lot about this."

"Well, it's just common sense really. Isn't it?" Mattie said looking over at Melissa and smiling. "Where was the article, by the way?"

And there it was; the long-sought-after, long-denied Mattie smile everybody treasured. Finally, it surfaced after all this time. Melissa sighed in relief, though inaudibly. What more than two years of maneuvering and machinations had failed to deliver, a stray comment, thrown up by chance, had succeeded in achieving. She and Mattie had bonded, or so she imagined. Whether or not it would last was an unknown, but for Melissa, it was a beginning. She now saw Mattie as her new best friend, taking her shopping, to clubs and fashion shoots in New York, meeting other celebrities. "Oh, I'm here with Mattie; we go to Princeton together," she would reply casually to whoever would listen. She would become a celebrity in her own right; the press would write about her; photograph them in their latest Valentino outfits. She wanted to reach over and hug Mattie.

By the time dinner was over, Melissa had offered to fetch the copy of *Vogue* in which the article had appeared and deliver it to Mattie, an offer that, to everyone's great surprise, was accepted.

The four of them left the Club together; no one recalled Eric's promise to have dessert with Consuelo who, in any event, was nowhere to be found. Mattie, who was walking to her off-campus flat, took her leave with a warmth and affability for all that enthralled Melissa.

"Thank you, Eric. That was an amazing dinner. One of the best I've ever had," she gushed.

"It was my pleasure. We did have a good laugh, didn't we," Eric added, who was also happy with the turn the evening had taken; the intimacy with Melissa that opened the door into Mark's social world. After Mattie's departure, Melissa exclaimed hastily:

"I hate to leave you guys, but I've got to run." Her mind was now focused on finding and delivering the magazine to Mattie. She was hoping that her roommate hadn't discarded it and didn't want to waste a minute.

"Ah, okay," replied Mark, as she hurried toward her dormitory, without a kiss or goodbye.

"How did you like dinner?" Eric asked of Mark, now that they were alone.

"It was fun, thanks. The girls enjoyed it, which is what I was concerned about. Melissa seemed happy enough."

"Yes, she and Mattie really hit it off," Eric said.

"That they did."

"What are you up to now?"

"Not sure. I was thinking we could have a French lesson," Mark said with a big smile.

"A French lesson? At this hour?" Eric feigned alarm, barely hiding his excitement.

"Yeah, at your place," Mark countered with a grin.

"I'm always up for French. You know that!" Eric replied as he touched Mark, ever so lightly on the shoulder.

"Up for French kissing, or French conjugation?" Mark asked coyly.

Eric smiled and led him back to his apartment for their overnight "French" lesson.

17

THE MAGAZINE had been crumpled up in a pile of other papers when Melissa retrieved it. Despite her best efforts, including the use of an iron to remove the creases, its poor condition remained. Nevertheless, she had delivered it in a large envelope with a typewritten cover note, which she had toiled on no less than two hours, reminding Mattie of their shared laugh, offering some awkward and sycophantic praise and concluding, with a hesitant yet ardent wish, to meet soon.

Mattie, who had not seen the envelope for a number of days after its delivery, had then reflexively discarded the magazine after glancing at the cover note. That would have marked her last thought of Melissa had it not been for a project in her contemporary dance class. Deborah Jowitt, the renowned dance critic at the *New York Times*, was teaching a course on twentieth-century dance, starting with Diaghilev's *Ballets Russes* and coming all the way up to the 1980s movements. She had required her students to prepare individual research projects on a topic of their own choosing and had indicated that the source documents for their projects would be found at the Juilliard School library in New York City. Mattie had chosen *Le Train Bleu*, a one-act ballet from the 1920s.

Yet she considered the prospect of conducting research at Juilliard incommodious; not so much due to its location—she traveled to New York City frequently—but because of her unfamiliarity with the library and the time it would take to locate the documents. She thought of asking someone in New York to retrieve them for her, and as she silently contemplated the list of her contacts, Mattie eliminated them one after another. Some of them would not know how to research and find the right documents; other names were discarded because of the need for discretion, and a few others because she did not wish to have to return the favor. "How frustrating; I shouldn't have taken this class," she told herself. "I thought it'd be an easy A and now look." Suddenly, Melissa's image flashed in her mind like a fulgurant burst of light and a smile came to her face. "Of course, she would be the perfect gofer for the project," she thought. "I wonder what would be the best way to approach her. What was it she had sent me?" Mattie couldn't remember the magazine or the contents of the cover note, but then she wouldn't need an entrée to solicit Melissa's help. The girl would jump off a cliff for her. Mattie looked up her number in the student directory and called. Melissa's roommate answered and passed the phone to Melissa without inquiring who the caller was.

"This is Melissa," she said in a flat, distracted tone.

"Hi, Melissa, how are you?" Mattie asked.

"Mattie?" she replied with incredulity, the tenor of her voice up several octaves.

"Yes, it's me," she laughed.

"Oh, I'm great, really great. How are things going with you?" she gushed, emphasizing the word "you."

"I'm also well, thanks. I wanted to thank you for leaving me the envelope. It was so kind of you!"

"Oh, it was my pleasure. I'm sorry the magazine was a bit crumpled. I hope you liked the article."

"I loved, absolutely loved it!" Mattie replied. "It was so ..." She tried to think of an inclusive word. "... interesting."

"Wasn't it, though? I'm so happy you liked it."

"I really did, and it made me think again of our lively evening together with the boys!'

"I know, what a wonderful evening," echoed Melissa, "we should do a repeat soon."

"Well, that's just it, you see. I was wondering if you'd be interested in getting together to discuss a dance project I'm working on."

"I definitely, definitely would be."

"Great. Have you heard of a ballet called *Le Train Bleu?*"

"Um ... yes, yes," she replied, never having heard of it. "Didn't it play at Lincoln Center," she ventured hesitantly, since everything had played there.

"Yes it did, but a long time ago. I'm writing a paper on this ballet and was wondering if you'd like to work on it with me?"

"I definitely would. But, I mean, I don't have any experience with ballet. How can I help?"

"We just need to do some research on it. I mean, its development and choreography. Would you be up for that?"

"Of course, I would love that! Research is right up my alley."

"Great," Mattie said, envisioning a collaboration where they wouldn't need to meet in person. "The thing is, all the materials are at Juilliard in New York."

"I love Juilliard! Do you want to go there together one day?"

"I would absolutely love to. It's just that right now I'm so tied up with my work. You know, my rehearsals don't leave me any free time. So I was wondering," Mattie purred, "if I could explain the project to you, and maybe you could go up there and do your own research and then we can compare notes. I mean, I've already done a fair bit of work on this, and when you could come up to speed, so to speak, we could then collaborate."

"I understand. Sounds like a great plan."

Mattie explained the scope of the paper and that Melissa should locate the appropriate source documents relating to the ballet, summarize them for her, and then they could meet to discuss the play's background.

Melissa agreed and was overjoyed with the assignment. When she hung up, she turned to her roommate and said, "I can't believe it. Mattie just asked me to work on a dance project with her."

To which her roommate replied, "Wow, that's amazing! Let me know if you need any help!"

"I definitely will," Melissa replied, though she had no intention of involving anyone else in their project, so as not to jeopardize her newfound access to Mattie.

The next weekend she took the train to New York and went directly from Penn Station to the Juilliard library. A helpful librarian directed her to the microfiche records on the arts from that period, where she discovered much information about the ballet, including articles about several performances dating back to its very first staging in the 1920s at the Théâtre des Champs-Élysées in Paris. There were even photographs of the dancers on and off stage. She found herself engrossed in the history and choreography of the ballet, as well as the colorful personalities involved in it: Jean Cocteau who had written the libretto; Bronislava Nijinska who choreographed and performed in it; Darius Milheaud who had composed the score; and of course, all performed under the auspices of Serge Diaghilev, the Grand Master of modern ballet. This appealed to her celebrity-worship syndrome, and she found herself drawn to each of these individuals, each peculiar in his or her own way, but especially to Serge Diaghilev and his not-so-secret homosexual relationship with Nijinska's celebrated brother Vaslav Nijinsky. All this she wrote down assiduously and made photocopies of the most relevant and interesting articles. She was surprised at how much she had enjoyed herself. She had never liked academic research, despite expressing a contrary opinion to Mattie; her preference was for celebrity gossip in magazines such as *Vogue* and *Vanity Fair*.

After finishing her research, Melissa went to the Upper West Side apartment of a friend who had graduated from Princeton the year prior. They had an early dinner before she caught the train back to New Jersey. The next day, she typed up her notes and left a message on Mattie's answering machine to let her know that the research had been completed. She called back, and they arranged to meet at Mattie's apartment to discuss the ballet.

When she read through the typed notes, Mattie couldn't hold back a sigh of relief. It was as if she were being handed a ready-made essay about the ballet.

"This is incredible, Melissa," she gushed.

"Thanks! I really got into it. I mean it was so interesting. All these people, especially Diaghilev. He's my favorite. How he started in Russia and then, after the Revolution, managed to create this incredible ballet company in Monte-Carlo. He was an international celebrity but at the same time the founder of modern ballet."

"Yes, exactly, and you know he's my favorite too." Mattie remembered Diaghilev's name from her class but not much more. "I also like Nijinsky; you know, who danced in the ballet."

Melissa realized Mattie's error—it was Nijinska who had choreographed and danced in the ballet, not Nijinsky—but she let it go, pretending that she had heard Nijinska instead.

"I know what you mean; Nijinsky and Nijinska were amazing dancers. By the way, did you know Diaghilev and Nijinsky were lovers?"

"No way," Mattie exclaimed, and then caught herself. "Oh wait, I think I knew that—" Melissa was too excited by Mattie's interest in her work and too eager to share her knowledge to notice Mattie's total ignorance of the subject.

"They were lovers until Nijinsky married Romola in South America. What an intrigue on the crossing. Diaghilev learned about it in the papers and was beside himself. He fired Nijinsky who then had a nervous breakdown from which he never recovered. He sank deeper and deeper into mental illness and was eventually committed, never again to dance. Imagine, the greatest ballet dancer of the twentieth century, sidelined by a lover's spat."

She had said all this in one breath. With wide eyes Mattie listened intently, drinking in every word about the tragedy Melissa recounted.

"I photocopied the articles and even some of the photos. Aren't they incredible?" she said, spreading the portfolio out on the coffee table. "I mean, look at Nijinska in this one," she said and pointed to one of the photographs in her pile.

Mattie nodded and then glanced over the documents, as well as the typed notes that Melissa had taken.

"This is incredible. And look at all the notes you took."

"I know, I got a little carried away."

"No, this is wonderful. More than I could have hoped for. We should hang out more often, Melissa. We have so much in common. Would you like to come to a performance in the city with me?"

"Of course, I'd love to. When?" she asked, trying to catch her breath.

"Next Tuesday evening. I'm actually performing in it."

Mattie walked over to a desk and picked up an oversized card and brought it over. "Here's the information. I'll put you on the list."

They stood, hugged each other, and as Melissa went out the door, Mattie turned back to her treasure trove of information thinking—another A in the making.

———

THE ALARM DIDN'T GO OFF, and Mark didn't wake up until after 6:00 A.M. He panicked and jumped out of bed. "Fuck, it's after six. I've got to get back."

Eric, who was still half asleep, said, "Why don't you pretend you went for an early run?"

Mark's eyes lit up. "Wow. That's a great idea," he said, wondering why he hadn't thought of it himself.

When he arrived back at his building, Mark went straight to the showers, which were down the hall, and then moseyed back to his quad. His roommates were still asleep. After that, he started coming back later, around 7:00, sometimes even

7:30 A.M., and if his roommates were up, which was rarely the case, he'd say he had been out for an early morning run. Either way, he always showered first, to cover himself.

Ever since Melissa had become increasingly preoccupied with Mattie, Mark found himself free most evenings, and he would go over to spend time with Eric. They would make love passionately, and then, one night, Mark asked Eric to penetrate him. The first few times were kind of excruciating, but he then relaxed and really began to enjoy it. More often than not, Mark wanted the bottom, and Eric was now happy to oblige. Afterward, they would lie in bed naked, discussing the rising stars of tennis. Mark was passionate about tennis and would attentively follow the international matches and players. Eric, who ordinarily didn't follow any professional sports, had begun to read up on tennis to converse with Mark. Bjorn Borg and John McEnroe's rivalry had dominated professional tennis in the late '70s and early '80s, but more recently, there were a number of rising stars, among them a young German named Boris Becker whom Mark followed ardently.

"What I'd give to watch Becker play. He's gonna win Wimbledon this year."

"Really? You think? What about McEnroe? And Ivan Lendl?"

"Eric, where you been, man? McEnroe's toast. I don't think he's even gonna play this year. And Lendl doesn't do well on grass."

"McEnroe's not toast. Granted he took some time off, but he's still a great player."

"You wanna bet?" Being lovers didn't forestall the aggression of a diehard tennis fan.

"I do, actually!" replied Eric, who had recognized a potential opportunity, however remote, to engineer a meeting with Mark over the summer holidays.

"Seriously? You don't stand a chance," Mark scoffed.

"We'll see," said Eric, smiling, as he reached over and kissed Mark.

Eric's mind went to work immediately. How to get two tickets to the finals of Wimbledon? Who could help him? His mother, of course. No one else he knew would, or could, do it. She knew a lot of connected people. But who did she know in London? He tried to remember some of his mother's friends there, but couldn't think of anyone with the right contacts. "I'll have to call her in the morning, after Mark's left," he told himself. His mind now drifted to hotel accommodations. Maybe they could stay at the Hilton on Hyde Park Corner. He'd stayed there before with his mother. Perfect location. They could take the tube, the Piccadilly line, and change at Earl's Court for Wimbledon. Much better and more economical than a cab. They'd spend the days at Wimbledon and nights making love. What could be more perfect?

———————

AS THE TERM WENT ON, Eric and Mark continued their three-night-a-week sleepover. This had assuaged Eric's febrile mind, allowing him to return to his studies, which is to say, to his life, with some tranquility. He had helped Mark with French to a point where even an A was within his grasp. As for his own scholarship, Eric had written an essay on *Madame Bovary* in French that Trompet had praised and read aloud in class. The essay, "Ses Rêves Trops Hauts, Sa Maison Trop Etroite," "Her Dreams Too Lofty, Her House Too Narrow," demonstrated in compelling detail, as Trompet phrased it, how Emma's delusional mind, like an untamed horse, carries her from one disastrous romantic obsession to the next, and ultimately to her doom. She turns to religion only to realize "que la religion n'est

qu'un leurre elle-meme," "that religion itself is b
Emma rebels against the reality of a monotono
with a dull husband—"Sa Maison Trop Etroite," "Her House
Too Narrow"—seeking fulfillment in a dream world that inevitably collapses, leading to her annihilation.

Remarkably, while Eric was astutely able to discern the
flaws in Emma Bovary's character that led to her downfall, he
was unable to draw any lessons from the novel or to recognize
that he, himself, was travelling along the same perilous path
that had led to the demise of Flaubert's heroine. Regrettably,
since his life took place outside of a French novel, he had no
help from Trompet or, for that matter, anyone. Where Flaubert
shone a light into the workings of the human mind—after all,
Emma Bovary's delusional obsessions are universal—academic
scholarship has the opposite effect; it obfuscates and prevari-
cates with linguistic gymnastics that prevent, rather than facil-
itate, the application of literary insights to the failings of the
human heart.

In this regard his mother was now becoming a
co-conspirator:

"Darling, I have some good news for you. I was able to get
two tickets to the finals at Wimbledon for you. Please call me
back."

Playing back this message, Eric dropped his book on the
floor and called his mother.

"Mummy, you're fantastic. I got your message. Thank you!
How did you do it?"

"You're welcome, darling. It was all luck. I called Princess
Fatemeh, who had two tickets for the finals, but as you know
she's quite ill and won't be able to go."

Princess Fatemeh Pahlavi was the Shah of Iran's younger
half-sister. She had moved to England during the Revolution

and now lived in London. She had been a tennis fan all her life. Recently, she had been diagnosed with cancer.

"Oh, God, poor Princess Fatemeh. How come she agreed to give you the tickets?"

"I called to inquire about her health. She asked how you were and I said you were driving me crazy for tickets to Wimbledon and, as she can't go, she offered to give you hers!"

"I'm so lucky, and you are so amazing. I love you, Mummy."

"I love you too, Darling."

Now that he had the tickets, he could approach Mark. Eric casually had asked on more than one occasion about his summer plans, but Mark had equivocated. He had mentioned traveling around Europe on a Eurorail pass if he wasn't able to obtain a job or an internship with a bank. That same evening, Mark had come over. And, as they lay in bed, Eric ventured:

"I have two tickets for the finals at Wimbledon."

"Do you? Nah, you're fucking with me."

"Honest! I really do! Want to come?" Eric asked, as offhandedly as he could.

Mark looked at him incredulously, the smile freezing on his face like candle wax.

"Well of course I do, but," he hesitated. "I mean I don't know if I can. I've applied for an internship."

Eric's heart sank. He looked at Mark beseechingly. "But this is Wimbledon, the finals. Becker will be playing. Surely you could take a few days off from your internship?"

"I know, I know," Mark said, his mind reeling. "You're killing me, man. You know that."

If Mark had been able to analyze his reluctance, he would have realized that it wasn't the possible internship, but rather his fear of commitment that was preventing him from accepting Eric's invitation. If his father or anyone else had offered a ticket to the finals of Wimbledon, he would have immediately and unhesitatingly welcomed it. But the Wimbledon ticket symbolized time alone with Eric abroad, the next step in their relationship that he wasn't yet prepared to take. While he vaguely considered what he had with Eric as a romance, he nevertheless felt that time abroad together would be going one step too far. But Mark did not have the self-awareness to fathom his own reluctance in this regard, and he convinced himself that it was the as yet unsettled internship that stood as an obstacle to their Wimbledon venture.

Eric for his part was equally and even more dangerously deluded. He had been certain that Mark wouldn't pass up the chance to see the finals of Wimbledon. Mark's hesitation was painful to him, not only because it was unexpected, but because it was also a rejection of their future together, though he didn't see it that clearly. In fact, Eric was so consumed by desire that he was unable to see the world as it was, or see the warning signs flashing red all around him. Through the haze of confusion, he was unable to detect Mark's fear but instead felt only his own pain. He wasn't able, or perhaps he was too fearful, to ask himself the most basic question: why wouldn't Mark want to spend time with him abroad, Wimbledon or not?

18

AT THE END OF EACH YEAR, the Princeton Clubs had "house parties," formal affairs to which each member invited a date. Obviously the dates were of the opposite sex, and it was always the men who asked the women, a tradition that persisted despite the social changes that raged beyond the gates of Nassau Hall in the 1980s. While underclassmen—freshmen and sophomores— were for the most part not invited to house parties, because they did not yet belong to a Club, Mark had invited Melissa the previous year, having received an invitation from one of his tennis teammates in T.I. This year, Mark and Melissa had the option of attending house parties at either T.I. or Cap and Gown. Mark hadn't even thought about the year-end house parties until a few days earlier when someone had asked him where he would be going. He had asked Melissa about her preferences, but she had told him that she wasn't going because she had an engagement in New York with Mattie that night. Mark was taken aback.

"What do you mean, you won't be here?"

"Well, Mattie is performing in a ballet, and I have to go to that."

"How come you didn't tell me before?"

"Honey, I've been gone almost every weekend in the last two months, and you haven't even noticed. So what's the big deal now?"

"It's not a big deal. It's just house parties. I'd have thought you'd wanna go with me."

"Well, I'd love to, but I've got to see Mattie perform, and then we're going out to an event in her honor afterward. So I can't skip that. Besides, house parties are so boring. They're no different than any other party, just everybody gets dressed up. Few of them even have the right clothes or makeup! Makes you wanna vomit. I'm wearing this new Valentino number to the event with Mattie."

Mark looked at Melissa as if her attitude had awoken him from a long sleep. It felt as if he were speaking to a complete stranger. He couldn't even remember the last time they had been intimate. Yes, she had been away virtually every weekend, and he now realized he hadn't cared. It was apparent that their relationship had ended, if, in fact, it had ever begun, for he now had a yardstick by which to measure intimacy. Though he was in general disconnected from his feelings, Melissa's abrupt statement had shaken him from his stupor, and in a concomitant moment of lucidity, he had glimpsed his own emotional sensibility and was frightened by it.

"What's the matter, Mark? Why are you looking at me like that?"

"Oh, no, nothing. I was just, um ... nothing."

"No, what? Tell me? I mean I didn't think you cared much about house parties anyway."

"You're right Melissa and I don't. Have a great time in New York with Mattie and say hello from me."

"I'll definitely do that. You are a darling," she said as she gave him a peck on the cheek, her disregard of his feelings matched only by her obsession with Mattie.

That same night, Mark went over to see Eric. He asked Eric if he had plans to go to the house parties, and Eric replied that he was taking his friend Sarah to the Campus party.

"Sarah? Should I be jealous?" Mark kidded.

"Just a friend, trust me." He paused to gauge Mark's mood. "How about you? Are you going to Cap or T.I.?"

"I'm not going at all."

"Really, how come?"

"Melissa's attending some bullshit event in New York with Mattie."

"I'm sorry. Are you miffed? Can you take someone else, or just go stag?"

"Nah. I don't really like them anyway." He paused, looked Eric in the eyes. "Listen, I was kind of thinking. Why don't we get out of here this weekend? Just you and me?"

Eric hesitated. He would normally jump at the opportunity, but he had invited Sarah and couldn't just cancel on her.

"Where do you wanna go?"

"I dunno. Somewhere, anywhere. Let's just get in my car and drive."

"Mark, I'd love to, but I've invited Sarah to the Campus party, which is in three days' time. Too late to cancel now."

"Ah, okay, forget it. Just a thought."

"No, no," said Eric in a panic, seeing Mark turning away from him. "I'd love to go on a road trip. Let me talk to Sarah. Okay? I'm sure I can arrange it," he said but felt that he might be jeopardizing his friendship with her.

"All right, man. It'll be awesome." He now added, "I've been thinking about the summer, you know Wimbledon."

"Yes," Eric replied expectantly.

"Well, I think I can come. See, my internship doesn't start 'til August, if I even get it, and my roommates and I have been talking about going on a Eurorail trip. So London can be my first stop."

"That's so great Mark!" exclaimed Eric and hugged him. They began to make out and soon were in his bed making love.

Afterward, as they lay naked in bed, Eric convinced himself that Sarah would forgive him if he cancelled at the last minute. His mind now raced forward to the weekend and London.

"So let's plan our weekend. Where are we gonna go?"

"I dunno. I thought we might drive to the Delaware beaches."

Eric didn't know about, nor had ever visited the beaches there and was by nature a cautious planner. He was about to disagree but held himself back. He was too consumed by his love for Mark to object to anything he wanted.

"That sounds exciting. When do you wanna leave?" Eric asked.

"How's Friday?"

"Okay. And I'm thrilled you can make Wimbledon. It'll be amazing. Maybe Becker will win."

"There's no maybe about it. He'll win it. He's been playing so well lately."

Mark soon fell asleep, but Eric couldn't. He lay there, bubbling over with excitement and anticipation. Never before had he experienced such romantic exaltation. He felt elated, as if entranced by some magical power. The moonlight shone through the window bathing Mark in its silvery glow. He listened to his gentle breathing and heard a rhapsody played upon the moon. He reached over and touched Mark's chest, to reassure himself this was real, that he wasn't in a dream; and at that moment, Mark, reflexively in his sleep, closed his hand over Eric's.

They checked into a motel room in Rehoboth Beach, a Delaware vacation town on the Atlantic Coast, which, unknown to either of them, was the vacation resort of choice for the gay communities of Washington D.C. and Philadelphia. They had chosen Rehoboth because it was the next town over from Dewey Beach, a popular destination for college students during spring break, which Mark knew and liked but didn't want to stay there because of the risk of accidentally encountering an acquaintance.

As the weather was resplendently sunny, they went to the beach every day. On the afternoon of their first day, they had observed two young men throwing a football to each other. Mark expressed regret at not having brought a ball. When the two guys had returned to lie on their towels, Eric approached them and asked if he could borrow the football and one of them pushed it over. After he and Mark tossed it a bit, they returned it and started up a conversation. Their names were Kyle and Jerry, and they attended Villanova. Kyle was on the football team and Jerry, who had played football in high school, had injured himself and couldn't play. They were typical college jocks; tall in stature with muscular physiques, though Kyle was decidedly leaner and more flexible. They were handsome, though with different looks; Kyle had rusty-blond hair and blue eyes, alabaster white skin and hardly any body hair; Jerry was swarthier with dark, curly hair, brown eyes, and a bushy chest.

Eric speculated that they were together but Mark denied it, insisting that they were "buddies" on vacation, probably on the hunt for girls. Little did they know that Jerry and Kyle were having a very similar conversation about them. It wasn't until their penultimate day before leaving that Jerry revealed his intimacy with Kyle to Eric. They had been intimate since their freshman year, though in complete secrecy. Eric, in turn, confessed to his relationship with Mark but had implored Jerry not to betray this confidence to Mark.

Mark was incredulous when Eric told him about Jerry's disclosure.

"No way," exclaimed Mark. "They look like totally straight, normal dudes."

"Well, aren't we?" laughed Eric.

"Yeah, but that's different. I mean, are you sure he wasn't fucking with you? Maybe he thinks you're a Eurofag and it's his way of finding out."

Eric was hurt by this slur. "No, he's not like that Mark. He's a decent guy and he's telling me the truth. They're together, though no one knows."

"So why is he suddenly telling you?"

"I guess he felt comfortable enough with me. I mean, I don't know anyone they know. Who would I tell anyway? And I think he suspects that we're sleeping together too."

"You didn't tell him, did you?" Mark quickly asked.

"Of course not."

Mark had never known any gay or bisexual athletes. Kyle and Jerry lacked the stereotypical homosexual traits and were not effete, dissolute, or lisping; and they were hyper-masculine when they played sports. In his mind, these were traits that precluded homosexuality. Yet, deep down, he had sensed the two were intimate, an impression now confirmed by Eric's revelation. But he could not bring himself to reconcile the reality of their relationship with being homosexual. For if they were gay, then how could he continue to persuade himself that he was not? It was these troubling velleities that had led to the "Eurofag" slip.

The night before they were to leave, Eric and Mark went out to a bar where they saw a fair number of typical homosexuals. They had peroxided hair, exaggerated body gestures, and called each other "dah-ling" and said "fah-bu-lous" in that unmistakably gay fashion. To Mark and Eric, they represented unpleasant caricatures with which they decidedly did not identify. They were about to leave when they ran into Jerry and Kyle who were visibly flushed with drink.

"Hey, where are you going?" exclaimed Jerry.

"We don't like the crowd here," Eric said, pointing toward a gaggle of queens hamming it up at the bar.

"Oh, them! Huh, harmless enough. I guess you guys didn't know this was kind of a gay resort?"

"What do you mean a gay resort?" asked Mark, breaking his silence.

"I mean it's a popular destination for the friends of Dorothy," jested Jerry with a laugh.

"Wait, how do you know this?" inquired Mark, a bit perplexed.

"It's a well-known fact, my friend," continued Jerry in the same bantering tone.

"It's well known? I didn't know. I mean Dewey Beach is right next door. I've been there for spring break."

"Two very different worlds," he said nodding his head up

and down in the manner of a person with confidence in his knowledge.

"Wait, so if you knew this, why did you guys come here?" Mark asked rather naively.

"Why do you think?"

"Beats me," Mark said.

"Oh, come on Mark, it's not like you're that innocent. We came here because we wanted to see what it was like. Why did you and Eric come?"

Mark glanced at Jerry and then over at Kyle who was nodding his head in affirmation. He didn't have an immediate reply to the question. Mark had had a fair amount to drink and felt confused, a bit discombobulated. The jumble of thoughts pulsated in his mind like the loud music thumping in the bar. Suddenly, he said in a quiet voice, "So Jerry, are you and Kyle together?"

"Yeah, we are," Jerry replied softly while casually laying his arm on Kyle's shoulder. The music was so loud that he wasn't sure if Mark and Eric had heard him properly. He now added, "Say it's really loud here. Do you want to take this to our rooftop? It's a bit more private, and we have some Sam Adams."

Eric looked over at Mark who appeared shaken but nodded his head. Intrigued by Jerry's frank avowal of their relationship, he wanted to continue the conversation, but not in this noisy, public setting beset by flamboyant queens.

The rooftop was a raw cement floor typical in cinder-block buildings from the 1960s that had been built on the cheap. Unlit and unfenced, it presented a real and present danger to drunken bar-goers. The four of them carried folding beach chairs, two packs of Sam Adams, and some candles up a dark staircase. It was a very hot and humid night, made tolerable by the ocean breeze. They were the only ones on the roof.

When they were ensconced in the chairs, each sipping on his beer, Jerry asked, "So, tell us a bit about you guys."

Silence followed. Eric, who contrary to his social nature had been subdued all evening, remained resolutely quiet. His hesitation to speak was not due to any concern for himself; instead, he realized that they were traversing an extremely perilous terrain for Mark whose anxiety was almost palpable to him.

The silence continued and was on the verge of becoming intolerable when Jerry added facetiously, "Gee, I won't grade you on your answer!"

This broke the ice and they all chuckled.

"We're together as well or ... kind of. It's complicated," Mark ventured. Ever since his conversation with Melissa about house parties, he had begun to consider his liaison with Eric in a different light. He had even admitted to himself that his relationship with Melissa had been a sham. After his first sexual encounter with Eric, he had immediately realized that sex could be more than "getting off," even gratifying, as he was enveloped by rhapsodic feelings that he had never experienced with her. Nevertheless, Mark had continued to suppress and stifle his natural urges, but with time's passage his feelings for Eric had gradually strengthened, loosening the hold on his fears, though he was not ready for a full acceptance of their relationship.

After another long silence, Mark finally asked, "How did you guys meet?"

"We're frat brothers," said Jerry glancing at Kyle affectionately. "I pledged him. He fell for me right then and there, didn't you?"

"That I did," responded Kyle, breaking his natural silence. "It was the second day of the pledge, and I passed out drunk in Jerry's room at the frat. His roommate was away, and Jerry fell asleep next to me. In the middle of the night, I felt his arm wrap around me, and I felt really excited. We fell asleep in that position, but I woke up and pushed myself closer, and he pulled me toward him. Our bodies were now touching, and though we were in T-shirts and boxers, I remember getting very excited and realizing I was rock hard."

"How about the next day? Did you guys let on?"

"No, we didn't. The first couple of months it was very awkward. Jerry had a girlfriend in college, and I was still officially with my high-school sweetheart who was at Vassar. But I really dug him and wanted to be around him all the time." He reached over and took Jerry's hand.

"As frat president, I had my own room in the frat, but my girlfriend was always there. She nearly caught us getting it on one day," Jerry chimed in.

"What happened? Are you still with her?" Mark asked.

"Nah, we broke up. I made my excuses to her, but it was because I'd fallen for Kyle."

"How about you guys, tell us about you," Jerry insisted.

"You tell them," Mark said, glancing over at Eric. Eric described how they had met over French lessons, slept together the first night, and continued with the rest of their story while Mark nodded his assent from time to time.

When Eric finished, Kyle asked Mark, "So what happened between you and Melissa? Are you guys still together?"

"I guess so, kind of. She blew me off for our year-end house party. I'm not sure, really." But, as he spoke these words, he knew his relationship with her was finished. At the same time, he felt as if a weight was being lifted off his shoulders. It was the first time that he had participated in a conversation of such deep, emotional significance and the first time that he had stuck his head outside the confining and emotionally draining space of the "closet." Jerry and Kyle's demeanor reminded him of his own circle of male friends. Their candor about their intimacy provided Mark with the courage to look, if not yet to step, outside the closet.

"Have you guys thought about what you would do after graduation?" Eric interjected.

"We've talked about it, but nothing concrete. I'll graduate a year before Kyle, and I was thinking of getting a job in New York or Philly. That way we could see each other on the weekends, and maybe Kyle will end up in the same city after graduation and we can share a place together."

"You're not worried that you'll be found out and it'll affect your employment?" Mark asked in an anxious tone.

"I don't want to be found out while I'm in college," Kyle said, "but I'm pretty relaxed about it afterward. All I know is, I care for this man and I want to be with him." He pulled Jerry toward him and gave him a hug, leaving his colossal left leg dangling in Jerry's lap.

"I feel the same way," Jerry cooed, stroking Kyle's leg.

The sight of these two hulking football players declaring their love for each other provided Mark a glimpse of what a future with Eric might be like.

———

CONSUELO was spending the summer in Paris. She was bunking in a small studio apartment on the Rue St. Jacques with an Italian girl whom she connected with through the agency that had helped arrange her summer abroad. Even before her arrival, she had managed to invite herself to dinner at Eric's, and though he had welcomed her visit, they hadn't fixed a specific date. In her first week there, Consuelo had called and left him several messages, but Eric had been too distracted by his impending rendezvous with Mark at Wimbledon and had been slow in returning her calls. Already insecure, she had felt rejected and unwanted, but when he eventually did contact her and invited her to dinner, she accepted without hesitation.

When she arrived at Eric's place, Consuelo marveled at the opulence and grandeur of their flat.

"This place must have cost a pretty penny. Can I have a tour?" she asked.

Eric cringed but was thankful that neither his mother nor her husband were within earshot of that tasteless comment. As for the "tour," he wasn't about to show her his parents' bedroom, or even his own for that matter.

"Here, come with me into the living room and let's have a drink. When did you get in?"

"Last Tuesday."

"So you must be over your jet lag. How are you holding up?"

"I'm doing okay, thanks! I've been going for long walks around the city. Paris is so beautiful, the architecture so grand, that it really grounded me and helped me adjust to the time zone change."

"Would you like a glass of red wine?"

"Sure, thanks. How about a tour of this amazing apartment?" she insisted.

"Um, sure. But let's just wait 'till my parents come in and then—"

His mother walked into the room before he had finished the sentence. She was impeccably made up and looked stunning in a red Valentino dress, black high-heeled shoes and a matching sapphire pendant and bracelet. The smile on her face faded as soon as she laid eyes on Consuelo, though she tried to disguise her disappointment in this short, unattractive girl in faded jeans and athletic shoes who wore no makeup. Eric read the concern on her face and was irritated by it.

"This is Consuelo, my friend from Princeton," he said.

"Hello, Consuelo. Welcome to our house. How are you?"

"I'm well, thanks. Thank you for having me over."

"Dinner's already on the table, so please come into the dining room and let's sit down."

The table was set for four. Lili asked the maid to call her husband and tell him that the food was on the table and was going cold—a ritual they went through every evening. After about ten minutes, Farzad emerged from his study with the triumphant strut of a man who had just negotiated nuclear détente between the major world powers.

"Please, please, go ahead and start," he intoned, and when he realized there was a guest at the table, he added, "I'm sorry, but I have been so tied up with work."

"This is Consuelo, my friend from Princeton," interjected Eric.

"Hello, hello. Nice to meet you, dear," Farzad said, as he reached over to shake her hand.

If she had been pretty, he would have endeavored to impress her with his list of accomplishments. As it was, he showed little interest in her, but when it was revealed that Consuelo was a comparative literature major, like his stepson, he warned her against imminent penury. She tried to protest, but his orotund tone and manner silenced her refutation. Eric, who had been long inured to these lectures, didn't perceive the consternation that his stepfather had caused in his friend. His mother saw her reaction but found Consuelo so lacking that she didn't feel like making amends for her husband's slight. For her part, Consuelo had expected Eric to intervene, if only because his stepfather's harsh words would have applied equally to him. But Eric had been only half listening. His mind kept wandering to Mark, to the remarkable weekend that they had spent together at the beach, and their meeting in London next week.

After dinner Consuelo, downtrodden and feeling unvalued, made a hasty exit. As she walked to the metro, a rage and resentment boiled up inside of her. "How dare they treat me so ignominiously," she thought to herself, "these white people so full of themselves, so privileged, yet so stupid." Images of Eric's grand apartment, his mother's sapphire jewelry, his stepfather's patrician condescension, and Eric's haughty detachment passed in quick succession before her. "We need another French Revolution to get rid of these aristocratic snobs for good," she thought, her resentment so powerful that it completely possessed her whole being. As she gritted her teeth and clenched her fists, her aggression physical and palpable, she wished to exact a revenge on Eric's family.

———

MEANWHILE, when the door had shut behind Consuelo, Eric's mother remarked, "That poor girl. She's so unattractive."

"Why would you even say that," Eric objected.

"Because it's true, Darling," she chirped merrily as if the girl's feelings meant nothing to her.

"Even if it were true, which it isn't, why does it matter? She's one of the smartest people at Princeton," he replied, exasperated by his mother's attitude.

"It matters a great deal because she's a woman. If she were a man, it wouldn't matter, and brains would suffice."

"What are you talking about?"

women, looks matter a great deal."

so opinionated," he declared.

why are you so angry, darling?" she asked defensively, using her typical diversionary tactic to deflect the question raised.

"I'm not angry; you're just so annoying at times!"

"Besides, you yourself ignored her at dinner, lost in thought the whole time."

"No, I wasn't," Eric rebutted, unconvincingly, even to himself. His mother's attitudes enervated him. He had also felt that her snide remarks were an implicit criticism of himself, almost an attack—that he would dare bring home such an unattractive girl. He hadn't even considered her appearance when he had invited Consuelo. What would his mother think if he invited Mark, as his boyfriend, he thought. She'd be very impressed with him until she found out her son was sleeping with him. Eric was unable to discern that his mother was expressing a viewpoint common among her generation. Nor was he aware that his own thoughts and feelings, perhaps even his attraction to Mark, had been shaped to a large extent by these very same social forces. It would require a degree of self-detachment of which he was, as of yet, incapable.

19

FINALLY the day he had been anticipating arrived. Eric checked into the Park Tower Hotel in London and awaited Mark's arrival. He unpacked his clothes, had a shower, and changed into fresh clothes. Two hours passed; he started to pace the room, and then went down to the lobby and approached the front desk to see if anyone had asked for him or left a message. None. He wasn't sure what to do with himself. He thought of going for a walk, but what if Mark arrived while he was out? He tried reading but couldn't concentrate. Television programs were more irksome than calming. What if Mark had mixed up the days or had taken down the hotel information incorrectly? They'd had a phone conversation in which he had provided Mark with the hotel's name. Mark had explained that he would meet Eric in London, and after Wimbledon would travel around Europe on the Eurorail with some friends. But now, he couldn't recall the details of the conversation and became concerned that he might have miscommunicated the hotel information. Eric had been so excited, his mind so completely overtaken by the upcoming reunion with Mark, that his perception of recent day-to-day events had been altered. Past, present, and future, as well as real and imagined, converged as if by a centrifugal force on a single focal point—his tryst with Mark.

Eric had absently drifted through the days since his arrival in Europe, mechanically going through the motions of life, which accounted for Consuelo's disastrous visit to their house in Paris. His mind told and retold the story of Mark and Eric's Wimbledon plans, like a projector showing the same film over and over. But now that the hour had at last arrived, Mark's absence was leading Eric to the dark recesses of his mind, where the multiheaded hydra of fear, doubt, and despair lay in wait. What if something had happened to Mark? Perhaps he had missed his plane? He should have asked him for the flight information; how stupid and foolish of him not to have inquired; at least he could then have checked to see if the flight had been cancelled or delayed. What if Mark had had a last minute change of heart and decided, instead, to just go travelling across Europe with his friends? He held his head in his hands and thought that the days ahead wouldn't be worth living if Mark didn't come. What would be the point? The ringing of the phone startled him out of his ruminations and he jumped to answer it. It was his mother, making sure that he had arrived safely in London and reminding him to write a thank you note to Princess Fatemeh.

"Do you have her address?" she asked.

"I'm sure I have it somewhere," he replied, trying to mask his impatience.

"Let me give it to you now," she insisted.

"I don't have a pen. Can we do this later?" he pleaded.

"No, you'll forget. Just take it down now and write the note on the hotel stationery." He sighed and reached for a pen. As he started to write, he heard a knock on the door.

"Hold on, Mother," he said.

"It'll take two seconds. It's Flat 5—"

There was another knock at the door.

"Mother, I need to get the door; I'll be right back."

Eric put her on hold and answered the door. Mark was standing there with his signature smile, a duffle bag, and a backpack. Eric's heart leapt as he motioned Mark inside. They hugged and Mark started to kiss him.

Eric said, "Hold that thought. I'm on the phone. I'll be right off."

After he wrote down Princess Fatemeh's address, he hurriedly said goodbye to his mother and hung up. He turned to Mark and they kissed passionately.

Mark was tired and jet-lagged, but Eric insisted they go for a walk in Hyde Park. Outside it was warm, but the rays of sunlight filtered through the treetops, as the light began to fade. They walked briskly into the rose garden on Hyde Park corner. The fresh air revived Mark's energy, as well as his appetite. They made their way back to the hotel and stopped at a small Italian restaurant on Beauchamp Place. Mark was relaxed; a very genuine smile appeared on his face. He reached under the table and touched Eric's knee, found his hand and interlaced his fingers with Eric's. He didn't talk. Eric, who was in the middle of a sentence discussing the menu, fell silent. He glanced up and caught Mark's eyes and knew at that moment that he loved and was loved in return.

———————

BORIS BECKER HAD BEATEN HENRI LECONTE and was now facing Ivan Lendl in the finals, which were being played that afternoon on Centre Court at Wimbledon. The day was overcast, and the rain threatened to delay the match. Mark and Eric had arrived by the underground in the morning, walked around the grounds and had sandwiches for lunch at one of the food tents. They then made their way to the stadium and their seats, which turned out to be in the fourth row on the opposite side from the umpire's chair, giving them an unobstructed and close-up view of the court. The match got underway, and when Becker took the first set, Mark jumped up with both hands in the air, crying out, "yeah man" and high-fiving Eric. Halfway through the second set, the game was paused and the players walked off as a drizzle turned into droplets of rain. "It's not even raining," complained Mark. "Why would they stop?"

"I guess it's because the grass gets slick. It may not be too long of a delay," Eric replied. "Let's go have a drink."

Mark bought them beers under a tent teeming with people waiting it out. They tried to negotiate some space but were jostled by the crowd. When a tall, highly inebriated middle-aged man stepped on Eric's foot, Mark pushed the fellow in a protective manner and uttered, "Watch it, buddy."

The man was too drunk to respond and merely stumbled on, but at that moment a fair-haired young man looked at them and said, "Eric, is that you?"

Campbell stood before them, holding a beer. He appeared to be alone.

"Campbell," stammered Eric, dazed by the unexpected and untimely encounter.

"How are you? How come I never heard from you?" he asked quizzically, then looking over at Mark:

"Oh, I see." He paused and gazed at Mark. "I'm Campbell by the way." He extended a hand out to Mark, who didn't catch the remark and merely shook his hand.

"Sorry," interjected Eric with a nervous laugh. "Mark this is Campbell; Campbell meet Mark."

"Nice to meet you," replied Mark.

They stood in uncomfortable silence before Campbell asked how long they were staying.

"Just for a few days, to see Wimbledon," Eric said.

"So I take it, you're visiting too?" Campbell asked, looking back at Mark.

"Yeah, I go to Princeton with Eric. I'm just here to watch the finals."

To Eric's great relief, Campbell was not only discreet but an easy conversationalist. He and Mark were soon talking about careers in banking and the stock market, topics that Eric ordinarily considered tedious at best but which now appeared to be saving him from an awkward and potentially perilous situation. It wasn't long before the rain stopped, and they were called back to Centre Court for the resumption of the match.

"It'll be nice to see you guys before you leave," Campbell said.

"That'll be great," replied Mark.

"You have my number, Eric, right? Just give me a ring."

"Um, sure, but I left my phone book in Paris. Can you please give it to me again?"

"Sure."

Campbell wrote his number on a napkin, but when he went to hand the napkin to Eric, Mark reached for it and stuffed it into his inside jacket pocket.

"Where are you staying, by the way?" Campbell asked as he handed over the napkin.

"At the Park Tower Hotel, in Knightsbridge," replied Eric.

"How posh of you, Eric," Campbell commented good-humoredly. "How about you Mark?"

Mark hesitated. He hadn't expected to be called on to answer this question.

"Um … uh, I'm just crashing with Eric for a couple of days."

"Ah, got you. Well, we best be moving along. They're starting. Hope to hear from you."

After he left and as they hurried back to Centre Court, Mark asked Eric how he knew Campbell.

"I forget now," replied Eric hesitantly. "I think we met at a party in Paris some time ago."

Mark accepted that statement at face value. He had had no experience with gay men and was not familiar with the subtleties of their communications, with their body language and gestures that, like Morse code, were decipherable by the initiates but remained inscrutable to everyone else. Even more, Mark did not discern the tinge of jealousy in Campbell's "I see" comment.

"Cool guy. He's in banking. We should meet up with him."

"Sure," replied Eric, flummoxed by their encounter and relieved that the match was starting up. Hopefully, Mark would forget about connecting with Campbell, or there wouldn't be enough time to meet.

————

ERIC HAD BOOKED A TABLE that night at San Lorenzo, an Italian restaurant that had been catapulted to the top of London's culinary destinations—not so much for its gastronomic qualities, though the food was excellent, but by the frequentation of Princess Diana. Eric had booked a table there a month in advance but told Mark it was to celebrate Becker's win. Though the restaurant was full when they arrived, they were quickly seated at a round table toward the front. Mark felt uneasy, not because of the lavish surroundings—he had frequently dined at upscale venues with his parents—but because he was uncomfortable being in such a place with Eric. With his friends, he would go to a sports bar, at best a diner. For guys, elegant restaurants were for dates, and even though he had progressed in terms of accepting his feelings for Eric, he was not yet ready to be seen on a date with another man in public.

"How about some red wine?" asked Eric and then to the waiter, "Can we have the wine card please?"

At that moment Campbell walked up to their table. "Uh oh, I hope I'm not late," he said.

Eric looked at him stunned. Mark finally said, "When you mentioned the restaurant, I called Campbell to meet up with us. Hope you don't mind. Wanted to grill him about his job."

Eric quickly recovered. "No, that's fine," he stammered. "Are you okay with some red wine, or do you want something else?"

"Red's perfect," replied Campbell as he pulled back a chair and sat down.

Eric ordered a bottle of St. Julien while Mark said to Campbell, "I'm glad you were able to come on such short notice."

"Thanks for asking me. I didn't have any plans."

After some talk of the tennis finals, Mark asked Campbell about his job. It turned out that Campbell worked for Goldman Sachs, where Mark had applied but had been denied a summer internship.

"Internships are pretty hard to get, but I can try to connect you with some people for next year when you finish your degree?"

"That'd be awesome. You would do that?"

"Sure. I know one of the partners in the London office. He's pretty senior. Actually helped set up the London office. It's a very new office. I'm one of the first hires here. It was made possible by Thatcher's Big Bang."

Mark nodded as if he knew about Thatcher's reforms to the financial industry and understood the expression "the Big Bang."

"I wonder why they call it that. What does it mean?" asked Eric, admitting to his total ignorance of the subject.

Campbell offered a convoluted explanation of the recent deregulation of the British financial industry, which was more a reflection of his own general confusion rather than the complexity of the subject matter. Mark, who knew nothing about the topic, was impressed and saw in Campbell a real connection for his career. He was feeling relaxed; his initial disquietude about dining out had given way to a slightly fuddled contentment. They were on their third bottle of wine when Campbell, who was drinking heavily, asked:

"So what's the story with you guys?"

"What do you mean?" asked Eric.

"You know what I mean!" he said with a wink.

Eric glanced at Mark whose startled reaction was like that of a criminal caught in the act. Eric himself felt as if he were trapped in a maze under blaring lights, not knowing in which direction to run.

"What? Why so shy guys?" insisted Campbell.

"I don't know what you're implying. We're just college friends, that's all," exclaimed Eric in exasperation.

"Well, does he know about you?" asked Campbell.

"Do I know what about him?" interjected Mark.

"Oh come on guys. That he's gay, which is how we met."

"I thought you met at a party," Mark said with an edgy tone.

"We met at a club and went home together," Campbell stated, provocatively.

Mark went pale and after a moment said, with gritted teeth, "I've got to go." He stood up and left the table without another word.

"Why did you say that?" Eric asked, irritated, confused, and not sure whether Mark had gone to the men's room or had left completely.

"I don't understand what you're trying to hide. It's obvious to anyone you two are together."

"Yes, but it's complicated. I thought you'd understand and be a bit more discreet, Campbell."

"It's not like I outed you to the world. It was just us."

"But you implied that we'd slept together."

"Oh, he didn't know that? You hadn't told him?"

"No."

"I'm sorry. You're right. I should've kept my mouth shut. I didn't think. I mean, I thought he would know. Wait! Are you two, like boyfriends?"

"No, we're not boyfriends."

"So then why do you care that I told him?"

"Campbell I told you it's complicated, please."

"Eric, we had an amazing night in Paris together. I really liked you. I was sure you were going to call me, but then you never did. Then I run into you at Wimbledon with this guy, and the next thing I know he's asking me to join you two for dinner. I didn't even know what to think. I figured he wanted job information, or maybe a threesome."

"A threesome?" asked Eric stupefied.

"Yeah, why not?"

"Mark didn't even know you're gay. He was definitely thinking business contact."

"I see. So it was his idea, not yours?" Eric nodded his head. "You didn't even know he'd called me?"

"I didn't and I wouldn't have. Sorry, but I've got to get back to the hotel, back to Mark."

"You said yourself he's not your boyfriend."

"I know I said that, but it's complicated. Listen, I need to go. Let's get the bill."

"Please don't go," Campbell said in a beseeching tone and took his hand.

Eric shook his head. "Campbell, I'm in love with Mark."

As soon as he had uttered this confession, Eric was flummoxed; it was as if someone else had made this declaration of love. "Did I just say that?" he thought, as the weight of the statement bore down on him. What did that actually entail? he wondered.

Campbell replied, "Does he love you back?"

"I, I don't know. I hope so," he replied in a low wistful voice.

Campbell let go of his hand and sat back. "He seems a bit of an arse-hole to me. At any rate, he's a lucky guy to have you." He now waved to the waiter, rubbing his fingers together and when the bill arrived, he pulled out his credit card to pay.

"Oh no, let me do this," Eric insisted, reaching for the bill.

"God, no. I've already fucked things up enough for you. The least I can do is pay the bill."

Outside the restaurant, Eric went to shake Campbell's hand, but Campbell pulled him toward him and kissed Eric, who didn't resist. For an instant, they stayed in each other's embrace and Campbell whispered, "You're a beautiful man Eric. Please don't let this guy mess with you. I don't feel good about him. Take care of yourself."

And with that, they parted. Eric rushed back to the hotel and went into the room where all the lights had been turned off; it was totally dark. He panicked that Mark might have packed his things and left. He switched on the nightstand lamps and found Mark lying on the bed. His eyes were open; he was staring up at the ceiling. Eric approached him tentatively, sat on the edge of the bed, and reached over to touch Mark's hand, which was resting on the blanket. Mark jerked his hand away. Eric could see the anger seething through his frigid expression, frozen like the face of a mummy painted on an Egyptian sarcophagus. Eric was relieved that he was still there but frightened for them both.

"I'm very sorry about Campbell," he finally said.

Mark didn't respond.

"Mark, talk to me?" Eric implored of him.

"Fuck you!"

"Mark, it's not what you think."

"Fuck you, you asshole."

Eric was taken aback. Whatever he'd done, he didn't deserve this level of belligerence. But he was too afraid of losing Mark to hold his ground in this standoff.

"Mark, please. Why are you so upset?"

"You fuckin' slept with him," fulminated Mark, his face red with rage.

"I, I ... didn't actually. I mean, what makes you say that?" stammered Eric in confusion.

"Stop fucking lying. He said it, for Pete's sake."

"He said we went home together. That's all. I ... I don't care about him. All I want is to be with you."

"But you slept with him? You're admitting it."

"Mark, it was a long time ago, before I knew you, and we didn't have sex."

"When was it?" Mark asked, who appeared slightly soothed by the revelation of this timeline.

"I don't remember exactly. I think it was last summer in Paris."

Mark scrutinized him intensely. It was as if he was plunging into the depths of Eric's being to discover the truth. Eric remained as still and silent as the Sphinx. They gazed at each other, not like lovers but as combatants. After a few moments, Mark's expression altered; a faint smile replaced the pursed lips, and he reached over and pulled Eric toward him and kissed him on the mouth. Eric opened up and let Mark's tongue plunge deep into his mouth. Mark, who was only wearing his underwear, now stripped Eric in a succession of quick movements, kissing him deeply in between the removal of each layer of clothing. He lay on top of Eric and held Eric's arms above his head as his continued to kiss him and murmured "I love you" in his ear.

"I love you Mark," exhaled Eric in a perfect mix of confusion and exhilaration.

20

BACK AT PRINCETON the new
academic year commenced
during a heat wave. Temperatures
rose into the high 90s and the humid
air felt blistering. The short bursts of
torrential rain, which sent students
scampering for shelter, brought no
relief from the oppressive sultriness
that weighed down on everybody
like the world on Atlas's shoulders.
Accustomed to the crisp Septembers
in Paris, Eric was wearing gabar-
dine trousers and a long-sleeved
shirt. He hadn't even brought back
summer clothes, which in his mind
were intended for holidays in places
like Cannes, Majorca, or the Amalfi
Coast rather than Princeton, where

it wouldn't be appropriate to wear beach clothes. He had never spent a summer in the States and in prior years had only encountered mild temperatures in September. When he first arrived at Princeton as a freshman, Eric had been surprised at what he considered the students' slovenly garb of torn jeans, sneakers, cargo shorts, Birkenstocks, duck boots, and other such sartorial lapses.

Now, as he walked to his first class, he strained under the weight of his heavy clothes. Yet, he was too preoccupied to notice the hot weather. He hadn't received a message from Mark, who had moved rooms and whose new on-campus contact information Eric didn't have. Surely Mark knew enough to leave a message with his new phone number. He wondered about the cause of this oversight. After London, Mark had spent a week in Paris with Eric when his parents were away for their summer holiday in Gstaad. They had had the flat to themselves; the anonymity of the city had provided cover for their love affair, which had started to blossom after its near crash a week earlier. Eric glanced back in his mind on those happy days of summer with a hint of nostalgia and groped for answers, but found himself continuously confronted by questions. Could Mark have had a change of heart? Could something have happened to him on the European trip with his friends? He hadn't written or called since they had parted. Distracted by these thoughts, he walked into his advance French classroom, sat down, but didn't even notice Ali two chairs away.

Ali reached over and tugged at his sleeve and jovially said, "Hello." They hadn't seen each other since the evening at Bain Douches last Christmas. Ali appeared to be in a cheerful mood and engaged in light banter with Eric:

"So now you pretend you don't even know me, huh," he said with a chuckle.

"Please forgive me, Your Royal Highness. I, I didn't see you sitting there," Eric replied, startled. He rose from his chair, shook the Prince's hand, then he took the chair next to Ali.

"I didn't realize that you were in this seminar."

"I chose it late. I thought Trompet is, or at least can be, as entertaining as Stendhal and Hugo."

The seminar was a graduate-level program on nineteenth-century French novelists. Eric was pleased to see Ali in the class. The others were all graduate students, none of whom he knew. The Prince's presence comforted him in his discombobulated state.

"I trust that your summer was enjoyable?" asked Eric.

"It was great. Um ... I, I didn't spend much time in Paris," replied Ali, who suddenly recalled the evening at Bain Douches and felt a tinge of guilt at deliberately losing Eric in the club. However, his pride prevented an apology or even an admission that his conduct had been insensitive. "I went to Morocco and the South of France," he continued nonchalantly.

Eric had not been offended by Ali and had at the time, attributed the bad manners to Sanam and his half-brother Kamran. Moreover, given his fixation with Mark last semester, he had long forgotten the incident. Eric had grown up in an environment of extreme deference to royalty with an unquestioned acceptance of their whims and caprices. Nothing that Ali said or did could offend him. As he was pondering the next item of polite small talk, Trompet walked into the class and everyone fell silent. Trompet looked around the room with his usual affable smile, and when he saw Ali and Eric, his eyes rested on them and his smile broadened. He then welcomed the class to the world of Victor Hugo.

When the class let out after three hours, torrential rain was beating down on the campus, creating large puddles and sending everyone scurrying for cover. After a while, as the downpour continued unabated, Eric thought of making a mad dash to the Campus Club. As he ran in the pounding rain, he began to soak through, and his socks became saturated. Then, he suddenly glimpsed a figure, dripping with water who also was frantically hurrying along. Though she was holding a book over her head in a futile attempt to shield her face from the rain, Eric had recognized her and called out. Melissa turned around in surprise. Recognizing Eric, she smiled and waved but made a gesture to indicate that she couldn't stop and continued on her sodden journey. Eric wasn't about to let her escape. He ran in her direction and finally caught up with her.

"I'm sorry Eric. I'd love to stop and chat but I'm really late," she said pointedly, with the exasperation of someone whose meticulous plans are suddenly frustrated by circumstance.

"Okay, no problem. Have you seen Mark? I've got something of his." Eric thought quickly, "A French book that I need to give him." This was a facile lie but it was the best he could think up.

For an instant, a quizzical look replaced the beleaguered expression on Melissa's face, as if she had surmised the real purpose of Eric's insistence, but her mission was too pressing to permit distraction, and she responded irritably as she continued to walk briskly:

"I've no idea where he is. We broke up. I'd have thought you'd have known."

"I'm so sorry. I had no idea," Eric replied, gasping at this sudden and unexpected news.

"Thanks. I've really got to go now. I'm horribly late. I'll talk to you later." And with that, she picked up the pace and began to run away.

Eric stood there, absorbing the tingling pleasure created by Melissa's disclosure of their breakup. But his exhilaration was short-lived and gave way to anxiety concerning Mark's whereabouts. He wondered why Mark hadn't informed him of the breakup, which brought back questions as to why he had failed to contact Eric. Uncertainty begot fear, and as these thoughts churned in his mind, he began to feel extremely agitated. He had noticed that his generally happy disposition could degenerate into despondency when issues of love were involved. He dismissed it as perhaps humanity's curse—that we cannot hold contentment, that all thought eventually leads to discontent. Yet, if he had probed deeper, he may have concluded that perhaps the true affliction is not so much the propensity of thought toward negativity but that we are so identified with thought as to be oblivious to its pull. Drenched and dispirited, he made his way to the Campus Club.

The rain brought much cooler temperatures. The torrid furnace of heat and humidity had given way to the gentle caress of a cool breeze that caused people to throw open their windows and switch off their air-conditioners. But for Eric, these crisp, almost autumnal days of brilliant sunshine were as harrowing as the sleepless nights, when he lay awake wondering what had become of Mark and of their relationship. Far from assuaging his concerns, the chance encounter with Melissa had raised more doubts in his mind. Obviously, nothing dire had happened to Mark, or Melissa would have mentioned something. Mark's behavior was mystifying. Why would he break up with Melissa but not call or contact him? Could Mark have met another guy? It's possible, and that would be a plausible explanation. At times his mind would flare up in jealousy at the thought of Mark with another man, and yet he couldn't quite conceive of Mark falling for someone else right now. How could he after their passionate confessions of love as recently as a month ago? The jealous thoughts inflicted wounds on his pride. Who would be better than me for him, Eric thought? Who would be more handsome or intelligent, more sociable and entertaining than he? He mentally competed against this mystery man and would win each contest easily and decisively. And yet envy waxed and waned and his doubts and fears returned, like receding waves that surge back at high tide.

Some days later, Mark finally called him. His grandfather had passed away, and he had left for the funeral and was just returning. He came over to Eric's right away, and as soon as he walked inside, they fell into each other's arms and made love, deeply and passionately. Eric's distress dissipated like the heat after the recent rainstorms. Afterward, as they lay in each other's arms, Eric recalled his jealousy and now considered it such folly and wondered why he had ever suspected Mark of infidelity. But his suffering had been too brief to give rise to self-examination. Like a patient recovering from a serious illness who seldom thinks about a relapse, he rejoiced in Mark's embrace. Now everything made sense; Mark had broken up with Melissa but hadn't called because he had to attend his grandfather's funeral and was grieving his loss. He told Mark he had run into Melissa who had informed him of their breakup.

"Yeah, she broke up with me; she met someone else over the summer."

"Oh, I thought you broke up with her."

"Nope."

"How do you feel about it?" Eric asked tentatively.

"I dunno. It's okay, I guess. We'd drifted apart anyway," he answered uncertainly.

While Mark decidedly did not love Melissa, he had become accustomed to her, or rather to the idea of having a girlfriend. Now that he found himself single, he was somewhat bewildered about it. Though he was unaware, at a conscious level at least, of the turmoil that the breakup had inflicted on his psyche, he felt an undercurrent of disquietude that he could neither fathom nor articulate.

Eric, however, felt a wave of disappointment. He had thought that Mark had left Melissa because of his love for Eric. Dazed by desire, he wasn't able to see that while Mark did, in his own way, love him, he was unable and perhaps never would be able to progress as far, or as fast, as Eric in their relationship.

"Aren't you relieved? I mean we're—" Eric stopped mid-sentence, sensing, despite himself that he may be treading into perilous territory. They had never broached the topic of their future liaison, and while Eric was keen, only in private to be sure, to invest in a dialogue with the semiosis of a romantic relationship, Mark remained aloof. "I mean, that just gives us more time together," he said and trailed off.

"I guess, but I don't want to talk about it," Mark responded gruffly, but then pulled Eric to him and started to kiss him. "I'm just happy to see you."

The melodrama having passed, Eric and Mark settled into the new term. They were now seniors, not only looked upon with awe by underclassmen but each in his own way had gained the respect of his peers—Mark due to his athletic prowess and Eric to his scholarship. Like their classmates, they also had a sense that there was a world beyond Princeton. They soon would be moving on from the insular and microcosmic preoccupations of campus life. Mark already had begun to apply for jobs with investment banks and, thanks to his family's connections at Banker's Trust, he almost had a foot in the door. Eric was considering pursuing a graduate program in comparative literature, as well as preparing for the LSATs, the entrance examinations for law schools in the States. They had the confidence of successful upperclassmen and the glowing innocence and enthusiasm of youth, uncurbed by the adversities or sorrows of worldly experience. Mark now spent three and sometimes four or five nights a week at Eric's. He was in a double this year, but his roommate had been absent due to a serious injury at hockey practice. Glowing with the boundless enthusiasm of youth, they cut a handsome figure together and in another, more liberal, time, would perhaps have made a lovely couple.

Life had also resumed as usual at the Campus Club, where the members came together at dinner to share stories about the past summer, discuss their new classes, professors, sports, and activities. Only Consuelo appeared out of sorts. While she smiled and was friendly enough, she seemed to go out of her way to avoid Eric. If he went to sit at her table for dinner, she would pretext her studies or a prior commitment and leave quickly. If he was sitting down, she never joined his table. When he tried to engage her in conversation in the sitting area, she responded politely enough to his questions but would excuse herself due to some engagement. While Eric did notice Consuelo's marked change toward him, he paid little attention to it, dismissing it in his mind as inconsequential, and to the extent he thought of her behavior, he considered her an ungrateful friend. After all, hadn't he invited her to dinner in Paris? His all-encompassing desire for Mark had inured him to disagreeable people and situations, like an anesthetic that numbs the body to pain. If he had been more alert, he may have discerned in her manner a certain resentment, a seething rancor that was biding its time before striking, and perhaps he might have attended to it more assiduously. Upon reflection Eric might have even realized that his parent's lavish household and his mother's aristocratic demeanor had weighed on her social insecurities, emphasizing her insignificance in the little studio apartment, or at least that she had felt belittled by his overbearing stepfather's pronouncements. Despite her misgivings, she had called and left several messages for him, out of loneliness, and he had failed to return any of her calls and had not bothered to see her again in Paris. Of course, he had spent the next several weeks with Mark, but after Mark had left, he could have made an effort. As it was now, Eric drifted away from her to the point where their interactions became limited to polite greetings.

Meanwhile, Eric had left a few phone messages for Mattie but hadn't heard back from her for several weeks. They were no longer in the same class, and since she no longer needed his assistance, it appeared she no longer desired his company. As with Consuelo, Eric bore this disappointment, which ordinarily would have caused him great consternation, with equanimity. Still, whether it was a trace of requital, or more likely an insurance against future needs, she eventually had called and invited him to lunch.

21

MATTIE HAD INVITED ERIC to lunch at Cap and Gown, the only co-educational eating Club whose membership was selective, and as with its all-male counterparts, it relied on a selection process known as "bicker"—which combined the brutality and vulgarity of the traditional fraternity hazing with a veneer of country club gentility. Though mixed in terms of gender, the Club's membership was strangely homogenous, resembling the golden-haired, milky-tooth boys and girls in nineteenth-century fairytales. And, while they had a reputation for heritage and breeding, they rather appeared as grownup Hansels and Gretels who had just jumped out of the pages of a Ralph Lauren or Laura Ashley catalogue.

Mattie had just arrived from a ballet rehearsal in New York City and met Eric in the lobby of the Club, wearing a pearl necklace.

"What a beautiful necklace!" Eric exclaimed.

"Oh, this little thing. A gift from a ballet admirer."

"An 'admirer?'" Eric inquired with raised eyebrows.

"Yes, and as close as he's going to get to me," replied Mattie with a carefree chuckle while she took Eric's arm and led him into the dining room.

As they entered, Eric's eyes scanned the room and discovered Ali and Khaled at one of the tables. Then he noticed Mark sitting at a separate table with other Hansel and Gretelesque types whom he didn't know. Why would Mark be here? he asked himself. He then recognized Melissa at his table, and the sight of the two of them together in this setting alarmed Eric. He was overcome by confusion and became self-conscious, instinctively sensing peril, yet he was at a loss as to how to comply.

"Let's go and say hello to Ali and Khaled," Mattie said, as she nudged him in their direction. He followed her mechanically, his mind frozen by this unexpected encounter. The two Princes stood up, kissed Mattie on both cheeks, shook hands with Eric, and invited the pair to join them for lunch.

Eric had carefully calibrated the movement of his head as he greeted Ali with a shallow bow that to others, unfamiliar with the formal gestures of the royal court, would most likely have appeared as a nod of the head. He noticed people staring at them and then quickly averting their eyes.

"What a pleasant surprise to see you here," he said, as he tried to smile, looking first at Ali and then Khaled. He regained his presence of mind and said, "I couldn't imagine any place I'd rather be than with the three of you here now," the timbre of his voice resonating just enough to be overheard but not to sound vulgarly loud. They all sat down and engaged in a light social banter. Eric, who was again keenly aware of the attention focused on them, was taken aback when Melissa unexpectedly strutted over and greeted Mattie. Mattie was visibly irritated but checked herself quickly. The girl pulled over a chair to sit next to her idol without asking. Mattie looked to Eric to intervene, but he was flummoxed by Melissa's seemingly aggressive and inappropriate intimacy.

After Eric introduced Melissa to the Princes, she held up a slim newspaper for all to see. "Have any of you seen the letter to the editor in the *Daily Princetonian?*" she asked, looking around the table. The *Daily Princetonian* was a local campus paper edited and put out by Princeton students.

"No, which letter?" Mattie asked, as unaware and perplexed as the others.

"Here, I'll read it to you," she announced flatly. Before anyone at the table could object, Melissa began to read out loud from the paper. The room went so silent you could hear a pin drop.

Dear Dean of Admissions,

We know that admission at Princeton is a black box, but we couldn't resist asking you to explain two particular choices that appear to fly in the face of everything this institution stands for. The first is the second son of the recently deposed tyrannical monarch of Iran, who not only brutally repressed his country for decades while his wife took baths in milk and he had his lunches flown in from Paris but was the very real cause of our own citizens being taken hostage. And while these innocent Americans languished in the prisons he had built to torture his countrymen, he checked into a top-notch hospital in New York for cancer treatment. And his son— now one of us Tigers, thanks to your admissions department—attended some of our best prep schools.

This so-called Prince is attended to by another one of your questionable admissions choices, who has taken sycophancy to a whole new level, fawning over his master whom he has known since childhood when doubtlessly they started their questionable "liaison." Yes, between his disingenuous smiles, we have, every once in a while, glimpsed a forlorn, rueful look appear on his face when licking the boot of his master. We suspect this gives away the Wildean nature of the relationship, or shall we say Proustian since our Iago is none other than a posing Proustian scholar, no doubt writing his thesis on the Sodom and Gomorrah chapter of Proust's masterpiece.

Mattie glared at Melissa. "Stop this immediately, Melissa. I demand it."

Melissa merely smirked. She was enjoying the spotlight. Holding her back now would be like trying to stop water from spilling from an overflowing dam. "Oh no, it gets much better," she said with relish.

Mattie stood up, threw her napkin on the table and stormed away, a gesture that could have encouraged the others to do likewise, but they were frozen in place as much by the outlandish incivility of these accusations as by its spiteful recitation.

Melissa continued to read:

> Don't blush, Dean, you guessed right. This
> relationship is far more sinister than the Bobbsey
> twins ever imagined. As I said, this odd couple appears
> to have known each other since the days when the
> Prince's father terrorized his people and Iago's parents
> did his bidding, and afterward absconded with some
> of the country's wealth. While the Prince parades
> around campus, tailed by a private security guard,
> paid, no doubt, by the money his father took from
> his country on his way out, we suspect the decision
> to apply to Princeton was a joint one so they could
> enjoy each other for four "bootylicious" years. We
> know that Princeton prides itself on the diversity of
> its student body, and we applaud your valiant efforts
> in this regard, but really, these two? Why the hell did
> you let them in, we'd like to know.

Melissa set the paper down. While a few gasps went up from
those in the room during the reading, a marked silence persisted afterward. Without a word Ali and Khaled rose and left
the Club. Eric, who had surreptitiously glanced over at Mark,
saw that he deliberately avoided looking in his direction. An
expression as cold as stone was fixed on Mark's face, like on the
Roman busts from antiquity. It frightened Eric. He hadn't had
time to process the full import of the letter, though he intuited
that its effect would be devastating in many ways. While he
was aware of the salacious accusations of impropriety, his main
concern was Mark's reaction to these lies.

Alone now with Melissa, he turned to her. "Who wrote this
drivel? You?"

She shook her head. "Not me, and it's unsigned," she smirked. Eric noted that she appeared to be enjoying his discomfort. But before he could inquire further, or rebuke her for this monumental lapse in etiquette, Melissa rose from her chair and went back to her table. This whole time Eric was having an internal dialogue with Mark; he was already explaining why none of this mattered; besides the fact that it was all made up and libelous, what difference did it all make? They'll be graduating in six months and leaving all this behind them, Princeton and all its petty, prattling people. But Mark's implacable expression flashed through his mind, annihilating, in one fell swoop, all his contrary arguments. Eric needed time to think; he had to get away.

He stood up and walked out. In the sitting room, Mattie was waiting for him.

"Eric, I'm so sorry. This is outrageous. I will never have anything to do with Melissa again. And you should sue the University, or at least the newspaper."

"I'd rather it just go away, but I have to see if Ali is okay. Would you please excuse me?" he stammered.

"Sure, there was just something I wanted to talk to you about. A project that might interest you," Mattie said, leaning into him.

"Sure. May I call you about it?" Eric asked hurriedly.

"Of course," she said, "but sooner rather than later if you don't mind. There's a deadline." Eric nodded his head. "It's right up your alley, too."

"I'll call you later today," he said absently while kissing her on the cheek, and then he left. Outside he watched Ali's limousine drive off.

Eric walked briskly to his apartment. A bitter wind churned the fallen autumn leaves, lifting and spreading them in upward circular motions. He pulled his coat collar up around his neck but was too preoccupied to feel the chill or notice the storm clouds that were rapidly gathering in a curious formation, as if the sky were frowning on him. His thoughts continued to swirl around Mark and his reaction. He wondered where he could find him right now. He had tried to catch his eye at the Club, but Mark had stubbornly refused to look in his direction. It was understandable. He was angry, confused, worried what people might think, given that Eric now was branded as a homosexual. But Mark would listen to Eric as he would explain to him how none of this mattered. He must recall their late-night conversation with Jerry and Kyle at the beach last May, and how neither of them cared about people's opinions of them once they left school. It would soon all be over, one more semester, and they could make a wonderful new life together away from this horrid place. As these thoughts churned in his mind, Eric arrived home. The message light on his machine was lit. He pressed it and sank down on the sofa as he heard Mark's voice.

"Hey there, Eric. Um … I think we should take a break from seeing each other. I mean, um … I don't know, man; it's just becoming too complicated. I know you understand. I'm, um, I'm sorry. Please try to understand. Don't call or contact me. Let's wait anyway until, until … well, anyway, I've got to go. I'll see ya."

The message was typical of Mark, too brief and vapid to be meaningful, yet sufficiently intelligible to inflict devastation on Eric. He played it several times with increasing incredulity. He must find Mark immediately and talk to him, he told himself. Eric disregarded the admonition not to contact him and dialed Mark's number, and to his great surprise, Mark answered the phone.

"Hi, it's me. Can we talk?"

"Didn't you get my message?" Mark asked gruffly.

"I did. But you can't leave it like that. I need to talk to you, please. The letter was rubbish."

"I can't really talk now." There was a long silence.

"Hello, are you there?" Eric asked.

"I'm here," Mark said faintly, his mouth away from the receiver. Eric could hear people talking in the background. A female voice. Was it Melissa?

"Is Melissa there? What were you doing at Cap anyway? With her?"

"Listen, man. I said I can't talk right now. I'm gonna hang up. I don't want to be rude, but I've got to go." And so Mark hung up and in effect ended their relationship.

Eric held onto to the receiver as the tone went flat and then started to beep. He set it down. A single tear gathered under his left eye and dropped down into his lap. All of a sudden he had an urge to leave his apartment, to escape this dreadful place, this Ivy League school where he felt persecuted and forlorn. He rose and walked to the Princeton train station where a small train called the "dinkey" would take him to Princeton Junction and from there to New York.

As he waited for the train, his mind drifted back to the *Princetonian* letter. Who could have written this venomous piece? It was transparently designed to inflict harm, but what would motivate someone to do this? he wondered. He pondered over the overt accusations of the Shah's corruption and wondered if the letter had been aimed at Ali. However, what about the insinuations of their homosexuality, which was a calumny far worse. The allegations about the Shah had been repeated in the media so often that they were more tiresome than scandalous. But the charge of homosexuality was personal and vindictive, and in a perverse twist of fate, Eric thought, it was true, though of course not how the letter had presented it. Whomever the slanderer, they had fathomed Eric's sexuality. "It was aimed at me, not Ali," he finally said to himself. But who would want to hurt me this badly? The first name that came to mind was Melissa's. Why had she been so keen to read out the letter? Had she caught on to him and Mark? Unlikely, as she had obviously invited Mark to lunch. She had denied penning the letter and Eric somehow believed her. Besides, she didn't have the cunning to write the piece. But who would? Who indeed.

As he considered his friends and acquaintances, suddenly the name Consuelo flashed before his eyes with the fulgurance of lightning. It was her. Yet, why would she libel him? How would she know about his homosexuality and why would she care? She didn't like Mark and didn't even know Ali. He now recalled her visit to his parents' flat in Paris and remembered their imperious behavior toward her. At the time he had paid it no mind, consumed as he had been with Mark. But now, he considered the events in a different light and realized how devastating it must have been for her, and especially his own careless and dismissive conduct. But even assuming she was the author, how could she have known that he was gay? She was a shrewd, intelligent girl and must have surmised it based on some conduct of his; perhaps he had been careless and let something slip. Even so, why would she think he was having an affair with Ali? He realized that he had been so distracted of late with Mark that he had paid little, if any attention, to anything or anybody else, and as a result, he had no answers. But while he was convinced that it was Consuelo, why she would implicate Ali remained a mystery.

22

I T WAS A LUGUBRIOUS JOURNEY; the other two passengers in Eric's compartment were silent, ashen figures. Rain rattled against the windows as the train swept across the dark and barren landscape. The conductor—tall, lanky, with dark beady eyes and dressed in clothes that appeared one size too large for him—reminded Eric of an undertaker. When Eric paid the fare, he intoned ominously, "Last train back is 11:00 P.M." Eric kept himself from crying in public by thinking about who had written this salacious letter.

By the time he arrived in New York City, it was already getting dark, every alley filled with lurking shadows and with the frigid rain beating him down even further. He took a cab to Christopher Street and wandered about cheerlessly. People darted in and out of cafes, shops, restaurants, escaping the cold, the wind, and the rain. He felt forlorn, alone in the midst of an anonymous, uncaring crowd and world. His thoughts spiraled like a whirlpool of black water. What's the point of all this? He thought of Kafka's Joseph K. He dies an ignominious death, no wiser for all his anguish and confusion. For the first time, he thought of his own mortality. That would be a way out, to end the suffering. How would I do it? The thought of cutting his wrists frightened him—he was squeamish and hated blood. There's got to be a better way. Pills? That's it. But which ones and how many? A young man, a bit older than him, stepped out of a pharmacy and smiled at Eric, like an angel parsing black clouds in a medieval painting.

Eric now found himself in Sheridan Square, facing The Monster, the notorious gay bar he had heard about. Did he really want to go inside? He plunged forward. It was already busy, and loud disco music dwarfed the hubbub of conversations from the men packed around the bar. This was even more outrageously gay than the bar in Rehoboth Beach. Eric made his way to the bar and ordered a beer, stood there, and almost gulped it down. He ordered another and another. The music seeped into him creating even more of a buzz. It was the heady days of *Frankie Goes to Hollywood* and *Dead or Alive*, but also Gloria Gaynor belting out her hit song, *I Will Survive*, along with the Weather Girls and Divine. As he began to sway to the music, he heard someone say: "Here's another beer for you. Your bottle was empty."

Eric looked over. Next to him was a guy about his own height, with dark hair and crystal blue eyes, and a very square jaw. Clean shaven, wearing a collared shirt and jeans, very preppy, clean-cut, and athletic-looking. He had a deep, resonating voice. Something about him reminded Eric of Mark, though they looked nothing alike. Perhaps it was a cross between frat-boy and casual suburban urbanity. He held out the bottle; Eric took it. They had to shout over the loud music. His name was Jim. He was twenty-eight-years-old, lived in the city, was married, and had a five-year-old daughter. He wasn't out to his wife or to anyone for that matter. Eric told him he was a student from Princeton, needed a break from the college grind, and had come to the city for the day.

"So you just happened to find your way here?" Jim asked with a smirk.

Eric smiled. "I wanted to get ... 'out' of the rain."

After another beer or two, they decided to go downstairs and dance. Somewhat shell-shocked by the day's events and still reeling from thoughts of suicide, dancing with a handsome stranger who kept on buying him beers seemed more life-affirming. After a while, Jim asked Eric if he wanted to go somewhere else.

Eric pulled back and stared at him. Did he really want to have sex with this man? Would this be another Campbell mistake he'd regret?

"Where?" Eric asked.

"How about your place?" Jim said.

"I live in Princeton, remember! Too far away."

"Ah, gotcha, that's a bummer." He paused, thinking about options. "I know a place we can go."

"Where?"

"A bathhouse."

"A bathhouse," Eric said, "but aren't they ... unsafe?"

"Depends on your partner," Jim said encouragingly, "and you can trust me."

Eric hesitated. He knew that AIDS was spreading through-out the gay community of New York.

Did he really want to risk it? Eric looked at Jim; he was so attractive, so sexy, and he now pulled Eric over and kissed him deeply on the mouth and said again, "Trust me." Eric relented.

"Okay, where is it? How far is it?"

"Oh, it's close. Just a short cab ride away."

It was still raining when they left The Monster but they managed to hail a cab. The bathhouse was on Eighth Avenue. They entered a small, shabby lobby, where a tattooed attendant guarded the entrance like a gorgon from behind a windowed opening. There were a few men before them, but they presently reached the front of the line. They had to pay and Eric handed Jim thirty dollars.

"Let me have your wallet," the attendant demanded.

"Why?" asked Eric, concerned.

Jim reassured him. "They just keep your valuables in a safe behind the desk. They also need something as a guarantee."

"I'd rather not," Eric stammered.

At that moment, time seemed to stop. He looked at the burly attendant, Jim, and other haunted gays standing in the desolate lobby, as if he were a long distance away. Was this what he was reduced to? The comfort of strangers? A voice deep down in him whispered that he should leave, that this is a dark and dangerous place. But it was a faint whisper that died down quickly when Jim moved up behind Eric, held him in his arms and rubbed his pelvis against him.

There were people waiting behind them and the attendant was impatient and surly.

"Come on, I don't have all night. Either stay or go," he barked at them.

"Okay, okay, here I'll leave this," Jim said and unbuckled a gold chain from around his neck and handed it to the attendant. The man looked at it in the light, then pressed a buzzer opening a door that led to a hallway. Here another attendant was waiting with two towels and a room key. They followed him through a dark maze of corridors where men walked around in nothing but towels, eyeing each other brazenly and lasciviously. The piped-in music sounded similar to the music in The Monster and played loudly throughout the establishment.

"Where are we going?" Eric asked, nervously.

"A private room," Jim said. "We can take a sauna afterward if you like."

They entered a small room, just a little larger than a walk-in closet, in which the only item of furniture was a small bed. The lights were very dim, but Eric could see that the sheets were clean. Jim tipped the attendant, who left them with the key and the towels.

Jim began to make out with Eric, stripping off his clothes slowly while whispering in his ear how sexy and beautiful he was. Eric became very excited. He thought of Mark and his own sweet-talk patter. Their clothes came off rapidly, and they began to kiss and rub against each other passionately. Eric wondered what came next. Jim said he needed to use the bathroom. He wrapped the towel around him and left the room. He was gone for a long time and Eric became concerned. What could he be doing? He couldn't have left; his clothes were still hanging in the room. He opened the door and a multitude of men streamed by the room, one after another stopping to eye him up and down as if examining merchandise. One or two attempted to come inside, but Eric shut and locked the door. Eventually, Jim returned, removed the towel, and began caressing him again. This time he asked to penetrate Eric, who hesitated.

"I don't know. It's painful. And do you have rubbers?"

"I'll do it nice and gentle, and who needs them. I want to come inside of you."

The drinks, the music, the touch of this sexy man was all too much to resist. Eric ceded and let Jim penetrate him. It didn't take long before they both climaxed again, and then they did it again and yet again, and the next time Eric penetrated Jim. Finally, exhausted, they lay there, on the small bed, holding each other and fell off to sleep.

It was almost 5:00 in the morning when they left the bathhouse. Eric asked for Jim's number but he refused, stating that he was married and needed to be discreet. Instead, he asked for Eric's number and promised to ring him.

Eric made his way to Penn Station and took the first train back to Princeton. He passed in and out of sleep on the short train trip. By the time he arrived home, he was shattered and felt unwell, hungover, and exhausted, and somehow anxious and uneasy about this venture. There were no messages for him, and he decided to go to bed and see if he could get some rest.

He fell into a shallow, restive, sleep and had a long dream:

It had been an unusually long and dark winter. In February and March it snowed on six Tuesdays in a row. April greeted him with a gray and dreary sky virtually every day. It was as if the sun had forsaken the world and him. The rain continued unabated into May cancelling all the barbeques on Memorial Day. And then all of a sudden, one day in June, as if by magic, the sun came out and shone brightly. He was walking on the beach early that morning. There was no one else there. There was a gentle breeze, and the sand had never felt so good beneath his feet. The light was strangely translucent and prismatic bestowing a diaphanous, almost chimerical quality on the world; it was as if God himself was smiling that morning. And then he saw him—the beautiful stranger. Slightly taller than he, the man had ash-brown hair that had turned golden in summer, hazel-green eyes set against a broad brow and with a firm chin. His body was toned but not overly muscular; he was lightly tanned and had some hair on his chest with a treasure trail down to his navel. His masculine beauty was as natural as the spots on a leopard's skin.

As he approached him, the stranger said in a rich baritone, "Isn't it a beautiful morning?" A breathtaking smile broke across his face to reveal perfectly white, milky teeth.

"Yes, it's truly marvelous," he responded, transfixed by his encounter with this extraordinary stranger on this entrancing day.

"Give me your hand, you handsome man, and follow me into the ocean," he said, laughing boyishly, as he exuded an energy and charm Eric had rarely encountered. Eric did so without hesitation. They swam away together like two swans. He had never swum so effortlessly. Their first twin strokes were intoxicating. He looked under the surface and glimpsed a school of multicolored fish; it was if they were smiling at them, speaking to them in their own way and encouraging them in their swim. He felt at one with this unknown sub-aquatic world.

After some time—who knows how long, for time itself had become elastic—the stranger let go of his hand so he could swim alone. In the same instant, Eric fell into despair. The golden aura that had surrounded him turned ominous and dark. He felt alone, afraid, and lonely.

"Clasp my hand again, handsome stranger," Eric cried but had no voice. "Don't you see that I will drown on my own?"

They were only a few feet apart, but the stranger appeared oblivious to his despair, unmoved by the shrieks that he dared not utter.

And then, as if hearing his silent entreaty, the man said, "Ah, what a day; here, give me your hand and let's dive down together and look at this coral."

He took Eric's hand and his world became a kaleidoscope of wonder. The coral was redder than the reddest rose he had ever seen; a stingray glided by gracefully and would have been invisible against the ocean floor were it not for the gentle flapping of its tail.

And then he felt it against his cheek, a gentle delectable, sweeter-than-honey kiss. Yes, the stranger kissed him, and he was magically transported into an even more enchanted world where he was invincible. He became Poseidon conducting the marine orchestra with his trident, banishing the winds—Euros and Zephyr, back to Aeolus, with a reminder that it was to him and not their master that fate had bestowed the Kingdom of the Sea—"sed mihi sorte datum!" "but Fate gave to me."

As these intoxicating thoughts filled his mind, they rose back up to the surface.

"Who are you, beguiling stranger?" he asked.

The man didn't respond; instead, he pulled Eric toward him, and, as he drank from the stranger's deep-set eyes, he kissed him on the lips and enveloped him in a tight grip between his arms and his powerful legs.

At that moment, Eric felt he had died and was reborn in a different world. He knew now what ambrosia tasted like. He was Sampson before his locks were cut off. He was Dido before Aeneas' departure. They stayed in that embrace as time evaporated and he glimpsed the eternal and the infinite.

But then he felt the stranger's grip loosen and again he was off swimming by himself. This time, while perturbed, he didn't panic. He knew that the stranger would again hold him, take him back to Eden with him, and all would be fine.

But he didn't, and Eric saw the distance that separated them grow farther. He tried to swim in his direction, but as in dreams, his strokes took him nowhere and the stranger appeared to be floating away on an ocean current that was gathering ever increasing speed.

"Why are you abandoning me?" he cried out, this time his voice loud and clear, but it was lost against the rising wind on the horizon.

The stranger was now gone, as were Eric's trident and kaleidoscope of ocean wonders. All that was left was space—empty, open, untenanted space, with no land in sight. Suddenly, Eric became aware of the dangers that surrounded him. He didn't know in which direction to swim. How shall he find his way back? The coral no longer was a magical vermillion, but ragged and poisonous; the stingray now appeared to be flapping toward him with ill intent; the sun itself hid behind a dark passing cloud, casting deep shadows on the ocean.

Eric felt as if he would drown here since there was no one to pull him out; no one knew where he was—no one except the stranger who had abandoned him. He felt forlorn, helpless, and unable to escape his perilous predicament. He felt as if he were floating between life and death. He stopped swimming and dunked his head beneath ocean's surface, swallowing some sea water, the salt burning his throat, his eyes, and nose. Then, just as he was about to sink into oblivion, a thought, like a fulgurant flash, ran through his mind:

"I don't want to die. I want to live."

"Why?" responded an echo, like a siren's song from nowhere. "The stranger is gone. It isn't worth it, is it?"

But it was enough—that instinct for survival, for life, an instinct more powerful than life itself, which pulled him out of the torpor that had seized his body, and he began to swim. He swam and swam, but there was nothing in sight other than the vastness of the empty ocean. His arms and legs started to feel numb and he felt the sting of a fish—maybe an electric eel—on his right calf. He persisted and continued to swim, to stay alive at all cost. He couldn't help thinking about the stranger. At times, he wondered if he had gone to get help and that he would come back to save him. The thought of him holding him, kissing him, gave Eric a sense of comfort and hope, but in the next instant that crumbled like a house of cards when there was no sign of him returning.

In the distance, he thought he saw a boat. Desperately, he now swam toward it, screaming for help. It turned out to be a mirage. He continued on, and by some miracle he thought he glimpsed land. Cautiously, he swam toward it; he was right, as he swam closer, the shore came into focus. It was far away but at least within sight. At this point, his whole body was numb from the cold water. Now, he didn't even feel the eel's stings. He oscillated between hope that the stranger would return and save him, and despair that he would drown, his body and mind overpowered by pain and numbness. As he swam closer to shore, he saw a group of swimmers. He cried out to them, "Please, help me; I'm drowning." It turned out they only spoke Spanish and didn't understand him. He was surprised that they couldn't spot the signs of distress from his anxious expression. It took all his remaining energy to remember a few Spanish words: "Donde la playa?" he screamed.

They pointed in the direction of the shore and continued on their way, leaving him in his distress and solitude.

Now, he spotted some other swimmers and called out for assistance. To his astonishment, no one offered their help and simply pointed toward the shore. He even came across a lifeguard swimming out and pleaded for help. The man said that he was out to help those in serious danger of drowning. He claimed that Eric appeared to be a healthy swimmer, but if he was a bit tired, he should find a vigorous swimmer and ask him to take his hand and lead him ashore. Eric took his expert advice and cast about looking for a good swimmer. The image of his handsome stranger clouded his vision, and he wasn't able to truly distinguish the good swimmers from the average or weak ones. Still, he approached several men and asked them to take his hand. They refused, perhaps recognizing his desperation and distress and fearing that it would drag them underwater.

Eventually, a handsome man, who was a vigorous swimmer, held out his hand. For a little while they swam together, and Eric regained some hope of surviving, but then the swimmer began to drag him underwater.

"What are you doing? You're going to drown me," he cried out, but the swimmer continued to pull him under. Eric heard the flapping rotors of a helicopter overhead and tried desperately to wave in the hope of catching their attention. He struggled but felt that the swimmer was stronger and was overpowering him, pulling him underwater, drowning him.

The ringing of the telephone woke him up, and he gasped for breath. After a moment he realized that he was in his bed and could breathe quite comfortably, though he had a banging headache and felt nauseated. He let the caller's message go to the answering machine and lay on his back, pondering the events of the previous evening. He now regretted having sex with Jim; he felt it was a betrayal of Mark. But then Mark had broken up with him and told him not to call him. Surely he didn't mean it. It was all due to that venomous letter to the editor. Why would Consuelo write such a thing? Who would even believe it? Insinuating that he and Ali were lovers. Preposterous, laughable. Why was Mark at Cap anyway, and with Melissa? They'd broken up before the beginning of the term. Mark had told him that he loved him. He wouldn't break up over such a silly accusation. Yet, that's what he had implied. Could he have gone back to Melissa? Impossible. She broke up with him; she was seeing someone else, and anyway, he didn't love her. But then why that insipid call? And who was in the room with him? Melissa? Eric felt sick, jumped up and ran to the bathroom and vomited, then came back to bed. Who had called him, he now wondered.

23

ERIC SPENT THE ENTIRE DAY in bed, drifting in and out of sleep. When he finally arose, it was early evening. He distractedly listened to the phone message. It was his mother. She sounded upset, worried. She mentioned that she had received a call from Princess Ashraf about something that had happened at Princeton and wanted him to call her right away. He groaned. This inquiry was the last thing he wanted to deal with, but it was already midnight in Paris and if he was going to call her, he had better not delay. He picked up the receiver and dialed her number. After a few rings, she answered. He had obviously awakened her, but she appeared anxious to speak with him. His mother confirmed that Princess Ashraf had called about a defamatory letter that had been published in the college's newspaper. She said that Ali would not be coming back the next term and that the royal family was getting legal advice as to whether or not they should sue the University for defamation. The Princess wanted to see Eric in New York as soon as possible.

"Why me? I had nothing to do with it."

"Why don't you first tell me what happened?" she asked.

"Someone wrote a ridiculous letter to the editor in the *Daily Princetonian*. That's all."

"What exactly did it say?"

"Nothing really. I mean, it made some distasteful insinuations about the Shah's rule, and how he was responsible for the American Embassy being sacked."

"What else. There must be more?"

Eric didn't want to tell his mother about the insinuations of sexual impropriety between him and Ali.

"I don't remember much. I'll try to get a copy and send it to you."

"There isn't time for all that. You must call the Princess at once and go to New York to see her."

"But I can't," he protested. "I've got so much work to do. It's the end of term and I'm coming back to Paris next week."

"Eric, darling, it's vital that you call her. This is a very serious matter. They have insulted our Royal Family and our own family, as she tells me. You must, must go to the Princess at once."

"Okay, mother. I'll take the train tomorrow," he replied, resigned, knowing that resistance would be futile at this point.

He called the Princess's house in New York and spoke to one

of her ladies-in-waiting, whom he didn't know. She was very nice on the phone and mentioned that they had been expecting his call. Would he be kind enough to come for lunch the next day at 2:00 P.M.? She mentioned that Prince Ali would be there too. He accepted the invitation reluctantly, knowing that he didn't have a choice in the matter.

Princess Ashraf lived on Park Avenue in the Sixties. The marble lobby of her building was attended by three liveried doormen in white gloves. One of them opened the heavy, bronze door and another escorted Eric up the ornate lift that opened into the royal residence. A valet in a tuxedo was waiting in the entrance gallery, where a grand, circular staircase, which would have been more common in a European palace, led up to a vast sitting room. The design was almost entirely French restoration and Empire, with silk and velvet upholstery and gueridons inlaid with marquetry and pedestals made of nacre. A portrait of the Princess, by Andy Warhol, hung above an exquisitely carved marble fireplace in which a welcoming fire was burning. Princess Ashraf, in a Valentino crepe de chine dress and wearing a signature Van Cleef & Arpel necklace made of white gold and diamonds, was enthroned on a large rosewood sofa inlaid with ivory and nacre, full of embroidered cushions in silk and brocade. She was accompanied by two ladies-in-waiting, two gentlemen in suits and Ali, in a white-collared shirt, jeans and a blazer. When Eric walked in, everyone except the Princess rose. He went over to the Princess and bowed down to her.

Eric said, "Taazim, ghorban," which in Farsi means, "I bow down to you, Highness."

She kissed him on both cheeks, and after he had greeted everyone else, including Ali, who also gave him a kiss on both cheeks, she asked him to sit next to her on the large sofa.

"I hear from your mother that you play bridge?"

"A little, Your Highness."

"How nice. We'll play after lunch then."

This exchange took place in Farsi. The two gentlemen in suits, who were American, apparently didn't understand but kept on smiling and nodding their heads anyway.

Presently, a butler appeared to announce that lunch was being served. The dining room, wallpapered in silk damask, had an inlaid mahogany table that would comfortably seat eighteen people and was surrounded by Chippendale chairs, whose silk coverings matched the wallpaper. The plates, made of porcelain de Limoges and patterned in tasteful floral patterns with gilt edges, bore the imperial insignia: a golden crown and the letters A.P., which also appeared on the hallmarked silver cutlery. The wine glasses and water goblets were made of Baccarat crystal, as was the ornate chandelier that hung above the table. The Princess sat at the head of the table, Ali to her right. The chef had prepared a classic Persian dish—a pomegranate stew served over white rice—full of spices whose rich scent permeated the room and reminded Eric of home, though he hadn't much of an appetite, despite having not eaten in two days.

He learned that the gentlemen in suits were partners in a major white-shoe New York law firm. One of them—the older of the two, who appeared to be in his sixties and seemed to know the Princess well—questioned Eric about the letter.

"Do you know who wrote this letter to the editor?"

"I don't. I ... I was as taken aback by it as the Prince and wondered who would write such a thing," Eric lied, for by now he was almost certain that it had been Consuelo.

"Precisely. But we thought you might have an idea. Maybe someone with a personal vendetta against you?"

"Me. My reference in it was only secondary."

Ali, who had remained silent, added, "Which coward would write such calumnies? We must find out and punish them."

"What will you do?" asked Eric of the lawyer who had addressed him.

"Well, we are exploring a number of avenues. However, before we do anything, we must make sure that we understand all the facts."

"Which facts?" asked Eric. "His Majesty was a public figure, and I guess you can say what you will about him, but the rest is pure fantasy. There is nothing to support the insinuations about the Royal Prince." Eric bowed his head at Ali who nodded back.

"That's exactly right, Eric, but you see if you threaten or do bring a defamation case, you need to be fully prepared—mole-hills can become mountains in such a case."

Eric nodded his head.

"That's why we need to speak with you privately."

"Privately? Why?" Eric asked.

"Because you are a potential witness and because of privilege issues."

"Witness to what? I don't know anything about who wrote this letter or why. What are privilege issues?"

"Attorney-client privilege. You are a potential witness and a claimant."

"Why don't you talk about this after lunch," the Princess interrupted, finding this legal exchange decidedly tiresome. She turned to Eric. "I just want to punish the people who libeled us, and these gentlemen are here to help us do that."

The rest of lunch was spent in discussion of the movie *Top Gun* and its newly minted star, Tom Cruise, how hand-some he was, "a real man." Soon the Princess and the ladies-in-waiting were going through the list of all the Hollywood male stars, dead or alive, arguing about who was the most handsome: Tyrone Power? Cary Grant? No, the most handsome of all was Paul Newman. "Bah, he was nothing compared to Rock Hudson," one of the ladies proffered.

"Isn't Rock Hudson the one who died of AIDS?" asked the Princess.

"Yes, Your Highness," the woman responded.

"It's strange. I would never have thought he swung the other way," she said in Farsi.

"It was a shock to the whole world, Your Highness," another woman added.

Eric went pale and a shiver ran down his back. He felt that all eyes were on him, especially the old lawyer's, who was staring at him strangely as if he were accusing him of the same. But then the Princess continued:

"I remember him so well with Elizabeth Taylor in the movie *Giant*. You know she came to Tehran."

"Elizabeth Taylor came to Tehran?" Eric asked, relieved to get off the topic of Rock Hudson's homosexuality.

"Yes, she did. To my palace. Many of the stars did."

"Oh, I remember well the evening she came to dinner," said one of the ladies-in-waiting. "You should have seen the Princess that night, dressed in these incredible, elaborate burgundy trousers that flared at the bottom, when she took the first step down the staircase, the whole room went silent."

"Really? I seem to recall something about those trousers," the Princess said nonchalantly.

After lunch Ali excused himself. Eric realized that they hadn't spoken at all; there had, in fact, not been any opportunity for them to speak. When he asked Ali if he would be in Paris over the Christmas holidays, he replied that he wasn't sure what his plans were and took his leave. Eric had the impression that Ali didn't want to meet up with him.

The Princess had retired to her sitting room for a few minutes before bridge. The two lawyers asked Eric if he wouldn't mind speaking with them in a private room. They went downstairs, back into the entrance gallery, and into a smaller sitting room.

"We won't take up much of your time Eric," the older lawyer said. "We just want to know if there is anything to these allegations, these statements in the letter."

"What do you mean? I don't understand. I already told you that it is a pure fabrication."

"Yes, but you see, from a legal perspective, we need to be able to prove that the allegations are false. So we need to look at each of the statements and make sure that there is not even the semblance of truth to them."

"Well, I don't recall the whole thing, but it was pure fiction, I assure you."

"Here's a copy. Why don't you read through it and refresh your memory."

Eric took the paper from him and quickly scanned the letter.

"Well," he said. "They're regurgitating the same lies that the Revolutionaries spread about the Shah. And some of the press. There is nothing new here."

"Yes, we know that. However, there's more to this letter than that. Surely you can see that," continued the older lawyer.

Eric wondered for a minute why the other lawyer wasn't saying anything. Not familiar with law firms, he didn't realize that their code of conduct was every bit as hierarchical and Byzantine as the Peacock Throne.

"I ... I don't know what you mean," Eric said haltingly.

"Okay, let me spell it out for you. They are implying that there is a homosexual relationship between you and the Prince. Do you realize how devastating that is for the Prince?"

"But it's not true," Eric protested.

"Of course it's not true. But, that's not the point," he insisted.

"Well, if that's not the point, then what do you want to know from me?" Eric asked a bit exasperated.

"Why don't you go ahead and explain it to him, Mitch," the old lawyer said to his younger colleague.

For the first time, Eric heard the man's voice.

"So the way the law works is that you can't defame someone who is dead. Therefore, although the allegations against the Shah are completely false, we can't do anything about them. However, the law prevents you from saying defamatory things about people who are alive, and if they do, you can bring a lawsuit in a court of law. So, we can bring a lawsuit on behalf of Prince Ali. And you, yourself, might be able to bring a lawsuit. Let me remind you we are not your lawyers and can't give you any legal advice. We represent the Prince and the Imperial Family."

"Okay," Eric said, nodding his head.

"But there are certain defenses to a claim for defamation. One of them is justification, which means that the statement was true. That's what we're trying to find out here, so we're not surprised afterward."

"You want to find out if I have a homosexual relationship with Ali?" Eric asked, shaking his head in disbelief over such a preposterous proposition.

"No, we know you don't," the lawyer replied. "What we want to know is whether you yourself, how shall I say it best, whether you are a practicing homosexual?"

"What?" exclaimed Eric, the timbre of his voice rising, his cheeks becoming flushed.

"We don't mean any disrespect to you, Eric," the older

lawyer interjected. "We are just preparing our case and we need to know the facts, what we might be confronted with."

"Well, I'm not," Eric protested, "and I don't understand why it would even be an issue. This whole thing is a piece of rubbish."

"I understand, and I know how upsetting this must be to you, as indeed it is to the Prince and his whole family. We are just here to help and are going to ask the paper to print a retraction, and we are considering taking the University to court. That's why we need to ensure that we know everything. We must avoid any surprises down the line."

As the lawyer was talking, Eric suddenly recalled the case of Oscar Wilde. Hadn't he also launched a defamation lawsuit against the Marquis of Queensbury before he was arrested? He didn't remember why Wilde had been apprehended but now he shuddered, thinking that the same thing could happen here.

"Wait, is there any chance I could be arrested?" Eric asked.

"Arrested? What for?" the younger lawyer asked in surprise.

"Well, like Oscar Wilde. Wasn't he arrested after he brought a defamation lawsuit?"

"I don't know about that—"

"That was a very different time," the older lawyer interjected. "But you make a good point, which is why we are asking these questions. Oscar Wilde brought a defamation lawsuit claiming that the Marquis of Queensbury had defamed him by calling him a homosexual. Under the law of defamation, if a defendant can establish that what he said was true, then he will be exonerated. That is exactly what Queensbury did. His lawyers proved that Oscar Wilde was, in fact, homosexual and Queensbury won the case. However, at the time, homosexuality was illegal and a crime. Because it had been determined by a court—albeit in a civil case—that Wilde was a homosexual, the prosecution arrested him and tried him, this time in a criminal context and he was sent to prison. Today, homosexuality no longer is a crime; however, 'justification,' or the truth of the statement, still is a complete defense to a claim for libel."

"So, you mean that if they could prove that Ali and I had a relationship, then they would win the case?"

"That's about right. But even if they couldn't prove that, which of course we believe that they can't, if they could show that either of you had such proclivities, we could face some serious obstacles. Perhaps now you understand our line of questioning a bit better?"

"Yes, I do, but I still don't see the connection. I mean there's obviously nothing between us, and they can never prove otherwise."

"Eric, if we go to trial, you will be asked, in court, if you are a homosexual. We want to know how you will answer that question, bearing in mind that you will be under oath."

Eric hesitated. The old man was a seasoned lawyer, and whether he had intuited something about Eric's sexuality or whether he was simply covering his options, he had touched a nerve.

"Well, I'm not," Eric responded defiantly, after a moment.

"Eric, we're on your side," the old lawyer said.

"It doesn't feel that way," he said. Eric suddenly felt lightheaded, as if he might faint. "I need to sit down." He dropped into one of the armchairs.

"Are you okay? You look very pale," the older lawyer said.

"Yes, I'm just very tired. It's been a long semester and now all of this."

"Well, we won't keep you any longer. Here's my card. If you have any questions, or if you want to retract anything you've told us, please call me," he said, as he drew a business card from his vest pocket and handed it to Eric.

When the lawyers left, Eric went back upstairs but found the sitting room in which he had first met the Princess empty. He walked into the neighboring room, which was a vast hall that must, at one point, have been a ballroom. It would easily have fit two hundred people, perhaps even more. It was also empty, as were all the other rooms upstairs. He went back downstairs and walked around opening various doors, each of which led to another large empty room. He came across another set of stairs and walked down them only to find an entire floor of empty bedrooms, one larger than the other, the smallest the size of a large living room. He went up to a half-landing, which led to more empty rooms. At this point, he was starting to panic, as if he were lost in a labyrinth from which there was no escape. Luckily, he ran into the footman who had been waiting in the entrance gallery. He showed Eric to a card room where the Princess was already at the table with the two ladies-in-waiting.

"What happened to you?" she asked.

"Your Highness, I got lost downstairs," he said, shaking his head.

"Yes, the place is rather large. Come and sit down," she said, shuffling the cards. "Coupe," and the Princess began to deal the hand.

24

IT WAS A WARM, SUNNY DAY IN early May as Eric walked down Fifty-Seventh Street toward First Avenue. He wore a short-sleeved collared shirt and a pair of blue trousers, which kept slipping down, despite his belt being fastened on the last notch. He had lost a great deal of weight in the last few months, and by the time he reached the doctor's office, he was out of breath.

"I'm here for my test results," he said to the smiling receptionist behind the counter.

She invited him to wait. He flipped through a magazine—*Men's Health*—showing pictures of muscular men exercising. The very thought of a gym workout exhausted him. But he couldn't concentrate on the magazine. He was too worried about the test results. What if he had AIDS? The shame associated with the disease was almost worse than its certain fatality. When he had arrived in Paris for Christmas, he already felt sick and soon became very ill. It was the worst flu of his life, even worse than the strep infection that had nearly killed him as a child in Iran. He had developed a high fever and vomited. The family doctor had diagnosed a severe case of the flu and had prescribed paracetamol, bed rest, and lots of fluids. After about two weeks, the fever abated, and he began to recover. However, he never fully regained his energy and a persistent cough had lingered.

When he had returned to Princeton, after Reading Period in late January, it was as if Eric didn't recognize the place. Not that anything had changed; his apartment, the campus, the class-rooms, the Club, they were all the same. Yet something had fundamentally altered. The campus itself seemed gray and life-less, like the barren trees and the gloomy sky. He hadn't had any contact with Mark since their phone call on that fateful day in early December. His mind went 'round and 'round about what had happened, and anytime he saw something that reminded him of Mark, which was often, given how much time they had spent together, he felt like crying. He had gone to Campus Club, but since his "outing" in the *Daily Princetonian*, Eric felt that people shied away from him. Those who had been his friends, whom he had laughed with and shared meals with all these years, now appeared to avoid him. Consuelo had been expelled after Ali's family had threatened a defamation suit, which had also caused the *Daily Princetonian* to print a retraction and apol-ogy. However, this was of no comfort or consolation. Neither was the fact that Mattie had shunned Melissa. In fact, he had heard that Melissa's vengeful declamation of the letter had been caused by her resentment of Mattie, who had dropped her after she no longer needed her help on the *Le Train Bleu* project.

Or was it that everything was now seen in gray tones because all color had gone out of his life without Mark. The days merged into one another, one gloomier than the next. He had only two classes, easy ones—an undergraduate French literature class and an Italian class. At some point he stopped attending both and stopped going to the Campus Club for dinner. As he made no effort to socialize with anyone, Eric remained alone in his apartment. He worked on his thesis day after day. He had lost his appetite but would go out and have soup or a salad at nonstudent restaurants, and in the mornings would sip on a cup of coffee. He went entire days without eating and felt listless. He would bring his papers to bed and would simply write there. What energy he had was entirely focused on writing his thesis on Proust's *La Recherche*.

Initially, he had felt the pain of his break-up acutely. There were times when he would break down and cry and was inconsolable. One day he went out and walked around campus in the hopes of glimpsing Mark, but never did. As time went by, sorrow possessed his whole being; it was as if the suffering had congealed in him; Eric had become his grief. He would go through the motions of sleeping and waking, though the days when he actually rose from his bed were less and less frequent as the spring semester rolled on. The one thing he found he could do and do well was write. Strangely this had become easier, almost effortless as if he were a vessel through which the writing came, rather like a prophet delivering God's word into the Bible. His ideas flowed, his thesis was far more fluent and creative, as if he were telling a story—his own story, or humanity's story, which is a story that all great writers tell each in his or her own unique manner. Proust had told it in his inimitable way, describing an ephemeral and meretricious world that captivates his characters as they are slowly pulverized by the inexorable vicissitudes of time. Yet, out of the great suffering, perhaps even as a result of the suffering, something else can emerge, like Vinteuil's sonata or Elstir's paintings. Eventually, the narrator discovers this inner voice that will lead to the creation of Proust's own work that, like the Cathedral of St. Hilaire, stands as a bulwark against the ravages of time.

By the time the first blossoms of spring started to sprout along the campus pathways, Eric couldn't leave his bed. The mere thought of getting out of it was daunting. From afar his mother had started to worry about him, despite his many assurances that he was doing fine, just busy working on his thesis, as with all seniors. She came to visit him in April and was appalled by what she discovered. Eric had lost so much weight that she barely recognized him. His apartment was in a state of complete disarray. After her initial shock, her motherly instincts kicked into high gear. She forced him up and out of bed and helped him walk the short distance to the Nassau Inn where she was staying. There she made him eat; at first some soup, then more solid food and gradually during the next few days, she nursed him back to a healthier state. During this time, Eric would protest her care and did not want to leave the bed in his room at the hotel.

"I'm fine. Why did you have to come and disturb my routine?" he complained.

"Disturb you? You were wasting away," she said, tears forming in her eyes.

"So let me. What's the point of this life anyway?"

"Darling, don't say such horrible things like that. You scare me. This must be your illness talking. I should never have let you leave Paris while you were still sick."

WHEN HE HAD REGAINED some of his strength, his mother took him to a doctor in New York. He was an internist who, when he heard Eric's list of symptoms, had asked him whether he had sex with men.

"Why is that relevant?" Eric had retorted.

"Young man, as you may well know, we have an epidemic going around. It's transmitted sexually, primarily among gay men."

Eric admitted that he had had sex with two men. He didn't have intercourse with Campbell, but he couldn't imagine that either of them would have had AIDS. Mark definitely hadn't had, but not Jim either; he was married and had a daughter. But, recalling Jim's bathhouse scene and his wandering around gave Eric reason to pause.

Still, the doctor thought that it would be prudent to have him tested. He took his blood and said the results would be available in approximately three weeks' time. He also gave Eric a B-12 shot for his general lethargy and a prescription for antibiotics to deal with some of his flu-related symptoms.

Eric asked the doctor not to discuss this aspect of his health with his mother. By law, the doctor had to accept that injunction. When she inquired of the doctor, he said that her son was generally run down and that he had given him a B-12 shot for that. He was running some blood tests and they would know more at his next appointment.

He told his mother that the doctor had said that he needed to eat healthy foods more regularly and avoid stress.

"What about your awful cough?"

"He gave me a prescription for antibiotics that should cover it."

Eric wanted his mother to return to Paris. He needed more

time on his own to think things out. She annoyed him with her constant questioning and fretting about his health. Finally, at the end of the second week in May, Eric persuaded her to go back home. He promised that he would continue to look after himself, would observe a proper diet, and take walks during the day. She would be coming back for his graduation anyway in less than a month.

When she left, Eric went back to his apartment, which she had had cleaned and dusted, and had had his sheets, towels, and clothes laundered. She had stocked his fridge full of food—peeled fruits and yogurt, easy-to-eat sandwiches, soups, and ice cream. At first, he consumed some of the food, but soon he lapsed into the same vapid torpor as before and stopped eating regularly.

When the doctor's office called and asked him to come in, he groaned and said he couldn't make it. It was only when the nurse had threatened to call his mother and tell her he had missed his appointment that he agreed to come in.

As he sat in the doctor's waiting room, the thought that he might actually have AIDS worried him. It was strange; hadn't he thought recently how empty and meaningless life was, how much better off he would be if he ended it. But now that he faced a potentially life-threatening diagnosis, he shirked from the thought that he might actually die.

When they called him into the doctor's private office, the doctor quickly gave him the result. He was HIV positive and needed to receive immediate care. The doctor started telling him that he must inform everyone whom he has had sex with in the last year, but he stopped listening.

"Has anyone survived this?" he asked.

The doctor was silent and then responded, "Yes, there are some patients who have the virus but never develop the full-blown symptoms."

"But how many? I mean as a percentage?"

"Very few. I won't lie to you. Less than one percent."

"So, I'm going to die."

"Well, there are some experimental medications."

"Doctor, what are my chances of survival?" he interrupted.

"They're not good," the doctor said, looking down. "I'm very sorry, Eric."

"Don't be. I need to go now."

"But, we could put you on a treatment program. As I said, there are some experimental treatments, and the FDA is about to approve a new drug known as AZT."

"Okay. May I come back for the treatment if I so decide?"

"Absolutely. Anytime. Just call and come in and we will look after you."

He thanked the doctor and walked out. It was a beautiful, sunny day, not unlike the one last year when he and Mark had walked to Central Park together. Yet, that day seemed as distant as Jupiter's red moon. He made his way back to Princeton on the train. Eric oscillated between fear and panic, but increasingly became resolved to end his life. Previously he had had velleities about suicide; now his thoughts went past the ideation stage and he began to consider methods. He wavered, thinking about his mother. She'd be the only person who would care, who would be truly upset. However, he convinced himself that she had a great life in Paris, a husband who provided for her, however parsimoniously, who, in any event, didn't want Eric around. Besides, he would die anyway and would suffer a great deal until then. He would spare himself and his mother the suffering. She would insist on caring for him in Paris, which would destroy her life there—the social stigma of it all, plus its effect on the royal family's suit. It would all be for the best.

By the time he reached home, his resolve was firmly made;

it was only as to the method that he was unsure. He went to Firestone Library where he quickly found the medical books in the science section. It didn't take long before he figured out the method. He decided on a bottle of Valium, together with a bottle of wine, and then he would tie a plastic bag on his head and sleep, never to wake again, or at least not in this world.

As he was leaving the library, he saw Mark coming in. Their eyes met and Eric smiled but continued to walk on. Mark slowed down as if to stop, and Eric felt that Mark wanted perhaps to say something. For an instant, Eric thought of telling Mark that he had AIDS, as the doctor had told him he should inform his sex partners. Then he thought of telling Mark how much he loved him. But instead, Eric continued to walk through the turnstile and out into the plaza. He went to the supermarket on Nassau Street and bought some plastic bags, the sort that you can tie at the top, and then walked home.

The message light blinked on his answering machine, but he didn't bother listening to his messages. He sat down at the table and composed a note:

My dearest, darling mother whom I love and adore,

Please don't be angry with me. I didn't have a choice.
You see I fell in love with a man but was too afraid
to tell you. At first, he loved me back, and I was so
happy, but then he rejected me. I was despondent
and had nowhere to turn. Foolishly, I went to New
York and slept with another man who gave me AIDS.
So you see, I don't have long to live anyway. I think
you know that in these last few months I had grown
tired, both physically and mentally. In some way, I felt
like I died last December when my heart died with the
loss of my friend.

Mummy, I love you. I want you to go on and live
a full and happy life. I want you to do that for me.
Every time you smile I want you to smile for me.
Every night, when you look up and see the moon,
I want you to see my face and know that I love you
and I'm looking back at you.

Love you,
Your son

He put the pen down and went straight for the wine and
opened it. He took two long gulps from the bottle and spilled
a little on his shirt. Then he went to his medicine cabinet and
reached for the bottle of Valium. He had brought the medica-
tion back from Paris, at Christmas, but had taken only one or
two. He swallowed the entire contents with the help of some
water that he had poured from the faucet into a glass.

As he walked to his bed, he again saw the message light on
the machine, and he pressed the "play" button and walked into
his bedroom. He lay on his bed and fastened the plastic bag to
his head. He made sure that it was sealed and airtight at the
bottom. As he lay there, breathing the ever scarcer oxygen, he
began to fall asleep, but he heard the message on the machine.
His senior thesis had won the thesis prize and was being put
up for publication. "It was the most creative and extraordinary thesis that I've read in my thirty years at Princeton," said
Trompet. A little smile formed on his lips, and when his body
was found a few days later, he looked as if he were smiling.

Third Noble Truth of Buddhism:
The suffering can come to an end
with the cessation of craving.

New York City 2015

25

"ERIC, ARE YOU STILL WITH ME?" Ramyar asked.

Eric nodded. "Sorry. It's just the conference name, 'Play and Win Every Time,' in the context of our reminiscence, had my mind drifting back in time."

While Ramyar was telling the story about Farhad's death on the minefields, Eric was transported in an alembic of time to a place so far away that in the misty recesses of his mind he had only remembered its contours.

Ramyar nodded his head in assent. "Yes. I can understand. We sit here chatting in this posh club, while the bones of our childhood friends rot away."

Eric agreed, "Well, you don't know how close I came to joining them, both in Iran and during my frivolous years at Princeton."

Ramyar leaned forward, one ear turned to Eric like a priest taking a confession, awaiting a recitation of his sins.

Eric blinked his eyes and then glanced down at his watch. "I'd love to talk more, but my daughter is in a school play, and I promised her and my wife I would be there. How long are you here for? Perhaps we can have dinner one evening?"

Ramyar sat upright. There would be no confession today. "I'm leaving tomorrow for L.A., but I'll be back."

They exchanged numbers and goodbyes, and Eric hurried onto the street and walked quickly away. He looked for taxis but they were full. He managed to order a car through Uber, though it would cost him fifty dollars instead of the ten by Yellow Cab. His Uber rider app showed the car would be there in four minutes. But after five minutes, the car hadn't arrived, and the app still showed it as being four minutes away. He saw a Yellow Cab pull up to let out its passengers. He hurried toward it, and at the same time pushed the cancel button on Uber. The app confirmed the cancellation and applied its ten-dollar cancel charge. Eric swore he would contest it.

On his way to the school, the taxi got stuck in heavily congested cross-town traffic.

"Why are you taking this route? You should've taken Seventy-Second or Seventy-Ninth. Now look where this is getting us."

The Indian or Pakistani cab driver shouted back, but Eric didn't understand a single word.

"I don't understand what you're saying. This is hopeless. Just let me out here, and I'll walk."

After a few more obscenities, the taxi driver pulled over and let him out. He was still a few blocks away and walked briskly. By the time he arrived at the school, which was in the East Eighties, the play had already begun. As he had forgotten his parent's badge, he was further delayed at the security gate. The hallways were empty. He found his way to the auditorium, which had one of those doors with a long metallic bar that you push to open. As he pressed it, the door banged open loudly and the audience members, sitting in the dark room, turned their heads toward the latecomer. The open door shone the light on him and he could feel their silent reproaches. He walked in and looked for an empty seat but then glimpsed a raised hand. It was his wife, Celia. She had saved him a seat; luckily it was on the aisle so he could join her without making anyone stand up. As he sat down, she glared at him. Even in the dim light, he could discern the censorious look in her eyes that gave her a mad look, rather like the woman in Gericault's *Insane Woman* painting.

Celia had an irascible temperament that was concealed by her petite frame, short snowy blond hair, and her blue eyes, which gave her an innocent, almost ingenuous look. They had met when Eric was an associate at the law firm where Celia's father, Michael Landauer III, whom Eric had just run into in the lift on his way down, had been the managing partner. Eric and Celia had met one summer at the Piping Rock Club in Oyster Bay where, thanks to her father's membership, the law firm held its annual summer outing for its lawyers. She had taken an instant liking to him; she considered him very handsome, and he was unlike the young men that she was accustomed to socializing with and dating. He spoke French flawlessly and had a remarkable knowledge of history and literature; she found him exquisitely polite and dignified, and even if his urbanity verged on the effete, she considered it charming. They had flirted, after copious amounts of red wine at the dinner. To her surprise, at the end of the evening, when she was leaving, he had not asked for her number. She was too drunk to be overly concerned, but in the course of the next few weeks, she found herself thinking of him. Celia eventually convinced her father to invite Eric to dinner at his house, a palatial apartment on Fifth Avenue overlooking Central Park; he did so, very reluctantly. Landauer didn't know Eric or any other associate at the law firm for that matter. Inviting him to his house for dinner would be similar to Louis the XIV inviting a commoner to dinner at Versailles.

After that evening Celia would pursue him with a vigor that surprised even herself. When they were alone that night, he was attentive; he would listen to her speak and she would gaze into his eyes as she drank glass after glass of red wine. He would smile and ask her questions that encouraged her to talk about herself, and occasionally he would reach for her hand, which she was quick to offer. But afterward he rarely called her, and when pressed he would contend that his work obligations left him little free time, which was legitimate, but which also inflamed her desire all the more. She would plead with her father to reduce Eric's workload. Her father would grumble that he had nothing to do with his work, but he quietly put in a good word for Eric. In such a law firm, where associates, hired by the dozens out of law school, were required to work excruciatingly long hours in a competitive and often hostile environment that caused the vast majority to leave after a year or two, a good word from the managing partner was like Moses parting the sea.

Suddenly Eric, who had been toiling at the end of his second year and, like his peers, hated the firm, became the golden boy. Ignored by the partners and mistreated by the more senior associates, as is customary at any large law firm, he now found that the junior partners were actually smiling at him in the hallways and the senior associates had become deferential. This radical departure from law firm practice, which had astounded the other lawyers at the firm, had coincided with regular invitations to dinner at Mr. Landauer's home. It hadn't taken long for Eric and indeed the other associates—law firms are notoriously gossip-ridden—to realize that a *deus ex machina*, in the form of Michael Landauer, was looking after him. While the others had initially been perplexed by this divine intervention, they had very quickly grasped the motives behind it.

For Eric, the boss's daughter was, as if a lifeboat had miraculously appeared for his exclusive use, an escape from the sinking *Titanic* of his life. It had been almost three years since he had moved to New York and commenced work at the law firm. Like the majority of his peers, he had not expected his job to be as devastating, psychologically and emotionally, as it turned out to be. Day and night he had worked at the firm; time had lost its meaning. To this was added the fact that he knew no one in New York, and because of the long hours at the law firm, had not been able to meet anyone other than the other associates at the firm, who considered him a competitor rather than a friend. Eric lived alone in a one-bedroom apartment in a highrise on the Upper East Side. He felt alone and lonely in a foreign city and in a job he hated.

Their wedding had been a sumptuous affair at the Landauers' estate in Oyster Bay. Eric's parents had swept in from Paris and had arranged a prenuptial dinner for one hundred and fifty guests at the Metropolitan Club, which Princess Ashraf of Iran, who lived in New York City, had attended.

After they were married, Mr. Landauer, or by now, Michael, shed his image as Darth Vader and became an avuncular and jovial father-in-law, who took Eric golfing on the weekends and introduced him to his friends. His mother-in-law, Helen, was consumed with a passion for horses and riding. She kept a stable of magnificent thoroughbreds and rarely would come to New York City, spending most of her time attending to her horses in Oyster Bay.

Celia had been obsessed with Eric and hung on every word he uttered. She paraded him around to her friends and family, ask him to speak French, and then would delight and laugh at his flawless accent. Eric, on the other hand, though very fond of her, was not in love with Celia. He hadn't married her to advance his career but was not oblivious to Michael's influence, which not only had saved him from the traumatizing experiences of the law firm but eventually had propelled him into the position of an equity partner. With the birth of their daughters, Eric became a dedicated family man and remained faithful to his wife. Yet, despite his efforts to please her, Celia rightly felt that her love was unrequited, which inflamed her passion even further. She experienced a succession of often contradictory emotions—elation and disappointment, desire and jealousy—that would leave her confused, exhausted, and increasingly brittle.

The first of his daughters, Helen, was her mother's child—the same blond hair and blue eyes, and the same temperament and taste for clothes and ostentation display. Eva was Papa's little girl. Every night he would read her a bedtime story that would carry her off into a distant land, the fairytale worlds of *Cinderella* and *Snow White,* or *Hansel and Gretel,* and of course, *Narnia.* He would also tell her stories of the Greek gods, of the golden apple and three goddesses.

"How beautiful were they, Papa?" she would ask in amazement. He read to her of *Jason and the Argonauts* and his witch wife, Medea, and of the tales of Zeus and Hera's endless jealousies. She delighted in these stories and would refuse to sleep until Papa had come home to read her another story.

Eva had been born long after Celia's obsession with Eric had worn off. Her passion for him had consumed all her energy and, as it abated, she became restless and her ill-temper, camouflaged by the warm glow of her beauty, flared up. She complained that Eric had changed, that he had become distant and aloof. Yet, he was the very same person; it was she who had altered. As the carefully constructed image of her husband in her mind had begun to fade, it gave way to the cool light of reality.

She adopted various projects and would, for a time, devote herself, almost frantically, to the endeavor at hand. The first of these had been the renovation and decoration of a pre-war duplex apartment on Park Avenue that they had purchased with the aid of a large mortgage, which made Eric very nervous. She had engaged one of the most sought-after interior designers in New York—a flamboyant gay man, who would wear outlandish outfits and drape himself in a cape. They would wander around New York City in search of furniture and artwork. The apartment had been designed in a minimalist style, with contemporary furniture and white walls, but accentuated by extraordinary eighteenth-century pieces such an original console signed by Sheridan, or a rosewood table by Chippendale.

It had four bedrooms, one for each of their daughters as well as a guest room. There was also a separate maid's room with its own small bathroom for their Guatemalan housekeeper, Carmen.

The apartment and its furnishings had cost a small fortune, financed mostly by debt. Moreover, Celia spent lavishly on herself and their two daughters, buying the latest designer outfits, hosting ten-thousand-dollar birthday parties, and making copious charitable contributions that paved the way for a glittering social life on the Upper East Side of Manhattan. As a partner at a major New York law firm, Eric made more than two million dollars a year, but after taxes and Celia's expenditures, there was nothing left for savings. Eric considered these outlays excessive and was alarmed by the debt they had undertaken, not only for their apartment but also for that "cute little house" in South Hampton, another one of her projects that required the "touch" of her decorator friend, whose services came with an astronomical price tag. Then there were the obligatory vacations, Christmases spent skiing in Aspen and winter breaks down in St. Barts. In the spring, they would visit Eric's family in Paris, where they habitually stayed at the Bristol on the Faubourg St. Honore, a perfect location for Celia to indulge in her shopping fantasies. These extravagant trips, which for Eric had started to verge on the monotonous, were the sine qua non of Celia's life, providing her with ample opportunity to engage in none-too-subtle one-upmanship with her coterie of friends, though perhaps a more accurate word would be her "contacts," because friendship implies a minimum level of concern and empathy that was decidedly lacking in these relationships.

He tolerated her spending because, as everyone knew but no one acknowledged, without Celia he would not have become a partner. But there was another, more profound reason, and it had to do with the sublimation of her energies from her Eros or love to her projects. At first, her all-consuming passion had all but suffocated Eric to the point where he had thought of at least a separation, if not a divorce. During that early period, she had not let him alone, demanding and pleading for his attention at all times of the day and night. She had wanted to make love twice, sometimes three times a day. His only escape had been his work, and even there she would contrive to reach him, through his secretary or even her father's secretary, who would come into his office with an urgent message to call his wife.

And so he was grateful when the flames of passion had cooled; there were no more messages from the secretaries at work; the lovemaking had slowed to a trickle, and she would often ask him to sleep in the guest room because his snoring bothered her. If the price he had to pay for his freedom was her outlandish expenditures, then so be it, he had thought. Better to go into debt than to suffocate to death.

Nevertheless, he had become restive by the sheer scale of her spending, which continued unabated, like a hurricane gathering force; but having accepted it for so long, Eric didn't know how to approach the problem and broach the subject, and therefore he did nothing. Instead, he withdrew, spending more time at work, at the gym, playing tennis and golf, going away on business trips. On the occasional weekend that he was home, he would take Eva out on the town, to her delight. They would go to playgrounds, indoor playrooms, the zoo, and more recently to the American Museum of Natural History, and even the Met, where he would show her paintings and sculptures linked to the stories he had read to her. Here was Perseus holding the head of Medusa, there was Hercules battling the Hydra,

Zeus in his many guises, Venus and Mars and the other dei-
ties. She would laugh and ask him questions only children ask,
questions that, in their innocence, made him stop and ponder
the great mysteries that lay behind the cultures and the myths
depicted in these great works of art.

Helen and Celia would go shopping and buy reams of
dresses, shoes, handbags—more than there was room for even
in their capacious apartment, more than any one person could
ever need or use. It seemed that they were always shopping,
and if they were not shopping, they were looking through
online catalogs. At fourteen, Helen appeared more grown-up
than some thirty year olds. Her nails were perfectly manicured
with red nail varnish; she applied what her mother called "very
light makeup," though there was nothing light about the shade
of her red lipstick, or the mascara and rouge that she applied on
a regular basis to her face.

With such different temperaments, the two sisters didn't get
along. Helen considered Eva a childish annoyance and ignored
her for the most part. Celia and Helen would go out shopping,
leaving Eva behind to sit at home watching Spanish soap operas
with Carmen.

The collapse of Lehman Brothers and the concomitant
financial crisis had spared him. There had been a moment of
panic at his firm in the autumn of 2008, but it was short-lived;
the fiscal and monetary stimuli had succeeded in bandaging
the wounded economy. In fact, through "quantitative easing"
and the reduction of interest rates to historic lows, the Federal
Reserve had made available vast sums of essentially free money
to corporations, which they used to go on a buying spree, creating a new wave of mergers and acquisitions and share repur-
chases that lifted the stock market and inflated the profits of

private equity firms. Because Eric and his firm were advi\: __ un many of these transactions they too benefited from the Federal Reserve's monetary policy. Nevertheless, the financial crisis had inflicted psychological anxiety on the partners of the law firm. There was a sense that the monetary stimulus was an economic tourniquet that had failed to address the root causes of the crisis and, in some cases, had exacerbated the problems—inequality had increased; banks were larger. It was as if everyone was waiting for the other shoe to drop; meanwhile, each partner jealously guarded his or her clients, creating an atmosphere of extreme distrust and caution, reminiscent of Catherine de Medici's medieval court of silk and blood where courtiers fell prey to poisoned dresses and oubliettes.

26

A WEEK OR SO AFTER his meeting with Ramyar, Eric received an email from a John Birch at Princeton's Development Office, inviting him to an event in New York City hosted by the university for its Department of Romance Language and Literatures. Eric had put his Princeton days behind him long ago. After his last tumultuous term there, he made a clean break with his past and his fellow students. Years later, Eric had seen a photo of Consuelo in the *Princeton Alumni Weekly*, known by the acronym *PAW*, which had mentioned some political activities she had engaged in at Wesleyan, and in another issue had seen a reference to Melissa and her wedding to someone he didn't know. Yet despite the many invitations, designed of course to solicit contributions, Eric had not returned to the university or participated in any reunions or other events. If he had thought more deeply about it, perhaps he would have recognized that he was still wounded by Consuelo's outing of him and his abandonment by everyone else, and that conceivably, this was why he preferred to leave Princeton behind him. He went to delete the email, but something, perhaps his recent encounter with Ramyar that had momentarily pivoted his mind to things past, made him read on:

> *. . . and remarks by Professor Trompet,*
> *Professor Emeritus of French and Comparative*
> *Literature.*

He stopped for a minute and thought of Trompet, and recalled his winning the senior thesis prize as his one triumph during those sad later days. Eric replied that he would attend.

THE EVENT WAS HELD at one of those private clubs in New York City whose entrance is unmarked, bastions of a fading past that have survived the onslaught of cultural transformations around them—from the black civil rights movement to women's equality and, more recently, gay marriage rights—surprisingly intact. A cursory glance at the membership of these clubs and the club rules would reveal more about the power structures of the United States than all the newspapers and television coverage of politics combined.

Eric walked in and was directed to a room on the second floor, which appeared larger than it actually was due to a soaring double-height ceiling, in the middle of which hung an imposing chandelier made of Baccarat crystal. A substantial portrait of a man in a nineteenth-century military uniform hung over a massive fireplace of black marble. There were no more than approximately twenty guests, some sitting on the sofas and side chairs, others standing in clusters, and several at an open bar ordering drinks. Eric didn't recognize anyone and made his way to the bar where he asked for a glass of red wine. He felt awkward standing alone, sipping from his glass as if all eyes were focused on him, which of course wasn't the case. To his relief, a man in a dark suit and red tie standing near the fireplace spoke up to ask for silence and to announce that the evening's program was beginning. He introduced another man, who must have been in his mid-forties, with ginger-colored hair receding on the sides and at the top. He wasn't tall, no more than about five foot eight and wearing a three-piece grey bespoke suit. He had a congenial smile and a handsome face that was starting to see the ravages of time. When his name, Peter, was announced, Eric believed that he recognized him but couldn't quite recollect how. The man started to speak in unambiguously Etonian English. He mentioned that he had been an undergraduate at Princeton majoring in comparative literature, but Eric didn't recall him from his days there. He continued on and praised the department in vague terms and then mentioned Khaled, whom he had known well at Princeton. Eric racked his mind to recall this somewhat familiar stranger, but as long and hard as he tried, he couldn't place him anywhere within his sphere of his Princeton acquaintances.

Peter, in turn, introduced Trompet, who of course needed no introduction. Trompet, who had suddenly appeared next to

Peter, spoke in his inimitable English, which is to say with perfect fluency and literary flourish, and with a tinge of a French accent. No sooner had Trompet began to speak than Eric was transported back in time. He saw Mattie raising half an arm in class and Trompet enthusiastically calling on her to discuss *Madame Bovary*. He was at the Palladium with Mattie, where he met her gay fashion designer. And then he was overcome by melancholy, a somber, wistful feeling, mixed with remorse bordering on despair. He recalled flashes of an insane and unspeakable love affair that had almost destroyed him and yet felt a yearning for the selfsame feelings of abandonment—the love or the madness that had led him to the edge of doom. Eric gasped and endeavored to escape from the thoughts that had hijacked his mind, but like the waters held back by a gate that flood in once the sluice is cracked open, the more he tried, the more agitated he became.

"Eric, Eric," he heard his name twice and was startled out of his thoughts by this summons. "I'm so glad you could come. Oh, I'm John Birch, from the development office," he said, in response to Eric's bewildered look, which he had mistakenly ascribed to Eric's failure to recognize him—understandable as they had never met in person.

"Ah, John, how are you doing? Thanks for inviting me."

"How did you like Trompet's talk?"

"It was great," Eric gushed. Lost in thought, he had not registered a word of what Trompet had said and so diverted from the subject. "He was my favorite professor at Princeton. I'd love to talk to him."

John Birch, who was no doubt targeting Eric for a substantial contribution, said without hesitation, "Of course, let's go over and chat with him."

Trompet was surrounded by a group that included Peter and was in conversation with an elderly lady. Despite his smile, Eric could see that he found the company rather tiresome. John Birch introduced Eric to Peter, who didn't recognize him. They began to speak, and it turned out that Peter had graduated two years after him. Eric mentioned that he knew Khaled at Princeton.

"Did you hear that he has become very Islamic, almost to the point of fanaticism?" Peter asked.

"Yes, I knew that. I haven't seen him in a long time, but remember him condemning Salman Rushdie for the *Satanic Verses*. I mean, I didn't like the book, but Khaled was vehement about it, supporting Khomeini's crazy death fatwah. That's when I wondered what had happened to him. It was almost like he'd been brainwashed."

"I know. He hasn't answered any of my letters either. When was the last time you saw him?"

"I don't remember exactly. It must have been in the mid-'90s. He used to come for dinner at my parents' place in Paris, and we would exchange letters. But then I received a letter where he seemed upset that I hadn't written to him earlier, and said that he had run into a mutual friend in London who had told him that I had become a "sell-out corporate lawyer" in New York. That was the last I heard from him. He didn't answer any of my letters after that. I don't know what had upset him: my corporate legal practice or my poor epistolary manners."

"Well, it's great to meet you, Eric. I have to go; I'm hosting an event at my Club in two weeks and there's lots of work still to do." He paused. "I'd like to invite you if you're interested," he said, reaching for his card.

"What sort of event?"

"It's a talk by two economists about the financial crisis and its aftermath. It should be really interesting, especially for a corporate lawyer. One of them has a very different perspective." He wrote the time and address on the back of the card. "Hope to see you there!"

Eric put the card away in his pocket, knowing that like all the other cards politely exchanged at such events, he would later discard it.

The group around Trompet had thinned out. The man looked exactly as Eric had remembered him. As he approached, he wondered if Trompet would remember or recognize him. He has had thousands of students over the years.

"Bonsoir Monsieur," he said.

"Bonsoir," responded Trompet, smiling in his usual affable way.

As they spoke, Eric reminded Trompet that he was a student of his back in the mid-'80s.

"I remember you," Trompet responded. "You won the senior thesis award, but wouldn't let us publish it."

Eric smiled. "Yes, I think I had decided to go into law and didn't see the point of it."

Trompet grabbed his elbow. "For future generations, my boy. We must think of them."

Eric nodded his head, but Trompet seemed a bit disappointed in him. Eric quickly asked about his publications and reminded him that he had read his books on Flaubert and Hugo.

"Ah, those were a long time ago. More recently, I've written on Baudelaire and Mallarme."

Eric thought how long it had been since he had read any

poems or even any literature at all. The closest he had come to a literary experience was seeing *Les Miserables* on Broadway, to which he had taken his daughters; he felt embarrassed to tell Trompet that. It was as if he had been a different person back then—an Eric who had read the great works of literature and could quote from them. Now he was a lawyer attending to M&A deals, and a husband in a loveless marriage. At the thought of Celia, he sighed. How had this happened to him? Then he recalled asking the same question on the day he met with Ramyar.

The evening drew to a close, and as he left he put his hand into his left pocket and felt the edge of something sharp. It was Peter's card. Maybe I will go to Peter's event after all, he thought. Perhaps the memories aren't all bad.

27

As Eric walked up the steps to Peter's Club two weeks later, he couldn't help but think of the title "Play and Win Every Time" and hoped these speakers had more to offer than a poker metaphor. The auditorium was overflowing with people and he didn't know a single one of them. There was no sign of Peter anywhere. Why did I bother coming all the way downtown? he asked himself. This was just another dreary excuse for people to drink and flirt and he didn't do either. He thought of leaving, but then he had already checked his coat and the lecture was beginning. He decided to sit in the back and if the speaker was

ly expected him to be, he could make an unob-
nlike his entrance to Helen's play.

veted by the talk. The professor's perspective
was refreshingly simple and rang so true to his own experience.
He explained that our current economic system—capitalism—
is defined by the wage-based employer-employee relationship. This system came into being in the eighteenth century in
the UK and was initially exported to North America, Europe,
and Japan, and more recently to the rest of the world. In the
nineteenth century and early twentieth century, the laborers
fought for and obtained from employers the promise of rising
wages. A bargain was struck that the employee would do what
the employer demanded, and the employer would pay a rising
wage. This bargain came to a halt in the Western world and
Japan when the employers discovered that they could move
manufacturing to low-cost labor markets such as China. "We
are all too familiar with the exodus of the large multinational
companies from the United States, Western Europe, and Japan,"
the professor noted.

But, as he explained, Marx, ever the prescient critique of
capitalism, predicted that it would eventually prey upon itself.
Indeed, workers in the United States, Europe, and Japan have
seen their wages stagnate, if not decline, in the last forty years
since the exodus began. Capitalism is destroying the very markets it relies on to buy its products. What's more, because
labor is so cheap in places like China, the corporations over-
built and now have an excess of supply. At first, from the 1980s
to the 2000s, Americans and Europeans borrowed money to
make purchases that their stagnating wages would not otherwise have afforded them. The debt binge led to the collapse
of 2008. The rescue packages appear to have remedied the
situation; however, by not addressing the underlying causes

of the economic crash—the excess of supply and a shrinking demand—they have only prolonged the day of reckoning. Indeed, the only thing that all economists agree on is that our worldwide economy is in dire straits and getting worse.

"Wow, I wonder why the markets haven't collapsed yet," Eric thought to himself. "We'll have to sell our shares in Apple and Amazon and the others. Buy gold, maybe. But Celia won't agree. She won't believe this assessment with her unhinged optimism; all she wants is to buy more and compete with our friends—no, her friends, they're not my friends. That's why she buys all these ridiculous clothes. And with the kids. God, they're spoiled, especially Helen, and the poor things don't even know it. How did this happen? How did I get locked into this life of unending consumption? Well, it's not all bad. I mean, I'm a partner in a major firm." But, when he thought about his firm, Eric realized that he didn't like any of his partners. They all wanted to take his clients from him, and every day was a Darwinian struggle, not only to keep the seemingly, ever more demanding clients happy but to prevent these greedy bastards from stealing them. Where did he fit into the capitalist system the professor was describing? Of course, he wasn't one of these downtrodden wage slaves, but neither was he the corporate titan who was able to influence policy and legislation. His absorption with his personal life situation and his apprehension about his family's overspending were so overwhelming that he missed the point of the lecture and was unable to discern his own role in a system that was collapsing, precisely because of the narcissism and greed that had possessed Eric and his peers.

"Life is a game of musical chairs," he thought. "Maybe the poker metaphor wasn't an overreach after all." He pictured all of humanity going around a vast number of chairs, as one by one they are eliminated with each pause of the music. "Of course, their chances aren't all equal; the world ring-fences a lot of the chairs for a small elite, but even they eventually lose out, stricken by illness and injury or by a tragedy of some kind, or the perfidious competition of their peers. The game itself is exhausting, and the onset of depression and mental illness eliminate rich and poor alike. Happiness is elusive; to be sure the game has its high moments, as when the lucky take their seats—a raise or promotion, an infatuation, the birth of a child—but ultimately, happiness is an illusion. The music starts up in a minute and you have to get up. And so we go 'round, 'hypocrite lecteur, mon semblable mon frère, hypocritical reader, my fellow being, my brother,' as Baudelaire well understood, anxious and bored by the game of life."

Baudelaire. When was the last time he had thought about such things? He had become an automaton, playing a game that he didn't even know he was part of. What if you don't want to play this game? That would be a nihilistic perspective that would inevitably lead to suicide. He now had a momentary recollection of another life on another course that had led down this path. Eric pulled back. "But what if there was another alternative." His mind went around and around in circles, not realizing that was also part of the game.

He recalled a book on Buddhist meditation from his undergraduate years that had discussed the cycle of Samsara: the circle of human suffering, not just old age, sickness, and death, but also the ephemeral nature of pleasure; what some people call the suffering of change, which was not unlike the game of musical chairs—the moment you sit down you have to get up! The book had said something about the wandering mind that clings to what it perceives to be desirable and avoids what it perceives as undesirable. This he hadn't understood at the time and had put aside the book. But now, years later, given his life experience, it seemed more relevant.

Eric had been so deeply caught up in this chain of thought that he missed the second speaker's presentation completely. The lecture was now over and people were leaving the room. As he was walking out, he ran into Peter.

"Glad to see you, Eric. How did you like the lectures?"

"I thought the first guy was very interesting. A very different perspective that made me really think about how shaky things are."

"Yes, I know. He can be a bit radical but nevertheless very thought-provoking. You are staying for drinks, I hope? There's a whole group of ex-Princetonians here tonight."

Eric was planning to leave but felt it would be awkward now, and besides, he was curious to see who was there; he hadn't recognized anyone coming in. As he walked with Peter into the adjoining room, he rehearsed in his mind what he would say should he recognize one of his former classmates. He's a partner at a top law firm; he's married, of course, with two girls who go to top private schools. He had nothing to be ashamed of; he had "played and won" as well as the next person he kept telling himself; and yet he was anxious, his stomach contracted like an unprepared student before an exam.

The lounge was already full and very loud. He ordered a glass of wine, wondering for an instant if he should order something more manly and then decided against it. Peter moved him toward a group of people amongst whom he recognized a few faces but was surprised that he couldn't attach a name to any of them. One of the women, dark-haired with glasses, approached him and said, "I remember you!"

Names popped into his head: Becky, Debbie, Mary, Lynn, Maryann.

"I remember you too! How are you doing? Eric Richardson here by the way."

"I knew that. Or maybe I didn't." The woman laughed; she was a little tipsy.

"What's your name? Sorry it's been so long!" he said apologetically.

"It's Lynn, now Lynn Sullivan." Eric peered at her. "I know I'm so old now and don't look the same," she said.

"Nonsense, you don't look a day older than when we were at Princeton."

He hadn't known her well at all and didn't recall what she had looked like. Nevertheless, she seemed pleased with the compliment.

"I don't, but compared to some of our classmates, I guess I'm well preserved. By the way, you look great," she said, looking him up and down, almost surprised. "You haven't changed a bit."

Eric had kept his hair and was in reasonably good shape from weekly workouts at the gym.

He flushed unexpectedly and stammered a reply, "I, I haven't really been in touch with too many people from Princeton."

"How come?" she asked, then remembered something and narrowed her eyes.

"I don't know. Just work, family. You know how it is."

"That I do. Well, we've got quite a few of us here tonight as you can see." She started to point and name people. One of them was Mark Kerrigan. Could it be? Eric didn't recognize this person. It's true that the lighting was dim, but the man who bore that name didn't look anything like the Mark he remembered. He had wisps of thinning grey hair, wrinkles that made him appear distinctly middle-aged, and a slight paunch that stuck out from under his suit jacket.

"Did you say Mark Kerrigan?" asked Eric, incredulously as if he had misheard her.

"Yeah, you know Mark?" she asked, again probing him, but before Eric could respond, she shouted, "Hey, Mark, come over here."

Lynn's voice was so loud that, despite the music, the small group around Mark stopped talking and looked over at her. Mark excused himself and walked over to them. As he came closer, his face came into full view, and Eric was able to recognize the handsome, chiseled features he had once known so well beneath the skin that had lost the shine and vigor of youth. Yet the contrast between the Mark whom he remembered and the man who now stood before him was so distinct that for an instant Eric was breathless and at a loss for words.

"I know you!" said Mark affably. "Eric Richardson, right?" he said and reached out to shake his hand.

"Yes, but I go by my first name, Eric, now," he smirked.

"Ah, gotcha, still clever with words. Well, how've you been?" Mark asked and slurred his words. He had obviously been drinking and Eric could smell the alcohol on his breath.

"I've been well, thanks. How about yourself?" Eric responded and suddenly began to feel slightly nauseated.

"I'm doing well. Better now after the government bailout. But, having a good time here tonight."

"You live in the city?" asked Eric.

"Nah, in Greenwich, but I work in the city and commute. How about you?"

"I live and work here."

For an instant they were silent. Lynn had moved away, and it was just the two of them now. Eric thought that Mark looked at him rather knowingly, but he couldn't be sure as his vision was obscured by gazing back into the past, through the telescope of time, where he saw those emerald eyes looking back at him, beckoning, inviting, infuriating, and devastating him.

The moment passed; the banal conversation returned, "What do you do, Eric?"

"I'm a lawyer. How about you?"

Mark explained that he was a private banker for UBS, and Eric told him about his job at the law firm. They shared superficial details of their families, how many children they each had—Mark had a teenage boy and a little girl. Eric felt that Mark was devouring him with his eyes, but he wasn't sure if he was just imagining it, or if he liked the feeling. There were awkward pauses as they ran out of social banalities but neither wanted to move on.

"How's your tennis game?" asked Eric.

"I still play. How about you?"

"I do, too, when I can."

"Where do you play?" inquired Mark.

"At Roosevelt Island. There's a tennis club there."

"Know it well. Want to play sometime?"

Ah, here it was, at last. The way to meet. Tennis. Another game. He thought of Wimbledon. Who had been playing in the finals that year? Was it Becker? That's right, it was Boris Becker. The Park Tower hotel and—

"Campbell," Eric said under his breath.

"What was that?" asked Mark, narrowing his eyes like Lynn had.

"Nothing, I'm sorry. I was just thinking ... I was just thinking that you're probably a lot better than me. You sure you want to play?"

"Absolutely. Let's do it. Let's set it up. How do I reach you?"

Eric reached out with his card, as he floated between past and present realities. This made him wonder about Campbell. He would Google him when he got home. And why did Mark want to play tennis? Well, it's just a tennis game; no harm would come of that. But did he want to reestablish contact after all this time? Did he not remember Mark's bitter betrayal? Images flashed in his mind in quick succession: his apartment in Princeton, the Campus Club, and nights of lovemaking, the only real passion he had ever really known, Wimbledon, Cap and Gown and "The Catastrophe." Eric cupped his forehead with his right hand as if to dismiss the thoughts. He felt an urge to leave, to run away from the past and its pull, to be alone to think or perhaps to not think. He felt the thumping of the music like a hammer in his head.

He handed Mark the card and looked at his watch. "I must go. I'm already late. But do send me an email and we'll catch up and play some tennis," he said, perhaps more formally than he had intended. He then reached out to shake Mark's hand and quickly left the Club without bothering to say goodbye to Peter. He would send him a note the next day.

28

ROOSEVELT ISLAND is a narrow strip of land on the East River between Manhattan and Queens. It can be reached by a tram located on Sixtieth Street that goes high above the river, offering spectacular views of the iconic Manhattan skyline. But the panoramic cityscape was not captivating Eric at all this evening; perhaps he was too used to it, having undertaken the trip countless times or, more likely, he was preoccupied with other thoughts. He had been surprised at his own reaction to meeting Mark at the Club. He had recalled the emotional turmoil that their affair at Princeton had caused him, but now he felt nothing for this man whom he had once loved with all his being. Eric was curious to see Mark again, which is why he accepted the tennis date. It wasn't so much to learn more about his life, but rather to experience the feeling of being with Mark, with this person who had once exercised such complete control and dominion over him, not to gloat like over a diminished enemy but simply to discover the sensations arising in himself.

When he arrived at the tennis club, which was simply a large bubble, like a tent, housing two dozen Astroturf courts, Mark was already changed and waiting for him. They greeted each other with a polite handshake, and Mark waited outside the locker room while Eric changed. As they were walking to the court, Eric listened as Mark endeavored to fill the silence with small talk; he explained that he had driven into work that morning instead of taking the train because he knew he would have to drive home after tennis. He had heard of the Roosevelt Island Club but had never played here. By the time Mark had finished, they were on the court and started to hit balls.

They played for an hour and a half and split sets. Mark wasn't in as good a shape as Eric, which helped him keep even. Afterward, they went to the men's locker room to change. When he was in the shower, Eric heard Mark say:

"Now I know how you took a set off me! I weigh seventy pounds more than you."

Eric had weighed himself on the way to the showers, and Mark must have stepped on the scales right after. Eric wasn't sure how to answer and contented himself with saying, "Ah, okay. That must be it."

It was around 11:00 P.M. and the locker room was completely empty when Eric came out of the shower and began to dry himself. He was sitting on the bench in front of his locker when Mark emerged from the shower and came and sat near him. Mark let the towel that he had draped around himself slip, revealing his semi-erection. When Eric saw that, he too started to become aroused, though he didn't feel drawn to Mark; it was more reflex than attraction. But Mark saw his arousal and reached over and touched Eric's penis.

"What are you doing?" Eric stammered, stunned by Mark's overture.

"Don't worry man; there's no one here," Mark added.

"No, no, someone might come," Eric replied, trying to gauge his reaction. He suddenly realized that didn't actually worry him; he just didn't want to have sex with Mark; the idea put him off. Not that he hadn't jerked off in locker rooms, not this one, but in gym steam rooms and saunas. But here, with Mark, he suddenly felt grubby, sullied, almost violated. He tried to move Mark's hand from his penis, but Mark only strengthened his grip and stood up, shoving his erect penis into Eric's face. He pushed him away forcefully; Mark fell back against the lockers.

"What's the matter? You don't wanna have some fun, for old times' sake?" Mark said with a leer.

Eric glared at him but remained silent.

"Oh, come on, don't give me that look. It's not like you don't like it anymore."

Images from times long since past flashed before his eyes, as in a promotional trailer of an old movie: the library at the Campus Club where they had first met, his apartment at Princeton, the French lessons and mornings in bed, out on the town with Mattie, Ali at the Club party, then Melissa and Consuelo, Campbell at Wimbledon, the momentous day at Cap and Gown.

"I was in love with you. You destroyed me," Eric muttered, as if to himself.

Mark, who wasn't sure if he had heard Eric correctly, asked, "What was that?"

"Nothing. Don't worry. Let's just get changed and go."

Mark didn't respond but began to dress. Eric felt a presence within him stir and gather strength, like a trickle of water turning into a flood. This inner voice, timid and taciturn, which had spoken in barely audible whispers, now stated in a measured and resounding tone:

"I was in love with you. You destroyed me."

"What are you talking about, man?" Mark replied, taken aback by the force of this pronouncement.

"I mean it, Mark. I loved you. I would have done anything for you. We could have made a life together. But you shredded me to pieces. Over nothing. Over some ridiculous fantasy letter to the editor."

"What is wrong with you, man? We're both married. We have kids. That was just a passing phase. Nothing more."

"Is that what it was for you? Well, it wasn't that for me. I was really hurt." Eric paused. That was an understatement. You recover from hurt. He had been annihilated, demolished, smashed into pieces like a porcelain vase shattering on a cement floor. "A part of me died after that day at lunch," he said resolutely, like someone who is suddenly able to identify the way out of a dense fog and exclaims, "Ah, there it is."

Mark, who was increasingly uncomfortable, had dressed quickly and said, "It's late. I need to get back home."

Eric disregarded Mark's remark and continued, "Did you hear what I said, Mark? A part of me died when you left me."

"Listen, Eric," replied Mark in an alarmed tone, "I'm sorry

you felt that way. But it was a long time ago. And I just wanted to play some tennis and catch up. I didn't expect this ...," his voice trailed off.

"Finish your sentence, Mark. You didn't expect what? For me to tell you the truth about how I felt about you? For what happened to me after you left me?"

For an instant, there was a look on Mark's face that betrayed an actual sincere emotion. Perhaps in that moment, the fog had cleared for him too, long enough to experience long forgotten feelings he had once harbored. But it was fleeting and he replied, "I don't remember things that way, and I didn't expect this conversation."

"How do you remember it, Mark?" Eric asked, emphasizing the word "do."

"We had a good time, a dalliance, and moved on. That's all."

Eric glanced at him. Could it be that that's all it was for Mark? He had always thought that Mark had loved him but had been held back expressing it by fear. Now, for the first time, he wondered if he had been deluding himself, if perhaps it was nothing more than "we had a good time and moved on." This thought, rolling in like a sandstorm in the desert, stunned him and he sat motionlessly and resigned on the bench.

Mark mistook his silence as a concession and relieved by it, he reached out to shake Eric's hand. "All right, man, it's late, and we played a lot. You must be really tired. A good night's sleep will do it."

Eric held out his hand mechanically, reflexively. He didn't notice when Mark left the locker room.

On the way back, Eric was sick to his stomach. Haphazard thoughts and images, some lurid and distasteful, bombarded him as in a fiercely pitched battle, causing him turmoil and confusion.

At home it was quiet. Everyone was asleep. He went to the guest room and began to undress. He felt like Atlas, holding up the sky after the Battle of the Titans, with no one to shoulder this burden for him, even for a minute. He wished to sleep and not wake up. As he took two valium tablets, he thought of emptying the whole bottle into his stomach, but it was an ephemeral thought, a dark remembrance; he didn't do it.

29

THAT NIGHT ERIC HAD A DREAM.

He was outside under a low, ashen sky. A massive volcanic eruption in Indonesia had released huge amounts of ash into the atmosphere, blocking out the sun and making a confinement of the most open of expanses.

The days collapsed into each other, permeated by a gray monotony from dawn to dusk. He moved mechanically from one day to the next as if on a long road, shrouded in dark mist, with no beginning and no end in sight. Time had either stopped or had accelerated so quickly it appeared to be still. Weeks and months rolled on as if he were on the same crepuscular road leading *nowhere in particular. Then suddenly, as happens only in dreams, Eric came upon a path of gravel and sand, leading into a forest. Here and there you could glimpse the sun through a morning mist that appeared to be lifting. He walked deeper into the woods, and the world around him appeared to be coming back to life. He noticed a squirrel darting about; a hedgehog burrowed into a hole as butterflies flapped their wings above him. Rays of sunlight piercing the canopy of branches cast little shadows here and there as in a chiaroscuro painting. Now the path became obscured, and he wondered where he was, not anxiously or fearfully, but with a calm and quiet composure he didn't recall feeling in the past.*

As he walked on, he saw a strange reflection in the distance. He continued in that direction and as he came closer, the reflection grew in brilliance. It appeared as if there were a structure, off of which light was being reflected in multiple directions, a sort of giant prism. He was drawn to it like metal to a magnet; the closer he approached, the faster it pulled him in. Now he was able to view the full structure; it was made of reflecting glass, a pentagonal house of mirrors. He had never seen anything like it with its talismanic-like quality as in an old fairytale. But he was drawn out of his bewilderment by a movement inside the glass house. As he peered closer, he noticed the figure of a young man with handsome features whom he appeared to recognize but couldn't recollect from exactly where. The young man beckoned him with a hand gesture, and as Eric approached he saw another figure, a boy of perhaps twelve or thirteen, whom he also had the impression of somehow knowing. The boy was playing by himself in a corner of the house.

Eric called out to the young man, who looked at him but did not respond. He wondered if he were deaf or didn't understand English.

"Vous parlez français?" "You speak French?" he asked, with no response. "Sprechen Sie Deutch?" "You speak German?" Still no response. "Farsi baladeen?" "You know Farsi?" No response.

"My God, what language do you speak?" Eric exclaimed in frustration.

"I speak all of them," the young man said in perfect English.

"Who are you?" asked Eric reflexively.

"What do you mean?"

"I mean, who are you?" Eric replied, opening the palm of his right hand as if to emphasize that the question was self-evident.

"Who are you?" he asked in return.

"Well, I'm Eric Richardson. I'm a corporate lawyer and live in New York City."

"Is that who you really are?" the young man asked pointedly.

"Of course that's who I am. What a question!"

At that point, the young man stepped closer and said, *"But have you always been a corporate lawyer who lives in New York?"*

"Well, for the last twenty-five years."

"What about before that?"

"Before that, I was in law school and before that in college."

"What college?" he asked with a bemused smile as if he already knew the answer.

"I went to Princeton," Eric said, then paused. *"What's the point of these questions?"*

"So do I," chimed in the young man.

"What do you mean 'so do I'"?

"I mean I go to Princeton."

"Oh really! What class are you in?"

"I'm in the class of '87," the young man said.

"Don't be ridiculous. I was in the class of 1987. You're too young to have been there at that time." Again the bemused smile. *"Tell me what class you're really in."*

"As I said, the class of 1987."

Eric began to think this young man was addle-brained or insane.

"*The class of 1987 graduated more than thirty years ago. You're not even twenty years old.*"

The young man didn't respond but just stared at Eric. He was calm and self-possessed and didn't appear at all insane. In fact, he seemed completely lucid.

"*Anyway, what's your name? Where do you live?*" asked Eric of the young man.

"*My name is Eric and I live in Paris; I mean my parents live in Paris, but I go to Princeton.*"

"*Wait, who are your parents?*" he asked uneasily.

"*So many questions! I'm tired.*"

"*Please, tell me who your parents are,*" Eric insisted.

"*What does it matter? I told you I'm tired, very tired. I think I'm coming down with the flu. But I can't afford to be sick; I have to finish my senior thesis and ...*" he said and trailed off with a sigh, glancing into the distance.

"*Oh, don't mind him,*" said the little boy, who had walked over during this exchange but had remained silent. "*He's in love,*" he continued, drawing out the word "*love*" mockingly.

Eric shuddered. It was as if he had been hit in the head by a heavy object. He was dazed and scrutinized the young man, now with more recognition. For the first time he became aware of his forlorn, rueful disposition as if it were his own.

"*What's your name?*" Eric asked, turning to the boy.

He didn't respond and kept looking around as if he had lost something.

"*What are you looking for?*" Eric asked very gently.

The boy looked back at Eric, who could see the wariness, almost a mistrust, in his eyes.

"*Don't be afraid. I won't hurt you. In fact, I'll help you, if I can.*"

"*I want to go home,*" blurted the boy and started to sob.

Eric wanted to hold and comfort him, as if he were his own son, but didn't feel it was appropriate.

"Where's home for you?"

"Tehran, but we're moving soon. We're moving out of Iran, and I need to get home before my mum leaves."

"She's not going to leave without you."

"How do you know?"

"I don't for sure, but I can't imagine a mother leaving her son behind."

"There you see; you don't know anything. You talk like the rest of them. The Islamics. You don't care what happens to me."

"Oh, don't listen to him. He's delusional," said the young man. "He actually thinks he's in Iran and it's the early 1980s. He doesn't realize we're in Princeton, in the U.S."

"I've never been to America you fool," retorted the boy.

The young man smacked the boy on the side of the head, and the boy kicked him back in the shins.

"Ow, you animal," the young man said. "You're a donkey, that's what you are. You even kick like a donkey."

"You're a donkey yourself," the boy said, then retreated to the back of the room.

"How long have you been here?" asked Eric of the young man.

"I'm in my final year."

"What did he mean when he said you're in love?" Eric asked heedfully.

The young man shook his head in frustration. "The boy doesn't know what he's talking about. I told you, he's delusional ... mad, batshit crazy."

"So you're not in love."

"Of course I'm not. That's ridiculous. Who even knows what that means?"

"You're not in love with Mark?" Eric persisted.

The young man looked at him suspiciously.

"What makes you say that?"

"I, I, because ... I was once in love ..." he said and trailed off. Was I really in love with Mark? he thought.

"Well, yes, I guess I am, if you put it that way," the young man said hesitantly, as if completing Eric's thought.

"I know," Eric replied, who had an impulse to draw the young man to him and hug him as he had wanted to do with the boy.

"I'm dying," said the young man.

"You'll get over him. Trust me, I know you will," Eric said with assurance.

"No, I won't. I'll die before that."

"What are you talking about? I know love hurts. I feel your pain, but it will pass. In time."

"No, it won't. The pain is too great. It'll kill me, or ... I'll kill myself."

"Don't say that. You won't do any such thing."

"Yes, I will. What's the point of going on anyway? Just to be ravaged by this stupid disease and die a slow, ignominious death?" he asked of Eric.

"Wait, what disease are you talking about?"

"AIDS, you fucking asshole. AIDS, AIDS, AIDS." He spat out the words, like venom from a snake.

"You don't have AIDS. You can't have it."

"Well, I do. I should know. I got the diagnosis, idiot."

"How did you contract it?" asked Eric incredulously.

"At the baths. A while ago. This guy I met at a bar took me there."

"But you didn't go in. You didn't want to leave your wallet."

"I know. But he left his gold chain and we went in."

"No, he didn't. He said he didn't have anything to leave."

"I just told you. He left his chain. We got a room. He fucked me."

A tear rolled down his face as he said this.

"I'm almost glad, because the pain of my loss is too much, and now I can end it all. I know I'll die anyway," continued the young man.

"Come here," Eric said. The young man hesitated. "Come with me. I'm going to take you home with me. To where you will be safe, where no one can hurt you. Do you hear me? I love you as I love my own children." The young man walked over hesitantly, and Eric held him in his arms. He began to sob quietly, as Eric patted him on the back for reassurance.

Eric saw the boy looking over at them, in confusion. He called the boy over to him, and as he approached, the young man receded to the back of the room.

"Look, I want to help you too, but you have to tell me where you are."

"Where am I? Same place as you! In this godforsaken desert with all these Islamic fanatics, the crazies."

"Okay," Eric said patiently. "How did you get here?"

"They brought me in the back of a military truck. With other kids."

"Do you know why?"

"How should I know? They're maniacs, bloodthirsty assholes, who knows what they think?" he said in anger and desperation.

"Does your mum know you're here? Does anyone?"

"No, except for that double-crossing math teacher. That snake who promised to help me, and then delivered me into the hands of these assholes."

"Wait, you mean Mr. Nasr?"

"The very one."

"How did it happen?"

"Well, he told me he could help me find Farhad. You see, they'd taken Farhad from his home, and I wanted to know if he was all right. Mr. Nasr told me that he would take me to him. Instead, he delivered me to these crazies."

"Farhad?" Eric asked, just to be sure he had heard right.

"He's my friend. My only friend, really. The only person who was nice to me at school after the—" The boy stopped, not able to articulate it. "We were supposed to move to England together. I mean our families were."

"And then they took Farhad away?"

"That's right."

"How come you didn't leave the country before that?"

"We tried but couldn't. I mean, they wouldn't let my mum go, then we got caught trying to escape."

"How?"

"Over the mountains to Turkey, and they caught us."

"This was after the Revolution then?"

"Of course it was after . . . that," he said with a snicker. "Why would we do that before? We could just take a plane and leave."

"But you did take a plane," Eric found himself saying, caught between two realities, two selves.

"No, I didn't. We tried at the end, with my mother and grand-mother, but they wouldn't let us leave the airport."

"But, but . . . I, I mean you left with your grandmother and your mother came out later."

"No, I didn't," the boy said impatiently.

The boy was trapped in this reality, and Eric couldn't persuade him otherwise.

"Well, I'm going to take you away from this place. I'm going to take you to my house where you will be safe. I'll introduce you to my

daughters. They would love to have a brother. You can live with us."
An expression of great relief appeared on the boy's face, but as Eric
went to hold his hand, he started to wake up from the dream.

For an instant he was suspended in the space between sleep
and wakefulness; his consciousness floating between dream and
reality, or his reality. He thought he was still speaking with the
boy and kept reaching for his hand. But, as his eyes opened, the
glass house faded away, giving way to the guest room. "Wait,
don't go," he found himself saying out loud to an empty room.
As the dream receded, he intuited that something exceptional
was happening; that he was in one of those transformative,
revelatory moments, so rarely experienced in life, whose significance was as yet hidden to him. He reached for a pen and paper
on the desk and wrote down the dream.

30

ERIC ROSE AND STEPPED OVER
to the window, looked out
onto a blue, cloudless sky and saw
a luminous reflection off his neigh-
bor's rooftop conservatory, which
reminded him of the house in his
dream. He felt somehow buoyed by
this revelation. He went to the closet
and retrieved a suit of clothing—he
slept in the guest room more often
than not—dressed and went down to
breakfast. The maid had prepared a
bowl of fruit for him, and when she
saw him arrive in the dining room,
she went to make coffee and toast
some bread. He stepped into the
kitchen and looked at her.

"Good morning, Sir," she said.

"Good morning, Carmen," he replied. For the first time, Eric looked at her as a person, saw her moving around the kitchen, inserting the capsule into the Nespresso machine, and then placing bread in the toaster.

"How are you today, Carmen, how did you sleep?"

A bit startled, she replied in broken English, "I sleep well, Sir."

"How is your family? How are your children doing? You have two grown children, don't you?"

"Yes, Sir. And they are fine, gracias a Dios."

As he looked closer, Eric could see a little tightness around her eyes. "No, I mean really tell me. How is everyone? I want to know."

Carmen hesitated. This familiarity was so unlike her employer. While always polite and correct, he remained aloof and reserved. Their interactions had been brief, and he was often irritated by her broken English. For the most part, he had kept their conversations to a bare minimum and limited to his domestic needs: such as the quantity of fruit that she would present on a plate for his breakfast. But today his smile was genuine. This encouraged her to tell him the truth.

"But my daughter mucho problem with her husband."

"Come into the dining room, Carmen, sit down and tell me all about it."

The coffee was ready; she first brought Eric a cup and then sat herself down and began describing her daughter's marital issues. One by one she went through the difficulties with her daughter's husband and five children; it all came down to money, or rather the lack thereof.

Eric listened to her intently with new compassion. It was as if he were hearing her speak for the very first time. His usual impatience with her poor English and her customary complaints about her personal life, gave way to a profound interest in her and her concerns. While he listened to her tale of woe, he considered Carmen's whole being, her worn-out hands, and the tired, wary look in her eyes. For the first time, he saw her as she really was, not as he had always pictured her—a dumb maid who didn't speak English—but as a fellow human being, with feelings and problems which, while superficially different than his, were fundamentally of the same order of suffering, as a Buddhist might call it. With this new understanding came empathy, and he squeezed her hand.

"I'm going to help you, Carmen. We are going to work on these problems together. I want to speak with your daughter and her husband, and I want to help them with their money problems."

"El Senor Dios, the Lord, answered my prayers. Bless you," she said.

At that moment Celia wafted into the room in an elaborate kimono. Carmen jumped up from the table, but Eric said, "Please sit down Carmen. We haven't finished."

"What's going on here?" Celia asked, looking at the two of them warily.

"Good morning, dear. Hope you slept well," Eric inquired, rising to give her a kiss on the cheek.

Celia was taken aback. "Really. You want to know how I slept?" she said, staring back at him in disbelief. "What's gotten into you this morning?" she exclaimed, frowning.

"Nothing. I just hoped you slept well."

"Well, if you must know, I didn't, as always. Now, Carmen, I'd like my coffee black this morning. And make some egg whites for me. Take care that none of the yokes gets in there ... the yellow part ... solo blanco, only white."

Carmen nodded her head and hurried into the kitchen. For a moment Eric was upset with his wife. "Typical of her to breeze in and start commandeering everyone," he said to himself. He was on the verge of snapping at her but then he looked at Celia more carefully, watched her pull out a chair and sit down, the kimono slipping off her thin bare legs, the sharp movement of her hand as she grabbed the newspaper. He watched her with focused attention, and, as with Carmen, it was as if he were seeing his wife with new eyes.

"I'm sorry you didn't sleep well. Why do you think it was?"

Celia looked up from the newspaper, almost astonished by this question. "I never sleep well. And since when do you care about that or anything to do with me?"

"I'm sorry you feel that way," Eric said, almost shuddering.

Celia saw his reaction and quickly deflected his concern. "And what were you talking to Carmen about?"

Behind her brittle façade, Eric glimpsed her insecurity, the disappointment and confusion about them and their life together. She had loved him once and he had hurt her greatly. The noise in his mind had covered all this up, but now it had abated, and with his new attentiveness, he saw her as she really was—wounded, vulnerable, and fragile.

He reached over and held her hand, "Celia, I'm sorry. You have the right to be mistrustful, but I've always cared about you and I care now more than ever."

She glared at him, mystified by his declaration of love, and not knowing how to respond. Their tacit antagonism had become so habitual by now that she thought he was mocking her.

"Stop it, Eric. I'm in no mood for your little jokes. Besides, you'd better leave, or you'll be late for work."

"My work can wait, and I'm not joking at all. I'm concerned about your lack of sleep; I'm concerned about you. I care for you."

Celia stared into eyes filled with compassion. His sincerity was no longer in doubt.

"Well, that's very nice, dear. What's caused this new concern for me?" she replied, her tone softening a bit.

"I don't know," he said, in a tone that reflected genuine perplexity. "I just woke up this morning and realized that ..." he paused, searching for the right words, "that ... you and the girls are the only things that really matter to me."

Celia's eyes widened. "My God, Eric. Do you really feel that way?" she asked, having to catch her breath.

"Yes, absolutely." He squeezed her hand as he said this. "Let's go to dinner tonight; just you and me, like we used to."

"If you like," she said tentatively, still in disbelief. "Where would you like to go?"

"How about Elio's? We always liked it there."

"Okay, I'll reserve. Shall we say around 8:30?"

"That sounds perfect."

At that moment Carmen walked in with Celia's coffee and eggs.

He rose from the table and kissed his wife on the cheek and walked off. They both watched him leave, mystified.

31

A T WORK THAT DAY, there was
a partners' meeting to discuss
associate compensation. Their firm
was among the trendsetters in first-
year associate salaries, which acted
as the benchmark for the industry.
Each year the top firms competed for
the best talent, usually from the top
Ivy League law schools. The Above
the Law website had turned what
once was a discrete and staid issue
into a highly public one and what
some would consider an unnecessar-
ily dissonant affair. The meeting did
not consist of the entire firm's partnership; rather it was a committee of
influential partners, mostly the rain-
makers who controlled the firm's

client relationships. This included the firm's formidable chairman, Theodore Crompton III, affectionately and some would say paradoxically, known as Ted. He opened the meeting and got straight to the point:

"Well, we've heard through the grapevine that Cravath is raising compensation to one-eighty. We've got to beat them to it."

A few of the partners grumbled. Associate salaries were the largest cost item for the firm, and while everyone in the room made more than two million a year, and some made in excess of that figure, they considered associate salaries as unjustly reducing their profits. That associates were made to work unreasonable hours, at great sacrifice to their families and personal lives, and, most importantly, that without them, the firm would not function, were immaterial considerations. Associates were uniformly considered to be overpaid and undeserving ingrates and any mention of augmenting their pay was consistently met with resounding disapproval.

"One hundred eighty thousand is too high to pay these numbskulls who take years to train properly. My clients don't want to pay for first- and, increasingly, second-year associates. We have to really think about this increase," said Brian, the head of litigation—a red-faced, Irish New Yorker in his mid-fifties from a working-class background in Brooklyn. He was a graduate of Brooklyn Law School who had pulled himself up by the bootstraps to become a partner at the firm.

"Well, if Cravath goes to one-eighty, everyone's gonna follow, and we'll eventually have to or be satisfied with second-tier applicants," responded the chair, who disliked associates and their compensation just as much as his fellow partners, but whose experience and judgment tempered his greed.

"It's all because of that fucking website. If it weren't for them, we wouldn't be having these issues," Brian retorted.

"Maybe, but Brian, Ted's right. We can't be looked at as 'second-best.' We need to be viewed as leaders in all aspects of this business," said another partner.

"I'm gonna put it to a vote," Ted said. "Please raise your hand if you think we should move up to 180 right away."

Four out of seven hands went up to win the issue.

"Well, it sure as hell isn't gonna come out of our pay. Make the juniors and counsel take the hit," Brian said, referring to the junior partners and the senior counsel who hadn't made partnership yet.

"We make more than everyone else in the firm," Eric spoke up for the first time. "More than any others, this group can afford to absorb some extra costs. Why not spread the cost to the whole partnership, with those who make most bearing more of the cost?"

The others just looked at him as if he had turned into a unicorn, reared his front legs, and pissed on them.

"I haven't worked my ass off here for the last thirty years to give it all away to a bunch of lazy undeserving ingrates," Brian spat out. "If you've suddenly become a limousine liberal, Eric, why don't you fund the increase out of your take, which is larger than most."

Eric felt the blood rising to his cheeks. He had never liked Brian; he considered him a quintessential bully, uncouth, with no refinement or polish whatsoever.

"You forget Brian," Eric said, slowly enunciating each word while he imperiously fixed his gaze on his opponent, "that your department services our clients. Many times I've had to explain away and take the brunt for your losses and defeats of my clients' cases, as I'm sure others around this table have done. All things considered, why don't we take the increase out of your take instead?"

Brian looked over at Ted and gestured toward Eric, "You're gonna let him talk like this to me?"

Ted almost smiled. "All right you guys, enough's enough. We're all in this together. Let's not get carried away. Time to vote on it."

One of the partners looked puzzled. "What are we voting on? I thought we'd agreed to the one-eighty increase?"

"On how we're going to absorb the increase in associate pay. Whether it's going to come out of the junior partners and counsel shares, or whether it's whole partnership, including this group. If you vote for the juniors and counsel, raise your hand." Six out of seven hands went up.

"That settles it then. We'll announce the raises tomorrow. Thank you."

With that, Ted adjourned the meeting. He was an effective chairman, Eric thought, or at least in the way he managed to keep these six prima donnas in check at meetings.

As they shuffled out of the room, Eric looked over at Brian. For an instant their eyes met, and he noticed something that stirred him. Instead of his brash, vulgar persona, he saw a human being who, like himself, suffered and sought to be happy and was mostly miserable. He recognized the insecurities that lurked beneath the pugnacious facade, insecurities doubtlessly linked as much to his corpulence and slovenly appearance as well as to his working-class background. Eric regretted his sharp words at the meeting and smiled at Brian, but the man had already averted his gaze and had turned to walk out of the room in a huff.

———

THAT EVENING, after a quick workout at the gym, Eric met Celia at Elio's for dinner. He complimented her on her dress, and she gave him a quizzical look. "Well, thank you! Since when do you notice my dresses?"

She remained mystified by her husband's early morning congeniality.

"I don't know," he said gently, "I suppose now. But, just know that you look great, that's all."

She smiled graciously, evidently softening up to him. They ordered a bottle of Chianti. As they took sips from their glasses, Celia leaned back in her seat and asked in a jocular tone, "So Eric, what's this all about? This change of heart. Has something happened? Are we risking financial ruin?"

"Nothing of the sort," he replied. "Why would you think that?"

"I don't know. I thought there has to be some reason that, after all these years, you've asked me to Elio's for dinner, where you first courted me."

Eric laughed. "Oh, I courted you?"

Celia smiled. "Well, if I'd waited until you made the first move, hell might have frozen over."

Eric nodded his head. "There's no reason at all. I just ... I just thought ..." Eric paused. Why had he asked her to dinner? he wondered. "I suppose I'm missing us, and just thought it would be nice to spend some quiet time together like we used to. Remember how we'd come here and drink wine until we closed the place down?"

Celia just gazed at him. "Yes, I remember," she replied. "We were so young and naïve."

"Young maybe, but we were never naïve," he riposted, and then lowering his voice, he added, "Celia, I'm sorry if I've let you down."

She looked at Eric in surprise. "My, my, this is a different

Eric. What have they put in your wine?" she joked, holding her glass up to the light.

"Well, maybe it's just taken awhile to breathe our vintage wine," he replied with a smile. He then reached out and took her hand. "Celia, I mean it. What I said this morning. I do care for you. I love you and our daughters and our family."

"Come on Eric, after all this time ... a profession of love. Really," she replied somewhat skeptically.

"I, I, care for you, Celia. I want to know what you think and feel about that."

"What I think and feel about you loving me?" she repeated, somewhat startled. "I don't know what to say."

"Well, can you tell me how you feel about me?"

Celia just stared back at him dumbfounded, then looked around hoping the waiter would rescue her.

She was beginning to frustrate him, and he felt himself retreat into his habitual protective shell, about to lash out with some cutting remark, but he caught himself. For a moment he felt uncertain, suspended between the momentum of habitual mental patterns and a new lucid awareness, like two children balanced on each end of a seesaw. After a moment of silence, he said, in a measured tone. "Celia, there is something I want to tell you."

"I knew it," she responded in a sing-song tone. "What? Another woman?" she said, almost skeptically.

Eric caught the nuance in her voice. "No, of course not." He paused, and then continued, "You see, all these years I've struggled with my sexuality. I find myself attracted to men." He waited for the full weight of this declaration to hit her, convinced that it would elicit either sarcasm or scorn, or perhaps both.

"I know," Celia responded calmly.

"What do you mean, you know?" Eric asked, stunned at her reaction.

"I mean I know about that. I've known for a long time."

"How do you know? How come you never said anything?" he asked stupefied.

"I'm not stupid, Eric. I may be a lot of things, but stupid I'm not."

"Is there something I did? I thought I was always—" He stopped mid-sentence.

"Discreet? Is that the word? Well, not sufficiently discreet, as it were."

"What do you mean? Please don't do this. Just tell me what you know."

"Well, years ago, I suspected that you might be cheating and had you followed. You went to a hotel with another guy. Shall I continue?" she asked rhetorically, the timbre of her voice revealing a tinge of triumph.

Eric was breathless, bewildered as much by the substance of Celia's revelation as by the perfect equanimity of her delivery.

"How come you didn't say anything?"

"I was going to. I was furious and I cried in private. I felt shattered. But I didn't want a divorce. I didn't want a broken home for our daughters. And I didn't want a scandal. Imagine what people would say if they thought we divorced because you were gay. I'd be the laughing stock of all New York," she said in the same imperturbable tone.

Eric noticed that she had referred to him as "gay" rather than "bisexual," and he knew that she was closer to the mark, but he felt too overwhelmed to respond. He needed time to process this startling information.

"It's funny how people think we have the perfect marriage," continued Celia. "So many husbands cheat, or they drink and are abusive or even worse: they're fat, have bad breath, and don't care about their appearance or lack of emotional responsiveness. They figure that giving their wives all this money should keep them happy. But you and I, we look great, no public displays of ill-temper or rumors of infidelity; we're the model of the happy New York family," she said with relish as if she were showing off a manicured garden that she had spent years cultivating.

"So what do you want to do now?" asked Eric, flummoxed and confused.

Celia smiled, enjoying her superior position for once. "I think perhaps order some dessert, and we can share one."

"I mean in terms of us?" he persisted.

"What do you mean in terms of us?" she asked, looking straight at him and shrugging her shoulders as if to say he was making no sense.

To Eric's bewildered look, she continued, "Nothing has changed Eric. We go on as we have. Would you like to share a crème brûlée?"

32

T HEY WERE SPENDING THE weekend in the Hamptons, and Celia and the girls had left early on Friday afternoon. Eric planned to drive out on Saturday morning. He rather enjoyed the occasional free evening to do as he wished, whether it was to catch up with a friend over a drink or a workout and steam at the gym. On this particular evening, he arrived home at around 6:00 P.M. The sun was still shining, and he looked forward to the quiet, cool, and shaded interior of their apartment. Carmen had left with the rest of the family, so he had the whole flat to himself. He fetched a cold bottle of Heineken from the fridge, and on the way to his study he picked up from the guest room the papers on which he had scribbled down his dream from the other night.

He sat down on the plush, black leather sofa and read through the papers, astonished by the dream he had recorded. Had he actually dreamt this, or was it his imagination going wild? It wasn't that he didn't recall having a strange dream two nights ago, but he remembered only fragments from it and had just jotted down the key points the next morning. He read it over several times. There was no doubt in his mind that the boy and the young man were aspects of himself. Indeed they were him and both expressed his state of mind at that stage of his life. But if so, what explained the boy being stuck in Iran after the Revolution while he had escaped? Eric thought about it now, the chaotic scene at the Tehran airport, the bearded man who had taken them to a different room, the appalling discovery that his mother was on a blacklist. But his mother had had the foresight to send him and his grandmother on to Paris, a decision he had embraced. She had joined them in Paris the following year when they moved in with his stepfather. But the boy in his dream had clearly stated that he hadn't left Iran.

As he read and reread the lines he had written, he began to recall the exchange in even greater detail. There was no doubt about it. They had gone to the airport, but had all three of them been turned back? He had occasionally pondered what life would have been like if he had not left Iran that day, if he had stayed during the tumultuous years after the Revolution, especially when he read books about that period. But each time, Eric would draw a blank; his mind could go no further into a palimpsestic past that eluded him. No doubt, due to the break caused by the Revolution, he could not picture himself in Iran, even during happier times, as if his entire childhood there had been a dream.

Now he dreamt that he had stayed, or at least a part of him had. "What can this mean?" he thought. The boy had referenced the desert, the frontlines of the war with Iraq. If he had stayed, he could have been forcibly taken to the front lines as a human mine detector as were many boys his age. He could have died; most likely would have died there. Eric paused and considered his own fragile mortality; he put his beer down and ran his hands over his arms; he was alive, he had survived. His mother's decision to send him with his grandmother had seemed so obvious in retrospect that he had never grasped its significance. Now, as he looked back on it, through the lens of the dream, he realized its fateful nature; he owed his life to it—a seemingly simple decision—he even remembered Lili's words to her mother, "Maman, why don't you and Keyvan go; I'll stay and sort this out. He shouldn't stay in this environment." He hadn't given it another thought afterward, and yet it was the most important turning point in his life and it hadn't even been his decision or initiated by him. He thought about the capriciousness of life. The words "play and win each time" echoed in his mind as he pondered all the struggles, the hard work, the heartache, and then thought about the young man in the dream.

Eric had no doubt that he, too, was an aspect of himself. But he had said he had AIDS. The young man insisted that he had gone into the bathhouse. But Eric knew that he himself had refused to hand over his wallet and they hadn't let him in. For a second he doubted his own memory; perhaps he had gone inside, but he knew that he had never contracted AIDS. He had been tested multiple times and he was fine. So what had happened? He went back in his mind and tried to recall

that evening, but only this pivotal momer
was a blur, as in a house that you have
and can only remember a vague outline
ollect much about those years, other than a jumbɪc ....
ria. It occurred to him those college years were like a fantasy,
as if they had not been real, much like his childhood in Iran.
Was it the fallibility of his memory? For surely our memories
are untrustworthy—like an old book out of which many pages
are torn. Or perhaps it was something else at work: an oblit-
eration, a subconscious deletion of painful experiences, like
a little death—la petite mort? For the boy and the young man
had each died tragically and been buried in the dark recesses of
his mind. "That's it," he thought, "they each represent a psychological death: an irredeemable part of me had died in Iran
and again at Princeton; I never recovered from those deaths or
reclaimed the lost vitality that they represented, and that's why
my life is like a gilded sepulcher."

His mind came back to the question of AIDS; how he had
escaped it while the young man in his dream had been laid low
by the disease? He had caught it at the bathhouse—the bathhouse that he had refused to enter because he wouldn't leave
behind his valuables—like his very life, which had been stolen
from the young man. So he had escaped AIDS and certain death
because of this refusal. He allowed this thought to sink in,
and as it did, the congruity with his fortuitous liberation from
Khomeini's Iran took shape, like a story told on a large tapestry.
This reflection led to a new insight—that free will, if it was not
an illusion, was a feckless mistress. What better proof than his
own experiences, his narrow and truly spectacular escapes from
the jowls of death twice, which he hadn't until this moment
even been aware of. The irony caused him to snicker.

Now he wondered what had obscured his vision, or what

...her parts of him had intervened? He had never considered himself lucky. He began to see himself in a new light as if he had hidden resources that his conscious self had been unaware of all these years.

Eric stepped over to a storage cabinet where he kept old, personal papers. He had retained his notebooks, essays, and old exams from his days at Princeton in a box but hadn't looked at these since he graduated years ago. He opened the box and looked through it. There were essays on Kafka, Flaubert, Shakespeare; he began to read through them. There was his award-winning senior thesis on Proust. But what intrigued him the most was an essay that explored the theme of blindness in literature, as exemplified in *Oedipus Rex* and *King Lear*—two powerful kings brought down by their own blindness, literally and figuratively.

Oedipus is the most valiant warrior in the realm—he defies and kills Laius, a powerful lord and unbeknownst to him, his own father. He is also the most intelligent and vanquishes the crafty Sphinx by solving her unsolvable riddle. Yet, he is destroyed, not by another man (or woman), but by himself, or rather by his blindness to who he is and where he originates. The aphorism "know thyself" was inscribed on Apollo's temple at Delphi, the very place from which emanates the portentous messages that Oedipus (and Laius before him) fatally misapprehend. The Sphinx's riddle and the Oracle's warnings represent two sides of the same coin: each in its own way points to the same primordial question of "who am I" or, "what is mankind?" Oedipus correctly answered the Sphinx's riddle: "What is the creature that walks on four legs in the morning, two legs at noon, and three in the evening?" "Man," he had replied, and by his verbal response had destroyed the primordial beast. But what is the answer to "who am I?" The only person who appears to know that answer is the blind seer Tiresias, to whom Oedipus turns when groping for the truth of his identity. Tiresias's response, that "Well, it will come what will, though I be mute," angers Oedipus, but points to the ultimate truth, a truth that Oedipus will only grasp when he is blinded and cast out of power.

All of a sudden, Eric felt that his questions were being answered from within himself, the locks unlocked. He thought about the Sphinx's riddle: "What is the creature that walks on four legs in the morning, two legs at noon and three in the evening?"

Wasn't that him? The boy and the young man in his dream, and now himself watching them? Wasn't that the answer to the Sphinx's riddle? Man is born, he grows up to be strong for a while, and then declines and dies. There's nothing to be done about that. And yet, that is just the surface, the first layer of the palimpsest as it were, which was readily uncovered by Oedipus's intelligence. A more fundamental truth behind the riddle is captured in Tiresias' words "it will come what will" and in that sense, the riddle is a microcosm of the play and of life itself. Man's journey is not only linear—from birth to death—but appears predestined, or in the hands of a higher order—Oedipus falls into the very trap that he tries to escape. Eric thought of his own life. He had escaped Khomeini's Iran and potential death, not due to any act of valor or intelligence on his part, but because of a last-minute suggestion by his mother and his agreement with it; was that luck? Was it destiny? Was it all preordained? Later on in life, at Princeton, he could have caught AIDS, almost surely would have and would likely have died; he didn't because of the adventitious and inadvertent intervention of a surly bathhouse attendant and his own auspicious refusal to part with his "valuables."

He paused for a minute and caught his breath. His dream had awakened him to some important truths, and now his own essays were clarifying the meaning behind these hidden truths. He had gone through life obliviously, almost as if he were sleepwalking. He thought of his past struggles, the energy expended trying to achieve fortune, stability, love (yes, he had to admit, love, which he had long ago given up on). Was it all for naught? If his life had been predestined, then what's the point of making any decision; what's the point of striving to achieve anything. "I can't imagine that this type of nihilism is what underlies Oedipus's story," he now thought, perplexed. And yet, Oedipus's fate appeared to be a foregone conclusion; his destiny ordained even as he was born, foretold by the first oracular message to Laius. Clearly, there was a force far more powerful and intelligent than Oedipus—a mere mortal—that was directing the course of his life. This force, whose source remains obscure in the play but which is hinted at and appears to be communicated through the god Apollo at his temple at Delphi, cries out to him to "know thyself." Oedipus is blind to this force; he struggles against it and loses, as he must.

It was as if his younger selves, the boy and young man in his dream, were sending him messages through time, answering questions to which perhaps he didn't have the answers but was receiving them from some hidden source as had Sophocles, Hugo, and Proust. They had obtained the information, or rather the inspiration, from the ultimate source to which all these works were pointing. He thought of the description of the Battle of Waterloo in *Les Miserables*, a chapter that had always perplexed him because it appeared to have no relevance whatsoever to the plot and the drama that unfolds in the novel. Now Eric glimpsed the pertinence of Waterloo. Napoleon is the most powerful man in the world, a mighty general before whom the

indomitable empires of Russia and Austria co
that fatal day in Waterloo, this omnipotent em
As in *Oedipus*, there is another force, even more powerful than
Napoleon himself that is hinted at:

"Un mystérieux froncement de sourcil devient visible au fond
du ciel." "A mysterious frown became visible deep in the sky."

This hidden power appears if not to orchestrate, then to
guide the lives of the characters in the novel. It is this same
power that underlies the conversion of Jean Valjean through
the beneficence of Bishop Myriel. While its mechanisms
may vary, it is always the same power, and if it overwhelms
Napoleon, it most certainly shapes the destinies of the mere
mortals like Valjean, Fantine, Javert, and Thenardier.

And now, Eric turned to Proust and his *A La Recherche du
Temps Perdu*, and there it was again, the same power; to be
sure described differently, but it had the same hallmarks: A lifetime wasted in pursuit of meaningless love affairs and enslaved
by jealousy; a brilliant but equally unfulfilling social life; and
that unflappable monster time, obscure, yet deadly and inexorable, triturating the lives of the characters in the novel. And
yet, there is something even more powerful than time itself, a
force that Marcel the narrator-persona glimpses on rare occasions such as when he dunks his Madeleine in his tea—a force
that has enabled Marcel the author to create such a monumental work, one that can withstand the tides of time. What is this
force and where does it come from? Proust suggests strongly
that it is innate, that it is within us and ever present, but we
are blind to it because we never look within ourselves; we seek
fulfillment outside, in love or society, but these are delusions
that eventually collapse like a house of cards, leaving behind
confusion and suffering, and in the case of Swann, mental and
physical destruction. It is not until the end of the novel that the

narrator finally appears to grasp the locus of this force when he encounters the book *Francois le Champis* in the library of the Hotel de Guermantes. Only then does he for the first time look inward to discover, or rather rediscover, that fatal night of his childhood in Combray. The pivot to the internal world is what connects Marcel to the force that enables him to vanquish his indolent habits, that liberates him of his habitual past—the one that he has lived in the external world of love and society—and empowers him to turn to another coexistent past, which Eric now was doing, that exists only within Marcel, to recreate that world in the form of a novel, which is, of course, the classic novel we have just finished reading!

At this juncture, Eric stopped reading. Like Oedipus, like Napoleon, like Marcel, like the rest of humankind, he had been mindlessly seeking happiness and salvation in the external world. Now, for the first time, he closed his eyes and turned inward; he noticed his body, the weight of his bottom on the chair, his left hand resting on his knee, his feet planted on the ground beneath him; he became aware that he blinked quite often, that his throat was dry. Then he began to notice something else—his thoughts—how quickly they arose and confounded him. Yet, as fast as they came, they dissolved even faster! "Wait, what is this idea?" he thought, and as soon as he had thought this, he was again lost in thought until, a few minutes later he became aware again, or some part of him, that he was thinking. Suddenly it occurred to him that his thoughts were not solid; that they were fleeting, ephemeral. "Where do they come from?" he wondered. He realized that he had no choice in the matter; it wasn't as if he chose his thoughts; they just came, one after another in quick succession. "Where do they come from?" he thought again. They're just like dreams, and so perhaps they come from the same place, from that part of the mind that lies below the consciousness, conditioned by the past, like a set of footprints in fresh snow that you would follow if you were lost in the woods.

His next realization was equally perplexing and profound: that a thought gave rise to an emotion. First came the thought, then the emotion. Once again he went down a rabbit hole of thought. He pondered why modern science had nothing to say about this; what is a thought? What is an emotion? How do they arise? Science was silent, or his purview of it. And what about Descartes' "I think; therefore I am." He should have said, "I think, therefore I am lost!" and then it struck him. Wait. Who is thinking? What entity is thinking? What is it, or who is it, that is observing these thoughts and emotions? There is something within him that is looking at these thoughts; that is aware that he is thinking and feeling them. What is that? Could it be the force alluded to in the works of literature he had just been reading, the hand that shapes our destinies? "That's it," he thought, and then he laughed, the wide-bellied Buddha laugh of awakening, of realizing for the first time that he was not synonymous with his thoughts. "I see," he thought, realizing, that until now, he had been blind. Blind to the thoughts that he had mistaken for reality and had driven him, that had incarcerated him in an invisible prison of his own making! It had been so all his life. Keyvan had been trapped in circles of thought—his concern for Farhad and his obsession with leaving Iran—it wasn't his physical confinement in Iran that had destroyed him; it was his mental confinement within a prison of thought that allowed him to be duped by his teacher; the very same thoughts that were intended to find him a way out of Iran but which had led to his demise. Eric, too, had been destroyed by his own thoughts; consumed by his love for Mark, he had been unaware that the emotion he called love was preceded, perhaps generated by a series of temporary, ephemeral thoughts from which his tragic attraction for Mark arose, creating a psychological prison from which he had been unable to escape. It was as if each loop of thought pushed him deeper into the recesses of a labyrinth from which there was no hope of finding a way out. Yet now, in the cool light of inner observation, the prison bars collapsed, the maze faded and he became aware that if there is an Eric, it isn't Eric the law partner, or Eric the father or husband, or Eric the disconsolate lover, or Eric/Keyvan the child victim of an Islamic Revolution; no, it's the Eric who observes all of them; in whom all the thoughts and emotions unfold. The true Eric is nameless; it is connected to the force that directs our lives, perhaps is the force and it comes into view when there is a gap in the stream of thought. This is why the Buddha smiles so enigmatically. Now he understood the young man's remark in his dream when, in response to Eric's statement that he was Eric Richardson and was a corporate lawyer who lived in New York, he had asked if that's who he really was. The young man was pointing to the same source from which universal truths emanate, the source that knows "who you are," who we all are—not our names or addresses, not our professions or affiliations, nor our degrees or accolades, but who we really are, as Tiresias knew about Oedipus.

This realization had a cathartic effect. It was as if a huge burden had been lifted from his shoulders; the burden that comes from acting out this flow of incessant and relentless mental chatter. He sighed and looked down at his hands. He put back the books and the papers and realized he was tired and went to bed.

When he woke the next morning, the sun was shining. He rose and went out to fetch his car to drive to East Hampton. He felt the warmth of the sun on his skin, and he stopped and purchased a cup of mocha coffee at the corner shop. It had a great aroma and when he sipped it, he felt the taste of the chocolate and cocoa on the tip of his tongue. When he was collecting his car at the garage, the Hispanic attendant smiled at him. He looked back and he thought that he recognized himself in the eyes of the attendant. He smiled and muttered to himself, "We are all the same in our essence." And so we beat on, poor little fragments of the same larger tapestry of life, so far away from where we came that we have forgotten our common origins, lost sight of the force that created us, which is the same power that created the stars and the sun. It is the force that resides within us and is obscured by thought—streams of solipsistic thought that create the illusion of separateness, that erect little prison cells of solitude from which we endeavor in vain to escape by going round and round, in ever-widening circles of thought, that take us deeper into the pyramidal quagmire of "me," of "my thoughts," and "my opinions."

Eric got into his car and when he got on the road, he rolled down his window, let in the warm air, took a deep breath, and went on his way.

The End

ACKNOWLEDGMENTS

I extend my profound gratitude to Haleh Esfandiari for painstakingly checking the historical aspects, and John Nelson for his help with the revisions of my manuscript. Thanks also to Max Blankenship for helping me research the topography of the Zagros mountains, to David Bellos for his helpful comments on my manuscript, and to Mike Pinelli, Cynthia Mitchell and Carole Claps for assistance with proofreading. I am grateful to Meryl Moss for her help and support, to Walker La Vardara for typing portions of my handwritten manuscript, and to Carolyn Blankenship, Elliott Rasmussen, my mother, Pari, and my sons, Michael and Mark, for their indefatigable support without which I would not have been able to write this book.

Alexandre Montagu is a lawyer living in New York. Fluent in English, French, Farsi, and German, he studied at the University of Cambridge, Harvard Law School, and Princeton University, where he teaches a course in the comparative literature department as an adjunct professor.